THE DREAM THIEVES

Also by Maggie Stiefvater

The Raven Boys

The Scorpio Races

Shiver
Linger
Forever
Sinner

Lament: The Faerie Queen's Deception
Ballad: A Gathering of Faerie

THE DREAM THIEVES

BOOK II OF THE RAVEN CYCLE

MAGGIE STIEFVATER

SCHOLASTIC INC.

*for Jackson,
and all her mqrvelous hours
[sic]*

This book was originally published in hardcover by Scholastic
Press in 2013.

ISBN 978-0-545-42495-0

12 11 10 9 8 7 6 5 4 3 2 1   14 15 16 17 18 19/0

Printed in the U.S.A.   40
First paperback printing, October 2014

The text type was set in Centaur MT.

Book design by
Christopher Stengel

What if you slept
And what if
In your sleep
You dreamed
And what if
In your dream
You went to heaven
And there plucked a strange and beautiful flower
And what if
When you awoke
You had that flower in your hand
Ah, what then?

— SAMUEL TAYLOR COLERIDGE

Those who dream by night in the dusty recesses
of their minds wake in the day to find that it
was vanity: but the dreamers of the day are
dangerous men, for they may act their dreams
with open eyes, to make it possible.

— T. E. LAWRENCE

I loathe people who keep dogs. They are cowards
who haven't got the guts to bite people themselves.

— AUGUST STRINDBERG

PROLOGUE

A secret is a strange thing.

There are three kinds of secrets. One is the sort everyone knows about, the sort you need at least two people for. One to keep it. One to never know. The second is a harder kind of secret: one you keep from yourself. Every day, thousands of confessions are kept from their would-be confessors, none of these people knowing that their never-admitted secrets all boil down to the same three words: *I am afraid.*

And then there is the third kind of secret, the most hidden kind. A secret no one knows about. Perhaps it was known once, but was taken to the grave. Or maybe it is a useless mystery, arcane and lonely, unfound because no one ever looked for it.

Sometimes, some rare times, a secret stays undiscovered because it is something too big for the mind to hold. It is too strange, too vast, too terrifying to contemplate.

All of us have secrets in our lives. We're keepers or kept-from, players or played. Secrets and cockroaches — that's what will be left at the end of it all.

Ronan Lynch lived with every sort of secret.

His first secret involved his father. Niall Lynch was a braggart poet, a loser musician, a charming bit of hard luck bred in Belfast but born in Cumbria, and Ronan loved him like he loved nothing else.

Though Niall was a rogue and a fiend, the Lynches were rich. Niall's employment was mysterious. He was gone for months at a time, though it was hard to say if this was because of his career or because of his being a scoundrel. He always returned with gifts, treasure, and unimaginable amounts of money, but to Ronan, the most wondrous thing was Niall himself. Every parting felt like it would be the last, and so every return was like a miracle.

"When I was born," Niall Lynch told his middle son, "God broke the mold so hard the ground shook."

This was already a lie, because if God truly had broken the mold for Niall, He'd made Himself a knockoff twenty years later to craft Ronan and his two brothers, Declan and Matthew. The three brothers were nothing if not handsome copies of their father, although each flattered a different side of Niall. Declan had the same way of taking a room and shaking its hand. Matthew's curls were netted with Niall's charm and humor. And Ronan was everything that was left: molten eyes and a smile made for war.

There was little to nothing of their mother in any of them.

"It was a proper earthquake," Niall clarified, as if anyone had asked him — and knowing Niall, they probably had. "Four point one on the Richter scale. Anything under four would've just cracked the mold, not broken it."

Back then, Ronan was not in the business of believing, but that was all right, because his father wanted adoration, not trust.

"And you, Ronan," Niall said. He always said *Ronan* differently from other words. As if he had meant to say another word entirely — something like *knife* or *poison* or *revenge* — and then swapped it out for Ronan's name at the last moment. "When you were born, the rivers dried up and the cattle in Rockingham County wept blood."

It was a story he had told more than once, but Ronan's mother, Aurora, insisted it was a lie. She said when Ronan emerged, the trees all grew flowers and the Henrietta ravens laughed. When his parents bickered back and forth about his birth, Ronan never pointed out that both versions could be true.

Declan, the oldest of the Lynch brothers, once asked, "And what happened when I was born?"

Niall Lynch looked at him and said, "I wouldn't know. I wasn't here."

When Niall said *Declan*, it always sounded like he meant to say *Declan*.

And then Niall vanished for another month. Ronan took the opportunity to search the Barns, which is what the sprawling Lynch farm was known as, for evidence of where Niall's money came from. He found no clues of his father's work, but he did discover a yellowed newspaper clipping in a rusting metal box. It was from the year his father was born. Drily it reported the story of the Kirkby Stephen earthquake, felt through northern England and southern Scotland. Four point one. Anything less than a four wouldn't have broken it, only cracked it.

That night, Niall Lynch came home in the blackness, and when he woke, he found Ronan standing above him in the small white master bedroom. The morning sun made them both snowy as angels, which was the better part of a lie already. Niall's face was smeared with blood and blue petals.

"I was just dreaming of the day you were born," Niall said, "Ronan."

He wiped the blood on his forehead to show Ronan that there was no wound beneath it. The petals snared in the blood were shaped like tiny stars. Ronan was struck with how sure he was that they had come from his father's mind. He'd never been more sure of anything.

The world gaped and stretched, suddenly infinite.

Ronan told him, "I know where the money comes from."

"Don't tell anyone," his father said.

That was the first secret.

The second secret was perfect in its concealment. Ronan did not say it. Ronan did not think it. He never put lyrics to the second secret, the one he kept from himself.

But it still played in the background.

And then there was this: three years later, Ronan dreaming of his friend Richard C. Gansey III's car. Gansey trusted him with all things, except for weapons. Never with weapons and never with this, not Gansey's hell-tinged '73 Camaro slicked with black stripes. In his waking hours, Ronan never got any farther than the passenger seat. When Gansey left town, he took the keys with him.

But in Ronan's dream, Gansey was not there and the Camaro was. The car was poised on the sloped corner of an abandoned parking lot, mountains ghosted blue in the distance. Ronan's hand closed around the driver's side door handle. He tried his grip. It was a dream strength, only substantial enough to cling to the idea of opening the door. That was all right. Ronan sank into the driver's seat. The mountains and the parking lot were a dream, but the smell of the interior was a memory: gasoline and vinyl and carpet and years whirring against one another.

The keys are in it, Ronan thought.

And they were.

The keys dangled from the ignition like metallic fruit, and Ronan spent a long moment holding them in his mind. He shuffled the keys from dream to memory and back again, and then he closed his palm around them. He felt the soft leather and the worn edge of the fob; the cold metal of the ring and the trunk key; the thin, sharp promise of the ignition key between his fingers.

Then he woke up.

When he opened his hand, the keys lay in his palm. Dream to reality.

This was his third secret.

I

Theoretically, Blue Sargent was probably going to kill one of these boys.

"Jane!" The shout came from across the hill. It was directed toward Blue, although Jane was not her real name. "Hurry up!"

As the only non-clairvoyant in a very psychic family, she'd had her future told again and again, and each time it said she would kill her true love if she tried to kiss him. Moreover, it had been foretold this was the year she'd fall in love. *And* both Blue and her clairvoyant half aunt, Neeve, had seen one of the boys walking along the invisible corpse road this April, which meant he was supposed to die in the next twelve months. It all added up to a fearful equation.

At the moment, that particular boy, Richard Campbell Gansey III, looked pretty unkillable. In the humid wind at the top of the wide green hill, an ardently yellow polo shirt flapped against his chest and a pair of khaki shorts slapped his gloriously tanned legs. Boys like him didn't die; they got bronzed and installed outside public libraries. He held a hand toward Blue as she climbed the hill from the car, a gesture that looked less like encouragement and more like he was directing air traffic.

"*Jane.* You've got to see this!" His voice was full of the honey-baked accent of old Virginia money.

As Blue staggered up the hill, telescope on her shoulder, she mentally tested the danger level: *Am I in love with him yet?*

Gansey galloped down the hill to snatch the telescope from her.

"This isn't that heavy," he told her, and strode back the way he'd come.

She did not think she was in love with him. She hadn't been in love before, but she was still pretty sure she'd be able to tell. Earlier in the year, she *had* had a vision of kissing him, and she could still picture *that* quite easily. But the sensible part of Blue, which was usually the only part of her, thought that had more to do with Richard Campbell Gansey III having a nice mouth than with any blossoming romance.

Anyway, if fate thought it could tell her who to fall for, fate had another thing coming.

Gansey added, "I would've thought you had more muscles. Don't feminists have big muscles?"

Decidedly not in love with him.

"Smiling when you say that doesn't make it funny," Blue said.

As the latest step in his quest to find the Welsh king Owen Glendower, Gansey had been requesting hiking permission from local landowners. Each lot crossed the Henrietta ley line — an invisible, perfectly straight energy line that connected spiritually significant places — and circled Cabeswater, a mystical forest that straddled it. Gansey was certain that Glendower was hidden somewhere within Cabeswater, sleeping away the centuries. Whoever woke the king was supposed to be granted a favor — something that had been on Blue's mind recently. It seemed to her that Gansey was the only one who really *needed* it. Not that Gansey knew he was supposed to be dead in a few months. And not that she was about to tell him.

If we find Glendower soon, Blue thought, *surely we can save Gansey.*

The steep climb brought them to a vast, grassy crest that arched above the forested foothills. Far, far below was Henrietta, Virginia. The town was flanked by pastures dotted with farmhouses and cattle, as small and tidy as a model railroad layout. Everything but the soaring blue mountain range was green and shimmery with the summer heat.

But the boys were not looking at the scenery. They stood in a close circle: Adam Parrish, gaunt and fair; Noah Czerny, smudgy and slouching; and Ronan Lynch, ferocious and dark. On Ronan's tattooed shoulder perched his pet raven, Chainsaw. Although her grip was careful, there were finely drawn lines from her claws on either side of the strap of his black muscle T. They all eyed something Ronan held in his hands. Gansey cavalierly tossed the telescope into the buoyant field grass and joined them.

Adam allowed Blue into their circle as well, his eyes meeting hers for a moment. As always, his features intrigued Blue. They were not quite conventionally handsome, but they were *interesting*. He had the typical Henrietta prominent cheekbones and deep-set eyes, but his version of them was more delicate. It made him seem a little alien. A little impenetrable.

I'm picking this one, Fate, she thought ferociously. *Not Richard Gansey III. You can't tell me what to do.*

Adam's hand glided over her bare elbow. The touch was a whisper in a language she didn't speak very well.

"Open it up," he ordered Ronan. His voice was dubious.

"Doubting Thomas," Ronan sneered, but without much vitriol. The tiny model plane in his hand spanned the same breadth as his fingers. It was formed of pure white, featureless plastic, almost ludicrously lacking in detail: a plane-shaped thing. He opened the battery hatch on the bottom. It was empty.

"Well, it's impossible, then," Adam said. He picked off a grasshopper that had hurled itself onto his collar. Everyone in the group watched him do it. Since he'd performed a strange ritual bargain the month before, they'd been scrutinizing all of his movements. If Adam noticed this extra attention, he didn't indicate it. "It won't fly if it has no battery and no engine."

Now Blue knew what this thing was. Ronan Lynch, keeper of secrets, fighter of men, devil of a boy, had told them all that he could take objects out of his dreams. Example A: Chainsaw. Gansey had been excited; he was the sort of boy who didn't necessarily believe everything, but wanted to. But Adam, who had only gotten this far in life by questioning every truth presented to him, had wanted proof.

"'It won't fly if it has no battery and no engine,'" Ronan mimicked in a higher-pitched version of Adam's faint Henrietta drawl. "Noah: the controller."

Noah scuffled in the clumpy grass for the radio controller. Like the plane, it was white and shiny, all the edges rounded. His hands looked solid around it. Though he had been dead for quite a while and by all rights should appear more ghostly, he was always rather living-looking when standing on the ley line.

"What's supposed to go inside the plane, if not a battery?" Gansey asked.

Ronan said, "I don't know. In the dream it was little missiles, but I guess they didn't come with."

Blue snarled a few seed heads off the tall grass. "Here."

"Good thinking, maggot." Ronan stuffed them into the hatch. He reached for the controller, but Adam intercepted it and shook it by his ear.

"This doesn't even weigh anything," he said, dropping the controller into Blue's palm.

It *was* very light, Blue thought. It had five tiny white buttons: four arranged in a cross shape, and one off by itself. To Blue, that fifth button was like Adam. Still working toward the same purpose as the other four. But no longer quite as close as the others.

"It will work," Ronan said, taking the controller and handing the plane to Noah. "It worked in the dream, so it'll work now. Hold it up."

Still slouching, Noah lifted the tiny plane between thumb and forefinger, as if he were getting ready to launch a pencil. Something in Blue's chest thrummed with excitement. It was impossible that Ronan had dreamt that little plane. But so many impossible things had happened already.

"*Kerah*," Chainsaw said. This was her name for Ronan.

"Yes," agreed Ronan. Then, to the others, he said imperiously, "Count it down."

Adam made a face, but Gansey, Noah, and Blue obligingly chanted, "Five-four-three —"

On *blast-off*, Ronan pressed one of the buttons.

Soundlessly, the tiny plane darted from Noah's hand and into the air.

It worked. It really worked.

Gansey laughed out loud as they all tipped their heads back to watch its ascent. Blue shielded her eyes to keep sight of the tiny white figure in the haze. It was so small and nimble that it looked like a real plane thousands of feet above the slope. With a frenzied cry, Chainsaw launched herself from Ronan's shoulder to chase it. Ronan pitched the plane left and right, looping it around the crest, Chainsaw close behind. When the plane passed back overhead, he hit that fifth button. Seed heads cascaded from the open hatch, rolling off their shoulders. Blue clapped and reached her palm out to catch one.

"You incredible creature," Gansey said. His delight was infectious and unconditional, broad as his grin. Adam tipped his head back to watch, something still and faraway around his eyes. Noah breathed *whoa*, his palm still lifted as if waiting for the plane to return to it. And Ronan stood there with his hands on the controller and his gaze on the sky, not smiling, but not frowning, either. His eyes were frighteningly alive, the curve of his mouth savage and pleased. It suddenly didn't seem at all surprising that he should be able to pull things from his dreams.

In that moment, Blue was a little in love with all of them. Their magic. Their quest. Their awfulness and strangeness. Her raven boys.

Gansey punched Ronan's shoulder. "Glendower traveled with magi, did you know? Magicians, I mean. Wizards. They helped him control the weather — maybe you could dream us a cold snap."

"Har."

"They also told the future," added Gansey, turning to Blue.

"Don't look at me," she said shortly. Her lack of psychic talents was legendary.

"Or helped *him* tell the future," Gansey went on, which did not particularly make sense, but indicated that he was trying to un-irritate her. Blue's short temper and her ability to make other people's psychic talents stronger were also legendary. "Shall we go?"

Blue hurried to pick up the telescope before he could get to it — he shot her a look — and the other boys fetched the maps and cameras and electromagnetic-frequency readers. They set off on the perfectly straight ley line, Ronan's gaze still directed up to his plane and to Chainsaw, a white bird and a black bird against the azure ceiling of the world. As they walked, a sudden rush of wind hurled low across the grass, bringing with it the scent of moving water and rocks hidden in shadows, and Blue thrilled again and again with the knowledge that magic was real, magic was real, magic was real.

2

Declan Lynch, the oldest of the Lynch brothers, was never alone. He was never with his brothers, but he was never alone. He was a perpetual-motion machine run by the energy of others: here leaning over a friend's table at a pizza joint, here drawn into an alcove with a girl's palm to his mouth, here laughing over the hood of an older man's Mercedes. The congregation was so natural that it was impossible to tell if Declan was the magnet attracting or the filings attracted.

It was giving the Gray Man a not inconsiderable difficulty in finding an opportunity to speak with him. He had to loiter around the Aglionby Academy campus for the better part of a day.

The waiting wasn't entirely disagreeable. The Gray Man found himself quite charmed by the oak-shaded school. The campus possessed a shabby gravitas that was only possible with age and affluence. The dorms were emptier than they would've been during school term, but they were not *empty*. There were still the sons of CEOs traveling to third-world countries for photo ops and the sons of touring punk musicians with heavier things to bring along than seventeen-year-old accidental progeny and the sons of men who were dead and never coming to retrieve them.

These summer sons, few as they were, were not entirely noiseless.

Declan Lynch's dorm was not quite as pretty as the other buildings, but it was still handsome with money. It was a remnant from the seventies, a Technicolor decade the Gray Man had enormous fondness for. The front door was meant to be accessible only with a key code, but someone had propped it open with a rubber door stopper. The Gray Man clucked in disapproval. A locked door wouldn't have kept him out, of course, but it was the thought that counted.

Actually, the Gray Man wasn't certain he believed that. It was the deed that counted.

Inside, the dorm offered the neutral-toned welcome of a decent hotel. From behind one of the closed doors, a Colombian hip-hop track raged, something seductive and violent. It wasn't the Gray Man's sort of music, but he could hear the appeal. He glanced at the door. The dorm rooms at Aglionby were not numbered. Instead, each door bore an attribute the administration hoped its students would walk away with. This door was labeled *Mercy*. It was not the one the Gray Man was looking for.

The Gray Man headed in the opposite direction, reading doors (*Diligence, Generosity, Piety*) until he got to Declan Lynch's. *Effervescence.*

The Gray Man had been called *effervescent*, once, in an article. He was fairly certain it was because he had very straight teeth. Even teeth seemed to be a prerequisite for effervescence.

He wondered if Declan Lynch had good teeth.

There was no sound coming from behind the door. He tried the doorknob, softly. Locked. *Good boy,* he thought.

Down the hall, the music pounded like the apocalypse. The Gray Man checked his watch. The rental-car place closed in an hour, and if he despised anything, it was public transportation. This would have to be brief.

He kicked in the door.

Declan Lynch sat on one of the two beds inside. He was very handsome, with a lot of dark hair and a rather distinguished Roman nose.

He had excellent teeth.

"What's this?" he said.

By way of answer, the Gray Man picked Declan up off his bed and slammed him against the adjacent window. The sound was curiously muffled; the loudest part of it was the boy's breath bursting from him as his spine railed against the sill. But then he was back up and fighting. He wasn't a shoddy boxer, and the Gray Man could tell that he expected this surprise to give him an advantage.

But the Gray Man had known before he arrived that Niall Lynch had taught his sons to box. The only thing the Gray Man's father had taught him was how to pronounce *trebuchet*.

For a moment they fought. Declan was skilled, but the Gray Man was more so. He tossed the boy about his dorm room and used Declan's shoulder to sweep awards and credit cards and car keys from the dresser. The thump of his head against a drawer was indistinguishable from the bass down the hall. Declan swung, missed. The Gray Man kicked Declan's legs from beneath him, hurled him to the wall next to the piece of furniture, and then approached for another round, pausing only to pick up a motorcycle helmet that had rolled into the middle of the floor.

With a sudden burst of speed, Declan used the dresser to haul himself up, then pulled a handgun from a drawer.

He pointed it at the Gray Man.

"Stop," he said simply. He flicked off the safety.

The Gray Man had not expected this.

He stopped.

Several different emotions battled for precedence on Declan's face, but shock was not one of them. It was clear the gun was not for the possibility of an attack; it was for the eventuality of one.

The Gray Man considered what it must've been like to live like that, always waiting for your door to be kicked in. *Not pleasant*, he thought. *Probably not pleasant at all.*

He didn't think Declan Lynch would balk at shooting him. There was no hesitation in his stance. His hand trembled a bit, but the Gray Man thought that was from injury, not fear.

The Gray Man considered for a moment, then he hurled the helmet. The boy fired a shot, but it was nothing but noise. The helmet crashed into his fingers, and while he was still stunned, the Gray Man stepped forward and plucked the gun from his numb hand. He took a moment to put the safety back on.

Then the Gray Man smashed the gun against Declan's cheek. He did it a few times, just to get his point across.

Finally, he allowed Declan to sink to his knees. The boy was holding on to consciousness quite valiantly. With his shoe, the Gray Man pressed him the rest of the way to the ground, and then eased him onto his back. Declan's eyes were focused on the ceiling fan. Blood ran out of his nose.

The Gray Man knelt and pressed the barrel of the gun to Declan's stomach, which rose and fell calamitously as he gasped for air. Tracing the gun over the boy's right kidney, he said conversationally, "If I shot you here, it would take you twenty minutes to die, and you'd be done no matter what the medics did for you. Where is the Greywaren?"

Declan said nothing. The Gray Man gave him some time to consider his reply. Head wounds tended to make thoughts slower.

When Declan remained quiet, he dragged the muzzle down to Declan's thigh. He pressed hard enough that the boy gasped. "Here, you'd die in five minutes. Of course, I don't need to shoot you for that. The point of your umbrella over there would do it just as well. You'd be gone in five minutes and wishing for it in three."

Declan closed his eyes. One of them, anyway. The left eye was already swollen most of the way shut.

"I don't know," he said eventually. His voice sounded full of sleep. "I don't know what that is."

"Lies are for your politicians," the Gray Man said, without vehemence. He just wanted Declan to know that he knew about his life, his internship. He wanted him to know that he'd done his research. "I know where your brothers are right now. I know where your mother lives. I know the name of your girlfriend. Are we clear?"

"I don't know where it is." Declan hesitated. "That's the truth. I don't know where it is. I just know it *is.*"

"Here is the plan." The Gray Man stood up. "You're going to find that thing for me, and when you do, you're going to give it to me. And then I will be gone."

"How do I find you to give it to you?"

"I don't think you understand. I am your shadow. I'm the spit you swallow. I'm the cough that keeps you up at night."

Declan asked, "Did you kill my father?"

"Niall Lynch." The Gray Man tried the words out in his mouth. In his opinion, Niall Lynch was a pretty lousy father, getting himself killed and then allowing his sons to live in a place where they propped the security doors open. The world, he felt, was full of bad fathers. "He asked me that question, too."

Declan Lynch exhaled unevenly: half a breath, and then the other half. Now, the Gray Man could see, he was finally afraid.

"Okay," Declan said. "I'll find it. Then you'll leave us alone. All of you."

The Gray Man set the pistol back in its drawer and pushed it closed. He checked his watch. He had twenty minutes to pick up his rental car. He might upgrade to a midsize. He hated compact cars nearly as much as he hated public transportation. "Yes."

"Okay," Declan said again.

The Gray Man withdrew from the room, shutting the door partway. It wouldn't quite close right; he had messed up one of the hinges when he'd entered. He was sure there was an endowment somewhere that would cover the damages.

He paused, watching through the crack of the door.

There was still more to learn from Declan Lynch today.

For several minutes, nothing happened. Declan lay there bleeding and crooked. Then the fingers of his right hand crabbed across the ground to where his cell phone had fallen. He didn't immediately dial 911, though. With agonizing slowness — his shoulder was almost certainly dislocated — he punched in another number. Immediately, a phone rang on the opposite bed. It was, the Gray Man knew already, the bed that belonged to Declan's youngest brother, Matthew. The ringtone was an Iglu & Hartly song that the Gray Man knew but couldn't condone. The Gray Man already knew where Matthew Lynch was: floating in a boat on the river with some local boys. Like his older brother, never content to be alone.

Declan let his youngest brother's phone ring for longer than it needed to, his eyes closed. Finally, he pressed END and dialed another number. It still wasn't 911. Whoever it was didn't pick up. And whoever it was made Declan's already strained expression even tighter. The Gray Man could hear the tinny sound of the phone ringing and ringing, then a brief voicemail that he couldn't catch.

Declan Lynch closed his eyes and breathed, "Ronan, where the hell are you?"

3

"The problem is exposure," Gansey told the phone, half-shouting to be heard over the engine. "If Glendower really could be found just walking along the ley line, I don't see how he wouldn't have already been found in the past few hundred years."

They were headed back to Henrietta in the Pig, Gansey's furiously orange-red ancient Camaro. Gansey drove, because when it was the Camaro, he always drove. And the conversation was about Glendower, because when you were with Gansey, the conversation was almost always about Glendower.

In the backseat, Adam's head was tipped back in a way that gave equal attention to the phone conversation and his fatigue. In the middle, Blue leaned forward to better eavesdrop as she picked grass seed off her crochet leggings. Noah was on her other side, although one could never be sure he'd stay corporeal the farther they got from the ley line. It was a tight fit, even tighter in this heat, with the air-conditioning straining, escaping through every crevice in the crevice-filled vehicle. The Camaro's air-conditioning had only two settings: on and broken.

To the phone, Gansey said, "That's the *only* thing."

Ronan leaned on the cracked black vinyl of the passenger-side door and chewed on the leather bands on his wrist. They tasted like gasoline, a flavor that struck Ronan as both sexy and summery.

For him, it was only sometimes about Glendower. Gansey

needed to find Glendower because he wanted proof of the impossible. Ronan already knew the impossible existed. His father had been impossible. *He* was impossible. Mostly, Ronan wanted to find Glendower because Gansey wanted to find Glendower. Only sometimes did he think about what would happen if they actually discovered him. He thought it might be a lot like dying. When Ronan had been smaller and more forgiving of miracles, he'd considered the moment of death with rhapsodic delight. His mother had told him that when you looked into the eyes of God at the pearly gates, all the questions you ever had were answered.

Ronan had a lot of questions.

Waking Glendower might be like that. Fewer angels attending, and maybe a heavier Welsh accent. Slightly less judgment.

"No, I understand that." Gansey was using his Mr. Gansey professorial voice, the one that exuded certainty and commanded rats and small children to *get up, get up, follow me!* It had worked on Ronan, anyway. "But if we assume Glendower was brought over between 1412 and 1420, and if we assume his tomb was left untended, natural soil accumulation would have hidden him. Starkman suggests that medieval layers of occupation might be under a sediment accumulation of five to seventeen feet. . . . Well, I *know* I'm not on a floodplain. But Starkman was working under the assumption that . . . right, sure. What do you think about GPR?"

Blue looked at Adam. He didn't lift his head as he translated in a low voice, "Ground-penetrating radar."

The person on the other end of the phone was Roger Malory, a stunningly old British professor Gansey had worked with back in Wales. Like Gansey, he had studied the ley lines for years. Unlike Gansey, he was not using them as a means to find an ancient king. Rather, he seemed to study them for a weekend diversion when there were no parades to attend. Ronan hadn't met him in person and didn't care to. The elderly made Ronan anxious.

"Fluxgrate gradiometry?" Gansey suggested. "We've already taken a plane up a few times. I just don't know if we'll see much more until winter when the leaves are gone."

Ronan shifted restlessly. The successful demonstration of the plane had left him hyper-alive. He felt like burning something to the ground. He pressed his hand directly over the air-conditioning vent to prevent heat exhaustion. "You're driving like an old woman."

Gansey waved a hand, the universal symbol for *Shut up*. Beside the interstate, four black cows lifted their heads to watch the Camaro go by.

If I was driving . . . Ronan thought about that set of Camaro keys he had dreamt into existence, shoved in a drawer in his room. He let the possibilities unwind slowly in his mind. He checked his phone. Fourteen missed calls. He dropped it back into the door pouch.

"What about a proton magnetometer?" Gansey asked Malory. Then he added crossly, "I know that's for underwater detection. I would want it *for* underwater detection."

It was water that had ended their work today. Gansey had decided that the next step in their search was to establish Cabeswater's boundaries. They'd only ever entered the forest from its eastern side and never made it to any of the other edges. This time, they'd approached the forest from well north of their previous entry points, devices trained to the ground to alert them to when they found the northern electromagnetic boundary of the forest. After a several-hour walk, the group had instead come to a lake.

Gansey had stopped dead in his tracks. It wasn't that the lake had been uncrossable: It only covered a few acres and the path around lacked treachery. And it wasn't that the lake had stunned him with its beauty. In fact, it was quite unlovely as far as lakes went: an unnaturally square pool sunk into a drowned field. Cattle or sheep had worn a mud path along one edge.

The thing that stopped Gansey cold was the obvious fact that the lake was man-made. The possibility that parts of the ley line might be flooded should have occurred to him before. But it hadn't. And for some reason, although it was not impossible to believe that Glendower was still somehow alive after hundreds of years, it was impossible to believe he was able to pull off this feat beneath tons of water.

Gansey had declared, "We have to find a way to look under it."

Adam had replied, "Oh, Gansey, *come on*. The odds —"

"We're looking under it."

Ronan's plane had crashed into the water and floated, unreachable. They'd walked the long way back to the car. Gansey had called Malory.

As if, Ronan thought, *a crusty old man three thousand miles away will have any bright ideas.*

Gansey hung up the phone.

"Well?" Adam asked.

Gansey met Adam's eyes in the rearview mirror. Adam sighed.

Ronan thought they could probably just go around the lake. But that would mean plunging into Cabeswater headlong. And although the ancient forest seemed like the most likely location for Glendower, the sizzling volatility of the newly woken ley line had rendered it a little unpredictable. Even Ronan, who had little care for whether or not he shuffled off this mortal coil, had to admit that the prospect of being trampled by beasts or accidentally getting stuck in a forty-year time loop was daunting.

The entire thing was Adam's fault — he'd been the one to wake the ley line, though Gansey preferred to pretend it had been a group decision. Whatever bargain Adam had struck in order to accomplish it seemed to have rendered *him* a little unpredictable as well. Ronan, a sinner himself, wasn't as struck by the transgression as he was by Gansey's insistence that they continue to pretend Adam was a saint.

Gansey was not a liar. This untruth didn't look good on him.

Gansey's phone chirruped. He read the message before letting it drop next to the gearshift with a strangled cry. Abruptly melancholy, he lolled his head dismally against the seat. Adam gestured for Ronan to pick up the phone, but Ronan despised phones above almost every other object in the world.

So it sat there with its eyebrows raised, waiting.

Finally, Blue strained forward far enough to snatch it. She read the message out loud: " 'Could really use you this weekend if not too much trouble. Helen can pick you up. Disregard if you have activities.' "

"Is this about Congress?" Adam asked.

The sound of the word *Congress* made Gansey sigh heavily and urged Blue to whisper in withering derision, "Congress!" It hadn't been long since Gansey's mother had announced she was running for office. In these early days, the campaign had yet to directly influence Gansey, but it was inevitable he'd be called upon. They all knew that clean, handsome Gansey, intrepid teen explorer and straight-A student, was a card that no hopeful politician could avoid playing.

"She can't make me," Gansey said.

"She doesn't have to," Ronan sniffed. "Mama's boy."

"Dream me a solution."

"Don't have to. Nature already gave you a spine. You know what I say? Fuck Washington."

"This is why *you* never have to go to things like this," Gansey replied.

In the other lane, a car pulled up beside the Camaro. Ronan, a connoisseur of street battles, noticed it first. A flash of white paint. Then a hand stretched out the driver's side window, a middle finger extended over the roof. The other car shot forward and then fell back, then shot forward again.

"Oh, Christ," Gansey said. "Is that Kavinsky?"

Of course it was Joseph Kavinsky, fellow Aglionby Academy student and Henrietta's most notorious recreational forger. Kavinsky's infamous Mitsubishi Evo was a thing of boyish beauty, moon-white with a voracious black mouth of a grille and an immense splattered graphic of a knife on either side of the body. The Mitsubishi had just been released from a month-long stint in the police impound. The judge had told him that if he was caught racing again, they'd crush the Mitsubishi and make him watch, like they did to the rich punks' street racers out in California. Rumor had it Kavinsky had laughed and told the judge he'd never get pulled over again.

He probably wouldn't. Rumor had it Kavinsky's father had bought off Henrietta's sheriff.

To celebrate the Mitsubishi's release from impound, Kavinsky had just put three coats of anti-laser paint on the headlights and bought himself a new radar detector.

Rumor had it.

"I hate that prick," Adam said.

Ronan knew he ought to hate him, too.

The window rolled down to reveal Joseph Kavinsky in the driver's seat, his eyes hidden behind white-rimmed sunglasses that reflected only the sky. The gold links of the chain around his neck glittered a grin. He had a refugee's face, hollow-eyed and innocent.

He wore a lazy smile, and he mouthed something to Gansey that ended with "— unt."

There was nothing about Kavinsky that wasn't despicable.

Ronan's heart surged. Muscle memory.

"Do it," he urged. The four-lane interstate, gray and baked, stretched in front of them. The sun ignited the red-orange of the Camaro's hood, and beneath it, the massively souped-up and tragically under utilized engine rumbled drowsily. Everything about the situation demanded someone's foot crushing an accelerator.

"I know you are not referring to street racing," Gansey said tersely.

Noah gave a hoarse laugh.

Gansey didn't make eye contact with Kavinsky or Kavinsky's passenger, the ever-present Prokopenko. The latter had always been friendly with Kavinsky, in the sort of way that an electron was friendly with a nucleus, but lately, he seemed to have acquired official crony status.

"Come on, man," Ronan said.

In a dismissive, sleepy voice, Adam said, "I don't know why you think that would work out. Pig's got a load of five people —"

"Noah doesn't count," Ronan replied.

Noah said, *"Hey."*

"You're *dead*. You don't weigh anything!"

Adam continued, "— we've got our air-co on, and he's probably in his Evo, right? Zero-to-sixty in four seconds. What's this do, zero-to-sixty in five? Six? Do the math."

"I've beaten him," Ronan said. There was something dreadful about seeing a race dissolving in front of him. It was *right there*, adrenaline waiting to happen. And Kavinsky, of all people. Every inch of Ronan's skin tingled with useless anticipation.

"Not in that car you haven't. Not in your BMW."

"In that car," countered Ronan. "In my BMW. He's a shitty driver."

Gansey said, "It's irrelevant. It's not happening. Kavinsky's a dirtbag."

In the other lane, Kavinsky lost patience and pulled slowly ahead. Blue caught sight of the car. She exclaimed, "*Him!* He's not a dirtbag. He's an *asshole*."

For a moment, all of the boys in the Camaro were quiet, contemplating where Blue might have learned that Joseph Kavinsky was an asshole. Not that she was wrong, of course.

"You see," Gansey said. "Jane concurs."

Ronan caught a glimpse of Kavinsky's face, looking back at them through his sunglasses. Judging them all cowards. Ronan's hands felt itchy. Then Kavinsky's white Mitsubishi charged ahead in a faint cloud of smoke. By the time the Camaro had reached the Henrietta exit, there was no sign of them. Heat rippled off the interstate, making a mirage of the memory of Kavinsky. Like he'd never been.

Ronan slumped in his seat, all the fight sucked out of him. "You never want to have any fun, old man."

"That's not fun," Gansey said, putting on his turn signal. "That's trouble."

4

The Gray Man had not always intended to be a heavy.

Point of fact, the Gray Man had a graduate degree in something completely unrelated to roughing people up. At one point, he had even written a not-unsuccessful book called *Fraternity in Anglo-Saxon Verse*, and it had been required reading in at least seventeen college courses across the country. The Gray Man had carefully collected as many of these course reading lists as he could find and placed them in a folder along with cover flats, first-pass pages, and two appreciative letters addressed to his pen name. Whenever he required a small burst of fireworks to his heart, he would remove the folder from the bedside drawer and look at the contents while enjoying a beer or seven. He had made a mark.

However, as delightful as Anglo-Saxon poetry was to the Gray Man, it served him better as a hobby than as a career. He preferred a job he could approach with pragmatism, one that gave him the freedom to read and study at his convenience. So here he was in Henrietta.

It was, the Gray Man thought, quite an agreeable life after all.

After chatting with Declan Lynch, he checked into the Pleasant Valley Bed and Breakfast just outside of town. It was quite late, but Shorty and Patty Wetzel didn't seem to mind.

"How long will you be with us?" Patty asked, handing the Gray Man a mug with an anatomically incorrect rooster on it.

She eyed his luggage on the portico: a gray duffel bag and a gray hard-sided suitcase.

"Probably two weeks to start," the Gray Man replied. "A fortnight in your company." The coffee was astonishingly terrible. He shouldered off his light gray jacket to reveal a dark gray V-neck. Both of the Wetzels gazed at his suddenly revealed shoulders and chest. He asked, "Do you have anything with a hair more spine to it?"

With a giggle, Patty obligingly produced three Coronas from the fridge. "We don't like to appear like lushes, but . . . lime?"

"Lime," agreed the Gray Man. For a moment, there was no sound but that of three consenting adults mutually enjoying an alcoholic beverage after a long day. The three emerged from the other side of the silence firm friends.

"Two weeks?" Shorty asked. The Gray Man was endlessly fascinated by the way Shorty formed words. The most basic premise of the Henrietta accent seemed to involve combining the five vowels basic to the English language into four.

"Give or take. I'm not sure how long this contract will last."

Shorty scratched his belly. "What do you do?"

"I'm a hit man."

"Hard to find work these days, is it?"

The Gray Man replied, "I would've had an easier time in accounting."

The Wetzels enjoyed this hugely. After a few minutes of home-baked laughter, Patty ventured, "You have such intense eyes!"

"I got them from my mother," he lied. The only thing he'd ever gotten from his mother was an inability to tan.

"Lucky woman!" Patty said.

The Wetzels hadn't had a boarder in several weeks, and the

Gray Man allowed himself to be the focus of their intense welcome for about an hour before excusing himself with another Corona. By the time the door shut behind him, the Wetzels were decided supporters of the Gray Man.

So many of the world's problems, he mused, were solved by sheer human decency.

The Gray Man's new home was the entire basement of the mansion. He stalked beneath the exposed beams, peering through each open door. It was all quilts and antique cradles and dim portraits of now-dead Victorian children. It smelled like two hundred years of salt ham. The Gray Man liked the sense of past. There were a lot of roosters, however.

Returning to the first bedroom, he unzipped the duffel he'd left there. He sorted through slacks and cosmetics and stolen artifacts wrapped in boxer briefs until he got to the smaller devices he'd been using to detect the Greywaren. On the small, high window beside the bed, he set an EMF detector, an old radio, and a geophone, and then he unpacked a seismograph, a measuring receiver, and a laptop from the suitcase. All of it was provided by the professor. Left to his own devices, the Gray Man used more primitive location tools.

At the moment, the dials and read-outs twitched crazily. He'd been told the Greywaren caused energy abnormalities, but this was just . . . noise. He reset the instruments that had reset buttons and shook the ones without. The readings remained nonsensical. Perhaps it was the town itself — the entire place seemed charged. It was possible, he thought without much dismay, that the instruments would be useless.

I have time, though. The first time the professor had put him onto this job, it had sounded impossible: a relic that allowed the owner to take objects out of dreams? Of course, he'd wanted to believe in it. Magic and intrigue — the stuff of sagas. And in the time since that first meeting, the professor had acquired countless other artifacts that shouldn't have existed.

The Gray Man tugged a folder out of his duffel and opened it on the bedspread. A course syllabus lay on top: Medieval History, Part I. Required reading: *Fraternity in Anglo-Saxon Verse*. Sliding on a set of headphones, he queued up a playlist of The Flaming Lips. He felt essentially happy.

Beside him, the phone rang. The Gray Man's burst of joy fizzled. The number on the screen was not a Boston number and therefore not his older brother. So he picked it up.

"Good evening," he said.

"Is it? I suppose." It was Dr. Colin Greenmantle, the professor who paid his rent. The only man with eyes more intense than the Gray Man's. "Do you know what would make calling you easier? If I knew your name, so I could say it."

The Gray Man didn't reply. Greenmantle had lasted five years without his name; he could last another five without it. Eventually, the Gray Man thought, if he resisted using it for long enough, he himself might forget his own name, and become someone else entirely.

"Did you find it?" Greenmantle asked.

"I've just arrived," the Gray Man reminded him.

"You could have just answered the question. You could have just said *no*."

"*No* isn't the same as *not yet*."

Now Greenmantle was silent. A cricket chirruped on the ground just outside the tiny window. Finally, he said, "I want you to move fast on this one."

For quite a long time now, the Gray Man had been hunting for things that couldn't be found, couldn't be bought, couldn't be acquired, and his instincts were telling him that the Greywaren was not a piece that was going to come quickly. He reminded Greenmantle that it had already been five years since they'd first begun looking for it.

"Irrelevant."

"Why the sudden hurry?"

"There are other people looking for it."

The Gray Man cast his eyes to the instruments. He was not eager to allow Greenmantle to ruin his leisurely exploration of Henrietta.

He said what Declan Lynch had already known. "There have always been other people looking for it."

"They haven't always been in Henrietta."

5

Later that night, back in Monmouth Manufacturing, Ronan woke up. He woke like a sailor scuttles a ship on rocks, plunging, heedless, with as much speed as he could muster, braced for the impact.

Ronan had dreamt he'd driven home. The way to the Barns was twisted as a lightbulb's filament, all corkscrew turns and breathless lifts through broken terrain. These were not Gansey's tamed mountains and foothills. These eastern hills of Singer's Falls were hasty green folds, sudden rises, and precipitous hatchet marks in the rock-strewn forests. Mist rose from them and clouds descended into them. Night, when it came to the Barns, was several shades darker than it was in Henrietta.

Ronan had dreamt this drive, again and again, more times than he'd ever driven it in real life. The pitch-black roads, the old farmhouse suddenly looming, the single, eternal light in the room with his silent mother. But in his sleep he never made it home.

He hadn't this time, either. But he had dreamt something he wanted to bring back.

In his bed, he struggled to move. Just after waking, after dreaming, his body belonged to no one. He looked at it from above, like a mourner at a funeral. The exterior of this early-morning Ronan didn't look at all like how he felt on the inside. Anything that didn't impale itself on the sharp line of this sleeping boy's cruel mouth would be tangled in the merciless hooks of his tattoo, pulled beneath his skin to drown.

Sometimes, Ronan thought he would be trapped like this, floating outside his body.

When he was awake, Ronan was not permitted to go to the Barns. When Niall Lynch had died — been killed, not died, beaten to death with a tire iron that was still lying beside him when Ronan had found him, a weapon still coated in his blood and his brains and the better part of his face, a face that had been alive maybe only an hour before, two hours before, while Ronan was dreaming only yards away, a full night's sleep, a feat never again to be performed — a lawyer had explained the details of their father's will to them. The Lynch brothers were wealthy, princes of Virginia, but they were exiles. All of the money was theirs, but on one condition: The boys were never to set foot on the property again. They were to disturb neither the house nor its contents.

Including their mother.

It will never stand up in court, Ronan had said. *We should fight it.*

Declan had said, *It doesn't matter. Mom is nothing without him. We might as well go.*

We have to fight, Ronan had insisted.

Declan had already turned away. *She's not fighting.*

Ronan could move his fingers. His body was his again. He felt the cool wooden surface of the box in his hands, his ever-present leather wristbands sliding toward his palms. He felt the ridges and valleys of the letters carved into the box. The crevices of the drawers and movable pieces. His pulse surged in him, the thrill of creation. The ragged awe of making something from nothing. It was not the easiest thing to take something from a dream.

It was not the easiest thing to take only one thing from a dream.

To bring even a pencil back was a small miracle. To bring any of the things from his nightmares — no one but Ronan knew the terrors that lived in his mind. Plagues and devils, conquerors and beasts.

Ronan had no secret more dangerous than this.

The night churned inside him. He tangled himself around the box, getting ahold of his thoughts again. Now he was beginning to shake a little. He remembered what Gansey had said:

You incredible creature!

Creature was a good word for him, Ronan thought. *What the hell am I?*

Maybe Gansey was awake.

Ronan and Gansey both suffered from insomnia, though they had very different solutions for it. When Ronan couldn't — or wouldn't — sleep, he listened to music or drank or went out into the streets looking for vehicular trouble. Or all three. When Gansey couldn't sleep, he studied the bristling journal he'd compiled of all things Glendower or, when he was too tired to read, used a cereal box and a bin of paints to add another building to the waist-high model of Henrietta he'd constructed. Neither could really help the other find sleep. But sometimes it was better just to know you weren't the only one awake.

Ronan padded out of his room with Chainsaw scooped in his arm. Sure enough, Gansey sat cross-legged on Main Street, slowly waving a newly painted piece of cardboard in the direction of the single window airconditioner. At night, he looked particularly small or the warehouse looked particularly large. Lit only by the small lamp he'd set on the floor beside his journal, the room yawned above, a wizard's cave full of books and maps and three-legged surveying devices. The night was flat black against the hundreds of windowpanes, making them just another wall.

Ronan placed the wooden box he'd just dreamt next to Gansey and then retreated to the other end of the tiny street.

Gansey was quaint and scholarly with his nighttime wireframes slid down his nose. He looked from Ronan to the box and back again and said nothing. But he did take one of his earbuds out as he continued running a line of glue along a miniature seam.

Popping a bone in his neck, Ronan let Chainsaw down to entertain herself. She proceeded to turn over the wastebasket and go through the contents. It was a noisy process, rustling like a secretary at work.

The scenario felt familiar and timeworn. The two of them had lived together at Monmouth for nearly as long as Gansey had been in Henrietta — almost two years. Of course, the building hadn't looked like this in the beginning. It had been just one of the many abandoned factories and warehouses in the valley. They never got torn down. They just got forgotten. Monmouth Manufacturing was no different.

But then Gansey had come to town with his crazy dream and his ridiculous Camaro, and he'd bought the building for cash. No one else noticed it, even though they drove by every day. It was on its knees in the rye grass and the creeper, and he saved it.

The fall after Ronan and Gansey had become friends, the summer before Adam, they'd spent half their free time hunting for Glendower and the other half hauling junk out of the second floor. The floor was furred with flaked curls of paint. Wires trailed from the ceiling like jungle vines. Chipped plywood made lean-tos against hideous desks from a nuclear age. The boys burned crap in the overgrown lot until the cops asked them to stop, and then Gansey had explained his situation and the cops had gotten out of their cars to help finish the job. Back then, it had surprised Ronan; he hadn't realized yet that Gansey could persuade even the sun to pause and give him the time.

They worked on Glendower and Monmouth Manufacturing for months. The first week of June, Gansey found a headless statue of a bird with *king* carved on its belly in Welsh. The second week, they wired a refrigerator in the upstairs bathroom, right next to the toilet. The third week, someone killed Niall Lynch. The fourth week, Ronan moved in.

Fixing a cereal-box front porch into place, Gansey asked, "What was the first thing you took out? Did you always know?"

Ronan found himself pleased to be quizzed. "No. It was a bunch of flowers. The first time."

He remembered that dream — a haunted old wood, blue, blousey flowers growing in the dapples. He'd walked through the whispering trees with an often-present dream companion, and then a huge presence had blown through the canopy, sudden as a storm cloud. Ronan, bereft with terror and the certainty that this alien force wanted *him*, only him, had snatched at anything he could before being ripped aloft.

When he'd woken, he'd clutched a pulpy handful of blue flowers of a sort no one had seen before. Ronan tried, now, to explain them to Gansey, the wrongness of the stamen, the furriness of the petals. The impossibility of them.

Even to Gansey, he couldn't admit the joy and terror of the moment. The heart-pounding thought: *I'm just like my father.*

As Ronan spoke, Gansey's eyes were half-closed, turned toward the night. His thoughtless expression was one of wonder or of pain; with Gansey, they were so often the same thing.

"That was an accident," Gansey reasoned. He capped the glue. "Now you can do it on purpose?"

Ronan couldn't decide if he should exaggerate his prowess or emphasize the difficulty of the task. "I can sometimes control what I bring, but I can't choose what I dream about."

"Tell me what it's like." Gansey stretched to get a mint leaf from his pocket. He put it on his tongue and spoke around it. "Walk me through it. What happens?"

From the vicinity of the wastebasket, there was a satisfying tearing sound as a small raven ripped a large envelope lengthwise.

"First," Ronan replied, "I get a beer."

Gansey shot him a withering look.

The truth was that Ronan didn't understand the process very well himself. He knew it had something to do with *how* he fell asleep. The dreams were more pliable when he drank. Less like taut anxiety and more like taffy, susceptible to careful manipulation until, all at once, they broke.

He was about to say this, but instead, what came out of his mouth was: "They're mostly in Latin."

"Beg pardon?"

"They always have been. I just didn't know it was Latin until I got older."

"Ronan, there's no reason for that," Gansey said sternly, as if Ronan had hurled a toy on the floor.

"No shit, Sherlock. But there it is."

"Is it your — your thoughts that are in Latin? Or the dialogue? Do other people speak Latin in them? Like, am I in your dreams?"

"Oh, yes, baby." It amused Ronan to say this, a lot. He laughed enough that Chainsaw abandoned her paper shredding to verify that he wasn't dying. Ronan sometimes dreamt of Adam, too, the latter boy sullen and elegant and fluently disdainful of dream-Ronan's clumsy attempts to communicate.

Gansey pressed on. "And I speak Latin?"

"Dude, you speak Latin in real life. That's not a good comparison. Yeah, fine, if you're there. But usually, it's strangers. Or the signs — the signs are in Latin. And the trees speak it."

"Like in Cabeswater."

Yes, like in Cabeswater. In familiar, familiar Cabeswater, although Ronan surely hadn't been there before this spring. Still, arriving there for the first time had felt like a dream he'd forgotten.

"Coincidence," Gansey said, because it wasn't, and because it had to be said. "And when you want something?"

"If I want something, I have to be, like, aware enough to know that I want it. Almost awake. And I have to really want it. And then I have to *hold* it." Ronan was about to use the example of the Camaro keys, but thought better of it. "I have to hold it not as a dream, but like it's real."

"I don't understand."

"I can't pretend to hold it. I have to really hold it."

"I still don't understand."

Neither did Ronan, but he didn't know how to say it any better. For a moment he was quiet, thinking, no sound but Chainsaw returning to the floor to pick at the corpse of the envelope.

"Look, it's like a handshake," he said finally. "You know when some guy goes in for the shake, and you've never met him before, and he puts it out there, and you just know in that moment right before the shake if it's going to be sweaty or not? It's like that."

"So what you're saying is you can't explain it."

"I *did* explain it."

"No, you used nouns and verbs together in a pleasing but illogical format."

"I *did* explain it," Ronan insisted, so ferociously that Chainsaw flapped, certain she was in trouble. "It's a nightmare, man — it's when you dream of getting bit and when you wake up your arm hurts. It's *that*."

"Oh," said Gansey. "Does it hurt?"

Sometimes, when he took something out of a dream, it was such a senseless rush that it left the real world pale and unsaturated for hours after. Sometimes he couldn't move his hands. Sometimes Gansey found him and thought he was drunk. Sometimes, he really was drunk.

"Does that mean yes? What is this thing, anyway?" Gansey had picked up the wooden box. When he turned one of the wheels, one of the buttons on the other side depressed.

"A puzzle box."

"What does that mean?"

"Fuck if I know. That's just what it was called in the dream."

Gansey eyed Ronan over the top of his wireframes. "Don't use that voice on *me*. You have no idea whatsoever?"

"I think it's supposed to translate things. That's what it did in the dream."

Up close, the carvings were letters and words. The buttons were so small and the letters so precise that it was impossible to see how it could've been made. Also impossible was how the wheels of characters could have been fixed into the box without there being any seams in the rainbow-striped grain of the wood.

"Latin on that side," Gansey observed. He turned it. "Greek here. What's that — Sanskrit, I think. Is this Coptic?"

Ronan said, "Who the hell knows what Coptic looks like?"

"You, apparently. I'm pretty sure that's what this is. And this side with the wheels is us. Well, our alphabet, anyway, and it's set to English words. But what is this side? The rest of these are dead languages, but I don't recognize this one."

"Look," Ronan said, pushing to his feet. "You're overcomplicating this." Stalking to Gansey, he took the box. He spun a few of the wheels on the English side, and at once buttons on the other sides began to move and shift. Something about their progress was illogical.

"That hurts my head," Gansey said.

Ronan showed the English side to him. The letters read *tree*. He flipped it to the Latin side. The letters had shifted to read *bratus*. Then round to the Greek side. δένδρον.

"So, it's translated the English into all those other languages. That's 'tree' in all those. I still don't know what language this is. *T'ire?* That doesn't sound like . . ." Gansey broke off, his knowledge of perished linguistic oddities exhausted. "God, I'm tired."

"So sleep."

Gansey gave him a look. It was a look that asked how Ronan, of all people, could be so stupid to think that sleep was just a thing that could be so easily acquired.

Ronan said, "So let's drive to the Barns."

Gansey gave him another look. It was a look that asked how Ronan, of all people, could be so stupid as to think that Gansey would agree to something so illegal on so little sleep.

Ronan said, "So let's go get some orange juice."

Gansey considered. He looked to where his keys sat on the desk beside his mint plant. The clock beside it, a repellently ugly vintage number Gansey had found lying by a bin at the dump, said *3:32*.

Gansey said, "Okay."

They went and got some orange juice.

6

"You are an unbelievable phone tramp," Blue said.

Orla, unoffended, replied, "You're just jealous that *this* isn't your job."

"I am not." Sitting on the floor of her mother's kitchen, Blue glared up at her older cousin as she tied her shoe. Orla towered over her in a shirt, stunning both for its skintight fit and its paisley print. The flare of her bell-bottoms was capacious enough to hide small animals in. She waved the phone above Blue in a hypnotic figure eight.

The phone in question was the psychic hotline that operated out of the second floor of 300 Fox Way. For a dollar a minute, customers received a gentle probing of their archetypes — a slightly more than gentle probing if Orla answered — and a host of tactful suggestions for how to improve their fates. Everyone in the house took turns answering it. Everyone, as Orla was pointing out, but Blue.

Blue's summer job required absolutely no extrasensory perception. In fact, working at Nino's would have probably been unbearable if she'd possessed any more than five senses. Blue generally had a policy of not doing things she despised, but she despised working at Nino's and had yet to quit. Or to get fired, for that matter. Waitressing required patience, a fixed and convincing smile, and the ability to continuously turn the other cheek while keeping diet sodas topped up. Blue possessed only one of these attributes at any given time, and it was never the one she needed. It didn't help that Nino's clientele was mostly Aglionby boys, who often thought rudeness was a louder sort of flirting.

The problem was that it paid well.

"Oh, please," Orla said. "Everyone knows that's why you're so irritable."

Blue stood up to face her cousin. Apart from her large nose, Orla was beautiful. She had long brown hair crowned with an embroidered headband, a long face pierced by a nose stud, and a long body made longer by platform wedges. Even when standing, Blue — barely five feet tall — only came to Orla's deeply brown throat.

"I don't care about being psychic or not." Which was partially true. Blue didn't envy Orla's clairvoyance. She *did* envy her ability to be different without even trying. Blue had to try. A lot.

Again with the waving of the phone. "Don't lie to me, Blue. I can read your *mind*."

"You can*not*," Blue replied tersely, scraping her button-covered wallet from the counter. Just because she wasn't psychic didn't mean she was clueless on the process. She glanced at the oven clock. Almost late. Practically late. Barely on time. "Unlike some people, my sense of self-worth isn't tied into my occupation."

"Ooooooooh," Orla crowed, galloping down the hall, stork-like. She traded her Henrietta accent for a gloriously snotty version of Old South. "Someone's been hanging out with Richard Campbell Gansey the third too much. 'My sense of self-worth isn't tied into my occupation.'" This last bit was said with the most exaggerated rendition of Gansey's accent possible. She sounded like a drunk Robert E. Lee.

Blue reached past Orla for the door. "Is this about me calling you a phone tramp? I don't take it back. No one needs to hear their future in that voice you do. Mom, make Orla go away. I have to go."

From her perch in the reading room, Maura looked up. She was a slightly taller version of her daughter, her features amused where Blue's were keen. "Are you going to Nino's? Come take a card."

Despite her lateness, Blue was unable to resist. *It'll only be a moment.* Ever since she was small, she'd loved the ritual of a single card reading. Unlike the elaborate Celtic cross tarot spreads her mother usually did for her clients, the single card reading she did for Blue was playful, fond, and brief. It wasn't so much a clairvoyant experience as a thirty-second bedtime story where Blue was always the hero.

Blue joined her mother, her spiky reflection dimly visible in the table's dull sheen. Not looking up from her tarot cards, Maura gave Blue's hand an affectionate shake and flipped over a card at random. "Ah, there you are."

It was the page of cups, the card Maura always said reminded her of Blue. In this deck, the art was of a fresh-faced young person holding a jewel-studded goblet. The suit of cups represented relationships — love and friendship — and the page stood for new and budding possibilities. This particular bedtime story was one Blue had heard too many times before. She could anticipate exactly what her mother was going to say next: *Look at all the potential she holds inside her!*

Blue cut her off. "When does the potential start being a real thing?"

"Ah, Blue."

"Don't 'ah, Blue' me." Blue released her mother's hand. "I just want to know when it stops being potential and starts being something more."

Maura briskly shuffled the card back into her deck. "Do you want the answer you're going to like, or the real one?"

Blue harrumphed. There was only one answer she ever wanted.

"Maybe you're already something more. You make other psychics so powerful just by being there. Maybe the potential you bring out in other people is your something more."

Blue had known her entire life that she was a rarity. And it was nice to be useful. But it wasn't enough. It was not, her soul thought, *something more.*

Very coolly, she said, "I'm not going to be a sidekick."

In the hallway, Orla repeated in Gansey's Southern nectar: "*I'm not gonna be a sidekick.* You should stop hanging out with millionaires, then."

Maura made an ill-tempered *tsss* between her teeth. "Orla, don't you have a call to make?"

"It doesn't matter. I'm going to work," Blue said, trying to keep Orla's words from digging in. But it was true that she looked a lot cooler at school than she did surrounded by psychics and rich boys.

No, she thought. *No, it's not about that. It's about what I do, not what I am.*

It felt a little feeble, though. It had been a lot easier when Adam, the poorest of the lot, had seemed more like her. Now she felt as if she had something to prove. The others were Team Power, and she was supposed to be Team Ingenuity or something.

Her mother waved a card at her in farewell. "Bye. Will you be home for dinner? I'm making midlife crisis."

"Oh," Blue said, "I guess I'll have a slice. If you're making it already."

When Blue got to Nino's, she discovered that Gansey, Adam, Noah, and Ronan had already commandeered one of the big tables in the back. Because she couldn't come to them, they'd brought the Glendower discussion to her.

Ha! she thought. *Take that, Orla!*

Adam and Gansey sat in a cracked orange booth along the wall. Noah and Ronan sat on chairs opposite. Resting in the spotlight provided by the hanging green light was a wooden box. A battalion of foreign language dictionaries surrounded it.

With effort, Blue compared her current image of the boys with the first time she'd seen them. They'd not only been strangers then, they'd been the enemy. It was hard to remember seeing them that way. Whatever her identity crisis was, it seemed to live at home, not with the boys.

She wouldn't have predicted that.

Blue brought a pitcher of iced tea to the table. "What's that?"

"Jane!" Gansey said joyfully.

Adam said, "It's a wizard in a box."

"It will do your homework," Noah added.

"And it's been dating your girlfriend," Ronan finished.

Blue scowled. "Are you all drunk?"

They dismissed her question and instead excitedly demonstrated the principles of the wooden box. She was less surprised than most people would have been to discover it was a magical translating box. She was more surprised to discover the boys had possessed the forethought to bring the other dictionaries.

"We wanted to know if it was always right," Gansey said. "And it seems to be."

"Hold on," Blue replied. She left the boys to take the drink orders of a couple at table fourteen. They both wanted iced tea.

Nino's was unfairly famous for its iced tea — there was even a sign in the window proclaiming that it had the best in Henrietta — despite the fact that Blue could attest to the tea-making process being completely unremarkable. *Raven boys must be easy prey to propaganda*, she thought.

When she returned, she leaned on the table beside Adam, who touched her wrist. She didn't know what to do in response. Touch it back? The moment had passed. She resented her body for not giving her the correct answer. She asked, "What is that other language, by the way?"

"We don't know," Gansey said, around his straw. "Why is the tea so good here?"

"I spit in it. Let me see this thing."

She accepted the box. It had some heft to it, as if one would find workings to all these dials inside. It felt, actually, a lot like Gansey's journal on Glendower. It had been lavishly dreamt — not what she'd expected of Ronan.

Fingers careful on the smooth, cool dials, Blue moved the wheels on the English side of the box so that they read *blue*. Buttons sucked in and wheels turned on the other sides of the box, fluid and silent.

Blue turned it slowly to read each side: *hyacinthus*, ⲩⲱⲩⲉⲛ, नील, *celea*. One side was blank.

Gansey pointed to each side for her. "Latin, Coptic, Sanskrit, something we don't know, and . . . this is supposed to be Greek. Isn't that funny that it's blank?"

Derisively, Ronan said, "No. The ancient Greeks didn't have a word for blue."

Everyone at the table looked at him.

"What the hell, Ronan?" said Adam.

"It's hard to imagine," Gansey mused, "how this evidently

successful classical education never seems to make it into your school papers."

"They never ask the right questions," Ronan replied.

At the front of the restaurant, the door opened. It would fall to Blue to seat the new party, but she lingered by the table, frowning at the box.

She said, "I have a right question. What is the language on this side?"

Ronan's expression was petulant.

Gansey tilted his head. "We don't know."

Blue pointed at Ronan, who curled a lip. "*He* does. Somewhere in there. I know it."

"You don't know shit," Ronan said.

There was the very briefest of pauses. It was true that this sort of venom was not unusual from Ronan. But it had been a very long while since it had been used so forcefully on Blue. She drew herself up, everything prickling.

Then Gansey said, very slowly, "Ronan, you're never going to talk to Jane like that again."

Both Adam and Blue stared at Gansey, who concentrated his gaze on his napkin. It wasn't what he said but how he looked at no one when he said it that made the moment strange.

Blue, feeling oddly warm around the cheeks, told Gansey, "I don't need you to stand up for me. Don't *you*" — this was directed at Ronan — "think I'll let you talk to me like that. Especially not just because you're mad I'm right."

As she whirled toward the front, she heard Adam say, "You're such a *dick*," and Noah laugh. Her spirits sank as she saw who stood at the hostess stand: Joseph Kavinsky. He was unmistakable: the sort of raven boy who was clearly an import from elsewhere. Everything about his facial structure — the long nose; the hollowed-out, heavy-lidded eyes; the dark arch of his eyebrows — was completely unlike the Valley faces she'd grown up with. Like many of the other raven boys, he sported massive sunglasses, spiked hair, a small earring, a chain around his neck, and a white tank top. But unlike the other raven boys, he terrified Blue.

"Hey, baby doll," he greeted Blue. He was already standing too close, moving restlessly. He was always moving. There was something erratic and vulgar about the full line of his lips, like he'd swallow her if he got close enough. She hated the smell of him.

He was infamous, even at her school. You wanted something to get you through your exams, he had it. You wanted a fake license, he could get it. You wanted something to hurt you, he was it.

"I am not a baby doll," Blue said icily, picking up a laminated menu. Her face was burning again. "Table for one?"

But he wasn't even listening to her. He rocked on his heels, jerking his chin up to see who else was in the restaurant. Without looking at her again, he said, "My party's already here."

He walked away. Like she'd never been there.

She wasn't sure if she couldn't forgive Kavinsky for always managing to make her feel so insignificant, or herself, for knowing it was coming and being unable to guard herself against it.

She stuffed the menu back in the hostess station and stood there for a second, hating them all, hating this job, feeling strangely humiliated.

Then she took a deep breath and filled up table fourteen's tea.

Kavinsky headed directly to the large table in the back, and the postures of the other boys all changed drastically. Adam looked at the table with a studied disinterest. Smudgy Noah ducked his head down into his shoulders, but couldn't take his eyes off the newcomer. Gansey stood, leaning against the table, and there was something threatening rather than respectful about it. Ronan, however, was the one who had transformed the most. Though his casual position — arms crossed — remained the same, his shoulders were knotted with visible tension. Something about his eyes was ferocious and alive in the same way that they had been when he'd launched the plane in the field.

"I saw your POS out front," Kavinsky told Gansey. "And I remembered I had something for Lynch."

Laughing, he dropped a dry, tangled pile in front of Ronan.

Ronan eyed the gift, one eyebrow raised in glorious disdain. Leaning back, he pulled one of the strands to reveal that it was a collection of wristbands identical to the ones he always wore.

"How sweet, man." Ronan lifted it higher, like spaghetti. "It goes with everything."

"Like your mom," Kavinsky agreed with good humor.

"What am I supposed to do with them?"

"Hell if I know. I just thought of you. Regift them. White rabbit shit."

"Elephant," murmured Gansey.

"Don't bring politics into this, Dick," Kavinsky replied. He slapped a palm on Ronan's shaved head and rubbed it. Ronan looked ready to bite him. "Well, I'm out. Things to do. Enjoy your book club, ladies."

He didn't even look at Blue as he left. *Him not hitting on you is a good thing*, she told herself. She felt invisible. Unseeable. *Is this how Noah feels?*

Gansey said, "The only thing that gives me any joy is imagining the used car dealership he'll be working in by the time he's thirty."

Ronan, head down, kept studying the leather bands. One of his hands was a fist. Blue wondered what the real meaning of Kavinsky's gift was. She wondered if Ronan knew the real meaning.

"Like I said," Gansey muttered. "Trouble."

7

The Gray Man hated his current rental car. He got the distinct impression it hadn't been handled enough by humans when it was young, and now would never be pleasant to be around. Since he'd picked it up, it had already tried to bite him several times and had spent a considerable amount of time resisting his efforts to achieve the speed limit.

Also, it was champagne. Ridiculous color for a car.

He would have returned it for another, but the Gray Man made a point of staying unmemorable if he could. His previous rental had acquired an unfortunate and possibly incriminating stain in the backseat. Better to put some distance between himself and it.

After dutifully filling the car with Greenmantle's machines and dials, the Gray Man went on an electrical goose chase. He didn't mind terribly that the flashing lights and humming alarms and scattered needles weren't painting a coherent map to the Greywaren. Henrietta had considerable charms. The downtown was populated by daintily greasy sandwich shops and aggressively down-home junk shops, swaybacked porches and square columns, all of the buildings tired but tidy as library books. He peered through the car window as he passed by. Locals on chairs on porches peered back.

The readings continued to be meaningless, so he parked the Champagne Monstrosity at the corner drugstore, which advertised BEST TUNA FISH IN TOWN! He ordered a sandwich and a milkshake from a red-lipped lady, and as he leaned on the stainless-steel counter, the power went out.

The red-lipped lady used a meaty fist to thump the now-dormant milkshake machine and swore in a soft accent that made it sound affectionate. She assured him, "It'll come back on in a minute."

All of the shelves and greeting cards and pharmaceuticals looked eerie and apocalyptic in the indirect light from the front windows. "Does this happen a lot?"

"Since this spring, yes, sir. Goes out. Gets them surges, too, blows out them transformers and everything catches fire. Turns on the stadium lights, too, down at Aglionby, when nobody's there for a game. Sure all those terrible boys are gone for the summer. Well, most all of them. But you're not staying, are you?"

"A few weeks."

"Then you'll be here for the Fourth."

The Gray Man had to drag up a mental calendar. He didn't celebrate many holidays.

"You come down here and see the county show," she said, giving his half-blended milkshake a dispirited twitch. "You get yourself a nice view of the fireworks from the courthouse. Don't be fooled by those other ones."

"The ones people do at home?"

"The Aglionby ones," she said. "Some of them boys blow up all kinds of things they shouldn't be getting into. Terrorize the old ladies. Don't know why the sheriff don't stop him."

"Him?" The Gray Man was interested in how the plural *Aglionby ones* suddenly became a singular *him*.

She seemed to be in a reverie, watching cars go slowly by the big pane-glass windows. Eventually, she continued, "Probably it's

HEPCO's fault; they knew their wires was old, but do they replace them? No."

He blinked at the sudden shift in conversation. "HEPCO?"

"Beg pardon? Oh, Henrietta Electric Power Company." Only, with her accent it sounded like *Henretta Lektrick Poywurr Cuhmpuhnnay.* As if invoked by her voice, the electricity came back on. "Oh, there it is back again. Told you there's no need for worries."

"Oh," the Gray Man said, with a glance at the crackling fluorescent lights overhead, "I wasn't worried."

She chuckled. It was a deeply satisfied and knowing sort of laugh. "I reckon not."

The tuna fish was good. It was the only one he'd had since he arrived, however, so he couldn't say whether it was the best in town.

He kept driving. Victorians turned into fields as he crossed over the interstate, past steepled barns and white farmhouses, active goats and deceased pickup trucks. Everything was painted in the same color palette, ruddy greens and deep-green reds; even the rubbish looked as if it had grown from the sloping hills. Only the mountains looked out of place, blue ghosts on every horizon.

Much to the Gray Man's surprise, Greenmantle's meters seemed to be coming to a consensus.

They led him onto another back road. Ramblers and mailboxes poked through the soil.

His phone rang.

It was his brother.

The Gray Man's stomach wrung itself out.

The phone rang only twice. *Missed call.* His brother had never intended for him to pick up; he merely wanted this: the Gray

Man stopping the car, wondering if he was supposed to return the call. Wondering if his brother was going to call back. Untangling the wired threads in his gut.

Finally, a Labrador retriever barking at the door grounded him again. He shut the phone into the glove box, out of sight.

Back to Greenmantle's devices.

They led him to a yellow house with an empty carport. With the EMF reader in one hand and a cesium magnetometer in the other, he climbed into the heat and followed the energy field.

He ducked under a desolate clothesline. There was a doghouse, but no dog. The air had the dry, complicated scent of a cornfield, but there was no cornfield. He was eerily reminded of the foreboding drugstore with the lights off.

In the backyard was an ambitious vegetable garden where seven impeccable rows flourished — textbook tomatoes, peas, beans, and carrots. The next four rows were not quite as productive. As he followed the increasingly frantic light on the EMF reader, the rows thinned further. The final three were merely strips of bare dirt pointed toward the distant fields. A few desiccated vines curled up the bamboo stakes, nothing but skeletons.

The instruments guided the Gray Man to a rosebush planted on the other side of the dead rows, directly in front of a concrete well cover. Unlike the dry vines, the rose was hyper-alive. Above an ordinary green trunk, dozens of twisted shoots clawed from the old canes, contorting tightly around one another. Each mutated cane was tinged the florid red of new growth; it looked eerily as if blood ran through them. The new shoots bristled with malevolent red spines.

The ultimate result of this furious growth was apparent in the blackened knots of branches above. Dead. The rose was growing itself to death.

The Gray Man was impressed by the deep *wrong*ness of it.

A few waves of the meters confirmed that the energy was centered directly on the bush or the ground beneath it. An energy anomaly could possibly explain its hideous overgrowth. He didn't see, however, how it could be connected to the Greywaren. Unless —

Glancing toward the house, he set down his machines and hefted up the well's lid.

The EMF reader screamed, every light furiously red. The magnetometer's reading spiked jaggedly.

Cool air spiraled out of the impenetrably dark opening. He had a flashlight in the car, but he didn't think it would begin to pierce the depths. He contemplated what it would take to retrieve an object hidden in a well, if it came to that.

Just as suddenly as they'd started, both of the machines went quiet.

Startled, he gave them an experimental swing of his arm — nothing. Carried them around the rosebush. Nothing. Hung them over the well. Nothing. Whatever spurt of wild energy had brought him here was gone.

It was possible, he thought, that the Greywaren was something that worked in pulses, and it had just shut off from its hiding place in the well.

But it was more possible, he thought, that this had to do with HEPCO's little problem. The same energy surges that affected the stadium power might be at work here. Escaping from this water source. Somehow poisoning that blackened rose.

The Gray Man replaced the well cover, wiped a sheen of sweat from the back of his neck, and straightened.

He took a photo of the rose with his phone. And then he headed back to the car.

8

Adam Parrish had bigger problems than Ronan's dreams. For starters, his new home. These days, he lived in a tiny room above the St. Agnes rectory. The entire place had been built in the late seventeen hundreds and looked it. Adam was constantly smashing his head heroically against sloped ceilings and jabbing lethal splinters into his sock feet. The entire room had that smell of very old houses — plaster must and timber dust and forgotten flowers. He had provided the furnishings: a flat IKEA mattress on the bare floor, plastic bins and cardboard boxes as nightstands and desk, a rug found on sale for three dollars.

It was nothing, but it was Adam Parrish's nothing. How he hated and loved it. How proud he was of it, how wretched it was.

Adam Parrish's nothing lacked air-conditioning. There was no escaping the heat of a Virginian summer. He was too familiar with the sensation of sweat trickling down the inside of his pants leg.

And then there were the three part-time jobs that paid his Aglionby tuition. He crammed in the work hours now to afford a more leisurely fall when school started. He'd spent just two hours at the easiest of the jobs — Boyd's Body & Paint, LLC, replacing brake pads and changing oil and finding what was making that squeaking noise there, no, *there* — and now, even though he was off, he was ruined for anything else. Sticky and sore and, above all else, tired, always tired.

Little lights danced at the corner of his vision as he chained his bike to the staircase outside his place. Swiping the back of his sweaty hand over the front of his sweaty forehead, he climbed the stairs, and realized Blue was waiting at the top.

Blue Sargent was pretty in a way that was physically painful to him. He was attracted to her like a heart attack. Currently, she sat against his door in lace leggings and a tunic made of a ripped-up oversized Beatles shirt. She had been paging idly through the supermarket's weekly saver, but she put it down when she saw him.

The only rub was, Blue was another troubling thing. She was like Gansey in that she wanted him to explain himself. What do you *want*, Adam? What do you *need*, Adam? *Want* and *need* were words that got eaten smaller and smaller: freedom, autonomy, a perennial bank balance, a stainless-steel condo in a dustless city, a silky black car, to make out with Blue, eight hours of sleep, a cell phone, a bed, to kiss Blue just once, a blister-less heel, bacon for breakfast, to hold Blue's hand, one hour of sleep, toilet paper, deodorant, a soda, a minute to close his eyes.

What do you *want*, Adam?

To feel awake when my eyes are open.

"Hey," she said. "You've got mail."

He knew. He'd already seen the ignored, unopened envelope emblazoned with Aglionby Academy's raven crest. For two days he'd been stepping over it, as if it might disappear if he failed to acknowledge it. He'd already gotten his grades, and the envelope wasn't fat enough for the quarterly fund-raising gala information. It might be just an alumni banquet or a photo book advertisement. The school was always sending out notices for opportunities to enhance the Aglionby experience. Summer camps and flying lessons, deluxe yearbooks and custom raven-emblazoned apparel. These Adam threw out. They were meant for the eyes of affluent parents in houses decorated with framed images of their children.

But this time, he didn't think it was a fund-raiser notification.

He stooped to retrieve it, then hesitated, fingers on the door-knob. "Are you coming in? I need a shower."

There was a beat. *This was easier,* Adam thought suddenly, *when we didn't know each other.*

Blue said, "You can take one. I don't mind. Just figured I'd come say hi before my shift."

He played the key in the lock and let them both in. They stopped in the center of the room, the only place they could stand without ducking.

"So," she said.

"So," he said.

"What's new at work?"

Adam struggled to think of an anecdote. His mind was a box he tipped out at the end of his shifts. "Yesterday, Boyd asked me if I wanted to be his tech for his next season. Rally season."

"What does that mean?"

"I'd have a job after I graduated. I'd be gone six or seven weeks out of the year." It had been a flattering offer, actually. Most of the mechanics who traveled with Boyd had been at it far longer than Adam.

Blue guessed, "You said no."

He glanced at her. He couldn't read her as easily as he could read Gansey. He couldn't tell if she was pleased or disappointed.

"I'm going to college." He didn't add that he wasn't killing himself at Aglionby to end up a fancy mechanic. That might have been good enough, if he hadn't known what else was out there. If he hadn't grown up next door to Aglionby Academy. If you never saw the stars, candles were enough.

She poked a toe at a half-rebuilt fuel pump sitting on newspapers. "Yep."

There was something there, lurking just behind her answer, some private distress. He touched her face. "Something wrong?"

It was not quite fair. He knew that his touch would distract both of them from the question. Sure enough, Blue closed her eyes. He pressed his palm on her cool cheek, then, after a pause, down her neck. His hand was hyperaware of what it was feeling: the stray hairs at the base of her neck, the faint tackiness of her skin that came from the memory of the sun, the lump of her throat moving as she swallowed.

He captured her with his other hand, pulling her closer. Carefully. Now she was pressed against him, close enough for him to be self-conscious of his sweaty T-shirt. His chin rested on the top of her head. Her arms linked loosely around him; he felt her breath heat the fabric of his shirt. He couldn't forget that his hip bone was pressed against her.

It wasn't enough. He ached inside. But there was a line he wasn't allowed to cross, and he was never sure where it started. Surely this was close to it. He felt dangerous and kinetic.

Then her fingers cautiously pressed into his back, feeling his spine. He hadn't gone too far, then.

He leaned in to kiss her.

Blue tore herself from his arms. She actually tripped in her haste to get away. Her head knocked against the slanted ceiling.

"I said *no*," she gasped, hand clapped on the back of her skull.

Something stung in him. "Like *six* weeks ago."

"It's still no!"

They stared at each other, both hurt.

"Just," she said, ". . . just, not kissing."

He still ached. His skin was a constellation of nerve endings. "I don't understand."

Blue touched her lips as if they *had* been kissed. "I *told* you."

He just wanted an answer. He wanted to know if it was him, or if it was her. He didn't know how to ask it, but he did anyway. "Did something . . . happen to you?"

Her face was blank for a moment. "What? Oh. *No.* Does there have to be a reason? The answer's just no! Isn't that good enough?"

The correct answer was yes. He knew it. But the real answer was that he wanted to know if he had bad breath or if she was only doing this with him because he was the first one to ask her or if there was some other obstruction that he wasn't considering.

"I'm going to take a shower," he said. He tried not to let it sound like he was still hurt, but he was, and it did. "You gonna be here when I get back out? When's your shift start?"

"I'll wait." She tried not to let it sound like she was hurt, but she was, and it did.

While Blue paged through a few maps he had on his plastic bed stand, Adam stood in a cold shower until his heart stopped steaming. *What do you* want, *Adam?* He didn't even know. From inside the sloped old shower, he caught a half-image of himself in the mirror and startled. For a moment something about his own reflection had seemed wrong. His wide eyes and gaunt face peered back at him, troubled but not unusual.

And just like that, he was thinking of Cabeswater again. Some days he felt he didn't think of anything else. He hadn't owned many things in his life, properly owned them, him and no one else, but now he did: this bargain. It had been a little over a month since he'd offered his sacrifice to Cabeswater in order to wake Gansey's ley line. The entire ritual felt swimmy and surreal in his mind, like he'd been watching himself perform it on a television screen. Adam had gone fully prepared to make a sacrifice. But he wasn't quite sure how the specific one he'd eventually made had come to him: *I will be your hands. I will be your eyes.*

So far, nothing had happened, not really. Which was almost worse. He was a patient with a diagnosis that he couldn't understand.

In the shower, Adam scratched a thumbnail across his summer-brown skin. The line of his nail went from white to angry red in a moment, and as he studied it, it struck him that there was something odd about the flow of the water across his skin. As if it was in slow-motion. He followed the stream of water up to the showerhead and spent a full minute watching it sputter from the metal. His thoughts were a confusion of translucent drops clinging to metal and rain trembling off green leaves.

He blinked.

There was nothing odd about the water. There were no leaves. He needed to get some sleep before he did something stupid on the job.

Climbing out of the shower, his spine aching, shoulders aching, soul aching, Adam dried and dressed slowly. He feared — hoped? — that Blue might have left after all, but when he opened the bathroom door, scrubbing his hair dry, he discovered that she stood at the door, talking cheerfully to someone.

The visitor turned out to be St. Agnes's office lady, her black hair curled in the humidity. She probably had an official title that Ronan knew, sub-nun, or something, but Adam only knew her as Mrs. Ramirez. She seemed to do everything a church required to keep it running, short of saying Mass.

Including the collection of Adam's monthly rent check.

When he saw her, his stomach plummeted. He was filled with the certainty that his last check had bounced. She would tell him there were insufficient funds, and Adam would scramble to push money into the yawning hole of the account, and then he'd have to pay a returned check fee to the bank and another one to Mrs. Ramirez, getting further behind on his next month's rent, an endless pathetic loop of insufficiency.

Voice thin, he asked, "What can I do for you, ma'am?"

Her expression shifted. She wasn't sure how to say what needed to be said.

Adam's fingers tightened on the door frame.

"Oh, sweetie," she said, "I'm just letting you know about the rent on your little room here."

I'm so done, he thought. *No more. Please, I can't take any more.*

"Well, we got a new — tax assessment," she started. "For this building. And you know how we charge you as a nonprofit. So we . . . your rent's going to change. It's got to stay the same percentage of the, uh, building costs. It's two hundred dollars less."

Adam heard *two hundred* and wilted, and then he heard the rest and thought he must have misunderstood. "Less? Each year?"

"Each month."

Blue looked delighted, but Adam couldn't quite accept that his rent had just dropped by two thirds. Twenty-four hundred dollars a year, suddenly freed up. His dubious Henrietta accent slid out before he could stop it. "Why did you say it was changing?"

"Tax assessment." She laughed at his suspicion. "Those taxes don't normally work out on the happy side, do they!"

She waited for Adam to answer, but he didn't know what to say. Finally, he managed, "Thank you, ma'am."

As Blue closed the door, he drifted back to the center of the room. He still couldn't quite believe it. No, *wouldn't* believe it. It just didn't track. He retrieved the letter from Aglionby. Sinking onto his flat mattress, he finally opened it.

Its contents were very thin indeed, just a single-spaced letter on Aglionby letterhead. It didn't take long to convey its message. The following year's tuition was increasing to cover additional costs, although his scholarship was not. They understood the tuition raise presented a hardship for him, and he was an exceptional student, but they needed to remind him, with as much kindness as possible, that the waiting list for Aglionby was quite long, inhabited by exceptional boys able to pay full tuition. In conclusion, they reminded Mr. Parrish that fifty percent of the next year's tuition was due by the end of the month in order to hold his place.

The difference in tuition between this year's and next was twenty-four hundred dollars.

That number again. It couldn't be a coincidence.

"Do you want to talk about it?" Blue asked, sitting down beside him.

He didn't want to talk about it.

Gansey had to be behind it. He knew Adam would never accept the money from him, so he'd engineered all of this. Persuaded Mrs. Ramirez to take a check and manufacture a tax assessment to cover his tracks. Gansey must have gotten a matching tuition notice two days ago. The raise wouldn't have meant anything to him.

For a brief moment, he imagined life as Gansey must live it. The car keys in his pocket. The brand-new shoes on his feet. The careless glance at the monthly bills. They couldn't hurt Gansey. Nothing could hurt him; people who said money couldn't buy everything hadn't seen anyone as rich as the Aglionby boys. They were untouchable, immune to life's troubles. Only death couldn't be swiped away by a credit card.

One day, Adam thought miserably, *one day that will be me.*

But this ruse wasn't right. He would have never asked for Gansey's help. Adam wasn't sure how he would have covered the tuition raise, but it was not *this,* not Gansey's money. He pictured it: a folded-over check, hastily pocketed, gazes not met. Gansey relieved that Adam had finally come to his senses. Adam unable to say thank you.

He became aware that Blue was watching him, her lips pursed, eyebrows tight.

"Don't look at me like that," he said.

"Like what? I'm not allowed to be worried about you?"

Heat hissed through his voice. "I don't want your pity."

If Gansey wasn't allowed to pity him, Blue sure as hell wasn't allowed to. She and Adam were in the same boat, after all. Wasn't she on her way to work, the same as he'd just come from it?

Blue said, "Then don't be pitiful!"

Anger snarled up in him, instantly owning him. It was a binary emotion in the Parrishes. No such thing as slightly mad. Only nothing, and then this: all-encompassing fury.

"What's pitiful about me, Blue? Tell me what's pitiful." He jumped up. "Is it 'cause I work for everything I get? Is that what makes me pitiful and Gansey not?" He shook the letter. "Is it because I don't get this *given* to me?"

She didn't flinch, but something simmered in her eyes. "No."

His voice was terrible; he heard it. *"I don't want your damn pity."*

Her face was shocked. "What did you say?"

She was looking at the box that served as his nightstand. Somehow it had moved several feet away from the bed. The side was badly dented, its former contents scattered violently across the floor. Only now did he remember the act of kicking the box, but not the *decision* to kick it.

It hadn't switched off the anger.

For a long moment, Blue stared at him, and then she stood up.

"You be careful, Adam Parrish. 'Cause one day you might get what you ask for. There might be girls in Henrietta who'll let you talk to them like that, but I'm not one of them. Now I'm going to go sit on those stairs out there until my shift. If you can be — be *human* before then, come get me. If not, I'll see you later."

She ducked a little to keep from smashing her head, and then she shut the door behind her. It would have been easier if she'd yelled or cried. Instead his words just kept hitting flint inside his thoughts, again and again, another spark, and another. She was just as bad as Gansey. *Where does she get off?* When he graduated and flew from this place, and she was still trapped here, she'd feel stupid about all this.

He wanted to open the door and shout this fact at her.

He made himself stay where he was.

After a moment, he calmed enough to see how his anger was a separate thing inside him, a dingy, surprise gift from his father. He calmed enough to remember that if he waited long enough, carefully analyzing how it felt, the emotion would lose its inertia. It was the same as physical pain. The more he tried to mentally decide what made pain hurt, the less his brain seemed able to remember the pain at all.

So he took apart the anger inside him.

Is this what he felt like, he wondered, *when he grabbed my sleeve as I was going out the door? Is this what made him shove my face into the fridge? Did he feel this when he passed by my bedroom door? Was this what he fought every time he remembered I existed?*

He calmed enough to realize it wasn't even Blue he had been angry at. She'd just been unlucky enough to be standing in the blast zone when he went off.

He'd never escape, not really. Too much monster blood in him. He'd left the den, but his breeding betrayed him. And he knew why he was pitiful. It wasn't because he had to pay for his school or because he had to work for a living. It was because he was trying to be something he could never be. The sham was pitiful. He didn't need to graduate. He needed Glendower.

Some nights he lured himself to sleep by imagining how he would word the favor for Glendower. He needed to get the words exactly right. Now he rolled phrases around his mouth, desperately reaching for one that would comfort him. Ordinarily, words would tumble and lull through his mind, but this time, all he could think was *Fix me.*

Suddenly, he caught another image.

Right after he did, he thought, *What does that mean?* One couldn't *catch* an image. And he certainly hadn't done it more than once. But the sensation lingered, an idea that he had glimpsed, or felt, or remembered some movement at the corner of his eye. A snapshot captured just behind his eyes.

He had a strange, disconcerting feeling that he couldn't trust his senses. Like he was tasting an image or smelling a feeling or touching a sound. It was the same as just a few minutes before, the idea that he'd glimpsed a slightly wrong reflection of himself.

Adam's previous worries vanished, replaced with a more immediate concern for this ragged body he was carting around in. He'd been hit so many times. He'd already lost his hearing in his left ear. Maybe something else had been destroyed on one of those tense, wretched nights.

Then he caught another image.

He turned.

9

When Adam called, Ronan, Noah, and Gansey were at the Dollar City in Henrietta, loitering. Theoretically, they were there for batteries. Practically, they were there because both Blue and Adam had work, Ronan's shapeless anger always got worse at night, and Dollar City was one of the few stores in Henrietta that allowed pets.

Gansey answered his phone as Ronan examined a package of erasers shaped like alligators. The Day-Glo animals wore an assortment of six aghast expressions. Noah tried to skew his mouth to match as Chainsaw, buried in the crook of Ronan's arm, eyed them suspiciously. At the end of the aisle, the clerk viewed Chainsaw with equal distrust. When Dollar City had said *Pets Welcome*, Dollar City wasn't certain they'd meant carrion birds.

Ronan was very much enjoying the clerk's petulant gaze.

"Hello? Oh, hey," Gansey said to the phone, touching a notebook with a handgun printed on the cover. The *oh, hey* was accompanied by a definite change in the timbre of his voice. That meant it was Adam, and that somehow stoked Ronan's anger. Everything was worse at night. "I thought you were still at work. What? Oh, we're at the Bourgeoisie Playground."

Ronan showed Gansey a plastic wall clock cleverly molded in the shape of a turkey. The wattle, hanging below the clock face, ticked off the seconds.

"Mon dieu!" Gansey said. To the phone, he said, "If you're not

sure, it probably wasn't. A woman is hard to mistake for anything else."

Ronan wasn't exactly sure why he was angry. Although Gansey had done nothing to invoke his ire, he was definitely part of the problem. Currently, he propped his cell between ear and shoulder as he eyed a pair of plastic plates printed with smiling tomatoes. His unbuttoned collar revealed a good bit of his collarbone. No one could deny that Gansey was a glorious portrait of youth, the well-tended product of a fortunate and moneyed pairing. Ordinarily, he was so polished that it was bearable, though, because he was clearly not the same species as Ronan's rough-and-ready family. But tonight, under the fluorescent lights of Dollar City, Gansey's hair was scuffed and his cargo shorts were a greasy ruin from mucking over the Pig. He was barelegged and sockless in his Top-Siders and very clearly a real human, an attainable human, and this, somehow, made Ronan want to smash his fist through a wall.

Holding the phone away from his mouth, Gansey told them, "Adam thinks he saw an apparition at his place."

Ronan eyed Noah. "I'm seeing an apparition right now."

Noah made a rude gesture, a hilariously unthreatening act coming from him, like a growl from a kitten. The clerk clucked audibly.

Chainsaw took the clucking as a personal affront. She plucked irritably at the leather bands on Ronan's wrist, reminding him of Kavinsky's strange gift earlier. It was not an entirely comfortable feeling to think of the other boy studying him that closely. Kavinsky had gotten the five bands precisely right, down to the tone of the leather. Ronan wondered what he was hoping to achieve.

"For how long?" Gansey asked the phone.

Ronan rested his forehead on the topmost shelf. The metal edge snarled against his skull, but he didn't move. At night, the longing for home was ceaseless and omniscient, an airborne contaminant. He saw it in Dollar City's cheap oven mitts — that was his mother at dinnertime. He heard it in the slam of the cash register drawer — that was his father coming home at midnight. He smelled it in the sudden whiff of air freshener — that was the family trips to New York.

Home was so close at night. He could be there in twenty minutes. He wanted to smash everything off these shelves.

Noah had wandered down the aisle, but now he gleefully returned with a snow globe. He stood behind Ronan until he pushed off the shelf to admire the atrocity. A seasonally decorated palm tree and two faceless sunbathers were trapped inside, along with a painted, erroneous statement: *IT'S ALWAYS CHRISTMAS SOMEWHERE.*

"Glitter," whispered Noah reverentially, giving it a shake. Sure enough, it was not fake snow but glitter that precipitated on the eternal holiday sands. Both Ronan and Chainsaw watched, transfixed, as the colorful bits caught in the palm tree.

Farther down the aisle, Gansey suggested to the phone, "You could come stay at Monmouth. For the night."

Ronan laughed sharply, loud enough for Gansey to hear. Adam was militant about staying at his place, even though it was horrible. Even if the room had been a five-star accommodation, it would have been hateful. Because it wasn't the bruised home Adam desperately and shamefully missed, nor was it Monmouth Manufacturing, the new home Adam's pride wouldn't allow. Sometimes Ronan thought Adam was so used to the right way being painful that he doubted any path that didn't come with agony.

Gansey's back was turned to them. "Look, I don't know what you're talking about. Ramirez? I didn't talk to anyone at the church. Yes, twenty-four hundred dollars. I know that part. I —"

This meant they were talking about the Aglionby letter; both Ronan and Gansey had gotten matching ones.

Now Gansey's voice was low and furious. "At some point it's not cheati — no, you're right. You're right, I absolutely don't understand. I don't know and I won't ever."

Probably, Adam had made the connection between his rent change and the tuition raise. It wasn't a complicated assumption, and he was clever. It was easy, too, to hang it on Gansey. If Adam had been thinking straight, though, he would've considered how it was Ronan who had infinite connections to St. Agnes. And how whoever was behind the rent change would have had to enter a church office with both a wad of cash and a burning intention to persuade a church lady to lie about a fake tax assessment. Taken apart that way, it seemed to have *Ronan* written all over it. But one of the marvelous things about being Ronan Lynch was that no one ever expected him to do anything nice for anyone.

"It wasn't me," Gansey said, "but I'm glad it happened that way. Fine. Take from that what you will."

The thing was, Ronan knew what a face looked like, just before it was about to break. He'd seen it in the mirror often enough. Adam had fracture lines all over him.

Next to Ronan, Noah said, "Oh!" in a very surprised way.

Then he flickered out.

The snow globe crashed onto the ground where Noah's feet used to be. It left a damp, wobbly ellipse as it rolled away. Chainsaw, shocked, bit Ronan. He'd squeezed her as he leapt back from the sound.

The clerk said, "Come *on.*"

She hadn't seen the travesty. But she clearly knew one had occurred.

"Don't get excited," Ronan said loudly. "I'll pay for it."

He would have never admitted how his heart pounded in his chest.

Gansey turned sharply, his face puzzled. The scene — Noah absent, ugly snow globe rolled half under a shelf — offered no immediate explanation. To Adam, he said, "Hold on."

Abruptly, Ronan's entire body went cold. Not a little chilly, but utterly cold. The sort of cold that dries the mouth and slows the blood. His toes went numb, and then his fingers. Chainsaw let out a terrified creaking sound.

She cried, *"Kerah!"*

He laid a frozen hand over her head, comforting her, though he was not comforted.

Then Noah reappeared in a violent sputter, like the power crackling back on. His fingers clutched Ronan's arm. Cold seeped from the point of contact as Noah dragged heat to become visible. An absolutely perfect breath of Henrietta summer air dissipated around them, the scent of the forest when Noah had died.

They all knew that Noah could drop the temperature in the room when he first manifested, but this scale was something new.

"Whoa! Way to ask first, asshole!" Ronan said. But he didn't push him off. "What was *that?*"

Noah's eyes were wide.

Gansey told Adam, "I'll call you back."

The clerk said, "Are you boys done yet?"

"Nearly!" Gansey called back in his reassuringly honeyed voice, shoving his phone in his back pocket. "I'll be up for paper

73

towels in a minute! *What's happening here?*" This last bit was hissed to Ronan and Noah.

"Noah took a personal day."

"I lost . . ." Noah struggled for words. "There wasn't air. It went *away*. The — the line!"

"The ley line?" Gansey asked.

Noah nodded once, a sloppy thing that was sort of a shrug at the same time. "There was nothing . . . left for me." Releasing Ronan, he shook out his hands.

"You're welcome, man," Ronan snarled. He still couldn't feel his toes.

"Thanks. I didn't mean to . . . you were there. Oh, the *glitter.*"

"Yes," Ronan replied crossly. "The glitter."

Gansey swiftly retrieved the leaking snow globe and disappeared for the front counter. He returned with a receipt and a roll of paper towels.

Ronan asked, "What was up with Parrish?"

"He saw a woman in his apartment. He said she was trying to talk to him. He seemed a little freaked out. I think the ley line must be surging."

He didn't say, *Or maybe something terrible happened to Adam that day he sacrificed himself in Cabeswater. Maybe he's messed up all of Henrietta by waking up the ley line.* Because they couldn't talk about that. Just like they couldn't talk about Adam stealing the Camaro that night. Or about him basically doing everything Gansey had asked him not to. If Adam was stupid about his pride, Gansey was stupid about Adam.

Ronan echoed, "Ley line surging. Right. Yeah, I'll bet that's it."

All the whimsy of Dollar City was ruined. As Gansey led the way out, Noah said to Ronan, "I know why you're mad."

Ronan sneered at him, but his pulse heaved. "Tell me then, Prophet."

Noah said, "It's not my job to tell other people's secrets."

10

I was thinking you could come with me," Gansey said carefully, two hours later. He pressed the phone to his ear with one shoulder as he unrolled a massive scroll of paper across the floor of Monmouth Manufacturing. The numerous low lamps through the room made an array of searchlights across the paper. "To the party at my mom's. There might be an internship in there, if you're good at it."

On the other end of the phone, Adam didn't immediately reply. It was hard to say if he was thinking about it or being irritated about the suggestion.

Gansey kept unrolling the paper. It was a high-resolution print of the ley line as seen from a casually interested satellite. It had cost a fortune to get the images spliced and then printed in color, but it would all be worth it if he spotted some oddity. If nothing else, they could use it to track their exploration. Also, it was pretty.

From Ronan's room, he heard Noah's laugh. He and Ronan were throwing various objects from the second-story window to the parking lot below. There was a terrific crash.

Ronan's voice rose, exasperated. "Not *that* one, Noah."

"I'd have to see if I could get off work," Adam replied. "I think I can. Do you think I should?"

Relieved, Gansey said, "Oh, yes." He dragged his desk chair onto the corner of the print. It kept trying to roll back up on itself. He put a copy of *Trioedd Ynys Prydein* on the other corner.

"Have you heard from Blue?" Adam asked.

"Tonight? She has work, doesn't she?" Roll, roll, roll. He nudged it with his foot to keep it straight. It was surprisingly satisfying to see acres and acres of forest and mountains and rivers unrolling across his floorboards. If he were a god, he thought, this would be precisely how he'd create his new world. Unrolling it like carpet.

"Yeah. I just . . . has she ever said anything to you about me?"

"Like what?"

A long silence. "About kissing, I guess."

Gansey paused in his rolling. As a point of fact, Blue had confessed a lot about kissing. Namely, that she'd been told her entire life that she'd kill her true love if she kissed him. It was strange to remember that moment. He'd doubted her, he recalled. He wouldn't have now. Blue was a fanciful but sensible thing, like a platypus, or one of those sandwiches that had been cut into circles for a fancy tea party.

She'd also asked Gansey not to tell Adam about her confession.

"Kissing?" he repeated evasively. "What's going on?"

Another crash from Ronan's room, followed by diabolical laughter. Gansey wondered if he should stop them before vehicles with strobe lights did.

"I dunno. She doesn't want to," Adam said. "I don't blame her, I guess. I don't know what I'm doing."

"Have you asked her why she doesn't want to?" Gansey asked, though he didn't want to hear the answer. He was abruptly tired of the conversation.

"She said she was very *young*."

"She probably is." Gansey had no idea how old Blue was. He knew she'd just finished eleventh grade. Maybe she was sixteen.

Maybe she was eighteen. Maybe she was twenty-two and just very short and remedial.

"I dunno, Gansey. Does that sound like a real thing? You've dated way more than me."

"I'm not dating *now*."

"Except for Glendower."

Gansey couldn't argue that point. "Look, Adam, I don't think it's about you. I think she likes you fine."

Adam clearly didn't like this answer, though, because he didn't reply. It gave Gansey enough time to remember the moment he'd first approached her at Nino's on Adam's behalf. How disastrous it had been. Since then, he'd considered a dozen different ways he could've done it better.

Which was foolish. It had all worked out, hadn't it? She was with Adam now. Whether or not Gansey had made a first-class prat of himself the moment they met didn't change anything.

"No way, man!" Noah shouted, but he didn't sound like he meant it. His words were most of the way to a laugh already. "No way —"

Gansey kicked the rolled print hard enough that it teetered crookedly out to its end, yards away, out of the circles of light. Standing, he walked to the windows on the eastern wall of the factory. Leaning an elbow on the frame, he pressed his forehead against the glass, to gaze on the great, black spread of Henrietta below.

Once, he had dreamt that he found Glendower. It wasn't the actual finding, but the day after. He wouldn't forget the sensation of the dream. It hadn't been joy, but instead, the absence of pain. He couldn't forget that lightness. The freedom.

"I don't want things to get ugly," Adam said finally.

"Are they ugly?"

"No. I guess not. But somehow they always seem to get that way."

Gansey watched tiny car lights diminish as they left Henrietta, reminding him of his miniature version of the town. An early, illicit firework sprayed up in the foreground. "Well, she's not really like a *girl*. I mean, sure she's a girl. But it's not like when I was dating someone. It's *Blue*. You could just ask her. We see her every day. Do you want me to talk to her?"

This was something he definitely, 100 percent felt certain in his guts that he had no interest in doing.

"I'm really bad at talking, Gansey," Adam said earnestly. "And you're really good at it. Maybe — maybe if it just comes up natural?"

Gansey's shoulders collapsed; his breath fogged the glass and vanished. "Of course."

"Thanks." Adam paused. "I just want something to be simple."

So do I, Adam. So do I.

Ronan's bedroom door burst open. Hanging on the door frame, Ronan leaned out to peer past Gansey. He was doing that thing where he looked like both the dangerous Ronan he was now and the cheerier Ronan he had been when Gansey had first met him. "Is Noah out here?"

"Hold on," Gansey told Adam. Then, to Ronan: "Why would he be?"

"No reason. Just no reason." Ronan slammed his door.

Gansey asked Adam, "Sorry. You still have that suit for the party?"

Adam's response was buried in the sound of the second-story door falling open. Noah slouched in. In a wounded tone, he said, "He threw me out the window!"

Ronan's voice sang out from behind his closed door: "You're already dead!"

"What's happening over there?" Adam asked.

Gansey eyed Noah. He didn't look any worse for wear. "I have no idea. You should come over."

"Not tonight," replied Adam.

I'm losing him, Gansey thought. *I'm losing him to Cabeswater.* He had thought that by staying away from the forest, he'd keep the old Adam — put off the consequences of whatever had happened that night when everything started to go awry. But maybe it just didn't matter. Cabeswater would take him regardless.

Gansey said, "Well. Just make sure you have a red tie."

II

That night, Ronan dreamt of trees.

It was a massive old forest, oaks and sycamores pushing up through the cold mountain soil. Leaves skittered in the breeze. Ronan could feel the size of the mountain under his feet. The oldness of it. Far below there was a heartbeat that wrapped around the world, slower and stronger and more inexorable than Ronan's own.

He had been here before, lots of times. He'd grown up with this recurring dream forest. Its roots were tangled in his veins.

The air moved around him, and in it, he heard his name.

Ronan Lynch Ronan Lynch Ronan Lynch

There was no one there but Ronan, the trees, and the things the trees dreamt of.

He danced on the knife's edge between awareness and sleep. When he dreamt like this, he was a king. The world was his to bend. His to burn.

Ronan Lynch, Greywaren, tu es Greywaren.

The voice came from everywhere and nowhere. The word *Greywaren* made his skin prickle.

"Girl?" he said.

And there she was, peering cautiously from behind a tree. When Ronan had first dreamt of her, she'd had long honey-blond hair, but after a few years it changed to a close-cropped pixie cut, mostly hidden by a white skullcap. Although he had aged, she had not. For some reason she reminded Ronan of the old black-and-white photos of laborers in New York City. She had the same sort of forlorn, orphan look. Her presence made it easier to pull things from his dreams.

He reached a hand toward her, but she didn't immediately emerge. She peered around fearfully. Ronan couldn't fault her. There were terrifying things in his head.

"Come on." He didn't yet know what he wanted to take from this dream, but he knew that he was so alive and aware in it that it would be easy. But Orphan Girl remained out of reach, her fingers clinging to the bark.

"*Ronan, manus vestras!*" she said. *Ronan, your hands!*

His skin shivered and crawled, and he realized it was crawling with hornets, the ones that had killed Gansey all those years ago. There weren't many this time, only a few hundred. Sometimes he dreamt cars full of them, houses full of them, worlds full of them. Sometimes these hornets killed Ronan, too, in his dreams.

But not tonight. Not when he was the most poisonous thing in these trees. Not when his sleep was clay in his fingers.

They aren't hornets, he thought.

And they weren't. When he lifted his hands, his fingers were coated with crimson ladybugs, each as vivid as a blood drop. They whirled into the air with their acrid summer scent. Every wing was a buzzing voice in a simple language.

Orphan Girl, ever a coward, emerged only after they were gone. She and Ronan moved from one part of the forest to the next. She hummed a refrain of a pop song over and over again as the trees murmured overhead.

Ronan Lynch, loquere pro nobis.

Speak for us.

Suddenly, he faced a striated rock nearly as tall as he was.

Thorns and berries grew at its base. It was familiar in a way that was too solid to be a dream, and Ronan felt a ripple of uncertainty. Was this a dream he was in now, or was it a memory? Was this really happening?

"You're sleeping," the girl reminded him in English.

He clung to her words, a king again. Facing the rock, he knew what he was meant to do — what he had *already* done. He knew it would hurt.

The girl turned her narrow face away as Ronan seized the thorns and the berries. Every thorn prick was a hornet sting, threatening to wake him. He crushed them until his fingers were dark with juice and blood, dark as the ink on his back. He slowly traced words on the rock:

Arbores loqui latine. The trees speak Latin.

"You've done this before," she said.

Time was a circle, a rut, a worn tape Ronan never tired of playing.

The voices whispered to him: *Gratias tibi ago.* Thank you.

The girl said, "Don't forget the glasses!"

Ronan followed her gaze. Between the flowers and broken vines and fallen leaves was a gleaming white object. When he plucked it free, Kavinsky's sunglasses looked back at him, eyeless. He ran his thumb over the smooth surface of the plastic, fogged his breath over the tinted lenses. He did it until he could feel even the etched circle of the tiny screw in the earpiece. Dream to memory to reality.

He lifted his eyes to the girl. She looked afraid. She always looked afraid, these days. The world was a scary place.

She said: "Take me with you."

He woke up.

That night, the Gray Man dreamt of being stabbed.

At first he felt each individual wound. Particularly that first one. He was unbroken and entire, and then that wholeness was stolen by that thief, the knife. So that piercing was the worst. A half inch above his left collarbone, pinning him to the ground for half a breath.

Then, again, but closer to the knob of his shoulder, glancing off his collarbone. And then two inches below his belly button. The word *gut* was a verb and a noun. Another cut and another cut. Slippery.

Then the Gray Man was the assailant. The hilt of the knife was ridged and permanent in his hand. He'd been stabbing this piece of meat for a lifetime. He'd been born when it started and he'd die when he was done. It was the bite that kept him alive: the moment the blade parted a new inch of skin. The resistance and then nothing. Catch and release.

Then the Gray Man was the knife. He was a blade in the air, gasping, and then he was a weapon inside, holding his breath. He was voracious, chewing, never satisfied. Hunger was a species, and he was the best of that kind.

The Gray Man opened his eyes.

He looked at the clock.

He rolled over and went back to sleep.

That night, Adam didn't dream.

Curled on the mattress, he covered his face with his summer-hot arm. Sometimes, if he blocked his mouth and nose, just this side of suffocation, sleep would overthrow him.

But both regret and the memory of the brief apparition kept slumber at bay. The wrongness, the deadness, of the woman still hung in the air of the room. Or maybe inside him. *What did I do?*

He was awake enough to think of home — *It's not home, it was never home, those people didn't exist, and if they did, they were nothing to you* — and to think of Blue's face when he lost his temper. He was awake enough to recall precisely the smell of the forest as he sacrificed himself. He was awake enough to wonder if he'd been making bad decisions for his entire life. If he'd been a bad decision, himself, even before he was born.

He wished summer was over. At least when he was at Aglionby he could turn over his papers to see the grades, concrete proof of his success at *something*.

He was awake enough to think of the invitation from Gansey. *There might be an internship in there.* Adam knew it was a favor. Did that make it wrong? He'd said no for so long that he didn't know when to say yes.

And maybe, a tiny, watchful part of his mind said, *maybe it will be for nothing anyway. When they smell the Henrietta dirt beneath your fingernails.*

He hated the careful way Gansey had asked him about it. Tiptoeing, just like Adam had learned to tiptoe around his father. He needed a reset button. Just push the reset button on Adam Parrish and start him again.

He didn't sleep, and when he did, he didn't dream.

12

The following morning, Blue was perusing school summer reading when her aunt Jimi brought a plate full of smoldering plant matter through her bedroom. Jimi, Orla's mother, was as tall as Orla, but several times wider. She had all of Orla's grace, too, which was to say that she knocked her hips into every piece of furniture in Blue's room. Every time she did, she said things like "mother lover!" and "fasten it *all*." They sounded worse than real swear words.

Blue lifted her bleary eyes from the page, her nostrils smarting from the smoke. "What are you doing?"

"Smudging," Jimi answered. She held the plate in front of the canvas trees Blue had stuck to her walls and blew on the bound herbs to direct the smoke at the art. "That terrible woman left so much bad energy."

The terrible woman was Neeve, Blue's half aunt, who had disappeared earlier that year after practicing black magic in their attic. And smudging was the practice of using the smoke of sympathetic herbs to clear negative energy. Personally, Blue had always thought there must be better ways to get on a plant's good side than by setting it on fire.

Now Jimi waved the lavender and sage in Blue's face. "Sacred smoke, cleanse the soul of this young woman before me and give her some common sense."

"*Hey!*" Blue protested, sitting up. "I think I'm very sensible, thanks! There isn't mugwort in that, is there? Because I have things to do!"

Jimi said mugwort improved her clairvoyance. She didn't seem to mind its temporarily mind-altering affects. Sullenly, sounding just like Orla, she said, "No, your mother wouldn't let me."

Blue silently thanked her mother. Gansey and Adam were supposed to be coming over, and the last thing she wanted was to be responsible for getting them mildly high. Although, she thought with more than a little discomfort, Adam might be improved by something that took the edge off. She wondered if he was ever going to say sorry.

"In that case," she said, "would you do my closet, too?"

Jimi frowned. "Was Neeve ever in there?"

"With Neeve," Blue replied, "you never know."

"I'll say an extra little prayer in there."

The little prayer turned out to be a little longer than Blue had expected, and she fled the smoke after a few minutes. In the hallway, she discovered Jimi had already opened the attic door in preparation for smudging Neeve's old quarters. It felt like an invitation.

With a glance down the hall, she stepped into the stairwell and climbed. Immediately, the air warmed and began to stink. The grubby smell of asafetida, one of the charms Neeve had used, still permeated the space, and the attic's summer heat did nothing to improve upon it.

At the top of the stairs, she hesitated. Most of Neeve's things were still up here, but they'd been heaped and boxed on the throw-covered mattress for later removal. All of the masks and symbols had been removed from the slanted, unfinished walls, and the candles had been carefully packed taper-side down in a plastic bin. But Neeve's mirrors were undisturbed — two full-length mirrors pointed directly at each other. And there was a deep black bowl sitting on the floor beside them. Neeve's scrying bowl.

The base was slicked with the memory of recent liquid, even though Neeve hadn't been in this room for nearly a month. Blue wasn't sure who else would use it. She knew that Maura, Persephone, and Calla generally frowned upon the ritual. The technique was theoretically simple: The scryer looked into a mirror or dark bowl full of liquid, drew her mind into a space outside itself, and saw the future or another location in the reflection.

In practice, Maura had told Blue that it was unpredictable and dangerous.

The soul, she'd said, *is vulnerable when it's outside the mind.*

The last time Blue had seen this bowl, Neeve had been scrying into someplace hidden on the ley line. Possibly somewhere in Cabeswater. And when Blue had interrupted her, she'd found Neeve *possessed* by whatever dark creature she'd discovered there.

Now, in the attic's suffocating heat, Blue shivered. It was easy to forget the terror that had accompanied their hunt for Cabeswater. But the shiny circle in the base of the scrying bowl brought it all back in a second.

Who's using you? Blue wondered. And of course, that was only the first half of the question.

The other half was: *And what are you looking for now?*

Ronan Lynch believed in heaven and hell.

Once, he'd seen the devil. It had been a low, late morning at the Barns when the sun had burned off the mist and then burned off the chill and then burned the edges off the ground until everything shimmered with heat. It never got hot in those protected fields, but that morning, the air sweated with it. Ronan had never seen cattle pant before. All of the cows heaved and stuck their tongues out as they frothed with the heat. His mother sent Ronan to put them in the shade of the cattle barn.

Ronan had gone to the searing metal gate, and as he did, he'd glimpsed his father, already in the barn. Four yards away from him had stood a red man. He was not truly red, but the burned orange of a fire ant. And he was not truly a man, because of the horns and the hooves. Ronan remembered the alienness of the creature, how *real* it had been. Every costume in the world had gotten it wrong; every drawing in every comic book. They'd all forgotten that the devil was an animal. Looking at the red man, Ronan had been struck by the intricacy of the body, how many miraculous pieces moved smoothly in harmony, no different from his own.

Niall Lynch had had a gun in hand — the Lynches had an enormous number of guns of all sizes — and just as Ronan had opened the gate, his father had shot the thing about thirteen times in the head. With a shake of its horns, the unharmed devil had presented its genitalia to Niall Lynch before bounding off. It was an image that had yet to leave Ronan.

And so Ronan became a reverse evangelist. The truth burst and grew inside him, and it was laid upon him to share it with no one. No one was meant to see hell before they got there. No one should have to live with the devil. So many homilies on faith were ruined once you no longer required it for belief.

Now it was Sunday, and as with every Sunday, he was headed to St. Agnes. Gansey wasn't with him — he belonged to some religion that only required church attendance on Christmas — but Noah came with. Noah had not been Catholic when he was alive, but recently he had decided to find religion. No one in the church ever noticed him and it was possible God didn't, either, but Ronan, as someone God possibly ignored as well, didn't mind the company.

Today Ronan grimly stepped through the great old doors and clawed some holy water from the font while the choir members narrowed their eyes at him. He scanned the pews for Declan. It was the devil who drove him to church every Sunday, but it was his brother Matthew who drove him to a pew beside Declan.

His older brother sat in the rearmost pew, the knob of his skull resting on the wood, his eyes closed. As always, he'd dressed for church: collared shirt white as innocence, knot of his tie tight and sanctified, slacks obediently pressed. This week, however, Declan had zombie bruising beneath both of his eyes, a terrifically red, sutured split across a cheekbone, and a decidedly broken nose.

Ronan's mood improved. He flicked holy water onto Declan's face from his still-damp fingers. "What the hell happened to you?"

The two women sitting three pews forward whispered to each other. The organ murmured in the background.

Declan didn't open his eyes. "Burglary." He muttered it with as little effort as humanly possible, opening his mouth only wide enough for the word to escape.

Ronan and Noah exchanged a look.

"Oh, come on," Ronan said. For starters, it was Henrietta. And for finishers, it was Henrietta. No one got burgled, and if they did, they didn't get beaten up. And if anyone *was* going to get beaten up, it wouldn't be the Lynch brothers. There was very little worse than Ronan in Henrietta, and what worse there was

was too busy racing around in a little white Mitsubishi to burgle the remaining Lynches. "What did they steal?"

"My computer. And a little money."

"And your face."

Declan just inhaled in response, slow and careful. Ronan slid into the pew, and Noah moved in beside him, sitting at the very end. As he lowered the kneeler, he smelled the sharp, antiseptic smell of hospital on his brother. For a moment, disoriented, he had to hold in his breath. He knelt and put his head down on his arms. The image behind his eyes was the bloody tire iron beside his father's head. *I didn't come out soon enough, I'm sorry, I'm sorry. Why of all the things I can do can I not change* — While whispered conversations ebbed and flowed around them, he focused on the image of his older brother's face and tried unsuccessfully to imagine the person that could beat Declan up. The only person who had ever succeeded in beating up a Lynch brother had been another Lynch brother.

After he had exhausted this line of thought, Ronan gave in to the brief privilege of hating himself, as he always did in church. There was something satisfying about acknowledging this hatred, something relieving about this little present he allowed himself each Sunday.

After a minute, the kneeler buckled as Matthew joined them. Even without the buck of the kneeler, Ronan would have known his presence by the heavy dose of cologne Matthew always seemed to think church required.

"Hey, pal," Matthew whispered. He was the only person who could get away with calling Ronan *pal*. Matthew Lynch was a bear of a boy, square and solid and earnest. His head was covered with soft, golden curls completely unlike any of his other family members. And in his case, the perfect Lynch teeth were framed by an easy, dimpled smile. He had two brands of smile: the one that was preceded by a shy dip of his chin, a dimple, and then BAM, smile. And the one that teased for a moment before BAM, an infectious laugh. Females of all ages called him *adorable*. Males of all ages called him *buddy*. Matthew failed at many more things than either of his older brothers, but unlike Declan or Ronan, he always tried his hardest.

Ronan had dreamt one thousand nightmares about something happening to him.

Matthew had unconsciously left enough room for Noah, but didn't offer a greeting. Ronan had once asked Noah if he chose to be invisible, and Noah, hurt, had replied enigmatically, "Rub it in, why don't you!"

"Did you see Declan's *face*?" Matthew whispered to Ronan. The organ played dolorously.

Declan kept his voice just low enough to be church-level. "I'm right *here*."

"Burglar," Ronan said. Really, it was like the truth was a disease Declan thought might kill him.

"Sometimes, when I call you," Declan muttered, still in the strange, low voice that came from him trying not to move his mouth while he spoke, "I actually need for you to pick up."

"Are we having a conversation?" Ronan asked. "Is that what's happening right now?"

Noah smirked. He didn't look very pious.

"By the way, Joseph Kavinsky isn't someone I want you being around," Declan added. "Don't snort. I'm serious."

Ronan merely invested a look with as much contempt as he could muster. A lady reached over the top of Noah to pat Matthew's head fondly before continuing down the aisle. She didn't seem to care that he was fifteen, which was all right, because he didn't, either. Both Ronan and Declan observed this interaction with the pleased expressions of parents watching their prodigy at work.

Declan repeated, "Like, actually dangerous."

Sometimes, Declan seemed to think that being a year older gave him special knowledge of the seedier side of Henrietta. What he meant was, did Ronan know that Kavinsky was a cokehead?

In his ear, Noah whispered, "Is crack the same thing as speed?"

Ronan didn't answer. He didn't think it was a very church-appropriate conversation.

"I *know* you think you're a punk," Declan said, "but you aren't nearly as badass as you think you are."

"Oh, go to hell," Ronan snapped, just as the altar boys broached the rear doors.

"Guys," Matthew pleaded. "Be *holy*."

Both Declan and Ronan fell silent. They were silent all through the opening hymn, which Matthew sang cheerily along to, and the readings, which Matthew smiled pleasantly through, and the homily, which Matthew slept gently through. They were silent through communion, as Noah remained in the pew and Declan limped up the aisle and accepted the host and Ronan closed his eyes to be blessed — *please God what am I tell me what I am* — and Matthew shook his head at the wine. And finally silent through the last hymn as the priest and the altar boys trailed back out of the church.

They found Declan's girlfriend, Ashley, waiting on the side-walk just outside the main doors. She was dressed in whatever had just been on the front page of *People* or *Cosmopolitan* and her hair was dyed whatever shade of blond matched it. She had three tiny gold earrings in each earlobe. She seemed oblivious to Declan's cheating, and Ronan hated her. To be fair, she also hated Ronan.

Ronan snarled a smile at her. "Afraid you'll catch fire if you come in?"

"I refuse to participate in a ceremony that doesn't, like, allow equal spiritual privileges to women," she said. She didn't meet Ronan's eyes when she said it, though, and she didn't look at Noah at all, though he'd snickered vaguely.

"Do you two buy your politics out of the same catalog?" Ronan asked.

"Ronan —" Declan started.

Ronan flipped out his car keys. "I was just leaving." He allowed Matthew to perform a brotherly handshake that they had invented four years previously, and then he advised Declan, "Stay away from burglars."

It was not as easy as one might expect for Ronan Lynch to street race. Most people obeyed the speed limit. For all the press road rage received, the majority of drivers were either too safety conscious, too shy, too principled, or too oblivious to provoke. Even those who might have considered a few minutes of traffic-light dragracing were generally aware that their vehicles were not suited to the task. Races were not to be found just lying on the street. They had to be cultivated.

So this was how Ronan Lynch found trouble.

A brightly colored car, for a start. Ronan had spent hours of his life as the only black car in a short, straightforward game of candy-coated vehicles. He looked for hatchbacks, coupes. Almost never a convertible. No one wanted to mess up their hair. This was a street racer's wish list: aftermarket parts on any sort of car, yawning exhaust pipes, asphalt-scraping ground-effects, cavernous hood scoops, smoked headlights, mismatched flames painted on fenders. Any car that came with a wing. The more it looked like a handle to lift the car, the better. The silhouette of a shaved head or a hat jerked sideways was a promising sign, as was an arm hanging over the door. A deeply tanned hand braced on the mirror was better. Thumping bass was a call to battle. So were vanity plates, so long as they didn't say things like HOTGURL or LVBUNY. Bumper stickers were a turnoff, unless they were college radio. Oh, and horsepower didn't count for anything. Half the time, the best sports cars were piloted by middle-aged bankers fearful of what might lie beneath their hood. Ronan used to avoid cars with multiple passengers, too, figuring that a solo driver was more likely to burn rubber at a light. But now he knew that the right sort of passengers would egg on an ordinarily tame driver. There was nothing Ronan liked better than a skinny tanned kid half-hanging out of a noisy, mostly dead red Honda full of his friends.

And this was how it started: Nose up to the light. Meet the driver's eyes. Shut off the air-co to give the car a few extra horsepower. Rev the engine. Smile like danger.

This was how Ronan found trouble, except for when the trouble was Kavinsky. Because then it found him.

After church, Ronan and Noah headed in the general direction of the hellish affluent subdivision where Kavinsky lived with his mother. Ronan had half a thought that he might put the dream pair of sunglasses in Kavinksy's mailbox, or tuck them in the windshield wipers of the Mitsubishi. The BMW's air-conditioning was on full blast beneath the furious midday glare. Cicadas shrilled at one another. There were no shadows anywhere.

"Company," said Noah.

Kavinsky rolled up beside the BMW at an intersection. Above them, the traffic light turned green, but the street behind them was empty and neither car moved. Ronan's palms were suddenly sweaty. Kavinsky rolled down his window. Ronan followed suit.

"Fag," Kavinsky said, stepping on his gas pedal. The Mitsubishi wailed and shuddered a bit. It was a glorious and hideous piece of work.

"Russian," Ronan replied. He stepped on his gas pedal, too. The BMW growled, a little lower.

"Hey now, let's not make this ugly."

Opening the center console, Ronan pulled out the sunglasses he'd dreamt the night before. He tossed them through his open window onto Kavinsky's passenger seat.

The light turned yellow, and then red. Kavinsky picked up the glasses and studied them. He knocked his own sunglasses halfway down his nose and studied them some more. Ronan was gratified to note how closely the new pair resembled them. The only thing he'd gotten wrong was that he'd made the tint a bit darker. Surely Kavinsky, master forger, should appreciate them.

Finally, Kavinsky slid his gaze over to Ronan. His smile was sly. Pleased that Ronan recognized the game. "Well done, Lynch. Where'd you find them?"

Ronan smiled thinly. He turned off the air-conditioning.

"That's how it's gonna be? Hard to get?"

The opposing light turned yellow.

"Yes," said Ronan.

The traffic light above them turned green. Without any particular prelude, both cars exploded off the mark. For two seconds, the Mitsubishi snarled ahead, but then Kavinsky screwed the shift from third to fourth.

Ronan did not.

He blew by.

Just as Ronan tore around a corner, Kavinsky honked his horn twice and made a rude gesture. Then Ronan was out of sight and speeding on his way back to Monmouth Manufacturing.

In the rearview mirror, he allowed himself the slightest of smiles.

This was what it felt like to be happy.

13

Blue very much liked having the boys over to her house.

Their presence at the house was agreeable for several different reasons. The absolute simplest one was that Blue sometimes got tired of being 100 percent of the non-psychic population of 300 Fox Way — more and more often, these days — and that percentage improved dramatically when the boys were over. The second reason was that Blue saw all the boys, particularly Richard Campbell Gansey III, in a very different light when they were there. Rather than the glossy, self-assured boy he'd been when she'd first met him, 300 Fox Way Gansey was a self-deprecating onlooker, at once eager and unsuited for all of the intuitive arts. He was a privileged tourist in a primitive country: flatteringly curious, unknowingly insulting, quite certainly unable to survive if left to his own devices.

And the third reason was that it suggested permanence. Blue had *acquaintances* at school, people she liked. But they weren't forever. While she was friendly with a lot of them, there was no one that she wanted to commit to for a lifetime. And she knew this was her fault. She'd never been any good at having casual friends. For Blue, there was family — which had never been about blood relation at 300 Fox Way — and then there was everyone else.

When the boys came to her house, they stopped being *everyone else*.

Currently, both Adam and Gansey were situated in the narrow bowels of the house. It was a wide open, promising sort of sunny day; it invaded through every window. Without any particular discussion, Gansey and Blue had come to the decision that today was a day for exploring, once Ronan arrived.

Gansey sat at the kitchen table in an aggressively green polo shirt. By his left hand was a glass bottle of a fancy coffee beverage he had brought with him. By his right hand was one of Maura's healing teas. For several months now, Blue's mother had been working on a line of healthful teas to augment their income. Blue had learned early on that *healthful* was not a synonym for *delicious*, and had very vocally removed herself from the test group.

Gansey didn't know any better, so he accepted what he was given.

"I don't think I can wait any longer. But I would like to minimize the risk," he said as Blue rummaged in the fridge. Someone had filled an entire shelf with disgusting store-brand pudding. "I don't think we can ever make it completely *safe*, but surely there is a way to be more cautious."

For a moment Blue thought he was talking about the process of drinking one of Maura's teas. Then she realized he was talking about Cabeswater. Blue loved it in a way that was hard to hold inside herself. She'd always loved the big beech tree in their backyard and the oaks that lined Fox Way, and forests in general, but nothing had prepared her for Cabeswater's trees. Ancient and twisted and *sentient*. And — they'd known her name.

It felt an awful lot like a hint of *something more*.

Maura watched Gansey carefully. Blue suspected this was not because of anything Gansey was saying but because she was waiting for him to take a drink of whatever horrid potion she had steeping in that cup in front of him.

"I know what you're going to say," Blue said, settling on a yogurt. It had fruit on the bottom, but she'd eat around it. She threw herself into a chair at the table. "You're going to say, 'Well, then, don't take Blue with you.'"

Her mother flipped a hand like, *If you knew, why'd you ask?*

Gansey said, "What? Oh, because Blue makes things louder?"

Crossly, Blue realized that Gansey had now called her *Jane* so often that it felt strange to hear him say her real name.

"Yes," Maura replied. "But I actually wasn't going to say that, even though it's true. I was going to say that this place must have rules. Everything involved in energy and spirit has rules — we just don't always know them. So it looks unpredictable to us. But it's really just because we're idiots. Are you sure you want to go back?"

Gansey took a drink of his healing tea. Maura's chin jutted as she observed the lump of it heading down his throat. His face remained precisely the same and he said absolutely nothing, but after a moment, he made a gentle fist of his hand and thumped his breastbone.

"What did you say that was good for?" he asked politely. His voice was a little odd until he cleared his throat.

"General wellness," Maura said. "Also, it's supposed to manage dreams."

"*My* dreams?" he asked.

Maura raised a very knowing eyebrow. "Who else's would you be managing?"

"Mm."

"Also, it helps with legal matters."

Gansey had been swallowing as much of his fancy coffee as he could possibly manage without breathing, but he stopped and put the bottle on the table with a *clink.* "Do I need help with legal matters?"

Maura shrugged. "Ask a psychic."

"Mom," Blue said. "Seriously." To Gansey, she prompted, "Cabeswater."

"Oh, right. Well, no one else has to go with me," he said. "But the incontrovertible fact remains that I am looking for a mystical king on a ley line and it is a mystical forest on a ley line. I can't discount that coincidence. We can look elsewhere, but I think Glendower's there. And I don't want to waste time now that the ley line's awake. I feel like time's running out."

"Are you sure you still want to find him?" Maura asked.

Blue already knew this question was irrelevant. Without cutting her gaze over to him, she already knew what she would see. She would see a rich boy dressed like a mannequin and coiffed like a newscaster — but his eyes were like the dreaming pool in Cabeswater. He hid the insatiable *wanting* well, but now that she'd seen it once, she couldn't stop seeing it. But he wouldn't be able to explain it to Maura.

And he would never really *have* to explain it to Blue.

It was his *something more.*

Very formally, he said, "Yes, I do."

"It could kill you," Maura said.

Then there was the awkward moment that arrives when two thirds of the people in the room know that the other third is supposed to die in fewer than nine months, and the person who is meant to die is not one of the ones in the know.

"Yes," Gansey said. "I know. I've done it once before. Die, I mean. Do you not like the fruit bits? That's the best part." He directed this last statement to Blue, who gave him her mostly empty yogurt cup. He was very clearly done with talking about death.

Maura sighed, giving up, just as Calla stormed into the kitchen. Calla was not angry. She merely stormed whenever possible. She ripped open the fridge and tore a pudding cup from it.

As Calla spun with the hated store-brand pudding in her hand, she shook it at Gansey and thundered, "Just remember that Cabeswater is a video game that everyone in it has been playing for a lot longer than you. They all know where to get the level ups."

She plowed from the room. Maura followed her.

"Well," said Gansey.

"Yes," agreed Blue. After a second, she pushed back her chair to follow Maura, but Gansey stretched a hand out.

"Wait," he said in a low voice.

"Wait what?"

With a glance out toward the hall and reading room, he said, "Um, Adam."

Instantly, Blue thought of Adam losing his temper. Her cheeks warmed. "What about him?"

Gansey rubbed a thumb over his lower lip. It was a pensive habit, performed so frequently that it was surprising he had anything left to cover his bottom teeth. "Have you told him about that no-kissing curse thing?"

If Blue had thought her cheeks were warm before, it was nothing compared to the blaze raging in them now. "You didn't tell him, did you?"

He looked delicately aggrieved. "You told me not to!"

"Well, no. I haven't."

"Don't you think you should?"

The kitchen didn't seem very private, and they'd both unconsciously leaned as close as possible to keep their voices from carrying. Blue hissed, "It's all very under control. I don't really want to be discussing this with *you*, of all people!"

"'Of all people'!" Gansey echoed. "What sort of all people am I?"

She had no idea, now. Flustered, she replied, "You're not my — my — grandmother, or something."

"You'd talk about *this* with your grandmother? I cannot possibly imagine discussing my dating life with mine. She's a lovely woman, I suppose. If you like them bald and racist." He glanced around the kitchen, as if he were looking for someone. "Where is yours, anyway? Isn't every female relative of yours in this house somewhere?"

Blue whispered furiously, "Don't be un — un —"

"Couth? Uncouth?"

"Disrespectful! My grandmothers are both dead."

"Well, Jesus. What did they die of?"

"Mom always said 'meddling.'"

Gansey completely forgot they were being secretive and let out a tremendous laugh. It was a powerful thing, that laugh. He only did it once, but his eyes remained shaped like it.

Something inside her did a complicated tug.

Oh no! she thought. But then she calmed herself. *Richard C. Gansey III has a nice mouth. Now I know he has nice eyes when he laughs, too. This still isn't love.*

She also thought: *Adam. Remember Adam.*

"It makes sense that there's a family history for your condition," he said. "Do you eat all of the men in the family? Where do they go? Does this house have a basement?"

Blue stood up. "It's like boot camp. They can't hack it. Poor things."

"Poor me," he said.

"Yup! Wait here." She was a little relieved to leave him at the table; her pulse felt like she'd been running. She found Maura and Calla still in the hall, conferring in low voices. She told her mother, "Look. We're definitely all going to Cabeswater. This afternoon, when Ronan's done. That's the plan. We're sticking to the plan."

Maura appeared a lot less distressed by this statement than Blue had feared. In fact, she didn't look very distressed at all.

"Why are you telling me?" Maura asked. "Why is your face so red?"

"Because you're my mother. Because you're an authority figure. Because you're supposed to inform people of your travel plans when you're hiking on dangerous trails. This is what my face always looks like."

"Hm," said Maura.

"Hm," said Calla.

Suspiciously, Blue asked, "You're not going to tell me not to go?"

"Not this time."

"No point," Calla agreed.

"Also, there's a scrying bowl in the attic," Blue said.

Her mother peered into the reading room. "No, there's not."

Blue insisted, "Someone's been using it."

"No, they haven't."

With an edge to her voice, Blue said, "You can't just say it's not there and no one's using it. Because I'm not an infant and I use my own eyes and brain *all the time*."

"What do you want me to tell you, then?" Maura asked.

"The truth. I just told *you* the truth."

"She did!" Gansey called from the kitchen.

"Shut up!" Blue and Calla said at once.

Maura lifted a hand. "Fine. I used it."

"For what?"

Calla said, "To look for Butternut."

My father! Blue probably shouldn't have been surprised — Neeve had been asked there to find her father, and although Neeve was gone, the mystery of her father's whereabouts remained. "I thought you said scrying was a bad idea."

"It's like vodka," Calla said. "It really depends on who's doing it." With her spoon poised over her pudding cup, she peered into the other room, just as Maura had.

Blue craned her neck to see what they were looking at. It was just Adam. He sat in the reading room by himself, the diffuse morning light rendering him soft and dusty. He had removed one of the tarot decks from its bag and lined all of the cards faceup in three long rows. Now he leaned on the table and studied the image on each, one at a time, shuffling on his elbows to the next when he was through. He looked nothing like the Adam who'd lost his temper and everything like the Adam she had first met. That was what was frightening, though — there'd been no warning.

Maura frowned. In a low voice, she said, "I think I need to have a conversation with that boy."

"Someone does," Calla replied, heading up the stairs. Each stair groaned a protest for which she punished the next with a stomp. "Not me. I've outgrown train wrecks."

Blue, alarmed, said, "Is he a train wreck?"

Her mother clucked her tongue. "Calla likes drama. Train wreck! When a train takes a long time to go off the tracks, I don't like to call it a *wreck.* I like to call it a *derailment.*"

From upstairs, Blue heard Calla's delighted cackle.

"I hate both of you," Blue said as her mother laughed and galloped up the stairs to join Calla. "You're supposed to use your powers for good, you know!"

After a moment, Adam said to her, without lifting his eyes, "I could hear y'all, you know."

Blue hoped fervently that he was only talking about Maura and Calla and not about her kitchen conversation with Gansey. "Do you think you're a train wreck?"

"That would mean I was on the tracks to start with," he replied. "Are we going to Cabeswater when Ronan's done?"

Gansey appeared beside Blue in the doorway. He shook his empty bottle at her.

"Fair trade," he told her in a way that indicated he had selected a fair-trade coffee beverage entirely so that he could tell Blue that he had selected a fair-trade coffee beverage so that she could tell him *Well done with your carbon footprint and all that jazz.*

Blue said, "Better recycle the bottle."

He dazzled a smile at her before knocking on the doorjamb with his fist. "Yes, Parrish. We're going to Cabeswater."

14

You could ask anyone: 300 Fox Way, Henrietta, Virginia, was the place to go for the spiritual, the unseen, the mysterious, and the yet-to-occur. For a not-unreasonable fee, any of the women under its roof would read your palm, pull your cards, cleanse your energy, connect you with deceased relatives, or listen to the dreadful week you had just lived through. During the business day, clairvoyance was often work.

But on days off, when the mixed drinks emerged, it often became a game. Maura, Calla, and Persephone scavenged the house for magazines, books, cereal boxes, old decks of tarot cards — anything with words or images. One woman selected an image and hid it from the others, and the other two experimented with how accurate they could get their guesses. They made predictions with their backs to one another, with the cards splayed, with different numbers of candles on the table, while standing in buckets of water, calling up and down three or seven stairs from the front hallway. Maura called it continuing education. Calla called it turning tricks. Persephone called it *that thing we could do if there's nothing on television?*

That day, after Blue and Gansey and Adam had gone, there was no work to be done. Sundays were quiet, even for non-churchgoers. It wasn't that the women of 300 Fox Way weren't spiritual on Sunday. It was that they were spiritual *every* day, and so Sunday didn't particularly stand out. After the teens left the house, the women abandoned work and set up the game in the shabby but comfortable living room.

"I'm very nearly drunk enough to be transcendent," Calla said after a space. She was not the only psychic drinking, but she was the closest one to transcendence.

Persephone peered dubiously into the bottom of her own glass. In a very small voice (her voice was always small), she said sadly, "I am not drunk at all."

Maura offered, "It's the Russian in you."

"Estonian," Persephone replied.

At that moment, the doorbell rang. Maura swore delicately: one well-chosen and highly specific word. Calla swore indelicately: several more words with rather fewer syllables. Then Maura went for the front door and reappeared in the living room with a tall man.

He was very . . . gray. He wore a dark gray V-neck T-shirt that emphasized the muscular slope to his shoulders. His slacks were a deeper gray. His hair was an ashy blond, drained of color, and so was the fashionable week-old facial hair round his mouth. Even his irises were gray. It escaped none of the women in the room that he was handsome.

"This is Mr. —?"

He smiled in a knowing sort of way. "Gray."

All of the women's mouths twisted into their own knowing sort of smile.

Maura said, "He wanted a reading."

"We're closed," Calla said, utterly dismissive.

"Calla is rude," Persephone said in her doll voice. "We are not closed, but we are busy?"

This was said with a question in her voice and an anxious glance toward Maura.

"That's what I told him," Maura said. "However, it turns out that Mr. . . . . Gray — doesn't really need a *reading*. He's a novelist, researching psychics. He just wants to observe."

Calla rattled the ice in her glass. One of her eyebrows looked exceptionally skeptical. "What do you write, Mr. *Gray*?"

He smiled easily at her. They noticed he had extraordinarily straight teeth. "Thrillers. Do you read much?"

She merely hissed and tipped her glass toward him, plum lip-mark first.

"Do you mind if he stays?" Maura asked. "He knows poetry."

Calla sneered. "Give me a stanza and I'll fetch you a drink."

Without the slightest hesitation or suggestion of self-consciousness, the Gray Man placed his hands in the pockets of his dark gray slacks and said, *"Where has gone the steed? Where has gone the youth? Where has gone the giver of treasure? Where are the feasting seats, where the revelry in the hall? Alas, bright goblet; alas, mailed warrior; alas, prince's glory! How that time has passed away, obscured beneath the crown of night as if it never were."*

Calla lifted her lips from her teeth. "Do it in the original Old English and I'll put alcohol in that drink."

He did.

Calla went to get him a drink.

After she had returned and the Gray Man had been encouraged to sit on the worn couch, Maura said, "I'll warn you that if you try anything, Calla has Mace."

By way of demonstration, Calla handed him his drink and then removed a small black container of pepper spray from her small red purse.

Maura gestured toward the third member of their group. "And Persephone is Russian."

"Estonian," Persephone corrected softly.

"And" — Maura made an extremely convincing fist — "I know how to punch a man's nose into his brain."

"What a coincidence," the Gray Man said genially. "So do I."

He watched with an attentiveness both polite and flattering as Maura scraped her cards up from the sofa cushions. He leaned to pick up one she had missed.

"This fellow looks unhappy," he observed. The art depicted a man stuck with ten swords. The victim lay on his face, as most people did after being stuck with ten swords.

"That's a fellow after Calla's done with him," Maura said. "Good news for him is that the tens represent the end of a cycle. This card represents the absolute worst it'll get."

"Does seem like there's not much worse than ten points in your back and dust in your mouth," the Gray Man agreed.

"Look," Maura said, "his face looks a little like yours."

The Gray Man studied the card. He placed his finger on the blade rammed through the victim's back. "And that sword looks a little like you."

He glanced at Maura. It was a *glance*. She glanced back. It was also a *glance*.

"*Well,*" said Calla.

"Would you do the honor, Mr. Gray?" Maura handed him the deck of cards. "You'll have to ask 'top or bottom.'"

Mr. Gray gravely accepted the responsibility. He asked Calla, "Top or bottom?"

"Three of cups. And top, of course," Calla said, her smile plum and wicked. "The only place to be."

Mr. Gray removed the card from the top and turned it over. Of course it was the three of cups.

Maura grinned. She said, "Empress, bottom."

The Gray Man removed the card from the bottom and

showed it to the room. The Empress's gown was suggested with a liberal swipe of charcoal, and her crown was studded with inky fruits or jewels.

The Gray Man clapped slowly.

"Four of wands, bottom," Calla said.

"Ten of coins, top," Maura shot back.

"Ace of cups, bottom," Calla fired out.

Maura slapped the arm of the sofa. "The Sun, bottom."

"Four of swords, top!" Calla returned, her mouth a deadly curl of purple. The Gray Man flipped the cards again and again, revealing the correct predictions.

Persephone's quiet voice cut through Maura's and Calla's increasingly loud competition. "The king of swords."

Everyone turned to look at Persephone, who sat with her knees together and her hands folded neatly in her lap. Occasionally Persephone appeared both eight years old and eighty at once; now was one of those times.

The Gray Man's hand hovered obediently over the deck. "Top or bottom?"

Persephone blinked. "Sixteen cards from the top, I believe."

Maura and Calla both raised an eyebrow. Calla's went up farther.

The Gray Man carefully counted the cards, double-checked his count, and then turned over the sixteenth card for the others to see. The king of swords, master of his own emotions, master of his own intellect, master of reason, gazed out at them, expression inscrutable.

"That's Mr. Gray's card," Persephone said.

Maura asked, "Are you sure?" At a wordless agreement from Persephone, Maura turned to the Gray Man. "Do you think that's your card?"

The Gray Man turned the card one way and another, as if it would reveal its secrets to him. "I don't know much about tarot. Is it a terrible card?"

"No card is a terrible card," Maura said. She eyed the Gray Man, fitting the king of swords into the man before her. "And the interpretation can be very different at each reading. But . . . the king of swords is a powerful card. He's strong, but impartial — cold. He is very, very good about making decisions based upon facts instead of emotion. No, it's not a terrible card. But I'm picking up something else off it. Something like . . ."

"Violence," Calla finished.

It was a word that had an immediate effect on everyone in the room. For Maura, Persephone, and Calla, memories of Maura's half sister came in first as they were the most recent, followed by the boy Gansey and his broken thumb. The Gray Man recalled Declan Lynch's swimming gaze, blood streaming from his nose. *Violence.*

"Yes, violence," Maura said. "Is that what you meant, Persephone? Yes."

All three of them had leaned unconsciously toward one another. Sometimes Maura, Persephone, and Calla seemed more like three parts of the same entity instead of three separate women. The three of them turned as one to Mr. Gray.

He admitted, "My work is sometimes violent."

"I thought you said you were researching a novel." Maura's tone was more than a little prickly.

"That was a lie," the Gray Man said. "I'm sorry. I had to think quickly when you said I couldn't have a reading."

"So what's the truth?"

"I'm a hit man."

This confession ushered in several moments of silence. The Gray Man's answer seemed very flippant but his voice suggested otherwise. It was the sort of answer that required an immediate clarification or qualification, but he offered nothing.

Maura said, "That's not very funny."

"No, it's not," the Gray Man agreed.

Everyone in the room was waiting for Maura's response. She asked, "And does *work* bring you here tonight?"

"Just research."

"For *work*?"

Unperturbed, Mr. Gray said, "Everything is research for work. In its way."

He did absolutely nothing to make his words easier to accept. It was impossible to tell if he was asking them to believe him or to humor him or to fear him. He merely laid out this confession and waited.

Finally, Maura said, "Might be nice to have someone deadlier than Calla in the room for a change."

She *glanced* at him. He *glanced* back. There was a wordless, tacit agreement in it.

They all had another drink. The Gray Man asked knowledgeable questions full of wry humor. Some time later, he stood, took everyone's empty glasses to the kitchen, and excused himself with a glance at his watch. "Not that I wouldn't like to stay."

Then he asked if he could return later in the week.

And Maura said yes.

After he had gone, Calla looked through his wallet, which she had stolen as he left. "The ID is fake," she remarked, closing the billfold and stuffing it into the couch cushions where he had been sitting. "But he'll miss his credit cards. Why ever did you say yes?"

"Something like that," Maura replied, "makes me feel better if I can keep my eye on it."

"Oh," Persephone said, "I think we all know what you're keeping your eye on."

15

Adam remembered how cruel he had thought Gansey would be. There wasn't a day during his first month at Aglionby Academy when he hadn't doubted his decision to come there. The other boys were so alien and daunting; he would never be able to look like one of them. How incredibly naive he'd been to think he would ever possess a room like one of the other Aglionby students did. And Gansey was the worst of them. The other boys attended Aglionby and fit in life around the edge. But Gansey — it was impossible to forget that he had arrived with a life intact, and instead fit Aglionby into it. He was the boy all eyes turned to when he strode into the gym. He was the student with the easiest smile when called on in Latin. He was forever loitering behind after classes to chat with the teachers like equals — *Mr. Gansey, would you hold up a moment? I found an article I think you'd be interested in* — and he was the boy with the most beautifully interesting car and the most savagely handsome of friends, Ronan Lynch. He was the opposite of Adam in every possible way.

They didn't speak. Why would they speak? Adam slid into class and kept his head down and listened, trying to learn how to clip his accent. Gansey, a furious sun, glowed from the other side of the universe, his gravitational pull too distant to affect Adam. Although Gansey seemed to be friends with the entire school, it was Ronan who was always with him. And it was this friendship, all wordless glances and wry twists of the mouth, that made

Adam think that Gansey must be cruel. Ronan and Gansey were laughing, he thought, at a joke where the rest of the world was the punch line.

No, Adam and Gansey didn't speak.

They didn't exchange a word until six weeks into the year, when Adam bicycled past the Camaro on the way to school. Dark tire tracks pointed its path to the side of the road; its hood stood open. It wasn't an unusual sight: Adam had seen the Camaro behind a tow truck at least twice already. There was no reason at all to think that Gansey, hovering by the engine, would want Adam's help. Probably he'd already called a mechanic he had at the ready.

But Adam stopped. He remembered how afraid he'd been right then. Of all of the agonizing days at Aglionby, that had been the worst moment so far: knocking down his old bike's kickstand next to Richard C. Gansey III's glorious burning-orange Camaro and waiting for him to turn. His stomach had been a ruin of fear.

Gansey had pivoted and in his slow, lovely accent, said, "Adam Parrish, right?"

"Yeah. Di — Richard Gansey?"

"Just Gansey."

Already Adam had spotted what had stopped the Camaro in its tracks. With daring, he'd asked, "Do you want me to fix it? I know a little about cars."

"No," Gansey had replied curtly.

Adam remembered how his ears had burned, how he'd wished he'd never stopped, how he hated Aglionby. He was nothing, he knew, and of course Gansey, of all of them, could see it on him. The worthlessness of him. His secondhand uniform, his shitty bike, his stupid accent. He didn't know what had possessed him to stop.

Then Gansey, his eyes full of the *real* Gansey, had said, "I'd like you to show me how to fix it myself, if you could. There's no point having this car if I can't speak its language. Speaking of languages, you school me at Latin *every day*. You're as good as Ronan."

It shouldn't have happened at all, but their friendship had been cemented in only the time it took to get to school that morning — Adam demonstrating how to fasten the Camaro's ground wire more securely, Gansey lifting Adam's bike halfway into the trunk so they could ride to school together, Adam confessing he worked at a mechanic's to put himself through Aglionby, and Gansey turning to the passenger seat and asking, "What do you know about Welsh kings?"

Sometimes Adam wondered what would've happened if he hadn't stopped that day. What would be happening to him right now?

He probably wouldn't still be at Aglionby. Surely he wouldn't be in the Camaro headed to a magical forest.

Gansey was giddy now that they'd decided to go back to Cabeswater. He hated nothing more than standing still. He ordered Ronan to put on some terrible music — Ronan was always too happy to oblige in this department — and then he abused the Camaro at every stoplight on the way out of town. "Put your back into it!" Gansey shouted breathlessly. He was talking to himself, of course, or to the gearbox. "Don't let it smell fear on you!" Blue wailed each time the engine revved up, but not unhappily. Noah played the drums on the back of Ronan's headrest. Adam, for his part, was not wild, but he did his best not to appear *un*wild, so as not to ruin it for the others.

They had not been back to Cabeswater since Adam had made his sacrifice.

Ronan rolled down his window, letting in a gust of hot air

and the scent of asphalt and mown grass. Gansey followed suit. Already Adam's lower back was sweaty against the vinyl seat, but his hands felt chilly. Would Cabeswater claim him once he returned to it?

What have I done?

Gansey, dangling his arm outside, patted the side of the car as if it were a horse. "That'll do, Pig. That'll do."

Adam felt like he was watching it all from outside. He felt like he was about to catch another image, like a flick of the tarot cards he'd looked at earlier. Was that someone standing by the side of the road?

I can't trust my eyes.

Gansey leaned back, head thrown to the side, drunken and silly with happiness. "I love this car," he said, loud to be heard over the engine. "I should buy four more of them. I'll just open the door of one to fall into the other. One can be a living room, one can be my kitchen, I'll sleep in one . . ."

"And the fourth? Butler's pantry?" Blue shouted.

"Don't be so selfish. Guest room." The Camaro charged down the gravel road that would take them to the forest, a cloud of dust parachuting behind it. As they climbed, the field stretched out, green and endless. Once they reached the crest, they'd be able to see the tree line where Cabeswater began.

Adam's stomach squeezed with sudden nerves, as ferocious as that day when he'd first stopped his bike by Gansey's car. He almost said something. He didn't know what he would've said. *Was that another image?* A blank screen.

They crested the hill.

The field went on and on. Scrubby grass gave way to a wash where a stream must have been, and then continued on through more acres of grass. Hundreds of acres of field.

There were no trees.

The car fell quiet.

Gansey drove a few feet farther before stepping on the parking brake. Every head in the car was turned toward that endless field and the old stream. It was not that there had been trees and now they were gone. There were no stumps or tire tracks. It was as if there had never been trees.

Gansey held out his hand, and immediately, Ronan opened the glove box and got the journal. Slowly, Gansey paged through to where he had neatly written the coordinates for Cabeswater. Blue's breath caught audibly.

This was all ridiculous. It was like checking the coordinates for Monmouth Manufacturing. They all knew where it was.

"Jane," Gansey said, handing his phone back to her, "please check the GPS."

He read the numbers from the page. Then he read them again.

Blue, thumbing through the map on the phone, read them back from the screen. They were the same. They were the coordinates that had brought them here every other time. The coordinates that had brought their Latin professor and Neeve here.

They hadn't made a wrong turn. They hadn't overshot the road or parked in the wrong place. This was where they'd found Cabeswater. This was where it had all begun.

Noah finally said it: "It's gone."

16

A nd the Camaro broke down.

Its sense of timing was impeccable. In ordinary circumstances, the car would've been full of sound: radio blaring, conversation firing. There would have been no audience for the first subtle sounds of fluid filling the Camaro's lungs. But now, quieted by the impossible, they all heard the engine seize for a moment. Heard the turned-down radio stutter, like it had lost its train of thought. Heard the air-conditioning blower cough politely into its fist.

They had enough time to lift their heads and look at one another.

Then the engine expired.

Suddenly robbed of power steering, Gansey wrestled the coasting car to the shoulder. He hissed between his teeth, the sound identical to the noise of the tires in the grubby gravel.

Then there was absolute silence.

Instantly, the heat began to press in. The engine ticked like the twitch of a dying man's foot. Adam rested his forehead on his knees and curled his arms behind his head.

All at once, Ronan snarled, "This car. This fucking *car*, man. If this was a Plymouth Voyager, it would have been crushed for war crimes a long time ago."

Adam felt that the Pig's status perfectly encapsulated how he felt. It was not really dead, just broken. He was held inside the question of what it meant for him if Cabeswater was gone. *Why can't things just be simple?*

"Adam?" Gansey asked.

Adam lifted his head. "Alternator. Maybe."

"I don't know what that means." Gansey seemed almost relieved that the Pig had died. Now he finally had something concrete to do. If he couldn't explore Cabeswater, he could at the very least get them from the side of the road. "Say it in a language I understand."

"In indiget homo battery," muttered Ronan.

"He's right," Adam said. "If we had a new battery to drop in there, we could make it back home until we looked at it."

A new battery would cost a hundred bucks, but Gansey wouldn't even feel the bite.

"Tow truck?"

"State inspections today," Adam replied. Boyd's was the only tow company in town, and he only retrieved breakdowns when he wasn't working in the garage. "It'll be forever."

Ronan leapt out of the car and slammed the door. The thing about Ronan Lynch, Adam had discovered, was that he wouldn't — or couldn't — express himself with words. So every emotion had to be spelled out in some other way. A fist, a fire, a bottle. Now Cabeswater was missing and the Pig was hobbled, and he needed to go have a silent shouting fit with his body. In the back window, Adam saw Ronan pick up a rock from the side of the road and hurl it into the creeper.

"Well, that's helpful," Blue said tersely. She slid from the back into the now-empty passenger seat and shouted out, "That's helpful!"

Adam didn't quite catch all of Ronan's growled reply, but he heard at least two of the swear words.

Blue, unimpressed, reached for Gansey's phone. "Is there a place we can walk to?"

She and Gansey ducked their heads together to examine the screen and mutter about map options. The image of her dark hair and his dusty hair touching seared something inside Adam, but it was just one more sting in a sea of jellyfish.

Ronan returned, leaning in the passenger window. Blue turned the phone to him. "Maybe we could walk to this place."

"The Deering General Store?" Ronan said, voice scathing. "Look at it. That's not a place to get a battery. That's a place to lose your wallet. Or your virginity."

"Do you have a better idea?" she demanded. "Maybe we can hurl some stuff into the underbrush! Or hit something! That solves everything! Maybe we can be really manly and break things!"

Though she was turned to Ronan, Adam knew these words were meant for him. He laid his face on the back of the driver's headrest and simmered in shame and indignation. He thought about the way the car had stammered before it died. Using up the last of the battery before it couldn't go on. Then he thought about how Noah had disappeared in Dollar City while he was talking to Gansey on the phone. And now Cabeswater was gone. Using up the last of the charge.

But that didn't make sense. He'd activated the ley line. It kept blowing out transformers in town because it was so strong. There shouldn't be a *lack* of energy.

"I'm calling Declan," Gansey said. "And telling him to bring a battery."

Ronan told Gansey what he thought of this plan, very precisely, with a lot of compound words that even Adam hadn't heard before. Gansey nodded, but he also dialed Declan's number.

Afterward, he turned to Ronan, who leaned his cheek hard enough against the top of the window to make a dent in his skin.

"Sorry. Everyone else I know's out of town. You don't have to talk to him. I'll do it."

Ronan punched the top of the Camaro and turned his back to it.

Gansey rounded on Adam, clutching his own headrest and looking behind him. "Why is it gone?"

Adam blinked at his sudden nearness. "I don't know."

Releasing the headrest, Gansey turned to Blue. "Why? Is it science, or is it magic?"

Adam made a dismissive sound.

"No," Blue said, "I know what you mean. Did it go, or was it taken?"

"Maybe it's invisible," Gansey suggested.

Adam wasn't sure he believed in true invisibility. He'd tried it and it never seemed to protect him. He asked Noah, "Are you still there when we can't see you?"

Noah just blinked at him from the dimness of the backseat, his eyes liquid and faraway. He was, Adam noted, nearly disappeared already. He was more the feeling of Noah than actually Noah.

Ronan had been listening, because he spun and leaned in the window. "At the store, when he disappeared, he didn't just become invisible. He *went away*. If you're saying Cabeswater's like Noah, it's not invisible. It's gone somewhere."

There was a breath's silence. This was where Gansey, if he were Ronan, would swear. Where if he were Adam, he'd close his eyes. If he were Blue, he'd snap in exasperation.

But Gansey merely rubbed a thumb over his lip and then drew himself up. He was instantly cool and elegant, all true emotions placed in an undisclosed location. He drew out his journal, jotted a note in the margin, and caged it with terse brackets. When he closed the pages, whatever anxiety he had over Cabeswater was closed in with the rest of his thoughts on Glendower.

Some time later, after Noah had discreetly disappeared, Declan's Volvo glided up, as quiet as the Pig was loud. Ronan said, "Move up, move up" to Blue until she scooted the passenger seat far enough for him to clamber behind it into the backseat. He hurriedly sprawled back in the seat, throwing one jean-covered leg over the top of Adam's and laying his head in a posture of thoughtless abandon. By the time Declan arrived at the driver's side window, Ronan looked as if he had been asleep for days.

"Lucky I was able to get away," Declan said. He peered into the car, eyes passing over Blue and snagging on Ronan in the backseat. His gaze followed his brother's leg to where it rested on top of Adam's, and his expression tightened.

"Thanks, D," Gansey said easily. With no effort, he pushed open the door, forcing Declan back without seeming to. He moved the conversation to the region of the front fender. It became a battle of genial smiles and deliberate hand gestures.

Blue watched disdainfully from the passenger seat as Adam watched sharply from the backseat. And as he sat there, observing the set of Declan's shoulders and the way his eyes looked, he realized something startling.

Declan was afraid.

Probably it wasn't apparent to Gansey, who was fairly oblivious, nor to Blue, who didn't know what Declan looked like ordinarily. And Ronan's feelings about his older brother were like blood in the water; he wouldn't be able to see through the bilious clouds.

But to Adam, who'd spent a fair amount of his life afraid — not only afraid, but trying to hide it — it was obvious.

The question was what Declan Lynch had to be afraid of.

"Who gave your brother that shiner, Ronan?" he asked.

Without opening his eyes, Ronan replied, "Same person who fucked his nose over."

"And who was that?"

Ronan laughed, just once, a *ha!* "Burglars."

The problem with getting the facts about Declan from Ronan was that Ronan always assumed that his brother was lying.

Of course, usually he was.

Suddenly, the driver's side door was ripped open. The sound and shock of it were so violent that Ronan forgot to look asleep and Adam and Blue both stared. Declan leaned in.

"I know you want to do the opposite of everything I say," he snapped, "but you need to keep your head down. Do you remember when I told you to keep it down, months ago? Have you forgotten?"

Ronan's voice was slow, petulant. His eyes, though, half-hidden in the dim, warm light of the Camaro's interior — they were terrible. "I haven't forgotten."

"Well, it feels like you have," Declan said. "People are watching. And if you slip up, you screw things up for all of us. So don't slip up. And I *know* you've been on the streets again. When you lose your license, I —"

"Declan." Gansey's voice cut through, deep and responsible. He placed a hand on Declan's shoulder, gently tugging him back. "We're cool here." When this didn't have the desired effect, Gansey added, "I know you don't want to make a scene in front of . . ."

Both boys looked at Blue.

Blue's lips parted with indignation, but Gansey's words worked magic. Declan retreated instantly.

A moment later, Gansey returned to the Pig. "Sorry, Jane," he said. Now his voice sounded weary, nothing like the broad persuasion he'd just exercised on Declan. He lifted the battery into view. "Adam, you want to do this thing?"

He said it like it was an ordinary day, like they'd come back from an ordinary trip, like nothing was wrong. The Lynch brothers had fought, but that was merely evidence that they were both still breathing. The Pig had died, but it was always either dying or rising again.

But in everything Gansey didn't say, in every feeling he didn't paint on his face, he was shouting:

It's gone.

17

The mask was his father's.

Even in his dreams, Ronan could not go back to the Barns, but here was something from the Barns coming to him. In reality, the mask hung on his parents' dining room wall, well out of reach of curious hands. But in his dream, it hung at eye-level on the wall of Adam's shabby apartment. It was carved of smooth, dark wood and looked like a cheap tourist souvenir. The eyeholes were round and surprised, the mouth parted in an easy smile big enough for lots of teeth.

"This is cheating," Orphan Girl said in Latin.

She hadn't been there before, but she was now. Her presence reminded Ronan all at once that he was dreaming. This moment, the one when he realized he'd already created everything here with his own mind, that was when he could take something back with him. It was his. He could do whatever he wanted to with it.

"Cheating," she insisted again. "Dreaming a dream thing."

She meant the mask, of course. It was surely from his father's mind.

"It's my dream," Ronan told her. "Here. I brought you some chicken."

And he had. He handed her a box of fried chicken, which she fell on voraciously.

"I think I'm a psychopomp," she said, with her mouth full.

"I don't even know that that means."

The ragged girl stuffed an entire chicken wing in her mouth, bones and all. "I think it means I'm a raven. That makes you a raven boy."

This irritated Ronan for some reason, so he took the rest of the chicken from her and placed it on a piece of furniture that vanished as soon as he turned away.

"Cabeswater's gone," he told her.

"Far away isn't the same thing as gone." This was Adam. He stood at Ronan's shoulder. He wore his Aglionby uniform, but his fingers were black with oil. He pressed his greasy hands to the mask. He didn't ask permission, but Ronan didn't stop him. After the briefest of pauses, Adam took the mask from the wall and held it up to his eyes.

Shrieking a terrified warning, Orphan Girl dove behind Ronan.

But Adam was already becoming something else. The mask was gone, or it had become Adam's face, or Adam was carved from wood. Every tooth behind the smile was hungry; Adam's elegant jaw was starving. His eyes were desperate and incensed. A long, fat vein stood out in his neck.

"*Occidet eum!*" begged Orphan Girl, clinging to Ronan's leg.

It was becoming a nightmare. Ronan could hear the night horrors coming, in love with his blood and his sadness. Their wings flapped in time with his heartbeat. He wasn't in control enough to drive them away.

Because Adam was the horror now. The teeth were something else, Adam was something else, he was a *creature*, close enough to touch. To think about it was to become immobilized with the horror of watching Adam be consumed from the inside out. Ronan couldn't even tell where the mask was now; there was only Adam, the monster, a toothful king.

The girl sobbed out, *"Ronan, imploro te!"*

Ronan took Adam's arm and said his name.

But Adam lunged. Tooth upon tooth upon tooth. Even as he went for Ronan, one of his hands still tugged at the now-invisible mask, trying to free himself. There was none of his face left.

Adam seized Ronan's neck, fingers hooked in his skin.

Ronan could not kill him, no matter how much Orphan Girl begged. It was *Adam.*

The mouth gaped, door to bloody ruin.

Niall Lynch had taught Ronan to box, and he had once told his son: *Clear your mind of whimsy.*

Ronan cleared his mind of whimsy.

He seized the mask. The only way he could find the edge was to snatch Adam's hand where it still doggedly clawed at the slender mask. Bracing himself for the effort, Ronan wrenched. But the mask came away as easily as a petal from a flower. It was only for Adam that it had been a prison.

Adam staggered back.

In Ronan's hand, the mask was as thin as a sheet of paper, still warm from Adam's gasped breaths. Orphan Girl buried her face in his side, her body shaking with sobs. Her tiny voice was muffled: *"Tollerere me a hic, tollerere me a hic . . ."*

Take me away from here, take me away from here.

In the background, Ronan's night horrors drew closer. Close enough to smell.

Adam was making peculiar, dreadful sounds. When Ronan lifted his eyes, he saw that the mask had been all that was left of Adam's face. When he'd pulled it from Adam, he'd revealed muscle and bone, teeth and eyeball. Adam's pulse pumped a globule of blood from every place a muscle met another muscle.

Adam slumped against the wall, life leaking from him.

Ronan gripped the mask, his limbs awash with adrenaline. "I'll put it back on."

Please work.

"Ronan!"

Ronan curled on his bed, half-propped against the wall, his headphones still around his neck. His body was frozen, as it always was after dreaming, but this time he could feel fire through every nerve. The nightmare still pumped adrenaline through him, although he couldn't move to use it. His breath came in great, uneven puffs. He couldn't uncurl or answer or stop seeing Adam's ruined face.

It was morning. Early, gray morning, rain beating on the window beside his head. He floated above himself. The boy below him was locked in an unseeable battle, every vein standing on his arms and neck.

"Ronan," whispered Noah. He crouched inches away, colorless in this light. He was solid enough for his knees to leave an impression on the bedspread but not enough to cast any sort of shadow. "You're awake, you're awake."

For a long minute, Noah blinked at him while Ronan looked back, wrung out. Gradually, his heart slowed. With an icy touch, Noah worked Ronan's fingers free of the dream's spoils. The mask. Ronan hadn't meant to bring it with him. He'd have to destroy it. Maybe he could burn it.

Noah lifted it into the window's diffuse light and shivered. The mask's surface was splattered with red-black drops. Whose DNA, Ronan wondered, would a lab find in that blood?

"Yours?" Noah asked, barely audible.

Ronan shook his head and sealed his eyes again. Behind his closed eyelids, it was Adam's dreadful face he saw, not Noah's.

In the corner of the room, there was a sound. Not the corner where Chainsaw's cage was. And not a sound like a young raven. It was a long, slow scrape on the wood floor. Then a rapid sound like a drinking straw in bicycle spokes. *Tck-tck-tck-tck-tck.*

It was a sound Ronan had heard before.

He swallowed.

He opened his eyes. Noah's eyes were already wide.

Noah said, "What were you dreaming about?"

18

Gansey had woken before dawn. It had been a while since he'd had to wake up early for crew team practice, but he still sometimes sat bolt upright at 4:45 A.M., ready to hit the river. Usually, he'd spend those sleepless early-morning hours quietly going through his books or surfing the Internet for new references to Glendower, but after the disappearance of Cabeswater, he couldn't bring himself to be productive. Instead he had retreated outside through the drizzle to the early-morning Pig. Immediately, he had been comforted. He'd spent so many hours sitting in it like this — doing his homework before going in to class, or stranded by the side of the road, or wondering what he would do if he never found Glendower — that it felt like home. Even when it wasn't running, the car smelled intimately of old vinyl and gasoline. As he sat, a single mosquito found its way into the car and worried at his ear, a high tremolo against the basso continuo of the rain and thunder.

Cabeswater's gone. Glendower is there — he must be — and it's gone.

The drops pattered and dispersed on the windshield. He thought about the day he'd been stung to death by hornets and lived anyway. Gansey ran over the memory until he no longer felt the thrill of hearing Glendower's name whispered in his ear, and then instead gave himself over to feeling sorry for himself, that he should have so many friends and yet feel so very alone. He felt it fell to him to comfort them, but never the other way around.

As it should be, he thought, abruptly angry with himself. *You've had it the easiest. What good is all your privilege, you soft, spoiled thing, if you can't stand on your own legs?*

The door to Monmouth opened. Noah immediately spotted Gansey and made a generalized flapping gesture. It seemed to mean he wanted Gansey and, furthermore, that he was feeling fairly urgent about it.

Ducking his head against the rain, Gansey joined Noah. "What?"

More hand flapping. In they went.

Inside, the small smells of the building — the rusty fixtures, the wormholed wood, his mint plants — had been overtaken by an unfamiliar odor. Something damp and strangely fertile and unpleasant. Perhaps it was brought out by the rain and the humidity. Perhaps an animal had died in a corner. At Noah's urging, Gansey cautiously stepped into the main room instead of continuing to the second-floor apartment. Unlike the second floor, the ground floor was dim, lit only by small windows high up on the walls. Rusty metal columns held the ceiling aloft, spaced wide to leave room for whatever the room had been designed for. Something substantial in both height and width. Everything was dust in this forgotten factory — the ground, the walls, the shifting shape of the air. It was unused, spacious, time-less. Eerie.

Ronan stood in the center of the room with his back to them. This Ronan Lynch was not the one that Gansey had first met. No. That Ronan, he thought, would've been intrigued but wary of the young man standing in the motes of dust. Ronan's close-shaved head was bowed, but everything else about his posture suggested vigilance, distrust. His wicked tattoo hooked out from behind his black muscle T. This Ronan Lynch was a dangerous and hollowed-out creature. He was a snare for you to step your foot in.

Do not think of this Ronan. Remember the other one.

"What are you doing down here?" Gansey asked, vaguely unnerved.

Ronan's posture didn't alter at the sound of Gansey's voice, and Gansey saw now that it was because he was already wound to the utmost. A muscle stood out on his neck. He was an animal poised for flight.

Chainsaw rolled in the dust between his feet. She appeared to be in the midst of ecstasy or seizure. When she saw Gansey, she stilled and studied him with one eye and then the other.

Outside, thunder rumbled. Rain pattered through the broken panes above the staircase. A whiff of that humid scent came through again.

Ronan's voice was flat. *"Quemadmodum gladius neminem occidit; occidentis telum est."*

Gansey had a strict policy of avoiding noun declension before breakfast. "If you're trying to be wise, you win. Is *quemadmodum* 'just like'?"

When Ronan turned, his eyes were shuttered and barred. His hands were also coated in blood.

Gansey had a pure, logicless moment where his stomach dropped and he thought, *I don't know who any of my friends really are.* Then reason filtered back in. "Jesus Christ. Is that yours?"

"Adam's."

"Dream Adam's," Noah corrected quickly. "Mostly."

In the rain, in the dim, the shadows shifted in the corners. It reminded Gansey of the first nights he'd spent here, when the only way he could sleep was to pretend that this vast room didn't exist beneath his bed. He could hear Ronan breathing.

"Do you remember last year?" Ronan asked. "When I told you . . . it wouldn't happen again?"

It was a foolish question. Gansey never forgot. Noah discovering Ronan in a slick of his own blood, veins ripped to shreds. Hours in the hospital. Counseling and promises.

No point being coy. Gansey said, "When you tried to kill yourself."

Ronan shook his head once. "It was a nightmare. They tore me apart in my dream, and when I woke up —" He gestured with his bloody hands. "I brought it with me. I couldn't tell you. My father told me to never tell."

"So you let me think you'd tried to kill yourself?"

Ronan allowed the weight of his blue-eyed gaze to rest heavily on Gansey, making him understand that he wasn't getting another answer. His father had told him to never tell. And so he had never told.

Gansey felt the entire year reshaping itself in his head. Every night he'd been terrified for Ronan's well-being. All of the times Ronan had said, *It's not like that.* At once he was incensed Ronan would have allowed him such continuous fear and relieved that Ronan was not such a foreign creature after all. It was easier for Gansey to wrap his head around a Ronan who made dreams real than a Ronan who wanted to die.

"Then why . . . why are you down here?" Gansey said finally.

Overhead, something banged. Both Ronan and Chainsaw snapped their chins upward.

"Noah?" Gansey asked.

"I'm still here," Noah replied from behind him. "But not for long."

Through the constant hiss of the rain, Gansey heard a scrape across the floor upstairs, and another bang as something fell over.

"It's not just the blood," Ronan said. His chest moved up and down with his breath. "Something else got out, too."

The door to Ronan's room was closed. A bookshelf had been emptied, tipped on its side, and pushed in front of it. The books were hastily piled beside the knocked-over telescope. Everything was silent and gray as the rain beaded on the windows. The smell Gansey had noticed downstairs was more prominent up here: moldy, sweet.

"*Kerah?*" croaked Chainsaw from Ronan's arm. He made a soft noise back at her before lowering her onto Gansey's desk; she disappeared into the rain-black shadow beneath it. Switching a crowbar to his right hand, Ronan pointed to the box cutter on the desk until Gansey realized he meant for him to take it. He dubiously extended and retracted the blade a few times before glancing at Noah. The latter looked ready to vanish, either from a lack of energy or a lack of courage.

"Are you ready?" Ronan asked.

"What is it I'm preparing myself for?"

Behind the door, something scratched on the floorboard. *Tck-tck-tck.* Like a mallet dragged across a washboard. Something in Gansey's heart thrilled with fear.

Ronan said, "What's in my head."

Gansey didn't think there was a way to steel oneself for *that*. But he helped Ronan push the bookshelf out of the way.

"Gansey," Ronan said. The doorknob was turning on its own accord. He reached out and held it still. "Watch — watch your eyes."

"What's our plan?" Gansey's attention was on Ronan's grip on the doorknob. His knuckles were white with the effort of keeping it from turning.

Ronan said, "Kill it."

He flung open the door.

The first thing Gansey saw was the disaster: Chainsaw's cage flattened, the perch splintered. The mesh cover of a speaker was bent like a clam near the threshold. A computer keyboard wedged beneath an overturned stool. A tattered shirt and pair of jeans sprawled on the floor, at first glance a corpse.

Then he saw the nightmare.

It moved from the rear corner. Like it was a shadow, and then it was a thing. Fast. Black. Bigger than he'd expected. Realer than he'd expected.

It was as tall as he was. Two-legged. Clothed in something torn, black, greasy.

Gansey couldn't stop staring at the beak.

"Gansey!" Ronan snarled, and then he swung the crowbar.

The creature hurtled to the floor. It twisted out of Ronan's reach as he swung again. Gansey became aware of a claw. No, *claws*, dozens of them. Massive, shiny, curled to needle points. They snatched at Ronan.

Gansey darted in, slashing at a limb. The creature's clothing parted beneath the blade. It leapt up, straight at Ronan, who blocked it with the crowbar. With a mighty flap, the creature launched itself through the air and perched on the doorjamb, hands between its legs, clinging like a spider. There was nothing human about it. It hissed at the boys. Red-pupiled eyes snapped shut and open. A bird. A dinosaur. A demon.

No wonder Ronan never sleeps.

"Close the door!" snapped Ronan. "We don't want to play hide-and-seek in there!"

The bedroom seemed too small to shut themselves in with a monster, but Gansey knew Ronan was right. He slammed the door just as the creature flew at him. Hooks and beak, black and twisted. At the same instant, Ronan hurled himself, pushing Gansey to the floor.

In a brief, crystal moment, pinned beneath both Ronan and the beaked creature, Gansey saw the thing's claws seize Ronan's arm, and with hyperawareness, saw matching scabs crisscrossed beneath the fresh ones. The beak darted for Ronan's face.

Gansey stabbed the box cutter blade into the waxy black flesh between the claws.

The thing made no sound as it reared back. Ronan swung again with the crowbar, and when it glanced off the creature, he aimed a fist instead. The two of them stumbled over the corner of the bed. The nightmare was on top of Ronan. Both of them fought soundlessly; Ronan could die, and Gansey wouldn't know it until after.

Sweeping a hand across Ronan's desk, Gansey seized a beer bottle and smashed it against the creature's skull. Instantly, the smell of alcohol filled the room. Ronan cursed from beneath the monster. Gansey snatched one of the thing's limbs — was it an arm? Was it a wing? Revulsion coursed up his throat — and swiped at its body with the box cutter. He felt the blade make contact, bite into greasy flesh. Suddenly, there was a claw around his neck, a claw shoved into the thin skin under his chin. Hooked like a fish.

He was aware of how tiny the blade of the box cutter was. How insubstantial in comparison to the bristling claws of this thing. He felt a warm trickle into the collar of his shirt. His lungs filled with the fecund smell of rot.

Ronan smashed the crowbar into the creature's head. And then he smashed it again. And once more. Both Gansey and the thing crumpled to the ground; the weight of it was an anchor on Gansey's skin. He was caught, impaled, snarled on this grip.

The box cutter was taken from Gansey. Gansey, seeing what Ronan meant to do, stretched his arms for that still-grasping beak. So it was the creature holding Gansey holding the creature. And then Ronan cutting its throat. It was neither fast nor blood-less. It was as ragged and slow as cutting wet cardboard.

Then it was over, and Ronan unhooked the claw carefully from Gansey's skin.

Released, Gansey scrambled back from the creature. He pressed the back of his hand to the wound on his chin. He couldn't tell what was his blood and what was its blood and what was Ronan's blood. Both of them were out of breath.

"Are you murdered?" Ronan asked Gansey. A scratch came down his temple and skipped across his eyebrow to his cheek. *Watch your eyes.*

A soft probe with Gansey's fingertips revealed that the actual wound under his chin was quite small. The memory of being caught on the claw wouldn't soon leave him though. He felt per-ilously undone, like he needed to hold on to something or be washed away. He kept his voice even. "I think so. Is it dead?"

"If it's not," Ronan said, "it's a worse nightmare than I thought."

Now Gansey did have to sit down, very slowly, on the edge of the torn-apart bedsheets. Because that *thing* had been impossible. The plane and the puzzle box, both inanimate objects, had been far easier to accept. Even Chainsaw, in all respects an ordinary raven apart from her origin, was easier to take in.

Ronan watched Gansey over the body of the creature — it seemed even larger in its death — and his expression was as unguarded as Gansey had ever seen it. He was being made to understand that this, all of it, was a confession. A look into who Ronan really had been the entire time he had known him.

What a world of wonders and horrors, and Glendower only one of them.

Gansey finally said, "Seneca. That's who said that, right?"

While his body had been fighting a nightmare, his subconscious had been battling the Latin Ronan had greeted him with.

Quemadmodum gladius neminem occidit; occidentis telum est.

Ronan's smile was sharp and hooked as one of the creature's claws. " 'A sword is never a killer; it is a tool in the killer's hand.' "

"I can't believe Noah didn't stick around to help."

"Sure you can. Never trust the dead."

Shaking his head, Gansey pointed at the scabs he had seen on Ronan's arm during the fight. "Your arm. Is that from fighting with it while I was in the Pig?"

Ronan shook his head slowly. In the other room, Chainsaw was making anxious noises, worried over the fate of him. *"Kerah?"*

"There was another one," he said. "It got away."

19

"Jane, how do you feel about doing something slightly illegal and definitely distasteful?" Gansey asked.

Ronan's back was already sticky with the heat. The bird man's corpse was in the BMW's trunk, and undoubtedly a dreadful scientific process was happening to it. Ronan was certain it was a process that was going to only get more odiferous as the day grew warmer.

"It depends on if it involves a helicopter," Blue replied, standing in the doorway of 300 Fox Way. She scratched her calf with her bare foot. She wore a dress Ronan thought looked like a lampshade. Whatever sort of lamp it belonged on, Gansey clearly wished he had one.

Ronan wasn't a fan of lamps.

And he had other things on his mind. Nerves tingled in his fingers.

Gansey shrugged. "No helicopters. This time."

"Is this about Cabeswater?"

"No," Gansey said sadly.

She looked past them to the BMW. "Why is there a bungee cord around the trunk?"

Although Ronan reckoned the Pig deserved it, Gansey had refused to put the corpse in the Camaro. "It's a long story. Why are you looking at me like that?"

"I guess I've never seen you in a T-shirt before. Or jeans."

Because Blue had been staring at Gansey in a way that was

more conspicuous for the fact that she was trying to be inconspicuous about it. It was equal parts startled and impressed. It was true that Gansey rarely wore jeans and a T-shirt, preferring collared shirts and cargo pants if he wasn't in a tie. And it was true he wore them well; the T-shirt hung on his shoulders in a way that revealed all kinds of pleasant nooks and corners that a button-down usually hid. But Ronan suspected that Blue was most shocked by how it made Gansey look like a boy, for once, something like one of them.

"It's for the distasteful thing," Gansey said. He plucked at the T-shirt with deprecating fingers. "I'm rather slovenly at the moment, I know."

Blue concurred, "Yes, slovenly, that's exactly what I was thinking. Ronan, I see that you're dressed slovenly as well."

This was meant to be mocking, as Ronan was in a fairly typical Ronan getup of jeans and black tank.

"Shall I get into something more slovenly, too?" she asked.

"At least put shoes on," Gansey replied somberly. "And a hat, if you must. It looks like rain."

"Tut tut," Blue said, glancing up to verify. But the sky was hidden by the leafy trees of her neighborhood. "Where's Adam?"

"Picking him up next."

"Where's Noah?"

Ronan said, "Same place Cabeswater is."

Gansey winced.

"Nice, Ronan," Blue said, annoyed. She left the door hanging open as she retreated into the house, calling, *"Mom! I'm going with the boys to . . . do . . . something!"*

As they waited, Gansey turned to Ronan. "Let me be very clear: If there was any other place we could bury this thing without fear of it being discovered, we'd be going there instead. I don't think it's a good idea to go to the Barns, and I wish you wouldn't come with us in any case. I want it to be on record."

"WHAT SORT OF SOMETHING?" This was Maura, from inside the house.

"Great, man," Ronan replied. Even the admonishment was electrifying. Proof that this was indeed happening. "I'm glad you got it out."

There was never a chance Ronan wasn't coming with.

"SOMETHING DISTASTEFUL!" Blue roared back. She reappeared at the door, her wardrobe essentially unchanged but for the addition of crochet tights and green rubber boots. "What *are* we doing, by the way?"

Home, Ronan thought. *I'm going home.*

"Well," Gansey said slowly, as thunder rumbled once more, "the illegal part is that we're going to Ronan's family's property, which he's not allowed to do."

Ronan flashed his teeth at her. "And the distasteful part is that we're burying a body."

Ronan had not been to the Barns in over a year, even in his dreams.

It was as he remembered it from countless summer afternoons: the two stone pillars half-hidden in ivy, tangled banks like a wall around the property, the oaks huddled close on either side of the pitted gravel driveway. The gray sky above made everything greens and blacks, forest and shade, growing and mysterious. The effect was to give the entrance to the Barns a sort of privacy. A reclusiveness.

As they ascended the drive, rain spattered on the BMW's windshield. Thunder rumbled. Ronan navigated the car up over a crest through the oak trees, around a tight turn, and there — a great sloping expanse, pure green, sheltered by trees on all sides. Once upon a time, cattle had grazed in these front pastures, cattle of every color. That herd, lovely as fairy animals, still populated Ronan's dreams, though in stranger fields. He wondered what had happened to the real cattle.

In the backseat, Blue and Adam craned their necks, looking at the approaching house. It was homely, unimpressive, a farmhouse that had been added on to every few decades. It was the namesake barns scattered through the saturated hills that were memorable, most of them chalk-white and tin-roofed, some of them still standing, some of them collapsing. Some were long and skinny livestock barns, others broad hay barns topped with pointy-hatted cupolas. There were ancient stone outbuildings and new, flat-roofed equipment sheds, still-rank goat houses and long-empty dog kennels. They dotted the fields as if they'd grown from them: smaller ones clustered like mushrooms, larger ones standing apart.

Over them all was the troubled sky, huge and purple with rain. Every color was deeper, truer, better. This was the reality, and last year had been the dream.

There was one light on in the farmhouse, the light to the sitting room. It was always on.

Am I really here? Ronan wondered.

Surely he would wake up soon and find himself again exiled in Monmouth Manufacturing or in the backseat of his car or lying on the floor beside Adam's bed at St. Agnes. In the oppressive light, the Barns was so green and beautiful that he felt sick.

In the rearview mirror, he caught a glimpse of Adam, his expression dreamy and ill, and then of Blue, her fingertips pressed to the glass as if she wanted to touch the damp grass.

The gravel parking area was empty, the home nurse nowhere in evidence. Ronan parked beside a plum tree laden with unpicked fruit. Once, he'd had a dream that he'd bitten into one of the fruits, and juice and seeds had exploded from inside. Another where the fruit bled and creatures came to lap it up before they burrowed under his skin, sweet-scented parasites.

When Ronan opened the door, the car was immediately filled with the damp-earth, green-walled, mold-stone scent of *home*.

"It looks like another country," Blue said.

It *was* another country. It was a country for the young, a country where you died before you got old. Climbing out, their feet sank into the summer-soft turf beside the gravel. Fine rain caught in their hair. The drops murmured on the leaves of the surrounding trees, an ascending hum.

The loveliness of the place couldn't even be marred by the knowledge that this was the place Ronan had found his father's body, and this was the car Ronan had found him lying near. Like Monmouth Manufacturing, the Barns was transformed utterly by the changing light. The body had been found on a cool, dark morning, and this was a shaggy, gray afternoon. So the memory became only a briefly noted thought, analytical rather than emotional.

The only reality was this: He was home.

How badly he wanted to stay.

A few minutes later, standing at the open trunk, they all realized neither Gansey nor Ronan had considered the plan deeply enough to procure a shovel.

"Einstein?" Ronan addressed Adam.

"Barn?" suggested Adam, coming awake. "Tools?"

"Oh, yeah. This way."

Climbing over a black four-board fence, they set off across the fields toward one of the main barns. The atmosphere encouraged silence. Adam took a few hurried steps to walk beside Blue, but neither spoke. On Ronan's shoulder, Chainsaw flapped to keep her balance. She was getting heavy, this dream of his. Beside Ronan, Gansey's head was ducked against the rain, his face pensive. He'd made this walk enough times himself, before.

How many times had Ronan made this walk? It could have been a year ago, five years ago.

Ronan was filled with a burst of fury at Declan, enforcer of his father's will. He couldn't have his father back, probably would never have his mother back. But if he was allowed to come back here — it wouldn't be the same, but it would be bearable.

Chainsaw saw the strange thing first. She remarked, *"Kreck."*

Ronan stopped.

"What's that?" he asked. A dozen yards away, a smooth brown object sat in the midst of all the green. It was waist-high in size and mountainous in texture.

Dubiously, Blue asked, "Is that . . . a cow?"

It was obvious once she had said it. It was certainly a cow, lying down as cattle do in the rain. And it was certainly one of the cattle that had occupied this pasture before Niall Lynch had died. Ronan couldn't quite work out how it was still here.

Adam made a face. "Is it dead?"

Ronan pointed to the cow's slowly moving side as he walked around it. Now he could see her finely sculpted face and the moisture around the nostrils. Her large black eyes were half-lidded. Both he and Chainsaw leaned in, heads identically cocked. When Ronan waved a hand in front of the cow's eyes, she didn't move.

"Non mortem," he muttered, narrowing his eyes, *"somni fratrem."*

Blue whispered, *"What?"*

Adam translated, " 'Not death, but his brother, sleep.' "

Gansey, a bit of the gallows in his voice, advised, "Poke its eye."

"Gansey!" Blue said.

Ronan did not poke the cow's eye, but he did brush a finger through her soft, unblinking eyelashes. Gansey held a palm in front of the cow's nostrils.

"It *is* breathing."

Huddled close, Blue stroked the cow's nose, leaving dark marks on the wet hair. "Poor thing. What do you think's wrong with it?"

Ronan wasn't certain there *was* anything wrong with it. It didn't look ill, aside from its lack of movement. It didn't smell terrible. And Chainsaw didn't seem abnormally distressed, although she did press her body against the side of Ronan's head as a warning to not set her down anywhere near it.

"There's a metaphor for the American public in here," Gansey murmured darkly, "but it escapes me at the moment."

Blue said, "Let's just go on before Gansey has time to say something that makes me hate him."

They left the cow behind and continued on to the largest of the barns. The big sliding door was worm-eaten and rotted near the bottom, and the metal edging was rusted.

Ronan put his hand on the uneven surface of the door handle. Out of habit, his palm memorized the feel of it. Not the idea of it, but the real *sensation* of it, the texture and shape and temperature of the metal, everything he'd need to bring it back from a dream.

"Wait," Adam said, wary. "What's that smell?"

The air was colored with a warm, claustrophobic odor — not unpleasant, but undeniably *agricultural*. It was not the smell of a barn that had been used in the past; it was one of a barn currently in use.

Frowning, Ronan slid open the creaking, massive door. It took a moment for their eyes to adjust.

"Oh," said Gansey.

Here was the rest of the herd. Dozens of cattle were dark silhouettes in the watery light through the door. There was not so much as a twitch over the clatter of the door opening. There was just the sound of several dozen very large animals breathing, and over all of it, the shushing of the light rain on the metal roof.

"Sleep mode," Gansey said, at the same time that Blue said, "Hypnosis."

Ronan's heart beat unevenly. There was a raw potential to the sleeping herd. Like someone with the correct word could rouse a stampede.

"Is this our fault, too?" Blue whispered. "Like the power outages?"

Adam looked away.

"No," Ronan answered, certain that this sleeping herd wasn't because of the ley line. "This is something else."

Gansey said, "Not to sound like Noah, but this is giving me the creeps. Let's find a shovel and get out of here."

Feet scuffing through sawdust, they wound their way through the motionless animals to a small equipment room made gray by the rain. Ronan found a spade. Adam picked up a snow shovel. Gansey tested a post-hole digger's weight as if checking the balance of a sword.

After a moment, Blue said, "Did you really grow up here, Ronan?"

"In this barn?"

"You know *exactly* what I mean."

He started to answer, but pain welled up, sudden and shocking. The only way he could get the sentiment out was by drowning the words with acid. It came out sounding like he hated the place. Like he couldn't wait to get away. Mocking and cruel, he said, "Yes. This was my castle."

"Wow," she replied, as if he hadn't been sarcastic. Then she whispered, "Look!"

Ronan followed her gaze. Where the corrugated roof imperfectly met the edge of the finished wall, a dusty brown bird was tucked away in a nest. Its chest looked black, bloody, but a closer look revealed that it was a trick of the dim light. Its chest plumage was a peacock's metallic emerald. Like the cattle, its eyes were open, its head unmoving. Ronan's pulse surged again.

On his shoulder, Chainsaw crouched low, pressing against his neck, a reaction to *his* reaction rather than to the other bird.

"Touch it," Blue whispered. "See if it's alive, too."

"One of you two Poverty Twins should touch it," Ronan said. "I touched the last one."

Her eyes blazed. "*What* did you just call me?"

"You heard me."

"*Gansey*," she said.

He put down his post-hole digger. "You told me you wanted to fight your Ronan battles on your own."

With a roll of his eyes, Adam dragged over a chair and investigated. "It's breathing, too. Same as the cows."

"Now check for eggs," Ronan said.

"Screw you."

They were all a little uneasy. It was impossible to tell if this slumber was natural or supernatural, and without that knowledge, it didn't seem impossible that it might happen to them, too.

Gansey said, "Are we the only things left awake?"

This inspired Ronan. Setting Chainsaw down on a table made of cinder blocks, he opened the old feed bin beside it. Even though it was empty, he suspected it would still be occupied. Sure enough, when he stuck his head inside, he discovered a sharp, living smell beneath the warm odor of grain.

Ronan ordered, "Light."

Flicking to his phone's flashlight function, Gansey illuminated the bin's interior.

"Hurry up," he said. "This cooks my phone."

Reaching all the way to the crumpled old feed bag in the bottom, Ronan found the mouse nest. He carefully pulled one of the young mice free. It was downy and weightless, so small that the warmth of its body barely registered. Though the mouse was old enough to be completely mobile, it remained calm in his cupped palm. He ran a finger gently along its spine.

"Why is it so tame?" Blue asked. "Is it sleeping, too?"

He tipped his hand just enough for her to see its alert, trustful eyes, but not enough for Chainsaw to glimpse it — she'd think it was food. He and Matthew used to find the mouse nests in the feed rooms and in the fields near the troughs. They would sit cross-legged for hours in the grass, letting the mice run back and forth across their hands. The young ones were never afraid.

"It's awake," he said. Lifting his hand, he pressed the tiny body to his cheek so that he could feel the flutter of its rapid heartbeat against his skin. Blue was staring at him, so he offered it to her. "You can feel its heart that way."

She looked suspicious. "Are you for real? Are you messing with me?"

"How do you figure?"

"You're a bastard, and this doesn't seem like a typical bastard activity."

He smiled thinly. "Don't get used to it."

Grudgingly, she accepted the tiny mouse and held it to her cheek. A surprised smile crept across her mouth. With a tiny, happy sigh, she offered it to Adam. He didn't seem eager, but at her insistence, he pressed the little body against his cheek. His mouth quirked. After a second, he passed the mouse on to Gansey. Gansey was the only one who smiled at it *before* he lifted it to his face. And it was his smile that buried Ronan; it reminded him of Matthew's easy expression when they'd first discovered the mice, back when they'd been the Lynch family.

"Astonishingly charming," Gansey reported. He tipped it into Ronan's hands.

Ronan held the mouse over the top of the bin. "Anyone want seconds before I put it back? Because it'll be dead in a year. Lifespan's shit for field mice."

"Nice, Ronan," said Adam, turning to go.

Blue's face had gone to lemons. "That didn't last long."

Gansey didn't add anything. His eyes merely lingered on Ronan, mouth rueful; he knew Ronan too well to be offended. Ronan felt he was being analyzed, and maybe he wanted to be. "Let's go bury this thing," he said.

Back at the BMW, Gansey was decent enough to not look smug when Blue slapped her hand over her mouth and Adam sucked in his breath at the first sight of the bird man. Ronan and Gansey had stuffed it into a speaker box as best they could, but enough of the corpse poked out of both ends to abuse the imagination. Several hours of deadness had not improved its appearance in any way.

"What is it?" Adam asked.

Ronan touched one of the ragged claws hooked around the edge of the box. It was terrible, chilling. He was afraid of it in a dull, primeval, permanent way that came from being killed by them again and again in his head. "They come when I'm having a nightmare. Like, it draws them. They hate me. In the dreams, they're called night horrors. Or . . . *niri viclis.*"

Adam frowned. "Is that Latin?"

Perplexed, Ronan considered. "I . . . don't think so."

Blue looked sharply to him, and immediately Ronan remembered when she'd accused him of knowing the other language on the puzzle box. It was possible she was right.

Between the four of them, they carried the speaker-box coffin to the tree line. As the rain drizzled on, they took turns digging in the storm-damp soil. Ronan glanced up every few seconds to check on Chainsaw. She didn't care for anything large and black, including herself, and so she kept her distance from the corpse, even after it was in the hole. But she adored Ronan above all things, so she loitered in the middle distance, poking the ground for invisible insects.

By the time they had tamped the last pile of dirt over the hole, they were soaked with rain and sweat. There was something warming, Ronan thought, about all of them burying a body on his behalf. He would've preferred it to stay in his dreams, but if it had to slip out, this was better than the last out-of-control nightmare.

With a gentle oath, Gansey jammed the tip of the shovel into the ground and wiped his forehead with the back of his hand. He stuffed a mint leaf into his mouth. "I have blisters. Nino's?"

Blue protested wordlessly.

Gansey looked to Adam.

"I'm fine with anything," Adam replied, his Henrietta accent snaking out, betraying his fatigue. It wasn't quite his usual tiredness. It was something deeper. It wasn't at all impossible for Ronan to imagine that bargain nesting in Adam's bones.

Gansey looked at Ronan.

Ronan rubbed a studious thumb beneath one of the leather straps, wiping away the grime and sweat. He wondered when he'd ever be back. Softly, just for Gansey, he asked, "Can I go and see Mom?"

20

Inside the farmhouse, everything was in black and white. The air was stained permanently with the pleasant odor of Ronan's childhood: hickory smoke and boxwood, grass seed and lemon cleaner.

"I remember," Gansey said thoughtfully to Ronan, "when you used to smell like this."

Gansey clucked at his bedraggled reflection in the dark-framed mirror hanging in the front hallway. Chainsaw eyed herself briefly before hiding on the other side of Ronan's neck; Adam did the same, but without the hiding-in-Ronan's-neck bit. Even Blue looked less fanciful than usual, the lighting rendering her lampshade dress and spiky hair as a melancholy Pierrot.

"It feels the same as when you guys lived here," Gansey said finally. "It seems like it should be different."

"Did you come here a lot?" Blue asked.

He exchanged a glance with Ronan. "Often enough."

He didn't say what Ronan was thinking, which was that Gansey was far more of a brother to Ronan than Declan had ever been.

Voice faded, Adam asked, "Could we get some water?"

Ronan led them to the kitchen. It was a farmhouse kitchen, no frills, worn smooth by use. Nothing had ever been repaired or updated until it had stopped working, and so the room was an amalgam of decades and styles: plain white cabinets decorated with a combination of old glass knobs and brass handles, counters that were half new butcher block and half dingy laminate, appliances a mixture of snowy white and polished stainless steel.

With Blue and Adam there, Ronan saw the Barns with fresh eyes. This was not the pretentious, beautiful old money of Gansey's family. This house was shabby rich, betraying its wealth not with culture or airs but because no comfort was wanting: mismatched antiques and copper pots, real hand-painted art on the walls and real hand-knotted rugs on the floors. Where Gansey's ancestral home was a no-touch museum of elegant, remote things, the Barns was a warren of pool tables and quilts, video game cords and shoddily expensive leather couches.

Ronan loved it so much. He nearly couldn't bear it. He wanted to destroy something.

Instead, he said, "Remember how I told you that Dad — that my father was like me?" He pointed to the toaster. It was an ordinary stainless-steel toaster, room for two slices of toast.

Gansey raised an eyebrow. "That? Is a toaster."

"Dream toaster."

Adam laughed soundlessly.

"How can you tell?" asked Gansey.

Ronan slid the toaster out from the wall. There was no wall plug, no battery panel. Yet when he pressed down on the lever, the filaments inside began to glow. For how many years had he used this toaster before he'd realized that it was impossible?

"What's it run on, then?" Adam asked.

"Dream energy," Ronan said. Chainsaw hopped untidily from Ronan's shoulder to the counter and had to be smacked away from the appliance. "Cleanest there is."

Adam's dusty eyebrows shot up toward his hairline. He replied, "Politicians wouldn't be pleased. No offense to your mother, Gansey."

"None taken," Gansey said cordially.

"Oh, and that," Ronan said, pointing at the calendar on the front of the fridge.

Blue paged through it. No one had been here to change over the month, but it didn't matter. Every page was the same — twelve pages of April, every photo displaying three black birds sitting on a fence. There had been a time when Ronan had thought it was merely a gag gift. Now he could readily recognize the artifact of a frustration dream. Blue peered at the birds, her nose nearly touching the image. "Are these vultures or crows?"

At the same time that Ronan said, "Crows," Adam said, "Vultures."

"What else is here?" Gansey asked. He was using his *deeply curious* voice and his *deeply curious* face, the ones he normally reserved for all things Glendower. "Dream things, I mean?"

"Damned if I know," Ronan replied. "Never made a study."

Gansey said, "Then let's make a study."

The four of them pushed out from the fridge, pulling open cabinets and shifting through items on the countertop.

"Phone doesn't plug into the wall," Adam noted, turning an old-fashioned rotary dial phone upside down to look at it. "But there's still a dial tone."

In the age of cell phones, Ronan found this discovery profoundly disinteresting. He had just found a pencil that was really a pen; even though an exploratory scratch of a fingernail on the side of lead revealed that it was a leaded pencil, the tip released a perfect line of blue ink when dragged across the notepad beside the pencil can.

"Microwave's not plugged in, either," Adam said.

"Here's a spoon with two ends," Gansey added.

A high-pitched whine filled the kitchen; Blue had discovered that when the seat was rotated on one of the high stools, it emitted a wail that sounded a little like "The Wind That Shakes the Barley" played several times faster than it had ever been meant to be played. She gave it a few spins to see if it made it all the way through the tune. It didn't. The product of another frustration dream.

"God*damn* it," said Gansey, dropping a knife onto the counter. He shook his hand out. "It's red-hot." Only it wasn't. The blade was ordinary stainless steel, its heat only evident by the faint scent of the counter finish melting beneath it. He tapped the handle a few times to verify that it was the entire knife that was hot, not just the blade, and then used a dish towel to replace it in the knife block.

Ronan had stopped searching in earnest and was merely opening and slamming drawers for the pleasure of hearing them crash. He wasn't sure what was worse: leaving or the anticipation of leaving.

"Well, this isn't frustrating at all," Adam remarked, demonstrating a tape measure he'd found. The tape tugged out to two feet, six inches, and no more. "I would've thrown this out the morning after."

"Perfect for measuring bread boxes," Gansey observed. "Maybe it has nostalgic value."

"How about this?" Blue, out in the hall, touched the petal of a perfect blue lily. It was one of a dozen gathered into a bouquet on the hall table. Ronan had never given much thought to the flowers, but when he did, he'd always assumed they were fake, as the vase they were displayed in had never contained water. The white and blue lilies were oversized and spidery with frothy golden stamen, blossoms like nothing he'd seen elsewhere. He should've known, in retrospect. Adam pinched off a bud and turned the moist end of the stem to the other two boys. "They're alive."

This was the sort of thing that Gansey couldn't resist, and so Adam and Ronan moved farther down the hall toward the dining room while Gansey lingered over the flowers. When Ronan glanced over his shoulder, Gansey stood with one of the blossoms cupped in his hand. There was something humble and awed in the way he stood, something grateful and wistful in his face as he gazed at the flower. It was a strangely deferential expression.

Somehow this made Ronan even angrier. He turned quickly away before Gansey could catch his eye. In the pale gray dining room, Adam was taking a wooden mask from a hook on the wall.

It was carved of a smooth, dark wood and looked like a cheap tourist souvenir. The eyeholes were round and surprised, the mouth parted in an easy smile big enough for lots of teeth.

Ronan hurled himself through the air.

"*No.*"

The mask clattered to the floor. Adam, startled, stared at where Ronan's hand gripped his wrist. Ronan could feel his own heart pounding and, in Adam's wrist, Adam's.

At once, he released him and fell back. He snatched up the mask instead. He hung it back on the wall, but his pulse didn't calm. He didn't look at Adam.

"Don't," he said. But he didn't know what he was telling Adam not to do. It was possible that his father's version of the mask was entirely harmless. It was possible that it only became deadly in Ronan's head.

Suddenly, he couldn't stand it, any of it, his father's dreams, his childhood home, his own skin.

He punched the wall. His knuckles bit plaster, and the plaster bit back. He felt the moment his skin split. He'd left a faint impression of his anger in the wall, but it hadn't cracked.

"Oh, come on, Lynch," Adam said. "Are you trying to break your hand?"

"What was that?" Gansey called from the other room.

Ronan had no idea what it was, but he did it again. And then he kicked one of the dining room chairs. He hurled a tall basket full of recorders and pennywhistles against the wall. Tore a handful of small frames from their hangers. He'd been angry before, but now he was nothing. Just knuckles and sparks of pain.

Abruptly, his arm stopped in midflight.

Gansey's grip was tight on it, and his expression, two inches away from Ronan's, was unamused. His countenance was at once young and old. More old than young.

"Ronan Lynch," he said. It was the voice Ronan couldn't *not* listen to. It was sure in every way that Ronan was not. "Stop this *right* now. Go see your mother. And then we're leaving."

Gansey held Ronan's arm a second longer to make sure he hadn't mistaken his meaning, and then he dropped it and turned to Adam. "Were you just going to stand there?"

"Yeah," replied Adam.

"Decent of you," Gansey said.

There was no heat in Adam's reply. "I can't kill his demons."

Blue said nothing at all, but she waited at the doorway until Ronan joined her. And then, as the other two began to tidy the dining room, she accompanied Ronan into the sitting room.

It was not really a sitting room; no one needed a sitting room anymore. Instead it had become a repository for everything that didn't seem to belong anywhere else. Three mismatched leather chairs faced one another on the uneven wood floor — that was the *sitting* part. Tall, thin crockery held umbrellas and dull swords. Rubber boots and pogo sticks lined the walls. Rugs made tight upholstery scrolls in a corner; one of them was marked with a sticky note that said *not this one* in Niall's handwriting. A strange iron chandelier, reminiscent of planetary orbits, hung in the center of the room. Niall had probably dreamt it. Certainly the other two chandeliers that hung in the corners, half light fixture, half potted plants, were dream things. Probably everything here was. Only now that Ronan had been away from home could he see how full of dreams it was.

And there, in the middle of it, was his beautiful mother. She had a silent audience of catheters and IVs and feeding tubes — all of the things that home nurses always felt she would need. But she required nothing. She was a sedentary queen from an old epic: golden hair swept away from her pale face, cheeks flushed, lips red as the devil, eyes gently closed. She looked nothing like her charismatic husband, her troubled sons.

Ronan walked directly up to her, close enough to see that she had not changed a bit since the last time he had seen her, months and months ago. Though his breath moved the fine hairs around her temples, she didn't react to her son's presence.

Her chest rose and fell. Her eyes stayed closed.

Non mortem, somni fratrem. Not death, but his brother, sleep.

Blue whispered, "Just like the other animals."

The truth — he'd known it all along, really, if he thought about it — burrowed into him. Blue was right.

His home was populated by things and creatures from Niall Lynch's dreams, and his mother was just another one of them.

21

Blue thought it was well past time they took Ronan to her family for a consultation. Dream monsters were one thing. Dream mothers were another. The following morning, she biked down to Monmouth Manufacturing and proposed her idea. There was silence, and then:

"No," Ronan said.

"Excuse me?" she asked.

"No," he replied. "I'm not going."

Gansey, lying on the floor beside his long aerial printout of the ley line, didn't look up. "Ronan, don't be difficult."

"I'm not being difficult. I'm just telling you I'm not going."

Blue said, "It's not the dentist."

Ronan, leaning against the doorway to his room, replied, "Exactly."

Gansey made a note on the printout. "That doesn't make sense."

But it did. Blue thought she knew precisely what was going on. Icily, she said, "This is a religion thing, isn't it?"

Ronan scoffed, "You don't have to say it like that."

"Actually, I do. Is this the part where you tell me my mom and I are going to hell?"

"I wouldn't rule it out," he said. "But I don't really have the inside line on that knowledge."

At this, Gansey rolled over onto his back and folded his hands on his chest. He wore a salmon polo shirt, which, in Blue's opinion, was far more hellish than anything they'd discussed to this point. "What's this all about now?"

Blue couldn't believe he didn't already know what the conflict was. Either he was incredibly oblivious or astonishingly enlightened. Knowing Gansey, it was undoubtedly the former.

"This is the part where Ronan starts using the word *occult*," Blue snapped. She'd heard versions of this conversation countless times in her life; it had become too commonplace to needle her anymore. But she hadn't expected it from her inner circle.

"I'm not using any word," Ronan said. The annoying thing about Ronan was always that he was angry when everyone else was calm, and calm when everyone else was angry. Because Blue was ready to bust a vein, his voice was utterly pacific. "I'm just telling you I'm not going. Maybe it's wrong, maybe it's not. My soul's in enough peril as it is."

At this, Gansey's face turned to a genuine frown and he looked as if he was about to say something. Then he just shook his head a little.

"Do you think we're in league with the devil, Ronan?" Blue asked. The question would've had a better effect if she'd asked it with sickly sweetness — she could just imagine Calla pulling it off — but she was too irritated to manage it. "They're evil soothsayers?"

He rolled his eyes luxuriously at her. It was like he merely absorbed her anger, saving it all up for when he needed it for himself.

"My mom first knew she was psychic because she saw the future in a dream," Blue said. "A *dream*, Ronan. It wasn't like she sacrificed a goat in the backyard to see it. She didn't *try* to see the future. It's not something she became; it's something she *is*. I could just as easily say that you're evil because you can take things from your dreams!"

Ronan said, "Yeah, you could."

Gansey's frown deepened. Again he opened his mouth and closed it.

Blue couldn't drop it. She said, "So even if it could help you understand you and your dad, you won't go talk to them."

He shrugged, as dismissive as Kavinsky. "Nope."

"Why, you close-minded —"

"Jane," Gansey rumbled. *Oblivious!* He cut his eyes to her, looking as stately as one could look lying on their back in a salmon polo shirt. "Ronan."

Ronan said, "I am being perfectly fucking civil."

"You're being medieval," Gansey replied. "Multiple studies have suggested that clairvoyance lies in the realm of science, not magic."

Oh. Enlightened.

"Come on, man," Ronan said.

Gansey sat up. "Come on, man, yourself. We're all aware here that Cabeswater bends time. You yourself somehow managed to write on that rock in Cabeswater before any of us ever got there. Time's not a line. It's a circle or a figure eight or a goddamn Slinky. If you can believe that, I don't know why you can't believe that someone might be able to glimpse something farther along the Slinky."

Ronan looked at him.

That look, Blue thought. Ronan Lynch would do anything for Gansey.

I probably would, too, she thought. It was impossible for her to understand how he managed to pull off such an effect in that polo shirt.

"Whatever," Ronan said. Which meant he'd do it.

Gansey looked at Blue. "Happy, Jane?"

Blue said, "Whatever."

Which meant she was.

Maura and Persephone were working, but Blue managed to corner Calla in the Phone/Sewing/Cat Room. If she couldn't have all three of them, Calla was the one she wanted anyway. Calla was as traditionally clairvoyant as the other two, but she had an additional, strange gift: psychometry. When she touched an object, she could often sense where it had come from, what the owner had been thinking when he or she used it, and where it might end up. As they seemed to be dealing with things that were both people *and* objects at the same time, Calla's talent seemed apropos.

Standing in the doorway with Ronan and Gansey, Blue said, "We need your advice."

"I'm sure you do," replied Calla, in not the warmest of ways. She had one of those low, smoky voices that always seemed more appropriate to a black-and-white movie. "Ask your question."

Politely, Gansey asked, "Are you sure you can think that way?"

"If you're doubting me," Calla snapped, "I don't see why you're here."

In Gansey's defense, Calla was upside down. She hung magnificently from the ceiling of the Phone/Sewing/Cat Room; the only thing preventing her from crashing to the floor was a deep purple swath of silk wrapped around one of her thighs.

Gansey averted his eyes. He whispered in Blue's ear, "Is this a ritual?"

There was something a bit magical about it, Blue supposed. Although the green gingham-wallpapered room was full of a multitude of odds and ends to lure the attention, it was difficult to look away from Calla's slowly spinning form. It seemed impossible the length of silk would hold her weight. Currently, she was rotated toward the corner, her back to them. Her tunic hung down, revealing a lot of dark brown skin, a pink bra strap, and four tiny tattooed coyotes running along her spine.

Blue, holding the puzzle box in her hands, whispered back: "It's aerial yoga." Louder, she said, "Calla, it's about Ronan."

Calla readjusted, wrapping the silk around her other thigh instead. "Which one's he again? The pretty one?"

Blue and Gansey exchanged a look. Blue's look said, *I'm so, so sorry.* Gansey's said, *Am I the pretty one?*

Calla continued turning, almost imperceptibly. It was becoming more obvious as she swiveled that she was not the thinnest woman on the planet, but that she had stomach muscles like *whoa*. "The Coca-Cola shirt?"

She meant Adam. He'd worn a red Coca-Cola shirt to the first reading and was now and forevermore identified by it.

Ronan said, his voice a low growl, "The snake."

Calla's rotation finished just as he said it. They looked at each other for a long moment, him right side up, her upside down. Chainsaw, on Ronan's shoulder, twisted her head to get a better look. There was nothing particularly sympathetic about Ronan just then, handsome mouth drawing a cruel line, eerie tattoo creeping out the collar of his black T-shirt, raven pressed against the side of his shaved head. It was hard to remember the Ronan who'd pressed that tiny mouse to his cheek back at the Barns.

Upside down, Calla was trying to look dismissive, but it was clear that one of her arched eyebrows was terribly interested.

"I see," she replied finally. "What sort of advice do you need, Snake?"

"My dreams," Ronan replied.

Now Calla's eyebrows matched her dismissive mouth. She allowed herself to circle away from them again. "Persephone's the one you'll want for dream interpretation. Have a nice life."

"They'll interest you," Ronan said.

Calla just cackled and stretched one of her legs out.

Blue made an irritated noise. Taking two strides across the room, she pressed the puzzle box to Calla's bare cheek.

Calla stopped spinning.

Slowly, she righted herself. The gesture was as elegant as a ballet move, a swan dancer unfolding. She said, "Why didn't you say so?"

Ronan said, "I did."

Her plum lips pursed. "Something you should know about me, Snake. I don't believe anyone."

Chainsaw hissed. Ronan said, "Something you should know about me. I never lie."

Calla continued performing aerial yoga for the entirety of the conversation.

Sometimes she was right side up, her legs curved beneath her. "All of these things are still a part of you. To me, they feel precisely the same as you feel. Well, mostly. They're like your nail clippings. So they all share the same life as you. The same soul. You're the same entity."

Ronan wanted to protest this — if Chainsaw fell off a table, he didn't feel her pain — but he wouldn't feel the pain of one of his nail clippings, either.

"So when you die, they'll stop."

"Stop? Not die themselves?" Gansey asked.

Calla turned herself upside down, her knees bent and her feet pressed to each other. It made her a cunning spider. "When you die, your computer doesn't die, too. They never really lived like you're thinking of life. It's not a soul that's animating them. Take away the dreamer and — they're a computer waiting for input."

Ronan thought of what Declan had said all those months before: *Mom is nothing without Dad.* He'd been right. "So my mother is never going to wake up."

Calla slid slowly upright, freeing her hands. "Snake, hand me that bird."

"Don't squeeze," Ronan said narrowly, folding the raven's wings against her body and relinquishing her.

Chainsaw promptly bit Calla's finger. Unimpressed, Calla snapped her teeth back at the raven.

"Careful, chickadee," she told Chainsaw, her smile deadly. "I bite, too. Blue?"

This meant she wanted to use Blue's invisible ability to hone her vision. Blue rested one hand on Calla's knee and used the other to keep Calla from rotating. For a long moment, Calla hung there with her eyes closed. Chainsaw was motionless in her hands, fluffed up over the ignominy of it all. Then Calla fixed her gaze on Ronan, a sharply structured smile manifesting on her plum-painted lips. "What *have* you done, Snake?"

Ronan didn't reply. Silence was never a wrong answer.

Calla stuffed the bird into Blue's hands, who tried to placate her before returning her to Ronan.

Calla said, "Here's the deal. Your mother was a dream. Your fool father took her out — what, there aren't enough women in the world without making one? — and now, she has no dreamer. You want her back, she has to go back in a dream."

She did several elaborate procedures then, all of them elegant and effortless looking. They reminded Ronan a bit of the movement of the puzzle box in that they seemed to be a little illogical, a little impossible. It was hard to understand how she extracted an arm from the silk without getting her torso tangled. Difficult to see how she twisted that leg without falling to the floor.

Ronan interrupted the silence. "Cabeswater. Cabeswater is a dream."

Calla stopped rotating.

"You don't have to tell me I'm right," Ronan said. He thought of all the times he had dreamt of Cabeswater's old trees; how familiar it had felt to walk there; how the trees had known his name. He was tangled in their roots, somehow, and they, in his veins. "If Mom is in Cabeswater, she'll wake up."

Calla stared at him. Silence was never a wrong answer.

Gansey said, "I guess we really do have to get Cabeswater back, then."

Blue tilted her head so that Calla was slightly less upside down to her. "Any ideas?"

"I'm not a magician," Calla said. Blue gave her a spin. Calla laughed all the way around, a filthy, pleased sound. She pointed to Ronan as he headed out the door. "But he is. Also, get rid of that mask. It's a nasty bit of work."

22

LAST WILL & TESTAMENT OF
NIALL T. LYNCH
ARTICLE 1
PRELIMINARY DECLARATIONS

I AM MARRIED TO AURORA LYNCH AND ALL REFERENCES IN
THIS WILL TO MY SPOUSE REFER TO AURORA LYNCH.

I HAVE THREE LIVING CHILDREN, NAMED DECLAN T. LYNCH,
RONAN N. LYNCH, AND MATTHEW A. LYNCH. ALL REFERENCES IN
THIS WILL TO MY "CHILD" OR "CHILDREN" OR "ISSUE" INCLUDE
THE ABOVE CHILD OR CHILDREN, AND ANY CHILD OR CHILDREN
HEREAFTER BORN TO OR ADOPTED BY ME. ALL REFERENCES TO
"MIDDLE SON" REFER TO RONAN N. LYNCH.

"I was thinking we could all get together for the Fourth of July,"
Matthew said, peering up at Ronan; the late evening light made
his curls cherubic. At Ronan's request, they'd met for dinner at
the downtown park square. It was a selfish act. Both Declan and
Ronan treated Matthew as their security blanket. "The three of
us. For fireworks."

Ronan hunched above him on the edge of the battered picnic
table. "No." Before his younger brother had a chance to say
something to unintentionally guilt him into it, Ronan gestured

to Matthew's paper-wrapped tuna fish sandwich with his own. "How's your sandwich?"

"Oh, it's good," Matthew said enthusiastically. It was not much of an endorsement. Matthew Lynch was a golden, indiscriminate pit into which the world threw food. "It's real good. I couldn't believe when you called. When I saw your phone number, I nearly shit myself! You could sell your phone, like, as new-in-box."

"Don't fucking swear," Ronan said.

ARTICLE 2
SPECIFIC BEQUESTS AND DEVISES

I GIVE THE SUM OF TWENTY-THREE MILLION DOLLARS ($23,000,000) TO A SEPARATE TRUST WHICH SHALL PROVIDE FOR THE PERPETUAL CARE AND MAINTENANCE OF THE PROPERTY REFERRED TO AS "THE BARNS" (SEE ITEM B) AND FOR THE CARE, EDUCATION, AND HOUSING OF MY SURVIVING CHILDREN. THIS TRUST SHALL BE EXECUTED BY DECLAN T. LYNCH UNTIL ALL CHILDREN HAVE REACHED THE AGE OF EIGHTEEN.

I GIVE THE SUM OF THREE MILLION DOLLARS ($3,000,000) TO MY SON DECLAN T. LYNCH, ONCE HE HAS REACHED THE AGE OF EIGHTEEN.

I GIVE THE SUM OF THREE MILLION DOLLARS ($3,000,000) TO MY SON RONAN N. LYNCH, ONCE HE HAS REACHED THE AGE OF EIGHTEEN.

I GIVE THE SUM OF THREE MILLION DOLLARS ($3,000,000) TO MY SON MATTHEW A. LYNCH, ONCE HE HAS REACHED THE AGE OF EIGHTEEN.

Ronan took one of Matthew's potato chips and gave it to Chainsaw, who mutilated it on the table's surface, more for the sound than the taste. On the sidewalk, a lady pushing a baby carriage gave him a dirty look for either sitting on top of the table or for looking disreputable while trafficking with carrion birds. Ronan reflected her look back at her after adding a few more degrees of shittiness to it. "Look, does Declan still have his panties in a twist over us going back to the Barns?"

Matthew, chewing fondly, waved at the contents of the baby carriage. The contents waved back. He spoke through his mouthful. "They always are. His panties, I mean. Twisted. Over it. And you. Is it true we'll lose our money if we go back? Was Dad really as bad as Declan says?"

Article 7
Further Condition

Upon my death, none of my children shall trespass the physical boundaries of "the Barns," nor disturb any of the contents there, living or inert, or the assets dealt within this Will shall be bequeathed instead to the New York-Roscommon Fund, apart from the Trust established for Aurora Lynch's continued care.

"What?" Ronan put his sandwich down. Chainsaw angled in. "What does he say about Dad?"

His younger brother shrugged. "I dunno, just he was never there, or something. You know. Hey, Declan's not that bad. I don't know why you guys can't get along."

Mommy and Daddy just don't love each other anymore, Ronan thought, but he couldn't say it to Matthew, who gazed up at him with the same trusting eyes the baby mouse had turned on him. This dinner wasn't enough to restore his balance. His illicit visit to the Barns, his realization about his mother, and Calla's assessment of the situation had badly shaken him. Suddenly, he was presented with a decision: whether or not to revive their mother. If he could have his mother back, that would help, surely, even if she had to live in Cabeswater. One parent was better than no parents. Life was better than death. Awake was better than asleep.

But those words of Declan's needled Ronan: *She's nothing without Dad.*

It was like he knew. Ronan wanted badly to know *how* much Declan knew, but it wasn't like he could ask him.

"Declan started hating me first," Ronan said. "In case you were wondering. So that wasn't me."

Matthew blew out a tuna-scented breath with the sanguine, pleasant air of either a nun or a pothead. "He was just upset Dad liked you the best. I didn't care. Everybody has favorite things. Mom liked *me* best anyway."

ARTICLE 2A
FURTHER BEQUESTS

I GIVE MY ENTIRE INTEREST IN THE REAL PROPERTY WHICH WAS MY RESIDENCE AT THE TIME OF MY DEATH ("THE BARNS"), TOGETHER WITH ANY INSURANCE ON SUCH PROPERTY, TO MY MIDDLE SON.

They both quietly ate their sandwiches. Ronan thought they were probably both considering how this left Declan as no one's favorite.

If I was your favorite, he asked his dead father, *why did you leave me a home I could never return to?*

Carefully — this was difficult, because Ronan never did anything carefully — he asked, "Does Declan ever talk about dreams?"

He had to repeat the question. Both Matthew and Chainsaw had gotten distracted by a circling pair of monarch butterflies.

"Like, his?" Matthew asked. He shrugged elaborately. "I don't think he dreams. He takes sleeping pills, did you know?"

Ronan didn't know. "What kind?"

"I dunno. I looked at the bottle, though. Doc Mac gave them to him."

"Doc the fuck who?"

"The Aglionby doctor?"

Ronan hissed. "He's not a doctor, man. He's a nurse practitioner or something. I don't think he's legal to give out drugs. Why does Declan take sleeping pills?"

Matthew stuffed the remaining quarter of his sandwich in his mouth. "Says you're giving him an ulcer."

"Ulcers are not sleeping problems. They are when acid eats a fucking hole through your stomach."

"Says you and Dad were both dreamers," Matthew said, "and you're going to make us lose everything."

Ronan sat very still. He was so still so quickly that Chainsaw froze as well, her head tilted toward the youngest Lynch brother, purloined tuna sandwich forgotten.

Declan knew about their father. Declan knew about their mother. Declan knew about *him*.

What did it change? Nothing, maybe.

"He put a gun under the seat of his car," Matthew said. "I saw it when my phone fell down between the seats."

Ronan realized that Matthew had stopped chewing and

moving and was instead just curved on the bench of the picnic table, his liquid eyes uncertain on his older brother's.

"Don't say burglars," Matthew said finally.

"I wasn't going to," Ronan replied. "You know I don't lie."

Matthew nodded, fast. He was biting his lip. His eyes were unselfconsciously damp.

"Look," Ronan said, and then, again, "look. I think I know how to fix Mom. She won't be able to stay at the Barns and — I mean, we can't go there anyway — I think I know how to fix her. So at least we'll have her."

NIALL LYNCH WAS, AT THE TIME OF SO EXECUTING SAID WILL, OF SOUND MIND, MEMORY, AND UNDERSTANDING AND NOT UNDER ANY RESTRAINT OR IN ANY RESPECT INCOMPETENT TO MAKE A WILL. THIS WILL STANDS AS FACT UNLESS A NEWER DOCUMENT IS CREATED.

SIGNED THIS DAY: T'LIBRE VERO-E BER NIVO LIBRE N'ACREA.

This was probably why he'd called Matthew. Probably he'd meant to promise this impossible hope from the very beginning. Probably he needed to say it out loud so it would stop chewing a fucking hole through his stomach.

His younger brother looked wary. "Really?"

The decision galvanized Ronan. "I promise."

23

It took the Gray Man several days to realize he had lost his wallet. He would have noticed it sooner if he hadn't been overcome by gray days — days where morning seemed bled of color and getting up unimportant. The Gray Man often didn't eat during them; he certainly didn't keep track of time. He was at once sleeping and awake, both of them the same, dreamless, listless. And then one morning he would open his eyes and find the sky had become blue again.

He had several gray days in the basement of Pleasant Valley Bed and Breakfast, and after he'd roused himself at dawn and shakily eaten something, he reached into the back pocket of his pants and found it empty. His fake ID and useless credit cards — the Gray Man paid for everything in cash — all gone. It must be at 300 Fox Way.

He'd try to swing back there later. He checked his phone for messages from Greenmantle, let his eyes skip unseeingly over his brother's missed call from days before, and finally consulted his jotted, coded notes to himself.

He glanced out the window. The sky was an unreal shade of blue. He always felt so alive that first day. Humming a bit, the Gray Man pocketed his keys. Next stop: Monmouth Manufacturing.

Gansey hadn't been doing well with Cabeswater's disappearance. He'd tried to come to grips with it. This was just another setback, and he knew he needed to treat it like every other setback: make a new plan, find another lead, throw all the resources in a new direction. But it didn't *feel* like any other setback.

He had spent forty-eight hours more or less awake and restless and then, on the third day, he had bought a side-scan sonar device, two window airconditioners, a leather sofa, and a pool table.

"Now do you feel better?" Adam had asked drily.

Gansey had replied, "I have no idea what you're talking about."

"Hey, man," Ronan said, "I like the pool table."

The entire situation made Blue apoplectic.

"There are children starving in the streets of Chicago," she said, her hair bristling with indignation. "Three species go extinct every hour because there's no funding to protect them. You are still wearing those incredibly stupid boat shoes, and of all the things that you have bought, you still haven't replaced them!"

Gansey, bewildered, observed his feet. The movement of his toes was barely visible through the tops of his Top-Siders. Really, in light of recent events, these shoes were the only things that *were* right in the world. "I *like* these shoes."

"Sometimes I hate you," Blue said. "And *Orla*, of all people!"

This was because Gansey had also rented a boat, a trailer, and a truck to pull it with, and then asked Blue's older cousin Orla to accompany them on their latest trip. The rental truck required a driver over twenty-one, and the mission, according to Gansey, required a psychic. Orla fit both purposes and was more than willing. She had arrived at Monmouth dressed for work: bell-bottoms, platform sandals, and an orange bikini top. There were acres of bare skin between the bell-bottoms and the bikini top. Her bare stomach was so clearly an invitation for admiration that Gansey could hear the dismissive voice of his father in his ear. *Girls these days.* But Gansey had seen photos of girls in his father's days, and they didn't look that different to him.

He exchanged a glance with Adam, because it had to be done, and of course Blue intercepted it. Her eyes narrowed. She wore two shredded tank tops and a pair of bleached cargo pants. In some parallel universe, there was a Gansey who could tell Blue that he found the ten inches of her bare calves far more tantalizing than the thirteen cubic feet of bare skin Orla sported. But in this universe, that was Adam's job.

He was in a terrible mood.

Somewhere across Henrietta, something crackled explosively. It was either a transformer falling prey to the electric whims of the ley line or Joseph Kavinsky having premature fun with one of his infamous Fourth of July explosives. Either way, it was a good day to get out of town.

"We should get moving," Gansey ordered. "It's only going to get hotter."

Just a few dozen yards away, the Gray Man sat in the Champagne Monster on Monmouth Avenue, paging through a history book and listening to *Muswell Hillbillies* while the air-conditioning played across his skin. Really, he should've been reading up on Welsh history — his cursory research on the Lynch brothers revealed that one of the boys they ran with was obsessed with it — but instead he indulged himself by trying his hand at a new translation of "Bede's Death Song." It was like an archaic crossword puzzle. When the text said *Fore ðæm nedfere nænig wiorðe,* would it be truer to the original intent of the writer to translate it as "Before the fated journey there" or "Facing the path to Death"? Pleasurable trials!

The Gray Man looked up as a boy emerged from Monmouth Manufacturing. The overgrown lot was already a mess of teens and rental vehicles and boats; they were clearly getting ready to go somewhere. The boy who had just exited was the square, showy one who looked like he was about to fall into the Senate — Richard Gansey. The third. That meant that somewhere there were at least two more Richard Ganseys. He didn't notice the Gray Man's rental car parallel parked in the shadows. Nor did he notice the white Mitsubishi parked just down the road. The Gray Man wasn't the only one waiting for the Monmouth Manufacturing building to be vacated.

A fellow academic had once asked the Gray Man: "Why Anglo-Saxon history?" At the time it had struck the Gray Man as a foolish and unanswerable question. The things that drew him to that time period were surely unconscious and many-headed, diffused through his blood from a lifetime of influences. One might as easily ask him why he preferred to wear gray, why he disliked gravy of all sorts, why he loved the seventies, why he was so fascinated by brothers when he couldn't seem to succeed at being one himself. He'd told the academic that guns had made history boring, which he knew was a lie even as he said it, and then he'd extricated himself from the conversation. Of course he thought of the true answer later, but it was too late then.

It was this: Alfred the Great. Alfred became king during one of the armpits of English history. There was no England, really, not back then. Just small kingdoms with bad teeth and abbreviated tempers. Life was, as the old saying went, nasty, brutish, short. When the Vikings came tearing onto the island, the kingdoms didn't stand a chance. But Alfred stepped in to unite them.

He made them a brotherhood, pushed out the Vikings. He'd promoted literacy and the translation of important books. Encouraged the poets and the artists and writers. He'd ushered in a renaissance before the Italians had ever considered the concept.

He was one man, but he'd changed Anglo-Saxon England forever. He imposed order and honor, and under that crushed-down grass of principle, the flower of poetry and civility had burst through.

What a hero, the Gray Man thought. *Another Arthur.*

His attention snapped up as Ronan Lynch stepped out of the old factory. He was clearly related to Declan: same nose, same dark eyebrows, same phenomenal teeth. But there was a carefully cultivated sense of danger to this Lynch brother. This was not a rattlesnake hidden in the grass, but a deadly coral snake striped with warning colors. Everything about him was a warning: If this snake bit you, you had no one to blame but yourself.

Ronan opened the driver's side door of the charcoal BMW hard enough that the car shook, then he threw himself in hard enough that the car kept shaking, and then he slammed the door hard enough that the car shook yet more. And then he left with enough speed to make the tires squeal.

"Hm," said the Gray Man, already preferring this Lynch brother to the last.

The rental truck pulled out with rather more care than the BMW had and headed down the street in the same direction. Then, although the lot was empty, the Gray Man waited. Sure enough, the white Mitsubishi he'd spotted before pulled in, the bass from its stereo slowly liquefying the pavement beneath it. A kid climbed out, carrying a plastic baggie full of something like business cards. He was the sort the Gray Man preferred to steer clear of; he hummed with a restless, unpredictable energy. The Gray Man didn't mind dangerous people, but he preferred sober dangerous people. He watched the kid enter the factory and return with only an empty bag. The Mitsubishi tore off, tires squalling.

Now the Gray Man turned off the Kinks, walked across the street, and climbed the stairs to the second-floor apartment. On the landing, he discovered the contents of Mitsubishi Boy's bag: a pile of identical Virginia driver's licenses. Each featured a sullen photograph of Ronan Lynch beside a birth date that would've had him a few months away from celebrating his seventy-fifth birthday. Aside from the clearly facetious birth date, they were very good forgeries. The Gray Man held one up to the light coming through the broken window. Its maker had done a tidy job of replicating the most difficult part, the hologram. The Gray Man was impressed.

He left the licenses lying outside the door and broke into Monmouth Manufacturing. He was careful about it. One could easily break a lock. One could not easily unbreak it. As he picked the lock, he dialed his phone and propped it on his shoulder. It only took a moment for someone to pick up.

"Oh, it's you," Maura Sargent said. "King of swords."

"And it's you. The sword in my spine. I seem to have lost my wallet somewhere." The Gray Man let the compromised door fall open. A smell of musty paper and mint rolled around him. Dust motes played over a thousand books; this wasn't quite what he'd expected. "When you were vacuuming under Calla, did you happen to see anything?"

"Vacuuming!" Maura said. "I'll look. Oh. Look at that. There *is* a wallet in the couch. I imagine you'll want to pick it up. How's work?"

"I'd love to chat about it." The Gray Man turned the lock behind himself. If the boys came back for something, he'd have a few seconds to make a plan of action. "Face-to-face."

"You're quite creepy."

"I imagine you like creepy men."

"Probably true," Maura admitted. "Mysterious, possibly. *Creepy* is a very strong word."

The Gray Man moved among the cluttered parts of Gansey's quest. He pulled down a map rolled on the wall. He wasn't sure what he was looking for yet.

"You could give me a reading." He smiled faintly as he said it, paging through a book on medieval weaponry that he also owned.

Maura heard the smile in his voice. "I most certainly cannot. Neither of us want that, I can promise."

"Are you sure? I could read you more poetry when you're done. I know a lot of poetry."

Maura clucked. "That's Calla's thing."

"And what is your thing?" The Gray Man poked at a stack of books on the Welsh language. He was so very charmed by all of these things of Richard Gansey's. He wasn't sure, though, that Gansey understood just how well Glendower would be hidden. History was always buried deep, even when you know where to look. And it was hard to excavate it without damaging it. Brushes and cotton swabs, not chisels and pickaxes. Slow work. You had to like doing it.

"My thing," Maura said, "is that I never tell my thing."

But she was pleased; he could hear it in her voice. He liked her voice, too. She had just enough Henrietta accent so you knew where she came from.

"Do I get three tries to guess it?"

She didn't immediately answer, and he didn't press her. Heart wounds, he knew, made one think more slowly.

While he waited, the Gray Man stooped to study Gansey's miniature model of Henrietta. Such affection in these tiny re-created streets! He straightened, careful not to harm any of the fond buildings, and headed for one of the two small bedrooms.

Ronan Lynch's room looked as if a bar fight had taken place within its walls. Every surface was covered with expensive bits of expensive speakers and pointy bits of pointy cages and stylishly distressed bits of stylishly distressed jeans.

"Tell me this, then, Mr. Gray: Are you dangerous?"

"To some people."

"I have a daughter."

"Oh. I'm not dangerous to *her*." The Gray Man picked up a box cutter from the desk and studied it. It had been used to wound something before being hastily cleaned.

Maura said, "I just don't know if this is a good idea."

"Don't you?"

He inverted a cowboy boot that seemed out of place. He gave it a shake, but nothing fell out. He couldn't say whether the Greywaren was anywhere in the building. Looking for something without a single description . . . he had to imagine what a loaf of bread looked like based upon the trail of crumbs it left behind.

"I just . . . tell me something true about you."

"I own a pair of bell-bottoms," he confessed. "And an orange disco shirt."

"I don't believe you. You must wear it, then, next time I see you."

"I couldn't," the Gray Man said, amused. "I'd have to change my name to Mr. Orange."

"Personally," Maura replied, "I don't think your sense of self should be flexible. Specially not if you're going to go around as the king of swords."

From the main room, the doorknob clicked audibly as the lock was tested. Someone was here. Someone without a key. He told Maura, "Hold that thought. I have to go."

"To kill someone?"

"Preferably not," the Gray Man said in a much lower voice. He ducked behind Ronan's half-open door. "There are nearly always easier ways."

"Mr. Gray —"

Someone kicked open the door. The Gray Man's careful lock-work was rendered irrelevant.

"I will," the Gray Man interrupted softly, "call you back."

Standing in the shadows of Ronan Lynch's room, he watched two men stalk in. One man wore an oversized polo shirt and the other wore a T-shirt printed with a missile. The two men took in the scope of the space with obvious annoyance, and then they spread out. The oversized polo shirt clung to the area near the windows to keep watch out in the parking lot, and the other crashed through the boys' belongings. They kicked over stacks of books and pulled out desk drawers and upended the bare mattress.

At one point, Missile turned to Polo Shirt. Missile Shirt held a pair of sunglasses up for inspection. "*Gucci.* Rich bastards."

He dropped the sunglasses before stepping on them. One of the fractured earpieces skittered across the wide floorboards. It made it all the way to the Gray Man's feet, but only the Gray Man was watching it. He leaned and picked up the shard, pensively thumbing the sharp, broken end.

So these were the people Greenmantle had warned him about. Fellow seekers of the Greywaren, whatever it might be.

The Gray Man picked his teeth with the broken edge of the sun-glasses and then used his phone to take photos of the men for Greenmantle.

Something about them was making him lose patience. Perhaps it was that they still hadn't noticed that he was watching them. Or perhaps it was the inefficiency of their process. Whatever it was, it solidified precisely as they began to trundle through the miniature model of Henrietta. He didn't know what the Greywaren looked like, but he was certain that he could find it without kicking in the front of a miniature cardboard courthouse.

He swiftly moved out of Ronan's room.

"Whoa!" said Missile from the middle of the destroyed Henrietta. "Don't move."

By way of reply, the Gray Man stuck the sharp end of the earpiece into Polo Shirt's neck. They fought briefly. The Gray Man used a combination of physics and the edge of the window airconditioner to gently lay the other man down on the floor.

It happened so quickly that Missile had only just reached them when the Gray Man wiped his hands on his slacks and stepped over the body.

"Jesus F. Christ," said Missile. He pointed a knife at the Gray Man.

This fight lasted slightly longer than the first. It was not that Missile was bad; it was that the Gray Man was better. And once the Gray Man had relieved the other man of his knife, it was over immediately. Missile crouched in the wreckage of Henrietta, fingers braced on the floorboards, gasping for breath.

"Why are you here?" the Gray Man asked him. He rested the tip of the knife as far into the man's ear as it would go without making a mess.

The man was already trembling, and unlike Declan Lynch, he folded at once. "Looking for an antique for an employer."

"Who is?" the Gray Man prompted.

"We didn't get his name. He's French."

The Gray Man licked his lips. He wondered if Maura Sargent's *thing* was environmental issues. She hadn't been wearing shoes, and that, to him, possibly was the sort of thing that someone interested in the environment might do. "French living in France or French living over here?"

"I don't know, man, what does it matter? He's got an accent!"

It would've mattered to the Gray Man. It occurred to him that he was going to have to change clothing before he went to 300 Fox Way for his wallet. He had intestinal matter on his slacks.

"Do you have a contact number? Of course you do not. What was this antique?"

"A, uh, box. He said it was probably a box. Called the Greywaren. That we'd know it when we saw it."

The Gray Man doubted that highly. He looked at his watch. It was nearly eleven; the day was racing by and he had so many plans. He said, "Do I kill you or let you go?"

"Please —"

The Gray Man shook his head. "It was a rhetorical question."

24

Would you like to explain, now, why we're in the middle of this puddle?" Adam asked.

"Godforsaken puddle," Ronan corrected from beside Gansey. As a pale-skinned, dark-haired Celtic sort, he didn't care for the heat.

The five of them — plus Chainsaw, minus Noah (he had been present, but feebly, when they'd left) — floated in the boat in the middle of the belligerently ugly man-made lake they had found before. It was relentlessly sunny. The smell of the field — warm dirt — reminded Gansey of all the mornings he'd picked up Adam from his parents' double-wide.

From shore, crows hollered apocalyptically at them. Chainsaw hollered back.

It really was some of the worst Henrietta had to offer.

"We're looking under it." Gansey eyed his laptop. He couldn't get the sonar device to communicate with it, despite a cursory examination of the instructional manual. Vexation was beginning to bead at his temples and on the back of his neck.

Blue, perched at the other end of the boat, asked, "Are we going to sonar every lake on the ley line? Or just the ones that piss you off?"

She was still angry about the couch and the pool table and Orla's bare midriff. Orla, tanning idly, wasn't helping. She took up most of the boat, her legs trailing up one side of it and her long bronze torso draped up the other. Every so often she opened her eyes to smile widely at one of the boys, twisting herself this way and that as if she were merely readjusting her spine.

"This is a pilot mission," said Gansey. He was more profoundly uncomfortable with Blue being angry at him than he cared to admit to anyone, least of all himself. "Odds suggest that Glendower's not under this lake. But I want to have recourse should we find a body of water we suspect he's under."

"Recourse," echoed Ronan, but without real force. The water reflected the sun at his face from beneath, rendering him a translucent and fretful god. "Shitdamn, it's hot."

Gansey's explanation was not precisely true. He occasionally had *hunches*, always about finding things, always about Glendower. They were a result of poring over maps and sorting through historical records and recalling the historical finds he'd made before. When you'd found impossible things before, it made the location of another impossible thing more predictable.

The hunch about this lake had something to do with this wide field looking like one of the only easy passes through this section of challenging mountains. Something to do with the name of the tiny lane at the bottom of the hill — Hanmer Road, Hanmer being the last name of Glendower's wife. Something to do with where it sat on the line, the look of the field, the prickling of *stop and look closer*.

"Is it possible that you've bought a sixty-five-hundred-dollar piece of junk?" Ronan pulled a cord out of the back of the laptop and hooked it up in a different way. The laptop pretended it couldn't tell the difference. Gansey hit some keys. The laptop pretended he hadn't. The entire process had looked a lot more straightforward on the instructional video online.

From the deck of the boat, Orla said, "I'm having a psychic moment. It involves you and me."

Distracted, Gansey glanced up from the computer screen. "Were you talking to me or Ronan?"

"Either. I'm flexible."

Blue made a small, terrible noise.

"I would appreciate if you'd turn your inner eye toward the water," Gansey said. "Because — goddamn it, Ronan, that made the screen go black."

He was beginning to think he *had* bought a sixty-five-hundred-dollar piece of junk. He hoped the pool table worked better.

"How long are we in D.C. for?" Adam asked suddenly.

Gansey said, "Three days."

Thank goodness Adam had agreed to go. There was plenty of opportunity to be had at a fund-raiser like this one. Internships, future positions, sponsors. An impressive-sounding name on the bottom of a college recommendation letter. So many pearls to be had, if you were in the mood to open oysters.

Gansey so hated oysters.

Ronan aggressively jerked a cable on the back of the laptop. The sonar device appeared on the laptop screen, shaped like a tiny submarine.

"You brilliant bastard!" Gansey said. "You've done it. What did you do?"

"Got tired of sweating is what I did. Let's look under this damn lake and get back into air-conditioning. Oh, don't even, Parrish."

Adam, on the other end of the boat, looked extremely unimpressed with Ronan's lack of heat tolerance. "I didn't say anything."

"Whatever, man," Ronan replied. "I know that face. You were born in hell, you're used to it."

"Ronan," Gansey said, "Lynch."

For quite a few minutes, they were all quiet as they puttered slowly through the water, watching the unspecific elements on the screen. Gansey felt the unpleasant and distinct sensation of a single drop of sweat rolling between his shoulder blades.

Orla declared, "I'm having a psychic moment."

"Pshaw!" Blue replied.

"No, really." Orla opened her eyes. "Is there something on the screen now?"

There was. On the laptop screen, the images tantalized him. One was a disc of some sort and the other was an indistinct raven. In reality, it could be any sort of bird. But for the group in this particular boat, a suggestion was all they needed. They needed it to be a raven. It was going to be a raven.

Gansey contemplated whether he could dive for the object. The first thing that occurred to him was his teal polo shirt — it would have to be removed. The next thing that occurred to him was his chinos — could they be removed in the presence of all these females? Dubious. And finally he considered his contact lenses. They rebelled even in pool water, and this was certainly not a swimming pool.

Blue peered over the edge into the brown water. "How deep is the water here?"

"It should say." Gansey squinted at the laptop. "Ten feet."

"Well, then." Blue flipped her sandals onto Orla's bare belly, ignoring Orla's vague protests.

Gansey said, "What! You can't go in."

"I actually can," she replied, twisting her vestigial ponytail into a tiny knot on the back of her skull. "I really, really can."

"But!" he tried. "You won't be able to open your eyes in that. Without irritating them."

"Your highly cultured eyes, maybe," Blue replied. Pulling off her topmost tank top, she tossed it on top of Orla as well. Bare skin flashed through the tears in the remaining tank. "My swamp eyes'll be great."

Gansey was stung, but before he could protest, he was forced to snatch the laptop as it toppled. Orla had suddenly and swiftly stood, sending the boat crazily off-kilter. Everyone in the boat braced themselves and gazed at the bell-bottomed giantess.

"Stop, Blue. I'll do it," Orla ordered. Her pierced belly button was precisely at Gansey's eye level. The silver ball winked at him. It said, *Watch this, boys!* "You're wearing clothing. I have a bikini."

Blue replied ferociously, "None of us can forget." If not for the sun, her voice would've iced the lake.

Orla tossed her head, her magnificently large nose describing a circle in the air. Then she tore off her bell-bottoms so fast that all the boys in the boat just stared at her, dazzled and stunned. Gansey couldn't understand the speed of it. One moment, she was wearing clothing, and the next moment, she was wearing a bikini. Fifty percent of the world was browned skin and fifty percent was orange nylon. From the Mona Lisa smile on Orla's lips, it was clear she was pleased to finally be allowed to demonstrate her true talents.

A tiny part of Gansey's brain said: *You have been staring for too long.*

The larger part of his brain said: *ORANGE.*

"Oh, for the love of God," Blue said, and jumped out of the boat.

Ronan began to laugh, and it was so unexpected that the spell was broken. He laughed as Chainsaw hurled herself into the air to circle where Blue had gone in, and he laughed as Orla let out a honking sound and cannonballed into the water. He laughed as the image on the laptop distorted with the rollicking water. He laughed as he stretched out his arm for Chainsaw to return to him, and then he sealed his lips with an expression that indicated he still found them all hilarious on the inside.

The boat, previously stuffed to capacity, now contained only three boys and a small, discarded pile of girls' shoes and clothing. Adam looked at Gansey, expression dazed. "Is this really happening?"

It *was* really happening, because the side-scan sonar showed two forms below the surface. One of them was nowhere near the objects and seemed to be moving in rather aimless circles. The other shot purposefully toward the vicinity of the raven, moving in brief surges that suggested a breaststroke. Gansey, former captain of the Aglionby crew team and a not untalented swimmer, approved.

"I feel rather ashamed," Gansey admitted.

Ronan ran a hand over his shaved head. "I didn't want to mess up my hair."

Adam just watched the ripples spread across the water.

Only a second later, Orla reemerged. Like her dive, her reappearance was dramatic: a great frothy breach that ended with her floating idly on her back, hands behind her head.

"It's too dark," she said, eyes closed against the sun. She seemed in no hurry to try again or get back into the boat. "But it's nice and cool. Y'all should come in."

Gansey had no desire to join her. He peered anxiously over the edge of the boat. One more second and he was going to —

Blue burst up beside them. Dark hair plastered her cheeks. With one white-knuckled hand, she clutched the edge of the boat, pulling herself half out of the water.

"Good God," Gansey said.

Blue cheerfully spit a mouthful of brown water on his boat shoes. It pooled in the canvas over his toes.

"Good *God*," he said.

"Now they're *really* boat shoes," she replied. Swinging her free arm, she tossed her prize in; it landed on the boards with a dense thud. Chainsaw immediately leapt down from Ronan's shoulder to investigate. "There's something else down there. I'm going back for it."

Before Gansey had time to say anything to her, the murky water closed over her head. He was struck by what a glorious and fearless animal Blue Sargent was, and he made a mental note to tell her that very thing, if she didn't drown getting whatever the second thing was.

She was only gone for a moment this time. The boat surged as she emerged again, gasping and triumphant. She hooked an elbow over the side. "Help me in!"

Adam hauled Blue in as if she were the catch of the day, stretched out on the base of the boat. Although she wore much more clothing than Orla, Gansey still felt he ought to avert his eyes. Everything was wet and clinging in ways that seemed more titillating than he'd come to expect from Blue's wardrobe.

Out of breath, Blue asked, "What's the first thing? Do you know?"

He accepted the first object from Ronan. Yes, he knew. Gansey rubbed his fingers over the slimy surface. It was a scarred metal disc about seven inches in diameter. There were three ravens embossed on it. The others must've been too buried in the silt to show on the sonar display. It was incredible that they'd seen even one of them. It would have been so easy for the disc to be completely obscured. Even easier for the identifying bird to be crusted and hidden by algae.

Some things want to be found.

"It's a boss," Gansey said with wonder. He ran his thumb around the uneven edge of it. Everything about it spoke to age. "Or an umbo. From a shield. This bit reinforced the middle of the shield. The rest of it must've rotted away. It would've been wood and leather, probably."

It wasn't what he would've expected to find here, or at all. From what he could remember of his history, shields like this weren't in popular use by Glendower's time. Good armor had rendered them unnecessary. It could've been a ceremonial shield, though. Certainly the fine workmanship seemed excessive for a working piece of weaponry. And it did seem like the sort of thing that would be brought along to bury with a king. He traced the ravens. Three ravens marked in a triangle — the coat of arms of Urien, Glendower's mythological father.

Who else had touched this boss? A craftsman, his mind busy with Glendower's purpose. A soldier, loading it into a boat to cross the Atlantic.

Maybe even Glendower himself.

His heart was on fire with it.

"So, it's ancient," Blue said from the other end of the boat.

"Right."

"And what about this?"

At the tone in her voice, he lifted his eyes to the large object that rested upright against the tops of her thighs.

He knew *what* it was. He just didn't know *why* it was.

He said, "Well, that's a wheel off the Camaro."

And it was.

It looked identical to the wheels currently residing on the Pig — except this wheel was clearly several hundred years old. The discolored surface was pocked and lumpy. With all of the deterioration, the elegantly symmetrical wheel didn't appear that out of place beside the shield boss. If you overlooked the tattered Chevrolet logo in the middle.

"Do you remember losing one a little while ago?" Ronan asked. "Like, five hundred years or so?"

"We know the ley line messes with time," Gansey said immediately, but he felt undone. Not exactly *undone*, but unmoored. Released from the ruts of logic. When the rules of time became flexible, the future seemed to hold too many possibilities to bear. This wheel promised a past with the Camaro in it, a past that both hadn't happened and had. Hadn't because the keys were still in Gansey's pocket and the car was still parked back at Monmouth Manufacturing. And had because Blue held the wheel in her still-damp hands.

"I think you should leave these with me while you go to your mom's this weekend," Blue said. "And I'll see if I can convince Calla to do her thing on them."

The boat was steered back toward shore, Orla was handed her bell-bottoms, the laptop was packed back into a bag, and the sonar device was dredged from the water. Adam wearily helped fix the boat to the trailer before climbing into the truck — Gansey was going to have to talk to him, though he didn't know what he would say; it would be good for them to get out of town together — and Ronan retreated to the BMW to drive back by himself. Probably Gansey needed to talk to him, too, though he didn't know what he would say to him, either.

Blue joined him in the shade of the boat, the shield boss in her hand. This discovery was not Cabeswater, and it was not Glendower, but it was something. Gansey was getting greedy, he realized, hungry for Glendower and Glendower alone. These tantalizing clues used to be enough to sustain him. Now it was only the grail he wanted. He felt grown old inside his young skin. *I tire of wonders*, he thought.

He watched Orla's orange bikini disappear hopefully into the BMW. His mind was far away, though: still absorbed with the mystery of the ancient Camaro wheel.

In a low voice, Blue asked meaningfully, "Seen enough?"

"Of — oh, Orla?"

"Yeah."

The question annoyed him. It judged him, and in this case, he didn't feel he'd done anything to deserve it. He was not Blue's business, not in that way.

"What care is it of yours," he asked, "what I think of Orla?"

This felt dangerous, for some reason. He possibly shouldn't have asked it. In retrospect, it wasn't the question itself at fault. It was the way that he'd asked it. His thoughts had been far away, and he hadn't been minding how he looked on the outside, and now, too late, he heard the dip of his own words. How the inflection seemed to contain a dare.

Come on, Gansey, he thought. *Don't ruin things.*

Blue held his gaze, unflinching. Crisp, she replied, "None at all."

And it was a lie.

It should not have been, but it was, and Gansey, who prized honesty above nearly every other thing, knew it when he heard it. Blue Sargent cared whether or not he was interested in Orla. She cared a lot. As she whirled toward the truck with a dismissive shake of her head, he felt a dirty sort of thrill.

Summer dug its way into his veins. He got into the truck.

"Let's go," he told the others, and he slid on his sunglasses.

25

Of course, the Gray Man had to get rid of the two bodies. It was a nuisance, but nothing more. The sort who would break into a house for supernatural artifacts also tended to be the sort who didn't get reported missing.

The Gray Man wouldn't be reported missing, for example.

Still, he needed to wipe the bodies for fingerprints and then drive them someplace more convenient for them to die. In the trunk of the Champagne Abomination, the Gray Man had fuel cans and two Peruvian pots that were too hot to sell yet wrapped in Dora the Explorer blankets, so he put the bodies in the backseat, buckling them so they wouldn't flop around too much. He was sadly on his way to creating an incriminating stain in yet another rental car. His father was right: past performance really *did* seem to be the best indicator of future performance.

While he drove, he called the Veranda Inn and Restaurant and canceled his dinner reservation.

"Would you like to change it to a later time?" the hostess asked. The Gray Man liked how she said *later*. It was something like *lyter*, but with a lot more vowels.

"Tonight just won't work, I think. Can I reschedule for . . . Thursday?" He took the exit for the Blue Ridge Parkway. The force of the turn knocked one of the thug's heads against the window. The thug was beyond caring.

"Table for one, was it?"

He thought about Maura Sargent and her slender, bare ankles. "Make it two."

He hung up the phone, put on the Kinks, and drove out along the parkway. He took turn after turn until the rental car's GPS was hopelessly confused. With the rental car, he made his own path into the woods past a copse of NO TRESPASSING signs (the Gray Man had never regretted paying for the additional damage insurance on a rental). He parked in a small, idyllic clearing, rolled down the window, and cranked up the stereo. Pulling out Missile and Polo Shirt, he untied their shoes.

He had just put Polo Shirt's shoes on his own feet when his phone rang.

The Gray Man picked it up. "Do you know who those men were?" he asked in place of a greeting.

Greenmantle's voice was frenzied. "I told you. I told you there were others there."

"You did," the Gray Man agreed. He stomped the treads of Polo Shirt's shoes full of good Virginia clay. "Are there more?"

"Of course," Greenmantle said tragically.

The Gray Man switched to Missile's shoes. The clearing was covered with their tracks. "Where are they coming from?"

"The readings! The machines! Anyone can follow the readings," Greenmantle said. "We're not the only ones with geophones lying about."

In the background, the Kinks sang about demon alcohol. "How is it that you knew this thing existed, again?"

"Same way we know anything. Rumors. Old books. Greedy old people. What is that sound?"

"The Kinks."

"I didn't know you were a fan. In fact, it's strange to think of you listening to music at all. Wait. I don't know why I said that. I'm sorry, that sounded terrible."

The Gray Man was not offended. It meant that Greenmantle thought of him as a thing instead of as a person, and he was all right with that. For a moment, they both listened to the Kinks sing about port, Pernod, and tequila. Every time the Gray Man put on the Kinks for any length of time, he considered getting back into academia. Two of the Kinks were brothers. *Fraternity in the Rock Music of the '60s and '70s* would be a fine title, he thought. The Kinks intrigued him because, although they fought continuously — one member famously spitting on another before kicking over the drums and storming offstage — they remained together for decades. That, he thought, was brotherhood.

"Will you be able to work around those two?" Greenmantle asked. "Will they be a problem?"

It took the Gray Man a moment to realize that he was referring to Missile and Polo Shirt.

"No," the Gray Man said. "They won't be."

"You're good," Greenmantle said. "It's why you're the only one."

"Yes," the Gray Man agreed. "I certainly am. Would you say that this thing is a box?"

"No, I wouldn't say that, because I don't know. Would *you* say that?"

"No. Probably not."

"Why did you ask, then?"

"If it was a box, I could stop looking at things that weren't boxes."

"If I'd thought it was a box, I would've told you to look for a box. *Would I say it's a box.* Why do you have to be so damn mysterious all the time? Do you get off on it? You want me thinking about boxes now? Because I am. I'll look it up. I'll see what I can do."

Hanging up, the Gray Man assessed the scene. In a fortunate world, the two bodies before him would lay undiscovered for years, picked at by animals and worn away by the weather. But in a world where lovebirds thought they caught a strange smell or poachers tripped on leg bones or buzzards inconveniently circled for days at a time, all there would be to the scene would be two men with mud-clotted shoes and defensive DNA clawed beneath their fingernails. In a way, two bodies made it easier. Made the story simpler. Two men up to no good on private property. A dispute between them. A fight that got out of hand.

One for loneliness. Two for a battle.

The Gray Man frowned and checked his watch. Hopefully, these were the only bodies he'd have to bury in Henrietta, but one could never say.

26

When Blue arrived home in her soaking-wet clothing, Noah was kneeling in the tiny, shaded front yard of 300 Fox Way. Orla breezed right inside without saying hello to him. As a psychic, she probably saw him, but as Orla, she didn't care. Blue stopped, though. She was pleased he was there. She rearranged the Camaro wheel under her arm and wiped damp hair off her forehead.

"Hey, Noah."

He was too busy being ghostly to attend to her, however.

Currently, he was engaged in one of his creepiest activities: reenacting his own death. He glanced around the tiny yard as if appraising the forest glen containing only himself and his friend Barrington Whelk. Then he let out a terrible, mangled cry as he was struck from behind by an invisible skateboard. He made no sound when he was hit again, but his body jerked convincingly. Blue tried not to look as he bucked a few more times before falling to the ground. His head jerked; his legs bicycled.

Blue took a deep, uneven breath. Though she had seen him do it four or five times now, it was always unsettling. Eleven minutes. That was how long the entire homicidal portrait lasted: one boy's life destroyed in less time than it took to cook a hamburger. The last six minutes, the ones that took place after Noah had first fallen but before he actually died, were excruciating. Blue considered herself a fairly steadfast, sensible girl, but no matter how many times she heard his torn-up breath seizing in his throat, she felt a little teary.

Between the twisted roots of the front yard, Noah's body jerked and stilled, finally dead. Again.

Gently, she asked, "Noah?"

He was on the ground and then, just like that, he was standing beside her. It was like a dream, where the middle part was cut out, the getting from point A to point B.

It was another of his creepy things.

"Blue!" he said, and patted her damp hair.

She hugged him tightly; he was chilly against her damp clothing. She was always so worried he wouldn't snap out of it at the end.

"Why do you do that?" she demanded.

Noah had reverted to his normal, safe self. The only evidence of his true nature was the ever-present smudge on his cheek where the bone had been smashed in. Otherwise he was once again slouched, mild, and eternally dressed in his Aglionby uniform.

He looked vaguely bewildered and pleased to have a girl clinging to him. "That?"

"What you did. Just *now*."

He shrugged, formless and amiable. "I wasn't here."

But you were, Noah, she thought. But whatever part of Noah that still existed to pour thoughts and memories into this form mercifully disappeared for the eleven minutes of his death. She wasn't sure if his amnesia over the whole thing made it more or less creepy.

"Ah, Noah."

He draped an arm over her shoulders, too cold and weird himself to notice that she was also damp and cold. They wandered to the door like that, a pretzel of dead boy and not-psychic girl.

Of course, he wouldn't come in. Blue suspected he couldn't. Ghosts and psychics competed for the same power source, and in an energy showdown between Noah and Calla, there was no doubt in Blue's mind who would come out the victor. She would have asked Noah to confirm this, but he was notoriously disinterested in the details of his afterlife. (Once, Gansey had tersely asked, "Don't you care how it is that you're still here?" and Noah had answered with remarkable acumen, "Do you care how your kidneys work?")

"*You* aren't going to D.C., are you?" Noah asked with some anxiety.

"Nope." She'd meant to just *say* it with no inflection whatsoever, but in truth, she felt curiously bereft at the idea of Gansey and Adam both leaving town. She felt, actually, exactly like Noah sounded.

Daringly, Noah offered, "I'll let you into Monmouth."

Blue blushed immediately. One of her most hidden and persistent fantasies was an impossible one: living in Monmouth. She'd never really be one of the group, she thought, as long as she was living here at 300 Fox Way. She'd never really be one of them as long as she wasn't an Aglionby student. Which meant she'd never really be one of them as long as she was a *girl*. The unfairness of it, the *wanting*, kept her up some nights. She couldn't believe Noah had guessed her desire so accurately. To cover her embarrassment, she huffed, "And I'd hang out all day with you and *Ronan*?"

Gleefully, Noah said, "There's a pool table now! I'm the worst at pool ever! It's *wonderful*." His arm tightened around her shoulders. "D'oh. Incoming."

A man headed up the sidewalk toward them. He was carefully put together and overwhelmingly . . . gray. At the same time that Blue appraised this Gray Man, she got the idea that she was also being appraised.

At the end of the moment, they both eyed each other with a sort of mutual decision to not underestimate the other.

"Hello," he said cordially. "I didn't mean to interrupt."

First of all, the way he phrased it meant that he could see Noah, which not everyone could. Second of all, he was polite in a way that was unlike anything Blue had encountered before. Gansey was polite in a way that squashed the other party smaller. Adam was polite to reassure. And this man was polite in a keen, questioning sort of way. He was polite like tentacles were polite, testing the surface carefully, checking to see how it reacted to his presence.

He was, Blue decided suddenly, very clever. Nothing to be trifled with.

She gestured to her soaked clothing. "This is performance art. We're reenacting 'The Little Mermaid.' Not the Disney version."

This was her own little tentacle test.

The Gray Man smiled agreeably. "Is he the prince? Do you stab him or do you turn into foam at the end?"

"Foam, of course," said Blue, enormously gratified.

"I always thought she should have stabbed him," he mused. "I'm looking for Maura."

"Ah." Now it all made sense. This was Mr. Gray. She'd heard his name whispered between Maura, Calla, and Persephone over the past few days. Especially between Calla and Persephone. "You're the hit man."

Mr. Gray had the good grace to look efficiently startled. "Oh. And you're the daughter. Blue."

"The one and only." Blue fixed a penetrating gaze on him. "So, do you have a favorite weapon?"

Without missing a beat, he replied, "Opportunity."

Now she raised an eyebrow. "Okay. Come on. Noah, I'll be back out in a sec."

She led the Gray Man inside. As always, new visitors made her over-aware of the house's unorthodox appearance. It was two houses knitted together, and neither structure had been a palace to begin with. Narrow hallways leaned eagerly toward one another. A stray toilet gurgled constantly. The wood floors were as buckled as the sidewalk out front, as if roots threatened to come between the boards. Some of the walls were painted in vivid purples and blues, and some of them maintained wallpaper from decades before. Faded black-and-white photographs hung beside Klimt prints and old metal scissors. The entire decor was a victim of too much thrift-store shopping and too many strong personalities.

Oddly enough, the Gray Man — a serene spot of neutral color in the middle of the riot — didn't look out of place. Blue watched him watching his surroundings as they made their way into the bowels of the house. He didn't seem like the sort of person one could sneak up on.

Again, she thought, *Don't underestimate him.*

"Oh!" croaked Jimi. She squeezed her ample mass past the Gray Man. "I'll get Maura!"

As Blue maneuvered him toward the kitchen, she asked, "What, precisely, is your intention with my mother?"

"That seems very frank," Mr. Gray said.

She stepped over two small girls (she wasn't certain who they belonged to) playing with tanks in the middle of the hall and snuck past a sort of possible second cousin carrying two lit candles. The Gray Man lifted his arms above his head to avoid being ignited by the second cousin, who clucked at him.

"Life's short."

"And getting shorter every day."

"So you see my point."

"I never disputed it."

Then they were in the kitchen, with all its mugs and half-packaged tea and boxes of essential oils waiting to be mailed and decapitated flowers waiting to be boiled.

Blue pointed to a chair beneath the fake Tiffany lamp. "Sit."

"I'd rather stand."

She made a neat rack of teeth at the Gray Man. "Sit."

The Gray Man sat. He glanced over his shoulder, back down the hall, then back to her. He had those bright, active eyes that Dobermans and blue jays had.

"No one's going to murder you here." She handed him a glass of water. "That's not poisoned."

"Thanks." He set it down but didn't drink it. "My only intentions right now are to ask her to dinner."

Leaning her butt on the counter, Blue crossed her arms and studied him. She was thinking about her biological father, Artemus. The truth was that Blue had never met him and in fact knew very little about him — little more than his name, Artemus. She felt strangely protective of him, though. She didn't like to think of him reappearing and finding a usurper in his place. But then again, it had been sixteen years. The likelihood of him coming back was a very narrow one.

And it was only dinner.

"You aren't staying here, are you?" Blue asked. She meant Henrietta, not the house.

She should've clarified, but he seemed to catch her meaning, because he replied, "I don't stay anywhere. Not for long."

"That doesn't seem very pleasant."

In the background, the phone rang. Not her problem. No one was calling *this* house for a non-psychic.

His keen expression didn't flag. "Got to keep moving."

Blue considered this wisdom before replying, "The planet spins at over a thousand miles an hour all the time. Actually, it's going around the sun at sixty-seven thousand miles an hour, even if it wasn't spinning. So you can move plenty fast without going anywhere."

Mr. Gray's mouth quirked. "That's a very philosophical loophole." After a pause, he said, *"Þing sceal gehegan / frod wiþ frodne. Biþ hyra ferð gelic."*

It sounded like German, but from hearing Calla's whispers about the Gray Man, she knew it was Old English.

"A dead language?" she asked, with interest. She seemed to be hearing a lot of them lately. "What's it mean?"

" 'Meetings are held, wise with the wise. Because their spirits are alike.' Or minds. The word *ferð* has the sense of mind or spirit or soul. It's one of the Anglo-Saxon Maxims. Wisdom poetry."

Blue wasn't certain that she and this Gray Man thought exactly alike, but she didn't think they were that different, either. She could hear the pragmatic beat of his heart, and she appreciated it.

"Look, she doesn't like pork," she said. "Take her someplace they use lots of butter. And don't ever say the word *chuckle* around her. She hates it."

The Gray Man drank his water. He flicked his eyes to the hall doorway, and a moment later, Maura appeared in it, phone in one hand.

"Hi, daughter," she said warily. For a millisecond, her expression was sharp as she analyzed whether or not Blue was in any danger from this strange man sitting at her kitchen table. She took in the glass of water in front of the Gray Man and Blue's casually folded arms. Only then did she relax. Blue, for her part, enjoyed the millisecond of her mother looking dangerous. "What can I do for you, Mr. Gray?"

What a strange thing this was that they all knew that Mr. Gray was certainly not Mr. Gray, and yet they all went along with it. This playacting should have rankled Blue's sensible side, but instead, it struck her as a reasonable solution. He didn't want to say who he was, and they needed to call him something.

The Gray Man said, "Dinner."

"If you mean me cooking it for you, no," Maura said. "If we're going out, maybe. Blue, this phone's for you. It's Gansey."

Blue noticed that the Gray Man was abruptly not interested in who was on the phone. Which was interesting because he had been so interested in absolutely everything else before.

Which Blue took to mean that, really, he was very interested in who might be on the phone, only he didn't want them to know he was interested.

Which was interesting.

"What's he want?" Blue asked.

Maura handed her the phone. "Apparently, someone broke into his place."

27

Although both Kavinsky and Gansey were hopelessly entwined in the infrastructure of Henrietta, Ronan had always done a fine job keeping them separate in his mind. Gansey held court over the tidier, brighter elements of the town; his was a sunshiney world of Aglionby desks, junior faculty waving at his car from the sidewalk, tow-truck drivers knowing his name. Even the apartment in Monmouth Manufacturing was typical Gansey: order and aesthete imposed on the ruined and abandoned. Kavinsky, on the other hand, ruled the night. He lived in the places that wouldn't even occur to Gansey: in the back parking lots of the public schools, the basements of McMansions, crouched behind the doors of public bathrooms. Kavinsky's kingdom was not so much conducted in the red-yellow-green glow of a traffic light, but in the black place just outside of the glow.

Ronan preferred them separate. He did not like his foods to touch.

And yet here he was, the night before Gansey left town, taking him to one of Kavinsky's coarsest rituals.

"I can do this without you," Ronan said, kneeling to pick up one of the dozens of identical fake licenses.

Gansey, pacing next to his ruined miniature Henrietta, set his eyes on Ronan. There was something intense and heedless in them. There were many versions of Gansey, but this one had been rare since the introduction of Adam's taming presence. It was also Ronan's favorite. It was the opposite of Gansey's most public face, which was pure control enclosed in a paper-thin wrapper of academia.

But this version of Gansey was Gansey the boy. This was the Gansey who bought the Camaro, the Gansey who asked Ronan to teach him to fight, the Gansey who contained every wild spark so that it wouldn't show up in other versions.

Was it the shield beneath the lake that had unleashed it? Orla's orange bikini? The bashed-up remains of his rebuilt Henrietta and the fake IDs they'd returned to?

Ronan didn't really care. All that mattered was that something had struck the match, and Gansey was burning.

They took the BMW. It would be easier to cope with a firework being inserted in its exhaust pipe than the Pig's. He left Chainsaw behind, much to her irritation. Ronan didn't want her to learn any bad language.

Ronan drove, since he knew where they were going. He didn't tell Gansey why he knew where to go, and Gansey didn't ask.

The sun had gone down by the time they arrived at the old county fairground, tucked away on a back road east of Henrietta. The site had not been used to host a fair since the county fair had run out of money two years previous. Now it was a great over-grown field studded with floodlights and strung with tattered bunting made colorless by months of exposure.

Ordinarily, the abandoned fairground was pitch-black at night, out of reach of the lights of Henrietta and far from any houses. But tonight, the floodlights splashed sterile white light over the grass, illuminating the restless forms of more than a dozen cars. There was something unbearably sexy about cars at night, Ronan thought. The way the fenders twisted the light and reflected the road, the way every driver became anonymous. The sight of them knocked his heartbeat askew.

As Ronan turned into the old drive, the headlights illuminated the familiar form of Kavinsky's white Mitsubishi, its black grille gaping. The trip of his pulse became a kick drum.

"Don't say anything stupid to him," he told Gansey. Already the beat of his stereo was being drowned out by Kavinsky's, the bass pulsing up through the ground itself.

Gansey rolled his sleeves up and studied his hand as he made a fist and released it. "What's stupid?"

It was hard to tell with Kavinsky.

To their left, two cars loomed out of the darkness, one red and one white, heading right toward each other. Neither vehicle flinched from the impending collision. Automotive chicken. At the last moment, the red car swerved, skidding sideways, and the white blared a horn. A guy half-hung out of the passenger seat of the white car, clinging to the roof with one hand and flipping the bird with the other. Dust wallowed round them both. Delighted screams filled the space between engine noises.

On the other side of this game, a tired Volvo was parked beneath a tattered, fallen string of flagged bunting. It was lit from within, like an entrance to hell. It took a moment to register that it was on fire, or at least working up to it. Boys stood around the Volvo, drinking and smoking, their forms distorted and dark against the smoldering upholstery. Goblins around a bonfire.

Something inside Ronan was anxious and moving, angry and restive. The fire ate him from the inside.

He pulled the BMW up to the Mitsubishi, nose to nose. Now he saw that Kavinsky had already been playing: the right side of the car was shockingly mutilated and crumpled. That felt like a dream — no way was the Mitsubishi so mangled; it was immortal. Kavinsky himself stood near it, bottle in hand, shirtless, the floodlights erasing the ribs from his concave torso. When he saw the BMW, he threw the bottle at the hood. It splintered on the metal, shivering glass and liquid everywhere.

"Jesus," Gansey said, in either surprise or admiration. At least they hadn't brought the Camaro.

Hauling up the parking brake, Ronan threw open the door. The air reeked of melting plastic and deceased clutches and, beneath it all, the warm scent of pot. It was noisy, though the symphony was constructed of so many instruments that it was hard to identify any individual timbres.

"Ronan," Gansey said, in the exact same way that he'd just invoked Jesus.

"Are we doing this?" Ronan replied.

Gansey threw open his door. Gripping the roof of the car, he slid himself out. Even that gesture, Ronan noted, was wild-Gansey, Gansey-on-fire. Like he pulled himself from the car because ordinary climbing out was too slow.

This was going to be a night.

The fire inside Ronan was what kept him alive.

Catching a glimpse of Ronan heading straight for him, Kavinsky spread a hand over his flat rib cage. "Hey, lady. This is a substance party. Nobody's in unless you brought a substance."

By way of reply, Ronan clasped one hand round Kavinsky's throat and the other around his shoulder, and hurled him tidily over the hood of the Mitsubishi. For punctuation, he rejoined him on the opposite side and slammed his fist into Kavinsky's nose.

As Kavinsky climbed back up, Ronan showed him his bloody knuckles. "Here's your substance."

Kavinsky wiped his nose on his bare arm, leaving a red streak. "Hey, man, you don't have to be so fucking antisocial."

Gansey, at Ronan's elbow, held up his hand in the universal sign for *Down, boy.* "I don't want to keep you from your revels," Gansey said, cold and glorious, "so I'm just going to say this: Stay out of my place."

Kavinsky replied, "I don't know what you're talking about. Babe, get me a smoke."

The last part seemed to be directed to a girl who lolled in the passenger seat of the crunched Mitsubishi, her eyes deeply stoned. She did not dignify his order with a response.

Ronan flicked out one of the fake IDs.

Kavinsky smiled broadly at his own work. With his hollow cheeks, he was a ghoul in this light. "You mad because I didn't leave you a mint, too?"

"No, I'm angry because you trashed my apartment," Gansey said. "You should be glad I'm here and not at the police station."

"Whoa, man," Kavinsky said. "Whoa, whoa. I can't tell which of us is high. Whoa. I didn't trash your place."

"Please don't insult my intelligence," Gansey replied, and there was just a hint of a glacial laugh in his voice. It was a terrifying and wonderful laugh, Ronan thought, because Gansey had measured out only contempt and not a touch of humor.

Their conversation was interrupted by the familiar, destructive sound of cars colliding. There was nothing dramatic about the sound of newer vehicles crashing: all the safety bumpers meant it was mostly the dull thud of plastic puncturing. It wasn't the volume, though, that sent a shiver up Ronan's spine — it was the specificity of the sound. There was no other sound in the world like a car crash.

Kavinsky caught the line of their attention. "Ah," he said, "you want in on this, don't you?"

"Where are these guys from?" Gansey squinted. "Is that Morris? I thought he was in New Haven."

Kavinsky shrugged. "It's a substance party."

Ronan growled, "They don't have substances in New Haven?"

"Not like these. It's Wonderland! Some make you big, some make you small . . ."

It was the wrong quote. Or rather, the right quote, done wrong. In the Lynch household, Ronan had grown up with two recurring stories, perennial favorites of his parents. Aurora Lynch's favorite had been an old black-and-white movie version of the myth *Pygmalion*, about a sculptor who falls in love with one of his statues. And Niall Lynch had had an extraordinary fondness for an ugly old edition of *Alice in Wonderland*, frequently read aloud to two or three reluctant, half-asleep Lynch brothers. Ronan had seen *Pygmalion* and heard *Alice in Wonderland* so often in his youth that he no longer could judge whether or not they were any good, whether or not he actually liked them. The movie and the novel were history now. They were his parents.

So he knew the quote was actually, "one side will make you grow taller, and the other side will make you grow shorter."

"Depends on which side of the mushroom you use," Ronan said, more to his dead father than to Kavinsky.

"True point," Kavinsky agreed. "So, what are you going to do about your rat problem?"

Gansey blinked. "Beg pardon?"

This made Kavinsky laugh uproariously, and when he was through, he said, "If I didn't trash your place, something else is infesting it."

Gansey's eyes flickered over to Ronan. *Possibility?*

Of course it was a possibility. Someone other than Ronan had smashed up Declan Lynch's face, so theoretically, something other than Kavinsky could have broken into Monmouth Manufacturing. *Possibility?* Anything was possible.

"Lynch!" One of the other partygoers drew closer, recognizing him. Ronan, in turn, recognized him: Prokopenko. His voice was milky with drugs, but Ronan would've recognized his silhouette anywhere, one shoulder crooked and higher than the other, ears like wing nuts. "And Gansey?"

"Yeah," Kavinsky said, thumbs hooked in his back pockets, hip bones poking out above his low-slung waistband. "Mommy *and* Daddy came. Hey, Gansey, you get a babysitter for Parrish? You know what, man, don't answer that; let's smoke a peace pipe."

Immediately, Gansey replied with precise disdain, "I'm not interested in your pills."

"Oh, Mr. Gansey," Kavinsky sneered. "Pills! First rule of substance party is, you don't talk about substance party. Second rule is, you *bring* a substance if you want another one."

Prokopenko chortled.

"Lucky for you, Mr. Gansey," Kavinsky continued, in what was probably supposed to be a posh accent, "I know what your dog wants."

Prokopenko chortled again. It was the sort of chortle that meant he would be vomiting soon. Gansey seemed to understand this, as he edged a foot back from him.

Ordinarily, Gansey would have done more than edge away. Having achieved all they'd needed to, he would have told Ronan it was time to go. He would have been frostily polite to Kavinsky. And then he would have been gone.

But this was not Gansey as usual.

This was Gansey with a lofty tilt to his chin, a condescending quirk to his mouth. A Gansey that was aware that no matter what went down here tonight, he would still go back to Monmouth Manufacturing and rule his particular corner of the world. This was a Gansey, Ronan realized, that Adam would hate.

Gansey said, "And what is it my dog needs?"

Ronan's lips curled into a smile.

Fuck the past. This was the present.

Kavinsky said, "Pyrotechnics. Boom!" He pounded the roof of his crumpled car. Amiably, he told the girl in the passenger seat, "Get out, bitch. Unless you wanna die. It's all the same to me."

It dawned on Ronan that Kavinsky meant to blow up the Mitsubishi.

In the state of Virginia, fireworks that exploded or emitted flame higher than twelve feet were illegal, unless you had a special permit. It wasn't a fact most residents of Henrietta had to remember, however, because it was impossible to find fireworks that did anything even slightly remarkable, much less illegal, within state borders. If you wanted something a bit more impressive for the holiday weekend, you headed for the city's fireworks display. If you were like some of the rowdier Aglionby boys or better-off rednecks of Henrietta, you drove over the state line and filled your trunk with illegal Pennsylvanian fireworks. If you were Kavinsky, you built your own.

"That dent will come out," Ronan said, equal parts exhilarated and horrified to think of the Mitsubishi perishing. So many times just the first glimpse of its taillights on the road ahead of him had been enough to pump an urgent spasm of adrenaline through him.

"I'll always know it was there," Kavinsky replied carelessly. "Cherry, popped. Prokopenko, make me a cocktail, man."

Prokopenko was happy to oblige.

"Take the edge off," Kavinsky said. He turned to Gansey, a bottle in hand. It sloshed with liquid; a T-shirt had been wound and stuffed through the mouth of it. It was on fire. It was, in fact, a Molotov cocktail.

To Ronan's surprise and delight, Gansey accepted it.

He was a striking version of himself, a dangerous version of himself, standing there before Kavinsky's despoiled Mitsubishi with a homemade bomb in hand. Ronan remembered the dream of Adam and the mask: the more toothful version of Adam.

Instead of throwing it at the Mitsubishi, however, Gansey sighted a line toward the distant Volvo. He hurled it, high and graceful and true. Heads curved up to watch its progress. A voice from the crowd shouted, *"Woop Woop, Gansey Boy!"* which meant that at least one member of the Aglionby crew team was present. A moment later, the bottle landed just short of the Volvo's rear tires. The simultaneous breaking of the glass and explosion made it seem as if the Molotov cocktail had sunk into the ground. Gansey wiped his hand on his pants and turned away.

"Good throw," Kavinsky said, "but wrong car. Proko!"

Prokopenko handed him another Molotov cocktail. This one Kavinsky pressed into Ronan's hand. He leaned close — too close — and said, "It's a bomb. Just like you."

Something thrilled through Ronan. It was like a dream, the sharpness of all this. The weight of the bottle in his hand, the heat from the flaming wick, the smell of this polluted pleasure.

Kavinsky pointed at the Mitsubishi.

"Aim high," he advised. His eyes glittered, black pits reflecting the small inferno in Ronan's grip. "And do it fast, man, or you'll blow your arm off. No one wants half a tattoo."

A curious thing happened when the bottle left Ronan's hand. As it arced through the air, trails of fire-orange in its wake, Ronan felt as if he had hurled his heart. There was a rip, just as he released it. And heat filling his body, pouring in through the hole he'd made. But now he could breathe, now that there was room in his suddenly light chest. The past was something that had happened to another version of himself, a version that could be lit and hurled away.

Then the bottle landed in the driver's window of the Mitsubishi. It was as if there was no liquid, only fire. Flames poured across the headrest like a living thing. Cheers erupted across the fairground. Partygoers moved toward the car, moths to a new lamp.

Ronan heaved a breath.

Kavinsky, his laugh high and manic, dashed another bomb through the window. Prokopenko threw another. Now the interior was catching, and the smell was becoming toxic.

Part of Ronan couldn't really believe the Mitsubishi was gone. But as the others began to add their cigarettes and drinks to the bonfire, the music abruptly vanished as the stereo melted. It seemed a vehicle was well and truly dead once the stereo had melted.

"Skov!" shouted Kavinsky. "Music!"

Another car's stereo boomed to life, taking up where the Mitsubishi had left off.

Kavinsky turned to Ronan with a sly grin. "You coming to Fourth of July this year?"

Ronan exchanged a look with Gansey, but the other boy was looking out over the numerous silhouettes, his eyes narrowed.

"Maybe," he said.

"It's a lot like a substance party," Kavinsky said. "You want to see something explode, bring something that explodes."

There was a dare there. It was a dare that could be satisfied, maybe, by a drive over the border or by the clever concoction of an explosive from plans found on the Internet.

But, Ronan thought, with the same thrill he'd felt before, it was also one that he could attack with a dream.

He was good at dangerous things, both in his sleep and while awake.

"Maybe," he replied. Gansey was moving toward the BMW. "I'll light a candle for your car."

"You aren't leaving? Harsh."

If Gansey was going, Ronan was going. He paused long enough to flick another fake ID at Kavinsky's bare chest. "Stay out of our place."

Kavinsky's smile was wide and crooked. "I only come where they invite me, man."

"Lynch," Gansey said. "We're gone."

"That's right," Kavinsky called after Ronan. "Call your dog!"

He said it like either Ronan or Gansey should be offended by it.

But Ronan felt nothing but that fiery, empty cavern in his chest. He slid himself into the driver's seat as Gansey shut the passenger door.

Ronan's phone buzzed in the door pocket. He looked at it — a message from Kavinsky.

see you on the streets

Dropping the phone back into the door, Ronan let the engine rev up high. He backed out with a dramatic spin in the dirt. Gansey made an approving noise.

"Kavinsky," Gansey said, with a little laugh in his voice, still dismissive. "He thinks he owns this place. He thinks life is a music video."

He gripped the door as Ronan let the BMW have its head. The car galloped joyfully and recklessly toward home for a few miles, the speedometer setting the pace of their pulses.

Ronan said, "You don't see the appeal?"

Closing his eyes, Gansey leaned his head back on his seat, chin tilted up, throat green in the dash lights. There was still an unsafe sort of smile about his mouth — what a torment the possibility in that smile was — and he said, "There was never a time when that could've been you and me. You know the difference between us and Kavinsky? We *matter*."

Just then, in that moment, the thought of Gansey leaving for D.C. without him was unbearable. They had been a two-headed creature for so long, Ronan-and-Gansey. He couldn't say it, though. There were a thousand reasons why he couldn't say it.

"While I'm gone," Gansey said, pausing, "dream me the world. Something new for every night."

28

"Good evening, king of swords."

"And good evening, noble blade. Did you do a reading before I came? To tell you how it all worked out?" the Gray Man asked as he walked with Maura down toward the Champagne Mutiny. He had showered before he came, though he had not shaved his trademark grizzle from his jaw, and he looked nice, although Maura didn't point this out.

"Did you kill someone before you left to pick me up?" Maura had traded her tattered blue jeans for a slightly less tattered pair of blue jeans and an off-the-shoulder cotton shirt that showed how well her collarbone and neck got along. She looked nice, although the Gray Man didn't point it out.

But they were both aware that the other had noticed.

"Of course not. I don't think I kill nearly as many people as you think I do," he said, opening the passenger door for her. "Do you know, this is the first time I've seen you wearing shoes. Oh, so — what's going on there?"

Maura glanced over her shoulder to where he pointed. A small, weary Ford had just pulled up behind the Gray Man's rental car. "Oh, that's Calla. She's following us to the restaurant to make sure you're really taking me there and not burying me in the woods."

The Gray Man said, "How ridiculous. I never bury anybody."

Calla gave a mean-spirited wave in his general direction. Her fingers were claws on the steering wheel.

"She likes you," Maura said. "You should be glad. She's a good friend to have."

The tired Ford followed them to the restaurant and waited on the curb until the Gray Man and Maura were seated at a table beneath a honeysuckle and Christmas-light-covered trellis. Fans fixed in the corners kept the humid night at bay.

Maura said, "I'm going to order for you."

She waited to see if he would challenge her, but he just said, "I'm allergic to strawberries."

"Six percent of the population is," she noted.

He said, "I see where your daughter came from."

She beamed at him. She had one of those lovely, open, perfect smiles, genuinely happy and very beautiful. The Gray Man thought, *This is the worst decision I've ever made.*

She ordered for them. Neither drank any wine. The appetizers were delicious, not because of the kitchen, but because all food eaten in anticipation of a kiss is delicious.

The Gray Man asked, "What is it like, being a seer?"

"That's a funny way to put it."

"I only mean, how much do you see, and how clearly? Did you know I would ask that question? Do you know what I'm thinking?"

Maura's smile curled cleverly. "It's like a dream or a memory, but forward. Most of it is fuzzy, but sometimes we'll see one particular element very sharply. And it's not always the future. Oftentimes, when people come for a reading, we're really telling them things they already know. So no, I didn't know you would ask that question. And yes, I know what you're thinking, but that's because I'm a good guesser, not a good psychic."

It was funny, the Gray Man thought, how humorous she always appeared, how that smile was always just a moment away from her lips. You really didn't see the sadness or the longing unless you already knew it was there. But that was the trick, wasn't it? Everyone had their disappointment and their baggage; only, some people carried it in their inside pockets and not on their backs. And here was the other trick: Maura was not faking her happiness. She was both very happy and very sad.

Later, their entrees arrived. Maura had ordered the salmon for the Gray Man.

"Because," she said, "there's something fishy about you."

The Gray Man was amused.

"What's it like, being a hit man?"

"That's a funny way to put it." But really, the Gray Man found that he didn't want to talk about his work. Not because he was ashamed of it — he was the best that he knew of — but because he was not defined by it. It wasn't what he did in his spare time. "It pays the bills. But I prefer my poetry."

Maura had ordered herself one of those small birds that was served looking like it had walked onto the plate under its own steam. She seemed to be doubting that decision now. "Your Old English poetry. Okay, I'll bite. Tell me why you like it."

He did. He did it as well as he could without telling her about where he had gone to school or what he had done before publishing his book. He mentioned he had a brother, but quickly backtracked and moved around that part of the story. He told her as much as he could about himself without telling her his name. His phone was buzzing against his leg, but he let it ring.

"So you are only a hit man to pay the rent," Maura said. "Do you not care about hurting people?"

The Gray Man considered. He didn't want to be untruthful. "I do," he said. "I just — turn that part of my brain off."

Maura pulled one of the legs off her tiny bird. "I don't suppose I have to tell you how psychologically unhealthy that is."

"There are more destructive impulses in the world," he replied. "I feel fairly balanced. What about you and your ambition?"

Her eyes widened in surprise. "What makes you say that?"

"The game you were playing that first night. When you were guessing the cards. Practicing. Experimenting."

"I just want to *understand* it," Maura said. "It's changed my entire life. It's a waste if I don't know as much as I can. I don't know if I'd call it ambition, though. Oh, I don't know. It has done its damage. . . . So, you mentioned a brother."

She somehow managed to link the word *brother* to *damage*. He felt as if she had already divined the nuances of their relationship.

"My brother," he said, and then he paused and regrouped. Very precisely, he replied, "My brother is very intelligent. He can create a map of a place if he's driven through it once. He can do great sums in his head. I always looked up to him when I was a child. He invented complicated games and spent all day at them. Sometimes he would include me, if I promised to follow the rules. Sometimes he'd take a game like chess or Risk and apply those rules to the entire neighborhood. Sometimes we built forts and hid in them. Sometimes he found things in other people's houses and hurt me with them. Sometimes he trapped animals and did things to them. Sometimes we dressed in costumes and put on plays."

Maura pushed her plate away. "So he was a sociopath."

"Probably, yes."

She sighed. It was a very sad sigh. "And now you're a hit man. What does he do? Is he in prison?"

The Gray Man said, "He invests other people's money in SEP accounts. He will never be in prison. He's too intelligent."

"And you?"

"I don't think I would do well in prison," he said. "I would rather not go."

Maura was quiet for a very long time. Then she folded her napkin and put it aside and leaned to him. "Does it bother you that he's made you this way? You know that's why you can do this, don't you?"

Any part of the Gray Man that had been bothered by this had died a long time before, burned with matches and gashed with scissors and picked at with straight pins, and when he looked at her, he didn't disguise that deadness in him.

"Oh," she said. Reaching across the table, she laid her palm on his cheek. It was cool and soft and entirely different, somehow, from what the Gray Man had expected. More real. Much more real. "I'm sorry no one saved you."

Was he unsaved? Would he have ever ended up any other way?

Maura called for the check. The Gray Man paid for it. He'd left two bites of salmon on his plate, and Maura used her fork to steal them.

"So we'll both have fish breath," she said.

And then, in the dark next to the Champagne Travesty, he kissed her. Neither of them had kissed someone else in a while, but it didn't much matter. Kissing's a lot like laughing. If the joke's funny, it doesn't matter how long it's been since you last heard one.

Finally, she murmured, her hand in his shirt, fingers tracing ribs, "This is a terrible idea."

"There aren't terrible ideas," the Gray Man said. "Just ideas done terribly."

"That's also a psychologically unhealthy concept."

Later, after he'd dropped her off and returned back to the Pleasant Valley Bed and Breakfast, he discovered that Shorty and

Patty Wetzel had been trying desperately to call him all through dinner to let him know that his rooms at the bed and breakfast had been ransacked.

"Didn't you hear us calling?" Patty asked urgently.

The Gray Man recalled the buzz of his phone and patted his pockets. His phone was missing, however. Maura Sargent had stolen it while they were making out.

In its place was the ten of swords: the Gray Man slain on the ground and Maura the sword driven through his heart.

29

"Y ou aren't sleeping," Persephone said as she woke Blue, "so would you come help us?"

Blue opened her eyes. Her mouth was pasted shut. A fan in the corner of the room rotated back and forth, drying sweat on the backs of her knees. Persephone knelt on the edge of her bed, draping a crimped pale cloud of hair around Blue's face. She smelled of roses and masking tape. The sky outside was black and blue. "I *was*."

In her tiny voice, Persephone pointed out, "But you aren't now."

There was absolutely no point in arguing with her; it was like fighting with a cat. Also, it wasn't strictly untrue. With an irritable stretch, she kicked Persephone off her bed and tossed off her sheet. Together they padded down the midnight stairs into the musty glow of the kitchen. Maura and Calla were already there, hunched over the table like a pair of conspirators, heads close together. The fake Tiffany lamp above them painted the backs of their heads in purple and orange. The night pressed in the glass door at their back; Blue could see the familiar, comforting silhouette of the beech tree in the yard.

At the sound of Blue's footfalls, Maura looked up. "Oh, good."

Blue gave her mother a heavy look. "Do I have time to make myself some tea?"

Maura flapped her hand. By the time Blue joined them at the table with her cup, all three women were drawn over a single object, one blond head, one brunette, one black. Three people but one entity.

Blue shivered a little as she sat down.

"Oh, *mint* tea," Calla said meaningfully, ruining the mood.

Rolling her eyes, Blue asked, "What is it I'm helping with?"

They opened their ranks enough for her to see what they clustered around: a cell phone. It was cupped in Calla's hand; clearly they'd been trying to get her reading on it.

"This is Mr. Gray's," Maura said. "Will you help us?"

Wearily, Blue placed her hand on Calla's shoulder.

"No," Maura said. "Not like that. We're trying to figure out how to access his email."

"Oh." She accepted the phone. "Kids these days."

"I know, right?"

Blue thumbed through the screens. Though she had no cell phone of her own, she had handled them plenty, and this was the same model as Gansey's. It took no particular skill to open Mr. Gray's email. She handed it back.

The three women leaned in.

"Did you steal that?" Blue asked.

There was no answer. Their necks were all craned, looking.

"Shall I light some orris? And celery?"

Persephone blinked up, her black eyes a little far away. "Oh, yes, please."

With a yawn, Blue pushed up from the table and prepared a little plate of celery seed and orris root from the cabinet. She used one of the candles on the counter to light it. Or sort of light it. The mixture smoked and popped, the celery seeds twitching like popcorn and the orris root smelling of burning violets. The smoke of them was meant to clarify psychic impressions.

She set the plate down on the table between them. It had begun to smell a little like fireworks. "So why are you going through his phone?"

"We all knew he was looking for something," Maura replied. "We just didn't know what. Now we know what."

"And what is that?"

"Your snake boy," Calla said. "Only he doesn't know it's a boy."

Maura said, "He calls it the Greywaren and says it's to take things out of dreams. You're going to have to be careful, Blue. I think that family is all tangled up in something messy."

Something messy that involved Ronan's father being beaten to death with a tire iron. That part Blue already knew.

"Do you think he's dangerous to Ronan?" Blue remembered Declan Lynch's battered face. "I mean, if he finds out that the Greywaren is a *he* and not an *it*?"

Calla said, "Absolutely" at the same time that Maura said, "Probably not."

Persephone and Calla shot looks at Maura.

"I'll take that as a maybe," Blue said.

At that moment, the phone leapt from the table surface. All four of them jumped. Blue was the first to calm; it was only ringing. Or rather, buzzing and vibrating its way across the table.

"Write down the number!" Calla called, but she must've been talking to herself, because she already was.

In a small voice, Persephone said, "It's a Henrietta number. Do you want to pick it up?"

Maura shook her head. After a moment, a voicemail buzzed through. "That we'll listen to, though. Uh. Blue? Make it work?"

Shaking her head, Blue swiped the phone and thumbed to the voicemail. She handed it to Maura.

"Oh," Maura said, listening. "It's him. Do I push this button to call him back —? Yes." She waited as the phone rang and then — "Ah, hello, Mr. Gray."

Blue loved that voice of her mother's, except for when it was being used on her. It was her authoritative, cheerful voice, the one that said she had all of the cards. Only now she was using it on a hit man whose phone she had just stolen. Blue couldn't decide if this was delightfully cheeky or incredibly foolish.

"Well, you didn't think I was going to answer a call on *your* phone, did you? That would be awfully rude. Did you get home all right? Oh, yes, you can have it back now. I'm sorry if you needed it. Did you — oh."

Whatever the Gray Man had said immediately shut Maura up. She dropped her eyes from the others and sucked her upper lip between her teeth. The tips of her ears were pink. She listened for a moment, swatting Calla and Persephone back.

"Well," she said finally. "Any time. I'd say that you should call first, but — well. You know. I have your phone. Ha. All right. All right. Don't sleep on your back. All the swords will go through to the other side. Yep, that's my professional advice."

Maura pressed END.

"What did he say?" Blue demanded.

"That we might as well just ask him which valuables we wanted from him next so he could plan for their absence," Maura said.

Calla's lips pursed. "Is that all?"

Maura busied herself moving the phone from her left hand to her right and back to her left. "Oh, just that he had a nice time at dinner."

Blue burst out, "But you haven't forgotten Butternut."

Her mother didn't protest the name, for once. She said, "I never do."

30

That night, Ronan dreamt of his tattoo.

He had gotten the spreading, intricate tattoo only months before, a little to irritate Declan, a little to see if it was really as bad as everyone said, and definitely so everyone who glimpsed the hooks of it had fair warning. It was full of things from his head, beaks and claws and flowers and vines stuffed into screaming mouths.

It took him a long time to fall asleep that night, his thoughts crowded with the burning Mitsubishi, Gansey holding the Molotov cocktail, the enigmatic language on the puzzle box, the dark bags beneath Adam's eyes.

And when he fell asleep, he dreamt of the tattoo. Ordinarily, Ronan only saw bits and pieces of it; he had not seen the full design since he'd gotten it. But tonight he saw the tattoo itself, from behind, as if he were outside of his own body, as if it were apart from his body. It was more complicated than he remembered. The road to the Barns was threaded through it, and Chainsaw peered out from a thicket of thorns. Adam was in the dream, too; he traced the tangled pattern of the ink with his finger. He said, *"Scio quid hoc est."* As he traced it farther and farther down on the bare skin of Ronan's back, Ronan himself disappeared entirely, and the tattoo got smaller and smaller. It was a Celtic knot the size of a wafer, and then Adam, who had become Kavinsky, said,

"Scio quid estis vos." He put the tattoo in his mouth and swallowed it.

Ronan woke with a start, ashamed and euphoric.

The euphoria wore off long before the shame did.

He was never sleeping again.

31

The next morning, Helen came in the helicopter for Gansey and Adam. As they took off, Adam leaned his head in his hands, his eyes glassily terrified, and Gansey, ordinarily a fan of flying, tried to be sympathetic. His head was a tumble of burning cars and ancient Camaro wheels and the deconstruction of everything Blue had said to him.

Below, he could still see Ronan where he lay on the roof of the BMW, watching them ascend. It felt ridiculous to leave Henrietta, the epicenter of the universe, for his parents' house.

As they sailed up and over the roof of Monmouth, Gansey caught a last image of Ronan sarcastically blowing him a kiss before turning his head away.

The rest of the flight left no time for introspection, however. Helen handed Gansey her phone and spent the entire flight dictating texts to him through the headphones. It was impossible for Gansey to consider what they'd do about Cabeswater when Helen's voice sounded directly in his head: *Tell her the centerpieces are in the garage. The bay farthest away from the house. Of course not where the Adenauer's parked! Do I look like an idiot? Don't type that. What does she say now? The extra champagne flutes are being delivered by Chelsea. Tell her if the cheese isn't in the fridge, I don't know where it is. Don't you have Beech's cell phone? Of course I know what a vegan is! Tell her they have to use olive oil instead of butter. Because cows make butter and Italians make olive oil! Fine! Tell her I will pick her up some vegan hors d'oeuvres. Vegans vote, too! Don't type that.*

If Gansey hadn't guessed the scope of the party, he would've gotten all the clues he needed during the flight. Of course, it wasn't just the party this evening. There was also the tea party the next morning and the book club speech the day after that. Adam looked as if he might throw up. Gansey wanted badly to tell him that he would be all right, but there was no way to be confidential with the headsets on. Adam would've been mortified for Helen to know how nervous he was.

Just forty-five minutes later, Helen landed the helicopter at the airfield and transferred herself, her overnight bag, the boys, and their suit bags to her silver Audi.

Gansey felt vaguely shell-shocked to be back in northern Virginia. Like he'd never left. The sun seemed more unforgiving on the backs of all the clean, new cars, and the air through the vents smelled like exhaust and someone else's cooking. Numerous archipelagos of stores thrust through seas of asphalt. It seemed like there were brake lights everywhere but nothing was actually motionless. Questing for hors d'oeuvres, Helen managed to find parking at the very back of the Whole Foods lot. She turned to face Gansey and Adam. "Do you want to come in and help me?"

They stared at her.

"What a royal shock. I'll leave it running," she said.

As soon as she'd shut the door, Gansey swiveled in the passenger seat to face Adam in the back, resting his cheek against the cool leather headrest. "How are you doing?"

Adam had melted across the length of the backseat. He said, "Praying I haven't grown since last year."

Gansey had gone with Adam to get fitted for a suit the winter before. He said, "I tried mine on before we left. I don't think you're any taller. It's only been a few months."

Adam closed his eyes.

"You'll be okay."

"Don't talk to me about it. I can't . . ." Adam slithered down even farther so that he lay on the seat and let his legs rest against the opposite door. "Talk about something else."

"What else is there to talk about?"

Blue.

He didn't say anything. *Knock it off, Gansey.*

Adam said, "Malory? Did he ever get back to you?"

He hadn't. Gansey dialed Malory's number. He heard the tinny, double ring of a UK number, and then Malory answered, "What?" He sounded confused that his phone had accepted a call. There was a tremendous amount of undefined background noise.

"It's Gansey. Is this a bad time?"

"No, no, no. No, no."

Putting the phone on speaker, Gansey slid it onto the dash. "Did you have any more thoughts by any chance? No? Well, we have a new problem."

"What's the trouble?"

He told him.

"Give me a moment to think," Malory said. Commotion hummed on the line. A dreadful shriek rang out.

"What in the world is that *noise*?"

"Birds, Gansey, the king of birds."

Gansey exchanged a look with Adam. "An eagle?"

"Don't be blasphemous. Pigeons! It's the regional today. I used to show them myself, you know. Don't have the time these days, but I still love the look of a quality Voorburg Shield Cropper."

Gansey said, "A pigeon show."

"If you could see them, Gansey!" On his end of the line, a loudspeaker blared.

Adam's mouth quirked. Gansey prompted, "The Voorburg Shield Croppers."

"There is so much more on offer here," Malory replied. "Much more than the Croppers."

"Tell me what you are looking at *right now.*"

Malory smacked his lips — he was really the absolute worst human to speak to on the telephone — and considered. "I'm looking at, what does this seem to be? West of England Tumbler, I should think. Yes. Lovely example. You should see his muffs. Right next to him is a dreadful little Thuringen Field Pigeon. I've never had them but I'm *quite* certain they aren't meant to have that hideous stallion neck. I have no idea what this one is. Let's read the card. Anatolian Ringbeater. Of course. Oh, and here's a German Beauty Homer."

"Oh, those are my favorite," Gansey said. "I am a fan of a good German Beauty Homer."

"Gansey, don't make light," Malory said sternly. "Those things look like bloody puffins."

Adam's body shook in silent convulsions of laughter.

Gansey took a moment to catch his breath before asking, "And what's that sound in the background?"

"Let me take a gander," Malory replied. There was a crackling sound, and then his voice, rather louder than before, said, "They're auctioning off some birds."

"What sort? Please tell me German Beauty Homers."

Adam, completely undone, bit his hand. Small gasps still managed to escape.

"Pigmy Pouters," Malory replied. "Feisty ones!"

Gansey mouthed *Blue* at Adam. Adam let out a little wail of helpless laughter.

"You never took *me* to any pigeon shows while I was there," Gansey said reproachfully.

"We had other tasks at hand, Gansey!" Malory said. "Such as now. This is what I think about your ley line. I think your forest is like an apparition, if I had to guess about these things. Without a solid source of energy, an apparition can only flicker."

"But we woke the ley line," replied Gansey. "It's so strong sometimes that it blows out the transformers here."

"Ah, but you said that the electricity goes out as well, did you not?"

Gansey grudgingly agreed. And now he was thinking of Noah vanishing in the Dollar City.

"So you see how your forest might be starved as well as over-fed. Good heavens, man, would you *watch* where you're carrying that thing! Sorry! I should think you are! I'd be sorry, too, if I had to claim that monstrosity as my own! That sausage neck . . . excuse *you!*" There was a scuffle, and then Malory said, "I apologize, Gansey. Some people! I should think you need to find out how to stabilize your line. The surges I'd expect, but certainly not the outages."

"Any ideas?"

"I've had quite a lot of ideas in just the last minute," Malory said. "I should like to see this line of yours. Are you opposed, one day . . . ?"

"You're welcome anytime," Gansey said, and meant it. For all his faults, Malory was still Gansey's oldest ally. He had earned it.

"Excellent, excellent. Now, if you don't mind," Malory said, "I have just spotted a pair of Shield Croppers."

They exchanged good-byes. Gansey turned his eyes to Adam, who looked more like himself than he had in ages. He silently vowed to do whatever it took to keep him that way. "Well. I don't know how helpful *that* was."

Adam said, "We found out German Beauty Homers look like bloody puffins."

The very first thing Ronan did after Gansey left was retrieve the keys to the Camaro. He had no immediate plan other than to see if they actually fit into the lock.

In the summer sun, the Pig glistened like a gem in the scrubby grass and gravel. Ronan lay a hand on the rear panel and slid his palm lightly up over the roof. Even that felt illicit; this car was so much Gansey's that it seemed as if, somewhere, Gansey must be able to feel this minor transgression. When Ronan lifted his hand, it was dusted green. He was struck by the details of the moment. This was something he needed to remember, when he dreamt. This feeling right here: heart thudding, pollen sticky on his fingertips, July pricking sweat at his breastbone, the smell of gasoline and someone else's charcoal grill. Every blade of grass was picked out in sharp detail. If Ronan could dream like this moment felt, he could take anything out. He could take this whole goddamn car out.

He put the key in the door.

It fit.

He turned it.

The lock popped up.

A smile was working over his mouth, though there was no one to see it. *Especially* because there was no one to see it.

Ronan sank into the driver's seat. The vinyl was infernally hot in the sun, but he just filed that information away. It was yet another sensation that made the moment real instead of a dream. Slowly, he ran a finger around the thin steering wheel, rested his palm on the slick gearshift.

Gansey's heart would stop if he saw Ronan Lynch right here.

Unless the key didn't work in the ignition.

Ronan put his feet on the clutch and brake, inserted the key, and turned it.

The engine roared to life.

Ronan grinned.

On cue, his phone buzzed as a text message came in. He slid it out of his pocket. Kavinsky.

my new wheels will blow you away. see you tonite @ 11.

An hour later, Noah let Blue into Monmouth Manufacturing. The sun had made the space vast and musty and lovely. The warm, trapped air was scented with old wood and mint and ten-thousand pages about Glendower. Although Gansey had been gone only hours, it suddenly seemed longer, like this was all that was left of him.

"Where's Ronan?" she whispered as Noah closed the door behind her.

"Making trouble," Noah whispered back. It was strange to be here without anyone else: speaking felt a little forbidden. "Nothing we can do anything about."

"Are you sure?" Blue murmured. "I can do a lot of things."

"Not about this."

She hesitated by the door. It felt like trespassing without Gansey or Ronan here. What she wanted was to somehow stuff all of Monmouth Manufacturing inside her head and keep it there. She was struck with anxious longing.

Noah held his hand out. She accepted it — it was bone-cold,

as always — and together they turned to face the huge room. Noah took a deep breath as if they were preparing to explore the jungle instead of stepping deeper into Monmouth Manufacturing.

It seemed bigger with just the two of them there. The cob-webbed ceiling soared, dust motes making mobiles overhead. They turned their heads sideways and read the titles of the books aloud. Blue peered at Henrietta through the telescope. Noah daringly reattached one of the broken miniature roofs on Gansey's scale town. They went through the fridge tucked in the bathroom. Blue selected a soda. Noah took a plastic spoon. He chewed on it as Blue fed Chainsaw a leftover hamburger. They closed Ronan's door — if Gansey still managed to inhabit the rest of the apartment, Ronan's presence was still decidedly pervasive in his room. Noah showed Blue his room. They jumped on his perfectly made bed and then they played a bad game of pool. Noah lounged on the new sofa while Blue persuaded the old record player to play an LP too clever to interest either of them. They opened all of the drawers on the desk in the main room. One of Gansey's EpiPens bounced against the interior of the topmost drawer as Blue withdrew a fancy pen. She copied Gansey's blocky handwriting onto a Nino's receipt as Noah put on a preppy sweater he'd found balled under the desk. She ate a mint leaf and breathed on Noah's face.

Crouching, they crab-walked along the aerial printout Gansey had spread the length of the room. He'd jotted enigmatic notes to himself all along the margin of it. Some of them were coordinates. Some of them were explanations of topography. Some of them were Beatles lyrics.

Finally, they regarded Gansey's bed, which was just a barely made mattress and box spring on a metal stand. It sat in a square of sunlight in the middle of the room, turned at an angle as if it had been driven into the building. Without any particular discussion, they curled on top of the blanket, each taking one of Gansey's pillows. It felt illicit and drowsy. Only inches away, Noah blinked sleepily at her. Blue crumpled the edge of the sheet against her nose. It smelled like mint and wheatgrass, which was to say, like Gansey.

As they baked in the sunlight, she let herself think it:

I have a crush on Richard Gansey.

In a way, it was easier than pretending otherwise. She couldn't do anything about it, of course, but letting herself think it was like popping a blister.

Of course, the opposite truth also seemed self-evident.

I don't have a crush on Adam Parrish.

She sighed.

Noah, his voice muffled, said, "Sometimes I pretend I'm like him."

"What part?"

He considered. "Alive."

Blue draped an arm over his cold neck. There wasn't really anything to say to make being dead better.

For a few sleepy minutes, they were silent, nested in the pillows, and then Noah said, "I heard about how you won't kiss Adam."

She turned her face into the pillow, cheeks hot.

"Well, *I* don't care," Noah said. With quiet delight, he guessed, "He smells, right?"

She turned back to him. "He does *not* smell. Ever since I was little, every psychic I know has told me that if I kiss my true love, he'll die."

Noah's brow furrowed, or at least the half of it that wasn't buried in pillow. His nose was more crooked than she'd ever noticed. "Adam's your true love?"

"No," Blue said. She was startled by how quickly she had answered. She couldn't stop seeing the dented side of the box he'd kicked. "I mean, I don't know. I just don't kiss anybody, just to be on the safe side."

Being dead made Noah more open-minded than most, so he didn't bother with doubt. "Is it *when* or *if*?"

"What do you mean?"

"Like, *if* you kiss your true love, he'll die," he said, "or is it *when* you kiss your true love, he'll die?"

"I don't get what the difference is."

He rubbed the side of his face on the pillow. "Mmmmsoft," he remarked, then added, "One's your fault. The other one, you just happen to be there when it happens. Like, when you kiss him, POW, he gets hit by a bear. Totally not your fault. You shouldn't feel bad about that. It's not your bear."

"I think it's *if*. They all say *if*."

"Bummer. So you're never going to kiss anyone?"

"Looks that way."

Noah rubbed the smudge on his cheek. It didn't go away. It never did. He said, "I know somebody you could kiss."

"Who?" She realized his eyes were amused. "Oh, wait."

He shrugged. He was maybe the only person Blue knew who could preserve the integrity of a shrug while lying down. "It's not like you're going to kill me. I mean, if you were curious."

She hadn't thought she was curious. It hadn't been an option, after all. Not being able to kiss someone was a lot like being poor. She tried not to dwell on the things she couldn't have.

But now —

"Okay," she said.

"What?"

"I said okay."

He blushed. Or rather, because he was dead, he became normal colored. "Uh." He propped himself on an elbow. "Well." She unburied her face from the pillow. "Just, like —"

He leaned toward her. Blue felt a thrill for a half a second. No, more like a quarter second. Because after that she felt the too-firm pucker of his tense lips. His mouth mashed her lips until it met teeth. The entire thing was at once slimy and ticklish and hilarious.

They both gasped an embarrassed laugh. Noah said, *"Bah!"* Blue considered wiping her mouth, but felt that would be rude. It was all fairly underwhelming.

She said, "Well."

"Wait," Noah replied, "waitwaitwait." He pulled one of Blue's hairs out of his mouth. "I wasn't ready."

He shook out his hands as if Blue's lips were a sporting event and cramping was a very real possibility.

"Go," Blue said.

This time they only got within a breath of each other's lips when they both began to laugh. She closed the distance and was rewarded with another kiss that felt a lot like kissing a dishwasher.

"I'm doing something wrong?" she suggested.

"Sometimes it's better with tongue," he replied dubiously.

They regarded each other.

Blue squinted. "Are you sure you've done this before?"

"Hey!" he protested. "It's weird for me, 'cause it's *you*."

"Well, it's weird for me because it's *you*."

"We can stop."

"Maybe we should."

Noah pushed himself up farther on his elbow and gazed at the ceiling vaguely. Finally, he dropped his eyes back to her.

"You've seen, like, movies. Of kisses, right? Your lips need to be, like, wanting to be kissed."

Blue touched her mouth. "What are they doing now?"

"Like, bracing themselves."

She pursed and unpursed her lips. She saw his point.

"So imagine one of those," Noah suggested.

She sighed and sifted through her memories until she found one that would do. It wasn't a movie kiss, however. It was the kiss the dreaming tree had showed her in Cabeswater. Her first and only kiss with Gansey, right before he died. She thought about his nice mouth when he smiled. About his pleasant eyes when he laughed. She closed her eyes.

Placing an elbow on the other side of her head, Noah leaned close and kissed her once more. This time, it was more of a thought than a feeling, a soft heat that began at her mouth and unfurled through the rest of her. One of his cold hands slid behind her neck and he kissed her again, lips parted. It was not just a touch, an action. It was a simplification of both of them: They were no longer Noah Czerny and Blue Sargent. They were now just *him* and *her*. Not even that. They were only the time that they held between them.

Oh, thought Blue. *So this is what I can't have.*

Not being able to kiss whoever she fell in love with didn't feel so different from not having a cell phone when everyone else at school did. It didn't feel very different from knowing she wasn't going to be studying ecology abroad for college, or going abroad period. It didn't feel very different from knowing that Cabeswater was going to be the only extraordinary thing about her life.

Which was to say that it was unbearable, but she had to bear it anyway.

Because there was nothing terrible about kissing Noah

Czerny, apart from him being cold. She let him kiss her, and kissed him back until he pulled back on an elbow and clumsily wiped away some of her tears with the heel of his fist. His smudge had gotten very dark, and he was cold enough that she shivered.

Blue gave him a watery smile. "That was super nice."

He shrugged, eyes doleful, shoulders curled in on themselves. He was fading. It wasn't that she could see through him. It was that it was hard to remember what he looked like, even while she was looking at him. When he turned his head, she saw him swallow. He mumbled, "I'd ask you out, if I was alive."

Nothing was fair.

"I'd say okay," she replied.

She only had time to see him smile faintly. And then he was gone.

She rolled onto her back in the middle of the suddenly empty bed. Above her, the rafters glowed with the summer sun. Blue touched her mouth. It felt the same as it always did. Not at all like she had just gotten her first and last kiss.

32

"G et in," Ronan said.

"Where are we going?" asked Matthew. But he was already climbing in, throwing his bag in the back. He shut the door. The interior of the car instantly smelled like a cologne sample.

Ronan put the BMW in gear. Aglionby shrank in the rearview mirror. "Home."

"Home!" yelped Matthew. Clutching the door handle, he stared over his shoulder as if bystanders would divine their destination. "Ronan, we *can't.* Declan said —"

Ronan slammed on the brakes. The tires squealed obligingly and the car jerked to a halt by the sidewalk. The car behind them honked and went around. "You can get out here and walk back, if you want. But I'm going. Do you want to or not?"

His younger brother's already round eyes were even rounder. "Declan —"

"Don't say his name."

Little dimples appeared in Matthew's chin, the sort that had meant, when he was three or four, that he was going to cry. He did not cry. Ronan wished for a half a second that he didn't hate Declan, for Matthew's sake.

"Okay," Matthew said. "Are you sure it will be okay?"

"No," Ronan replied, because he always told the truth.

Matthew put on his seat belt.

Ronan rummaged through his MP3 player until he found a playlist of bouzouki music. Matthew hadn't played since Niall Lynch died, but he'd been pretty good at it before then. It felt indulgent. Ronan rationed the music from their old life, as if he used up a bit of his memories of his father every time he played it. Surely this occasion warranted it, though.

As the tune plucked through the speakers, his younger brother let all of the air escape from his lungs. And Ronan drove home for the second time.

This time felt different. Having Matthew along should have made returning to the Barns feel more familiar than before, but instead it only served to remind Ronan of how forbidden this was. The sunshine made it a more anxious trip as well, as if the bright light left them more exposed as they drove down the driveway.

Ronan went slowly until he verified that the home nurse's car wasn't there, and then he drove around the back of the house to where an overgrown, mildew-green equipment shed stood.

"Open that door," he ordered Matthew. "Hurry up."

Matthew scrambled out, pawed away some of the creeper, and struggled to lift the metal door. He dragged a small, rusted lawn mower out of the way, and Ronan backed the BMW in. He turned it off, pulled down the door again, and checked to be sure the tires hadn't left obvious marks.

"James Bond," Matthew remarked inexplicably. He was incredibly cheerful. "What's that?"

Ronan held the puzzle box under his arm. "A shoe box."

Matthew cocked his head, working this out. He took in the facts: The perfectly square box was clearly wooden, covered with strange markings, and several inches shorter than his older brother's feet.

Matthew blinked. Then he said, "Okay!" Trotting ahead to the back door, he found the key hidden by the boot pull.

"Wait," Ronan warned. "Keep an ear out. If someone comes down the driveway, get in the basement. And turn off your phone, for God's sake."

"Right! Sure! Clever!"

He gallumphed into the house before Ronan, who looked over his shoulder before he locked the back door behind them. He heard Matthew's feet head toward the sitting room, hesitate, and then pound percussively up the stairs to his bedroom. Matthew's affection was a sloppy, demonstrative thing, and he had not seemed to know what to make of their now-motionless mother.

Ronan followed the hall to the sitting room more slowly, listening for the sounds of an approaching car between each footfall. The sitting room was dimmer and quieter than the hall, with no windows to let in the simmering afternoon or the trilling birds. The door to the basement was on the far wall, so he'd be able to intercept Matthew if anyone else arrived.

Ronan went directly to the desk against the wall, not looking at his mother. His father had called this desk his "office," as if his work had required a legitimate form of paperwork. Ronan wondered if his mother had known what Niall Lynch did for a living. Surely she must have. She must have known she was a dream thing.

Suddenly, for the briefest of moments, panic forced itself up.

Am I a dream creature? Would I know?

Then he let reason tamp the thought down. All of the boys had baby books, with photos and hospital records. He had a blood type. And if his father had dreamt him, he'd be motionless like his mother. He had been born, not conjured. He was real.

What is real?

Was something real once it had been taken from a dream? If so, was it real the moment he thought it?

He stole a glance over his shoulder at his mother. She didn't seem particularly logical *now*, sitting motionless and uncaring for months and months. But he had never doubted her before her father's death, even when she was the only parent for months at a time.

She's nothing without Dad.

Declan was wrong. She existed apart from Niall Lynch, even if he was her sole creator.

Ronan turned back to the desk. Setting the puzzle box on it, he pulled open the main drawer. A copy of his father's will sat on the very top of the contents, just as he remembered it.

Not bothering to reread the earlier clauses of the document — they would only anger him — he flipped directly to the last page. There, right before his father's signature.

NIALL LYNCH WAS, AT THE TIME OF SO EXECUTING SAID WILL, OF SOUND MIND, MEMORY, AND UNDERSTANDING AND NOT UNDER ANY RESTRAINT OR IN ANY RESPECT INCOMPETENT TO MAKE A WILL. THIS WILL STANDS AS FACT UNLESS A NEWER DOCUMENT IS CREATED.

SIGNED THIS DAY: T'LIBRE VERO-E BER NIVO LIBRE N'ACREA.

Ronan squinted at the final phrase. Picking up the puzzle box, he turned it around until the side with the unknown language faced him. It was painstaking work to plug in each word. Though he couldn't understand how the box managed it, it held the previously entered words in its workings in order to translate the grammar as well. That was how it had worked in the dream, after all.

If it worked in the dream, it worked in real life.

He frowned at the translation it provided.

This Will stands as fact unless a newer document is created.

Pressing his finger on the paper to keep his place, he compared it. Sure enough, the translated sentence was identical to the final sentence in English. But why would his father write the same thing in two different languages?

Hope — he hadn't realized what the feeling was until it abandoned him — slowly trailed out of him. He'd been right about the language, but wrong that there was a secret message. Or if it was a secret message, he wasn't clever enough to decode it.

Ronan shoved the drawer shut and folded the will into his back pocket to take with him. Just as he turned with the puzzle box, Matthew appeared in the doorway. He arrived with such speed that his shoulder crashed into the doorjamb.

"Nice," Ronan said thinly.

Matthew waved a hand and panted, voice low, "I think someone's here."

They both looked behind them at the basement door.

Ronan asked, "What kind of car?"

Matthew shook his head wildly. "In the house."

It was impossible, but the hair on Ronan's neck crept up.

And then he heard it, distantly, from somewhere else in the house:

Tck-tck-tck-tck.

The night horror. Ronan didn't think. He threw himself across the room and dragged Matthew inside.

There was a slow scrape from the direction of the kitchen.

"Basement?" gulped Matthew, shocked.

Ronan didn't answer. He shoved closed the sitting room door and looked wildly around. "Chair!" he hissed at his younger brother. *"Hurry!"*

Matthew cast about before carrying a flimsy, armless chair over. Ronan tried to work out a door jam, but the old-fashioned door hook resisted his efforts. Even if it had been an ordinary knob, the chair wasn't tall enough to provide a whisper of leverage.

Tck-tck-tck-tck.

"Ronan?" Matthew whispered.

Ronan leapt over three old flour crocks to where a cedar chest was pressed against the wall. He tested the weight and then began to shove.

"Come on, help me," he grunted. Matthew skidded over and threw his shoulder against it.

The claws tapped on the hallway floorboards. Scuffling.

The cedar chest scraped to a halt in front of the door. Back in Monmouth, the bookshelf had been heavy enough to keep the night horror in his bedroom. Ronan could only hope that the chest would be as effective.

Matthew looked up at Ronan, bewildered, as his older brother climbed on top of the cedar chest. Ronan stretched out an arm and hugged his brother's curly head, once, hard. He pushed him away.

"Sit next to Mom," he hissed. "It doesn't want you. It's me."

"Ro —"

"But if it gets past me, don't wait. Just fight."

Matthew retreated to where Aurora Lynch sat on her chair in the middle of the room, tranquil and motionless. Ronan saw him crouched there in the dim space, holding their mother's hand.

He should have never brought him with.

The door bucked.

Matthew jerked in surprise. Aurora didn't.

Ronan held the doorknob as it jiggled. There was a slow sound like water tapping out of a faucet.

The door jumped again.

Again Matthew started. But the cedar chest didn't budge. It was heavy, and the night horror was not. Its strength was in those claws and that beak.

Three more times the door jerked on its hinges. Then there was a long, long pause.

It was possible it had given up.

But Ronan hadn't considered what their next step would be. They couldn't risk opening the door if the night horror was on the other side. Perhaps he should go out by himself — the bird men never wanted anyone else. It was only Ronan they despised. Everything in him was loath to leave his brother and mother behind, but they would both be safer without him.

Long minutes stretched out in silence. And then, somewhere in the house, a door shut.

Matthew and Ronan stared at each other. Something about the sound had been very unhurried and human — not at all what Ronan would have expected from the night horror.

Sure enough, ordinary footsteps began to creak down the hall. Possibilities unwound in Ronan's mind, none of them good. There was no time to move the cedar chest without drawing attention to it. No wisdom to warning this newcomer of the nightmare, either — Ronan's presence would only make it more dangerous.

"Hide," Ronan ordered Matthew. His younger brother was frozen, so he grabbed his sleeve and tugged him away from their mother. There was just room for them to tuck themselves behind the rolled-up rugs in the corner of the room. It wouldn't withstand careful study, but in the dimness, there was no reason why they'd be discovered.

Many minutes later, after much creaking of floorboards elsewhere in the house, someone gave the door an experimental shove. This time, it was quite clearly a some*one* rather than a some*thing*. There was an audible, human-sounding sigh on the other side, and the shuffling of feet on the floorboards was clearly produced by shoes.

Ronan held a finger to his lips.

There was only one more shove, and then the door cracked an inch. Another grunt, another shove, and the door came open far enough to admit a person.

Ronan wasn't sure who he had expected. The home nurse, probably. Maybe even Declan, visiting illegally.

But this was a handsome, wiry man all dressed in gray; Ronan had never seen him before. The way he flicked his gaze around the room was so keen Ronan was afraid he would see them behind the rugs after all. But the man's interest was snagged by Aurora Lynch on her chair in the middle of the room.

Ronan tensed.

It would take nothing at all to spring him from his hiding place. If he so much as touched her —

But the Gray Man didn't touch Aurora. Instead, he bent over to look into her face. It was a curious, piercing study, over in a few seconds. He toed the tubes and wires that led from machines to nowhere. He rubbed his jaw and puzzled.

Finally, the Gray Man asked, "Why are you walled up in here?"

Aurora Lynch didn't answer.

The Gray Man turned to go, but paused. The language box, still sitting on the desk, had caught his eye. Retrieving the box, he turned it over and over in his hands, experimentally scrolling one of the wheels and watching the effect it had on the other sides.

And then he took it with him.

Ronan put a fist to his forehead. He wanted to go after him and recover it, but he couldn't risk discovery. Where would he get another puzzle box? He had no way of knowing if he'd ever dream of it again. Ronan tensed, thought about emerging, thought about hiding, thought about emerging. Matthew put a hand on his arm.

They waited a long time. Finally, a car rumbled out front before receding down the driveway.

They unhid themselves. Matthew pressed up against Ronan's side, reminding Ronan of Chainsaw when she was frightened. Ordinarily, Ronan would have protested, but this time, he allowed it.

"What was that?" Matthew whispered.

"There are," Ronan replied, "bad things in the world. Let's get out of here."

Matthew kissed his mother's cheek. Ronan made sure he had the will still tucked in his back pocket. The loss of the puzzle box still smarted, but at least he had this puzzle of his father's with him. Two lines, two languages. *What are you trying to say, Dad?*

"Bye, Mom," he told Aurora. He felt in his pocket for his keys. There were two sets: the BMW's and the false Camaro's keys. "See you later."

33

At that particular moment in time, Richard Campbell Gansey III was ninety-two miles away from his beloved car. He stood in the sun-soaked driveway of the Ganseys' Washington, D.C., mansion, wearing a furiously red tie and a suit made of tasteful pinstripe and regal swagger. Beside him stood Adam, his strange and beautiful face pale above the slender dark of his own suit. Tailored by the same clever Italian man who did Gansey's shirts, the suit was Adam's silken armor for the night ahead. It was the most expensive thing he had ever owned, a month's wages translated into worsted wool. The air was humid with teriyaki and Cabernet Sauvignon and premium-grade fuel. Somewhere, a violin sang with vicious victory. It was impossibly hot.

They were ninety-seven miles and several million dollars away from Adam's childhood home.

The sweeping circular driveway was a puzzle game of vehicles: tuxedo-black sedans, cello-brown SUVs, silvery two-seaters that could fit in the palm of your hand, sweating white coupes with diplomatic plates. Two valets, having exhausted every parking solution, smoked cigarettes and blew smoke curls over the fenders of a Mercedes beached on the curb beside them. Rose blooms rotted on the bushes beside them, sweet and black.

Gansey snaked between cars. "Lucky thing we didn't have to trouble ourselves with parking."

The helicopter ride still rested uneasily in Adam's stomach. He didn't care for flying or for being seen arriving in a helicopter. He'd spent thirty minutes scrubbing grease from his fingertips before they'd left. Was this the dream, or was his life back in Henrietta?

He echoed, "Lucky thing."

Two men and one woman stepped out of the front door of the house. Hands chopped at air; bits of the conversation exploded off the gutters overhead. *Already been passed — legislation — damn idiot — also his wife is a cow.* A murmur of guests passed through the open door behind them as if the threesome had pulled the sound out with them. The view through the doorway was a collage of pants suits and pearl necklaces, Vuitton and damask. So very many. So very, very many of them.

"Jesus Christ," Gansey said tragically, his eyes on the gathering. "Oh well." He flicked an invisible piece of lint off the shoulder of Adam's suit and placed a mint leaf on his own tongue. "Good for them to see your face."

Them. Somewhere in there was Gansey's mother, stretching her hands out to the hungry D.C. off-the-rack suit crowd, offering them treasure in heaven in return for votes. And Gansey was part of the sales package; there was nothing more Congressional than the entire Gansey family under one roof. Because those dripping necklaces and red ties were the captivated retinue who would fund Mrs. Richard Gansey II's run for office. And those shiny oxfords and velvet pumps were the nobles Adam sought squireship from.

Good for them to see your face.

A laugh, high and confident, pierced the air. Conversation swelled to accept it.

Who are these people, Adam thought, *to think they know anything about the rest of the world?*

He must not let it show in his eyes. If he reminded himself that he needed them, *these people*, if he reminded himself it was only a means to an end, it was a little easier.

Besides, Adam was good at hiding things.

Gansey greeted the guests standing outside the door. Despite his previous complaint, he was completely at ease, a lion on the Serengeti.

"In we go," he said grandly. And just like that, the Gansey who Adam had befriended — the Gansey he would do anything for — vanished, and in his place was the heir born with a silk umbilical cord wrapped round his blue-blooded neck.

The Gansey mansion spread out before them. There was Helen, now deliberately effete and decidedly unattainable in a black sheath, her legs longer than the driveway. *What shall we toast to? Toast to me, of course. Oh, yes, my mother, too.* There was ex-Congressman Bullock and there was the head of the Vann-Shoaling Committee and there were Mr. and Mrs. John Benderham, the largest single donors to the last Eighth District Republican campaign. Everywhere were faces Adam had seen in newspapers and on television. Everything smelled of puff pastry and ambition.

Seventeen years before, Adam had been born in a trailer. They could see it on him. He knew it.

"What are you two handsome devils up to?"

Gansey laughed: *ha ha ha*. Adam turned, but the speaker was already gone. Someone grabbed Gansey's hand. "Dick! Good to see you." The unseen violin wailed. The acoustics gave the impression the instrument was imprisoned in the chesterfield by the door. A man in a white shirt pressed champagne flutes into their hands. It was ginger ale, sweet and fraudulent.

A hand slapped the back of Adam's neck; he flinched badly. In his head, he fell down his father's stairs, fingers grabbing dirt. He could never seem to leave Henrietta behind. He could feel an image, an apparition, looming behind his eyes, but he pushed it away. Not here, not now.

"We always need young blood!" boomed the man. Adam was sweating, flipping between the memory of biting stars overhead, the fact of this present-day assault. Gansey took the man's hand from Adam's neck and shook it instead. Adam knew he was being rescued, but the room was too loud and too close for gratitude.

Gansey said, "We're young as they come."

"You're pretty damn young," the man said.

"This is Adam Parrish," Gansey said. "Shake his hand. He's more clever than I am. One day we'll be throwing one of these shindigs for him."

Somehow Adam had a business card pressed into his hand; someone else gave him more ginger ale. No, this one was actually champagne. Adam did not drink alcohol. Gansey smoothly took the champagne flute from him and placed it on an antique desk with ivory inlay. With a finger he slicked off a single drop of red wine that stained the surface. Voices wrestled with one another; the deepest voice won. *Eight months ago we were in the same place as this on that campaign,* a man with an enormous tie pin said to a man with an enormously shiny forehead. *Sometimes you just throw funds at it and hope it sticks.* Gansey shook hands and clasped shoulders. He talked women into confessing their names and then made them believe that he'd known them all along. He always called Adam *Adam Parrish.* Everyone always called him *Dick.* Adam gathered a bouquet of business cards. His hip smashed into a piece of lion-pawed furniture; Irish crystal jingled from the lamp sitting on it. A spirit touched his elbow. Not here, not now.

"Having fun?" Gansey asked. It did not sound as if he was, but his smile was bulletproof. His eyes roved the room as he knocked back his ginger ale or his champagne. He accepted another flute from a faceless serving tray.

They moved to the next person, and the next. Ten, fifteen, twenty people in and Gansey was an embroidered tapestry of a young man, the hoped-for youth of America, the educated princeling son of Mrs. Richard Gansey II. The room adored him.

Adam wondered if there was a true smile among this herd of wealthy animals.

"Dick, finally, do you have the keys to the Fiat?" Helen came close to them, eye to eye with Gansey in a pair of black pumps that were sensible on every other woman in the room and unreasonably sexy on her. She was, Adam thought, the sort of woman Declan was always trying to obtain, not realizing that Helen was not the obtainable sort. You could love the sleek, efficient beauty of a brand-new bullet train, but only a fool could imagine it would love you back.

"Why would I?" Gansey asked.

"Oh, I don't know. Every car is blocked in except that one. Those idiot valets." She tipped her head back and looked at the tree-painted ceiling; to Adam, the intricate branches seemed to be moving. "Mom wants me to do a booze run. If you come with, I can use the HOV lanes and not spend the rest of my life getting wine." She noticed Adam. "Oh, Parrish. You clean up well."

She meant nothing by it, nothing at all, but Adam felt an ice chip pierce his heart.

"Helen," Gansey said. "Shut up."

"It's a compliment," Helen said. A server replaced their empty drinks with full ones.

Remember why you're here. Get in, get what you need, get out. You're not one of them.

Adam said evenly, flattening his accent, "It's all right."

"I meant that you two were always in your school uniforms," Helen said. "Not, like —"

"Shut up, Helen," Gansey said.

"Don't PMS on me," Helen replied, "just because you wish you were with your beloved Henrietta."

A fleeting expression passed across Gansey's face then; she'd guessed right. It was killing him to be here.

"Why is it, again, you didn't bring the other one?" Helen asked. But before Gansey could reply, someone else caught her eye and she allowed herself to be swept away as swiftly as she'd appeared.

"What a dreadful thought," Gansey observed suddenly. "Ronan among this crowd."

For a fleeting moment, Adam could imagine it: the brocade curtains in decaying flames, the decorated consorts screaming from beneath the harpsichord, Ronan standing among it all saying *Fuck Washington.*

Gansey said, "Ready for the next round?"

The evening would never end.

But Adam kept watching.

He swallowed his ginger ale. He wasn't sure it hadn't actually been champagne, now, all along. The party had become a devil's feast: will-o'-the-wisps caught in brass hunting lamps, impossibly bright meats presented on ivy-filagreed platters, men in black, women jeweled in green and red. The painted trees of the ceiling bent low overhead. Adam was wired and exhausted, here and somewhere else. Nothing was real but him and Gansey.

Before them was a woman who had just spoken with Gansey's mother. Everyone who caught Gansey had either just conversed with his mother or just shook her hand or just glimpsed her moving between the dark-clad partygoers. It was an elaborate political play where his mother played a beloved but rare wraith; although everyone recalled seeing her, no one could actually locate her at the moment of recollection.

"You have," the woman said to Gansey, "grown so much since the last time I've seen you. You must be nearly . . ." and at that, at the moment of guessing Gansey's age, she hesitated. Adam knew that she had sensed that *otherness* to his friend: that sense that Gansey was both young and old, that he'd only just arrived, or he'd always been.

She was saved by a glance at Adam. Quickly assessing his age, she finished, "Seventeen? Eighteen?"

"Seventeen, ma'am," Gansey said warmly. And he was, as soon as he'd said it. Of course he was seventeen, and nothing else. Something like relief passed over the woman's face.

Adam felt the press of the candied tree branches overhead; to his right, he caught a half-image of himself in a gold-framed mirror and startled. For a moment, his reflection had seemed wrong.

It was happening. *No, no, it's not happening. Not here, not now.*

A second glance revealed a clearer image. Nothing strange. Yet.

"Did I read in the paper that you're still looking for those crown jewels?" the woman asked Gansey.

"Oh, I'm looking for an actual king," Gansey said, speaking loudly to be heard over the violin (there were three of them, actually; the last man had informed him that they were students from Peabody). The strings wavered as if the sound came from underwater. "A Welsh king from the fifteenth century."

The woman laughed delightedly. She'd misheard Gansey and thought he'd made a joke. Gansey laughed, too, as if he had, and any awkwardness that might have arisen was swiftly averted.

Adam made a note of that.

And now, finally, there was Mrs. Gansey, looming at the corner of his vision like a materialized dream. Like Gansey himself, she was intrinsically beautiful in the way that only someone who has always had money can be. It seemed right that an entire party should be thrown in her honor. She was a worthy queen for the evening.

"Gloria," Mrs. Gansey said to the woman. "I love that necklace. You of course remember my son, Dick?"

"Of course," Gloria said. "He is so very tall. You must be off to college soon?"

Both women turned for his answer. Violins shrilled up the scale.

"Well, it —" And then, all at once, Gansey faltered. It was not quite a full stop. Just a failure to slide smoothly from moment to moment. There was only time enough for Adam to see the gap, and then Gansey said, "I'm sorry, I thought I saw someone."

Adam caught his eye. There was a question there, unspoken. Gansey's return gaze was complicated; no, he was not all right, but no, there was nothing Adam could do about it. Adam had a brief, ferocious joy, that they could get to Gansey as well. How he hated them.

"Oh, I *do* see someone. I must leave you," Gansey said, impeccably polite. "I'm sorry. But I'll leave you with — Mrs. Elgin, this is my friend Adam Parrish. He has interesting thoughts about travelers' rights. Have you thought about travelers' rights lately?"

Adam tried to remember the last time he and Gansey had spoken about travelers' rights. He was pretty sure the entire discussion had taken place over a lukewarm pizza and had had something to do with the body scanners microwaving the brain cells of frequent flyers. But now that he'd seen Gansey at work, he knew Gansey would spool that out into a political epidemic solvable by his mother.

"I haven't," Gloria Elgin replied, dazzled by Gansey's Ganseyness. "We usually take Ben's Cessna these days. But I would like to hear about it."

When she turned to Adam, Gansey vanished into the crowd.

For a moment, Adam said nothing. He was not Gansey, he did not dazzle, he was a pretender with a flute of false champagne in his slender hand made from dust. He looked at Mrs. Elgin. She looked back at him through her eyelashes.

With a jolt, he realized that he intimidated her. Standing there in his impervious suit with its red-knotted tie, young and straight-shouldered and clean, he had pulled off whatever strange alchemy Gansey performed. For perhaps the first time in his life, someone was looking at him and seeing power.

He tried to conjure up the magic he'd already seen Gansey do this evening. His mind swam with the noise of this glittering company, the shimmer in the bottom of his champagne glass, the knowledge that this was the future, if he speared it.

he was in a forest, whispers pursued him

Not here

He said, "Can I refill your drink first?"

Mrs. Elgin's face melted with pleasure as she offered up her glass.

Don't you know? Adam wondered. He, at least, could still smell diesel fuel on his hands. *Don't you know what I am?*

But this flock of peacocks was too busy fooling to notice they were being fooled.

Adam couldn't remember why he was here. He was dissolving in a hallucination of ghostly guests alongside the real ones.

Because this is Aglionby, he thought, desperately trying to ground himself. *This is what happens to Aglionby in the real world. This is how you use that education you've worked so hard for. This is how you get out.*

Suddenly, an electric buzz groaned through the room. The lights dipped and crackled. The clinking of glasses paused as the lamps swelled once more.

And then the lights went out entirely.

Was this real?

Not now

The sun had set, and the interior of the house was close and dark brown around the guests. The windows were unfocused squares of gray street light. Scents seemed strangely pronounced: lilac and carpet cleaner, cinnamon and mold. The room was full of the wordless shuffle of a stockyard.

And in that brief pause in the conversation, in that shocked silence filled with neither the hum of voices nor of electronics, a high song floated through the dark. A precise, archaic melody, sung by a chorus of women's voices. Pure and thin, spreading from a thread of sound to a river of one. It took only a moment for Adam to realize that the words were not in English:

Rex Corvus, parate Regis Corvi.

Adam felt charged from his feet to his fingertips.

Somewhere in this darkness, Gansey was hearing this, too. Adam could *sense* him hearing it. These voices were true in a way that nothing else had been that day. Adam remembered all at once what it felt like to feel, to be real, to be *Adam*, instead of *my friend, Adam Parrish, give him your card.* He couldn't believe what a huge difference there was between those two things.

The lights surged back on. Conversation collapsed back into place.

Some part of Adam was still lodged back there in the dark.

"Was that Spanish?" Gloria Elgin asked, her hand pressed to her throat. Adam could see the line of her makeup on her jaw.

"Latin," Adam said, trying to find Gansey's face in the crowd. His pulse still galloped. "It was Latin."

The Raven King, make way for the Raven King.

"What a funny thing," said Gloria Elgin.

Owen Glendower was the Raven King. There were so many stories of Glendower knowing the language of birds. So many stories of ravens whispering secrets to him.

"Probably a brownout," Adam replied. The business cards in his pocket felt irrelevant. He was still searching for the only pair of eyes in the room that mattered. Where *was* Gansey? "Everyone's air-conditioning on at the same time."

"That's probably true," Gloria Elgin said, comforted.

The conversation around them muttered, *Peabody kids have a funny sense of humor! I'll have another of those shrimp things. What were you saying? What did you do when the marble was cracked?*

There, across the room, was Gansey. His gaze seized Adam's and held it. Even though the lights were back on, the voices long dissipated, Adam could still sense the power of the newly wakened ley line surging beneath him, all the way back to Henrietta.

This glittering host had already moved on, but not Adam. Not Gansey. They were the only two living things in this room.

Do you see? Adam felt like shouting. *This is why I made the sacrifice.*

This was how he would find Glendower.

34

The inside of the old Camaro smelled like asphalt and desire, gasoline and dreams. Ronan sat behind the wheel, eyes on the midnight street. Streetlights fenced the asphalt, slashing reflections over the atomic orange hood. On either side of the road, the barren lots of car dealerships sprawled, eerie and silent.

He was as hungry as the night.

The color of the dash turned green-yellow-red under the traffic light above. In the cracked passenger-side mirror, Noah appeared anxious. He checked over his shoulder for cops. Ronan checked his teeth.

"Nice to see you, Noah," he said. He could feel every pump of his heart, every surge through his veins. "Been a while."

I did this, Ronan thought. The keys trembled against one another in the ignition. *I made this happen.*

Kavinsky was late, as always. Time, as he liked to say, was money, and though he had plenty of both, he enjoyed the thieving nonetheless.

"I've been trying," Noah said. He added: "I don't want to watch you die."

Without answering, Ronan rubbed a thumb over the worn numbers on the gearshift. The engine pounded his shoes through the pedals. If anything about the Camaro had been built for comfort, those features had been worn away by forty years of use. The small of his back was sticky against the cracked vinyl seat.

The clock didn't work, but the tachometer did. The reluctant sigh of air through the vents was feeble, but the crash of the pistons was anything but. The engine was the loudest concert in the world, slowly thrashing itself to pieces under the hood. The speedometer was numbered all the way up to 140. That was insanity. The car felt dangerous, and it felt fast.

"I'll get Gansey," Noah threatened.

"I don't think you can."

"How long till Kavinsky gets here?"

"Noah," Ronan said tenderly, placing his palm on top of Noah's cold, seven-years-dead hand, "you're starting to piss me off."

Headlights sliced across the rearview mirror. Seventeen minutes after he was due, Kavinsky arrived.

In the rearview mirror, Ronan watched a white Mitsubishi slow as it pulled up. Its black mouth yawned; the gritty knife on the side was identical to Kavinsky's previous car.

The Mitsubishi pulled up alongside the Camaro. The passenger window rolled down. Kavinsky wore his white-rimmed sunglasses.

"Lynch, you bastard," he said, by way of greeting. He didn't acknowledge Noah; he probably couldn't see him. Ronan rolled his wrist to flip his middle finger at Kavinsky. Muscle memory.

Kavinsky appraised the Pig. "I'm impressed."

I dreamt this. Ronan wanted to shout it.

But instead he jerked his chin at the Mitsubishi. It was hard to believe that it was real. He had just seen the last one burning from the inside out. Kavinsky must've run out and replaced it the very next morning. And the graphic? Maybe he'd done it himself, though it was hard to imagine Kavinsky really devoting time to anything that wasn't powdered.

Ronan said, "That makes one of us."

"Oh, this one's got a bit more going on. You don't like it?"

On the gearshift, Ronan's hand shivered a little. More headlights glittered across the mirrors — Kavinsky's pack of dogs. Their faces were anonymous behind dark-tinted windows, but Ronan knew the cars: Jiang's Supra, Skov's RX-7, Swan's and Prokopenko's matching Golfs. He'd beaten them all before.

"Brought the whole family," Ronan observed. In a few minutes, they'd all disperse to look out for cops. First glimpse of a radar and Kavinsky would be warned off, gone before the asphalt had cooled.

"You know me," Kavinsky said warmly. "I just hate to be alone. So, are you gonna fuck that old lady you're in, or are you just gonna hold her hand?"

Ronan raised his eyebrow.

Noah said, "Ronan, don't. Gansey'll kill you. Ronan —"

Through the open window, Ronan asked evenly, "You gonna race with those shades on, you Bulgarian mobster Jersey trash piece of shit?"

Kavinsky nodded slowly through the question as if he agreed, scratching his wrist on the top of his steering wheel. He looked very tired or very bored as he replied, "What I can never figure out —" the traffic light flicked to red, turning his tinted lenses crimson "— is if you or Gansey is on top."

Something black simmered inside Ronan, slow and ugly. His voice was cyanide and kerosene as he said, "What's going to happen is I'm going to beat *that* car and then I'm going to get out of *this* car and then I'm going to beat the shit out of you."

"Three-hundred-twenty horses say you're wrong, man." Kavinsky touched his neck. He wore a white tank, and his exposed shoulder was raw and beautiful as a corpse. "But keep dreaming."

His window slid back up. Barely visible through the asphalt-black tint, Kavinsky tossed his sunglasses onto the passenger seat.

The whole world was now the traffic lights above the two cars.

"Ronan," Noah said, "I have a super bad feeling."

"It's called being dead," Ronan replied.

"That's the sort of joke that's only funny if you're alive."

"Good thing I am."

"For *now*."

Wait for the green. Ronan's eyes were not on the traffic light overhead but on the light on the opposing street. When it turned yellow, he had two seconds to get off the line.

Ronan eased his foot off the clutch, pressed down on the gas, held the car in check. The tach quivered just below the red line. The engine was alive, snarling, rattling. The sound replaced Ronan's pulse. Smoke from the rear tires crept from beneath the car and into the still-open windows. Kavinsky's Mitsubishi was barely audible over the howl of the Pig.

For a single second, Ronan allowed himself to think of his father and the Barns and his dreams stretching out before him full of impossible things. He allowed himself to think of the part of himself that was a bomb, the wick burning fast and destructive, nearly gone.

The opposing light was still solid green. The traffic light overhead was red as a warning.

Want was eating him alive.

The opposing traffic light went yellow. One second. He slid his foot farther off the clutch. One second. The gearshift knob sweated beneath his palm.

Green.

The cars burst from the line. It was growl, growl, growl, and this, strangely audible: Kavinsky's primal laugh.

Shift.

Immediately, the Mitsubishi was nearly a length ahead. On either side of the street, the streetlights flickered and flared, measuring out life in epileptic bursts of light:

flash

cracked asphalt

flash

Aglionby sticker on the dashboard

flash

Noah's widened eyes

They were bodies electric.

The Camaro caught the Mitsubishi in the second half, just as Ronan had expected. The engine raged at the top of second gear, and there it was. Crouched somewhere between second and third gear, somewhere between four thousand and five thousand RPMs, there was pure joy. Screaming along with the thousands of tiny explosions beneath the hood was a place where Ronan felt nothing but uncomplicated happiness, a dead and empty place in his heart where he needed nothing else.

Beside them, the Mitsubishi sagged. Kavinsky had buggered the shift from third to fourth. Like he always did.

Ronan did not.

Shift.

The engine roared anew. The car was Gansey's religion, and Ronan found it a worthy god. Its slender hood nosed ahead of the Mitsubishi. Put a length between them. Another half. It was nothing but up from here.

There was nothing inside Ronan. Glorious nothing, and behind that, more nothing.

But —

Something was wrong.

Kavinsky's window rolled down. He craned his head to meet Ronan's gaze in the rearview mirror, and he shouted something. The words were lost in the noise, but their meaning was visible. Teeth bared for a —*k* and then lips pursed —*ou*. Spat in a joyful curse.

The Mitsubishi exploded away from the Camaro. The streetlights snaked over the black windows, winking off and on across the widened gap.

It wasn't possible.

Ronan grabbed another gear — the only one left. The gas pedal crouched against the floor. Everything in the vehicle was shaking itself apart.

The Mitsubishi was still pulling away. Kavinsky's hand extended, middle finger waving.

Noah shouted, *"Impossible!"*

Ronan knew the numbers. He'd ridden in the Camaro. He knew Kavinsky's car. He'd beaten Kavinsky's car. Feeling was coming back to him like blood into a numb limb, stabbing him in fits and starts.

White as a fang, the Mitsubishi careened into the darkness in front of them. It was the sort of fast that didn't belong to cars. It was the sort of fast that wasn't a speed, it was a distance. Like a plane was here, and then it was there, in a moment. A comet was on this side of the sky, and then the other. The Mitsubishi was beside the Camaro, and then it wasn't.

It was so far gone into victory that the only engine note left was the Camaro's. Sparks rained down from the streetlights, searing tears dissipating on the pavement.

Only one month ago, Ronan had smoked the Mitsubishi in a far lesser car than the Camaro. There wasn't a reality that permitted Kavinsky's car to possess that sort of performance.

The streetlights flickered above them and went out. The Camaro smelled like a furnace. The keys dangled in the ignition, chinking metal against metal. It was slowly dawning on Ronan that he had been badly beaten.

This wasn't how it was supposed to end. He'd dreamt the keys, he'd gotten the Camaro, he'd made all the shifts and Kavinsky had not.

I dreamt this.

"Now you're done, right?" Noah asked. "Now you stop?"

But the dream was fading away. *Like they all do*, he thought. His joy was dissolving, plastic in acid.

"Stop," Noah repeated.

There was nothing left to do but stop.

But that was when one of the night horrors landed on the roof of the Camaro.

Ronan's first thought was the paint — the Pig was a piece of shit, but the paint was beyond reproach. And then one of the claws punched neatly through the windshield.

Whether or not it was in a dream or in reality, the night horror wanted the same thing: to kill Ronan.

35

onan!" Noah yelled.

The road spread out in front of them, black and empty. Ronan stepped on the accelerator. The Camaro responded with a churlish and enthusiastic growl.

Noah craned his neck. "Not working!"

A long splinter was forming in the glass of the windshield with the point of the night horror's claw as its epicenter. Ronan jerked the wheel back and forth. The Camaro skidded violently sideways, the body rolling back and forth.

"Goddamn it," Ronan muttered, fighting for control. This was not the BMW. Steering was an imaginary creature.

"Still there!" Noah reported.

The Camaro shuddered, the rear fishtailing.

Ronan's eyes darted to the rearview mirror. A second bird creature clung to the trunk.

This was bad.

Ronan snapped, "You could help!"

Noah fluttered his hands, pressing them on the window crank and then the back of the seat and finally the dash. He clearly didn't want to do whatever he was considering.

A squeal raked through the air. It was difficult to tell if it was a nail on metal or the sound of the bird man crying out. It clawed the hair up Ronan's arms.

"Noah, man, come on!"

Noah vanished.

Ronan craned his neck, looking.

With a tremendous crack, the bottom right corner of the windshield collapsed onto the dash. A claw snaked in.

Noah shouted, *"Brake!"*

Ronan slammed on the brakes. He had too much speed, too much brakes, too little steering. The Camaro swept from side to side as it hurtled on. The steering wheel did nothing.

Noah and a flash of black tumbled over the left side of the hood, leaving the windshield suddenly clear. The car kicked up as one of the tires ran over the bundle.

There was no time to see where the two of them went, because the jolt had unsettled the car — *Noah's already dead, he's all right*, Ronan thought frantically — and the Camaro was running out of road fast.

The smell of rubber and brake filled the car. It was an accident without a collision. The road went left but the car kept going straight.

No.

In agonizing detail, Ronan saw the telephone pole just as the passenger door made contact.

There was nothing gentle about this sound. It was not at all like the cars colliding at Kavinsky's substance party. This was metal rending. Glass shrieking. It was a five-finger metallic punch in Ronan's side.

Then it was over.

The car was utterly silent. Ronan didn't know if it had stalled or if he had killed it. The passenger-side door was buckled in halfway to the gearshift. The glove-box door had burst off entirely and the contents, including Gansey's EpiPen, had exploded throughout the front seat.

The realization was slowly dawning that everything had gone to shit.

Tck-tck-tck-tck.

The second night horror looked at Ronan, upside down. It was on the roof, staring through the windshield at him. Close enough for Ronan to see each individual scale around its sullen red pupil. With an experimental shove, the creature drummed nails on the windshield. What remained of the glass groaned where it met the car. With just a bit more weight it would all collapse.

"Do something." Noah was a voice, but nothing more, his energy expended.

But the impact had frozen Ronan. His ears rang.

The bird man hissed.

Ronan knew. He knew what he always did: It wanted him dead.

In his dreams, it didn't matter.

But he wasn't dreaming.

The night horror's head jerked up as a car slid by the Camaro. It was a sexy, messy, stylish slide, and the car performing it was a white Mitsubishi. The car spun round so the driver's side was illuminated by the Pig's headlights.

The night horror clambered down the windshield. Crouching on the hood, it hissed at the newcomer.

The driver's side window of the Mitsubishi slid down. Behind it was Kavinsky, his expression impossible to determine behind his white sunglasses. He leaned to get something from beneath his seat, and then he pointed it at the night horror. It took a moment for Ronan to realize what it was. It was a small, imaginary-looking gun, shiny as chrome.

Ronan dove down beneath the dash, curled small as he could.

Outside of the car, Kavinsky fired the gun. At the first shot, the bird man's hiss stopped abruptly. At the second, its weight slumped audibly against the hood. It didn't move after that, but Kavinsky fired four more times, until splatter appeared on the upper few inches of the Camaro's windshield.

There was no sound except for the sly growl of the Mitsubishi's engine. Ronan slowly sat up.

Kavinsky still leaned out his window, chrome gun hanging casually from his hand. He seemed to be enjoying himself, or at least seemed to be untroubled.

Ronan had to keep reminding himself he was awake. Not because he didn't feel awake, but because everything that had just happened felt so acutely like something he would dream. He opened the door — it seemed pointless to stay where he was, as the Camaro was clearly headed nowhere — and got out.

Standing on the asphalt, he stared at the dead night horror draped over the front of the ruined Camaro, and then he stared at Kavinsky.

"Try to keep up, Lynch," Kavinsky said. He withdrew into the car, and for a moment, Ronan was worried that he was leaving. Kavinsky was no ally, but he was human, and he was alive, and he had just saved Ronan's life, and that was something. But Kavinsky was just returning the gun to wherever he'd got it from and backing the Mitsubishi farther onto the shoulder.

He rejoined Ronan beside the Camaro, shoes crunching on grains of glass.

"Well, that's fucked," Kavinsky said approvingly.

And it was. The smooth line Ronan had run his hand along only hours before was now torqued, the metal hugged around the telephone pole. One of the wheels had come free and lay in the ditch several feet away. Even the smell in the air was disaster: chemicals spilling and substances melting.

Ronan scraped a hand over the back of his head. He felt like his heart was collapsing inside him. Each wall came down individually, crushing the one before it. "He's going to kill me. Goddamn it. He's going to kill me."

Kavinsky pointed to the night horror. "No, *that* was going to kill you, man. Gansey'll forgive you, man. He doesn't want to sleep alone."

All at once, Ronan was done. He seized the straps of Kavinsky's tank top and shoved him. "*Enough*, already! This isn't your fucking Mitsu. I can't go out and buy another one tomorrow morning."

With a knowing look, Kavinsky unhooked Ronan's fingers. He watched as Ronan pushed off, pacing, hands behind his head, eyes darting down the road to see if any other cars were coming. But there was no fixing this, no matter how Ronan looked at it.

"Look, Lynch," Kavinsky said. "It's simple. Wrap your tiny Celtic brain around this concept. What did your mom do when your goldfish died?"

Ronan stopped pacing. "I told you. It's not your rice rocket. I can get him another, but it won't be the same. He doesn't want another one. He wants this one."

"I'm going to be fucking patient with you," Kavinsky said, "because you've had a head injury. You're not listening to the words I say."

Ronan threw a hand toward the Pig. "This is not a goldfish."

"You people are such drama queens. I'm going to pop the trunk and you're going to scrape that thing into it. And then we're going to take a field trip to concept-land."

Ronan stared at him mistrustfully.

"Look, you're having a life-changing experience here. Get in the car before I need to get high again."

Ronan had nowhere else to go. He got in the car.

36

Several hours into the party, Gansey and Adam found themselves in the north-wing hallway between the back kitchen stairs and Gansey's old room. Vigorous conversation still murmured up through the floor. Adam wasn't sure of Gansey's situation, but he was aware that he himself was drunk. At least, his mouth tasted of champagne and the world seemed blunted and dark. He had not been drunk before. His father had done all of that for him.

They stood side by side on a lush purple Persian runner beside a docile Queen Anne side table covered with hunt-themed knickknacks. Dim gold versions of Adam and Gansey stood in a crazed black mirror hung on the wall. In the reflection, the ordinarily assured line of Gansey's mouth was twisted into something troubled. He tore the knot of his tie to a rakish angle.

"Can you believe," he asked tragically, "that I grew up in a place like this?"

Adam did not tell Gansey that he usually couldn't forget.

"I wish we could go back tomorrow," Gansey said. "I wish we could drive back and see if Cabeswater appeared."

When he said the word *Cabeswater*, Adam's neck spasmed, like a sly finger plucked a taut, anxious ligament. Another image tried to work its way through — a blink, and he'd see a man in the corner of his eye, standing behind his shoulder, looking at him in the mirror. Sad eyes and a bowler hat. *Why not?* Adam thought angrily. *Why the hell not?* "*Rex Corvus.* I'm never drinking again."

"You're not drunk," said Gansey. "It was ginger ale. Mostly. Look at our faces in there. We're older than we used to be."

"When?"

"Just a minute ago. We're getting older all the time. Adam — Adam, is this what you want? This?" He made an elegant, dismissive gesture toward the lower floor, pushing it all away from himself.

Adam said, "I want to get out of Henrietta."

He knew it was cruel to say, even if it was the truth. Because of course Gansey would say —

"I don't."

"I know you don't. Look, it's not like I'm trying to . . ." He was going to say *leave you behind*, but that was too much, even with the champagne lapping shores.

Gansey laughed terribly. "I'm a fish who's forgotten how to breathe in water."

But Adam was thinking about the suppressed truth: The two of them were on perpendicular paths, not parallel ones, and eventually, they'd have to go different ways. By college, probably. If not college, then after. A tension was building in him, like the one that sometimes haunted him late at night, where he wanted to save Gansey, or *be* Gansey.

Gansey turned to him; his breath was all mint leaves and champagne, him and them. He asked, "Why did you go to Cabeswater without me, Adam?"

Here it was, finally.

The truth was a complicated thing. Adam shrugged.

"No," said Gansey. "Not that."

"I don't know what to tell you."

"How about the truth?"

"I don't know what the truth is."

"I just don't believe that," Gansey said. He was starting to use *the voice*. The Richard Gansey III voice. "You don't do something without knowing why."

"That whole deal might work on Ronan," Adam replied. "But it doesn't work on me."

The Gansey in the mirror laughed humorlessly. "Ronan never took my car. He didn't lie to me."

"Oh, come on. I didn't lie. Something had to be done, or Whelk would've had control of the line right now." Adam cast a hand out in the direction of the stairs, back toward the party, toward the singing Latin. "*He* would be the one hearing that. I did the right thing."

"That wasn't the question. The question is: *that night*. You had to *walk right by me* to go. It's like you're so keen on being Adam Parrish, army of one."

He *was* Adam Parrish, army of one. Gansey, raised by these adoring courtiers, would never be able to understand that.

Adam's voice was heating. "What do you want me to say, Gansey?"

"Just tell me why. I've defended you to Blue and Ronan for weeks now."

The idea of his behavior being a topic of conversation infuriated Adam. "If the others have a problem with me, they can take it up with me."

"Damn it, Adam. *That's* not the point, either. The point is — just tell me it's not going to happen again."

"What's 'it'? Someone doing something you didn't ask for? If you wanted someone you could control, you picked the wrong person."

There was a pause, full of the distant ringing of silverware and glasses. Someone laughed, high and delighted.

Gansey just sighed.

And that sigh was the final straw. Because it didn't whisper of pity. It drowned in it.

"Oh, don't even," snapped Adam. "Don't you dare."

There was no switch this time. No flip from ordinary to angry. Because he'd already been angry. It was already dark, and now it was black.

"Look at you, Adam." Gansey held up a hand, demonstrating. Exhibit A, Adam Parrish, impostor. "Just *look*."

Adam felt stuffed full of the partygoers, their false civility, the glittering lights, the fakery of everything. He struggled for words. "That's right. 'There's Adam, what a mess. What do you reckon he was trying to say when he woke the ley line by himself? I don't know, Ronan. Let's not ask *him*.' How about this, Gansey? *It wasn't about you.* I was doing what needed to be done."

"Oh, don't lie to me. There were so many other ways."

"You weren't doing them. Either you want to find this thing or you don't." There was something brutally freeing about being able to say it out loud, everything he'd been thinking. He shouted, "And you don't need him. *I* do. I'm not going to sit back and let someone else take my shot out of this."

Gansey's eyes darted down the hall and back to Adam. *That's right, Gansey, don't wake the baby.* His voice was very low. "Glendower was not yours, Adam. This was mine first."

"You asked us. Either you meant it or you didn't. You did this."

Gansey lightly pressed a finger into Adam's chest. "*This?* I don't think so."

Adam seized Gansey's wrist. He wasn't nice about it. The suit was slippery as blood under his fingers. "I'm not going to be your minion, Gansey. Was that what you wanted? You want me to help you find him, you let me look *my* way."

Gansey jerked his arm out of Adam's grasp. Again his eyes darted down the hall and back. "You should look at yourself in the mirror."

Adam didn't.

"We do this, we do it as equals," Adam said.

Gansey glanced over his shoulder, furtive. His mouth made the *shh* shape, but not the sound.

"Oh, what?" Adam demanded. "You're afraid someone will hear? They'll know everything isn't perfect in the land of Dick Gansey? A dose of reality could only help those people!"

With a sudden twist, he swept all of the figurines from the Queen Anne table. Foxes in breeches and terriers seized in mid-flight. They all plunged to the floor with a satisfying and diseased smash. He raised his voice. "World's ending, folks!"

"Adam —"

"I don't need your wisdom, Gansey," he said. "I don't need you to babysit me. I got into Aglionby without you. I got Blue without you. I woke the ley line without you. *I won't take your pity*."

Now, finally, Gansey was silenced. There was something very remote about his eyes, or the set of his lips, or the lift of his chin.

He didn't say anything else. He just gave a tiny shake to the sleeve Adam had grabbed, letting the wrinkles fall out. His eyebrows were pulled together as if the action required most of his attention. Then he left Adam standing in the hall.

Next to Adam, the mirror reflected both him and the flickering form of a ghost no one but Adam could see. She was screaming, but there was no sound.

37

This was the dream: sitting in the passenger seat of Joseph Kavinsky's Mitsubishi, the odor of a crash clinging to Ronan's clothing, the white dash lights carving Kavinsky a gaunt and wild face, foully seductive lyrics spitting from the speakers, the vein-covered peaks of Kavinsky's knuckles on the gearshift between them. The smell in the car was sweet and unfamiliar, toxic and pleasant in the way Ronan had always thought marijuana would be before he came to Aglionby. Even the feel of the racing seats was unfamiliar; they held Ronan's shoulders and sucked his legs into the very depths of the car like a trap. Every bump in the road transferred directly to Ronan's bones, sharp and immediate. A touch of the wheel and they darted one way or another. It was like a car built to both feed on and produce anxiety.

Ronan didn't know if he loved it or hated it.

They didn't speak. Ronan didn't know what he would say anyway. It felt like anything could happen. All of his secrets felt dangerously close to the surface.

Kavinsky drove out of Henrietta, past Deering, into nowhere. The road turned from four lanes to two, and pure black trees pressed out the dull black sky overhead. Ronan's palms sweated. He watched Kavinsky change gears as he snaked along the back roads. Every time he shifted into the fourth gear, he missed the sweet spot. Couldn't he feel the car hanging when he did?

"My eyes are up here, sweetheart," Kavinsky said.

With a dismissive noise, Ronan lay his head back in the seat and looked out into the night. He could tell where they were now; they were nearly to the fairground where the substance party had been. Tonight the great floodlights were dark; the only evidence of the fairground was when the headlights swept over the bunting. They were only in the light for a moment, like color-less ghosts of flags, and then there was nothing but brush as Kavinsky pulled onto an overgrown gravel track before the fairground.

A few yards in, Kavinsky stopped. He looked at Ronan. "I know what you are."

It was like after the crash. After waking from a dream. Ronan was frozen in the sea, staring back at him.

The Mitsubishi charged forward, and the road gave way to a limitless clearing. In the headlights, Ronan saw another white car parked up ahead. As they pulled closer, the lights illuminated a huge spoiler on the trunk, and then revealed a portion of a knife graphic on the side. It was another Mitsubishi. For a moment, Ronan thought that it might be the old one, somehow, its dam-age miraculously hidden by the poor light. But then the headlights swung to another car parked beside it. This second car was also white with a large spoiler. Another Mitsubishi. A knife graphic peeked around the shadowed side.

Kavinsky pulled forward another few feet. It brought a third car into focus. A white Mitsubishi. They kept creeping forward, field grass rustling against the low bumper. Another Mitsubishi. Another. Another.

"Goldfish," Kavinsky said.

It wouldn't be the same.

But these were the same. Dozens upon dozens — now Ronan saw that the Mitsubishis were parked at least two deep —

of identical cars. Only they were not quite identical. The longer Ronan looked, the more differences he saw. A bigger wing here. A splattered dragon graphic there. Some had strange headlights that spread across their entire fronts. Some had no lights at all, just blank sheet metal where they should've been. Some were slightly taller, some were slightly longer. Some of the cars had only two doors. Some had none.

Kavinsky got to the end of the first uneven row and turned to the next. There had to be more than one hundred of them.

It wasn't possible.

Ronan's hands fisted. He said, "I guess I'm not the only one with recurring dreams."

Because of course these were from Kavinsky's head. Like the fake licenses, like the leather bands he'd given Ronan, like the incredible substances his friends would travel hours for, like every impossible firework he sent up each year on the Fourth, like every forgery he was known for in Henrietta.

He was a Greywaren.

Kavinsky hauled up the parking brake. They were a white Mitsubishi in a world of white Mitsubishis. Every thought in Ronan's head was a shard of light, gone before he could hold it.

"I told you, man," Kavinsky said. "Simple solution."

Ronan's voice was low. "Cars. An entire *car.*"

He hadn't even imagined it was possible. He had never even thought to try for more than the Camaro's keys. He'd never thought there was anyone outside of himself and his father.

"No — world," Kavinsky said. "An entire *world.*"

38

After the party had dwindled to nothing, Gansey crept down the back staircase, avoiding his family. He didn't know where Adam was — he was supposed to stay in Gansey's old room as guests of his mother occupied all of the other spare bedrooms — and he didn't go looking for him. Gansey was meant to sleep on the couch, but there would be no sleep for him tonight. So he quietly went outside to the back garden.

With a sigh, he sat on the edge of the concrete fountain. The nuances and wonders of the English garden were many, but most of them were lost after dark. The air was thick with the scent of boxwood, gardenias, and Chinese food. The only flowers he could see were white and drowsy.

His soul felt raw and battered inside him.

What he needed was to sleep, so this day would be over and he could start a new one. What he needed was to be able to turn off his memories, so that he could stop replaying the fight with Adam.

He hates me.

What he wanted was to be home, and home wasn't here.

He was stretched too thin to consider what was wise or what was not. He called Blue.

"Hello?"

He pressed his eyes closed. Just the sound of her voice, the Henrietta lull to it, made him feel uneven and shattered.

"Hel*lo*?" she echoed.

"Did I wake you up?"

"Oh, Gansey! No, you didn't. I had Nino's tonight. Is your thing done with?"

Gansey lay down, his cheek against the still sun-hot concrete of the fountain bench, and looked out of the midnight garden at the sodium-vapor paradise that was Washington, D.C. He held his phone to his other ear. His homesickness devoured him. "For now."

"Sorry for the noise," Blue said. "It's a zoo here, like always. And I'm just getting some — uh — yogurt and I'm — there we go. So what *do* you need?"

He took a deep breath.

What do I need?

He saw Adam's face again. He replayed his own answers. He didn't know which of them was wrong.

"Do you think . . ." he began, "you could tell me what is happening at your house right now?"

"What? Like, what Mom's doing?"

A large insect buzzed by his ear, coming in like a passenger jet. It kept going, though the flyby was close enough to tickle his skin. "Or Persephone. Or Calla. Or anyone. Just describe it to me."

"Oh," she said. Her voice had changed a little. He heard a chair scraping on her side of the phone. "Well, okay."

And she did. Sometimes she spoke with her mouth full, and sometimes she had to pause to answer someone else, but she took her time with the story and gave each of the women in the house full measure. Gansey blinked, slower. The take-out dinner smell had gone away and all that remained was the heavy, pleasant smell of growing things. That, and Blue's voice on the other end of the phone.

"Like that?" she asked finally.

"Yes," said Gansey. "Thanks."

39

Something strange and chemical was happening to the Gray Man. Once, he'd been stabbed with a screwdriver — Phillips head, bright blue handle — and falling in love with Maura Sargent was exactly the same. He hadn't felt a thing when the screwdriver had pierced his side. It hadn't been unbearable when he'd stitched it up as he watched *The Last Knight* on the television by the bed (Arbor Palace Inn and Lodging, local color!). No, it had gotten terrible only when the wound had begun to close. When he'd begun to regrow skin where it had been chewed away.

Now the ragged hole in his heart was regrowing out of the scar tissue, and he couldn't stop feeling it.

He felt it as he installed a new bank of meters in the Champagne Pogrom. They grinned and winked and chirruped at him.

He felt it as he sliced open the soles of his second pair of shoes and retrieved his spending cash from within. The bills ruffled fondly against his hand.

He felt it as he tried the doorknob of the Kavinskys' vinyl mansion. The front door swung wide open without resistance. He found a house full of wonders, none of them the Greywaren. Mrs. Kavinsky lifted her cheek slowly from the toilet, lashes fluttering blearily, nostrils snotty.

"I am a figment of your imagination," he told her.

She nodded.

He felt it as he leaned over Ronan Lynch's BMW in the parking lot of Monmouth Manufacturing and checked the VIN number. Ordinary VIN numbers were seventeen digits long and indicated what sort of car it was and where the car was made. This BMW's VIN number was only eight numbers long and corresponded to the date of Niall Lynch's birth. The Gray Man was senselessly delighted by this.

He felt it when Greenmantle called and railed angrily and anxiously about the length of time that had passed.

"Are you listening to me?" Greenmantle demanded. "Do I need to come there myself?"

The Gray Man replied, "Henrietta *is* a nice little town."

He felt it as he let himself into the rectory of St. Agnes and asked the priest inside if the Lynch brothers had ever confessed anything of note. The priest made a variety of shocked noises as the Gray Man dragged him across the small laminate counter of the kitchenette and the round breakfast table and through the automatic cat feeder provided for the use of the two rectory cats, Joan and Dymphna.

"You're a very sick man," the priest told the Gray Man. "I can find you help."

"I think," the Gray Man said, lowering the priest onto a case of new missals, "I've found some."

He felt it when every single machine in the Champagne Blight illuminated like a Christmas tree, flashing and wailing and surging for all that they were worth. When it first began, his first thought was: *Yes. Yes, that is exactly what it feels like.*

And then he remembered why he was there.

The lights flared, the meters surged, the alerts screamed.

This was not a test.

Slowly, inexorably, the readings drew him out of town, rewarding him with ever stronger results. The Gray Man felt it even now, in the inevitability of this treasure hunt. Every so often the machines would sag, the readings flickering. And then, just as he began to suspect the abnormality had vanished for good, leaving him adrift, the meters would explode in light and sound again, even stronger than before.

This was not a test.

He was finding the Greywaren today.

He could feel it.

40

At eleven the next morning, Gansey received a series of texts from Ronan. The first was merely a photograph. It was a close-up of a part of Ronan's anatomy that he hadn't seen before. An Irish flag was twist-tied to it. It was not the most grotesque display of nationalism Gansey had ever seen, but it was close.

Gansey received the text while in the middle of his mother's tea party. Drugged by the poor sleep on the sofa, numbed by the demure socialization occurring all around him, and haunted by the fight with Adam, he didn't immediately process the possible implications of such a photograph. Understanding was only beginning to prickle when a second text came in.

before you hear it from anyone else, i wrecked the pig

Gansey was suddenly very awake.

but don't worry man i got it under control say hi to your mom for me

In most ways, the timing was lucky. Because Gansey had inherited from his mother an extreme distaste of showing the uglier emotions in public ("Everyone's face is a mirror, Dick — endeavor to make them reflect a smile"), receiving the news while surrounded by an audience of fine china and laughing ladies in their fifties bought him time to figure out how to react.

"Is everything all right?" asked the woman across from him.

Gansey blinked at her. "Oh, yes, thank you."

There were no circumstances under which he would've

answered that question in any other way. Possibly if he'd discovered a family member had died. Possibly if one of his limbs had been separated from his body.

Possibly.

As he accepted a tray of cucumber sandwiches from the woman on his right to pass to the woman on his left, he wondered if Adam had woken up yet. He suspected Adam wouldn't come down, even if he were awake.

His mind replayed the image of Adam casting the figurines to the floor.

"These sandwiches are delightful," said the woman on his right to the woman on his left. Or possibly to him.

"They're from Clarissa's," Gansey said automatically. "The cucumbers are local."

Ronan took my car.

At that moment, Gansey's memory of Ronan and his filthy smile didn't look very different from Joseph Kavinsky and his matching dirty grin. Gansey had to remind himself that they had very important differences. Ronan was broken; Ronan was fixable; Ronan had a soul.

"I'm so pleased with the movement to keep food local," said the woman on his right, possibly to the woman on his left. Or maybe to him.

Ronan had charm. It was just buried deep.

Very deep.

"It tastes fresher," said the woman on his left.

The thing was, Gansey had known what happened on Friday nights when Ronan's BMW had come back smelling of burning brakes and a clutch under duress. And he'd taken the Camaro keys with him when he left for a reason. So this wasn't a surprise.

"Really, the advantages are in the reduced fuel and transportation costs," Gansey said, "that are passed on to the consumer. And to the environment."

But what did he mean *wrecked*?

Gansey's mind was on overload. He could feel his synapses murdering one another.

"One wonders about those trucking jobs that are lost, though," said the woman on the right. "Pass the sugar, would you?"

Say hi to your mom?

"I sort of feel the local infrastructure needed to process and sell the produce will end up with a null sum job loss," Gansey said. "The biggest challenge will be adjusting people's expectations to the seasonality of produce they've come to expect year-round."

Wrecked.

"You're probably right," said the woman on his left. "Though I do love having peaches in winter. I'll take the sugar, too, if you would?"

He passed a bowl of lumpy brown sugar cubes from the woman on his right to the woman on his left. Across the table, Helen was animatedly gesturing to a creamer shaped like a genie's lamp. She looked fresh as a newscaster.

Glancing up, she caught Gansey's eye, and then she tapped the corners of her mouth with her napkin, said something to her conversation partner, and stood up. She pointed at Gansey and gestured toward the door to the kitchen.

Gansey excused himself and joined her in the kitchen. It was the only part of the house that hadn't been renovated in the last two decades, and it was always dark and vaguely scented by onions. Gansey stopped by the espresso machine. He had an immediate, distant memory of his glamorous mother placing a frothing pitcher's thermometer under his tongue to check for fever. Time felt irrelevant.

The door swung shut behind Helen.

"What?" he asked in a low voice.

"You looked like you spent your last joy bill."

He hissed, "What does that even mean?"

"I don't know. I was just trying it out."

"Well, it doesn't work. It doesn't make sense. And anyway, I've got plenty of joy bills. Loads."

Helen said, "What's happening there on your phone?"

"A very small joy debit."

His older sister's smile shone brightly. "You see, it does work. Now, did you or did you not need to get out of that room?"

Gansey inclined his head in slight acknowledgment. Gansey siblings knew each other well.

"You're so welcome," Helen said. "Let me know if you need me to write a joy check."

"I really don't think it works."

"Oh, I think it has promise," she replied. "Now, if you excuse me, I must get back to Ms. Capelli. We're talking about space adaptation syndrome and the Coriolis effect. I just wanted you to know what you're missing."

"*Missing* is a strong term."

"Yes. Yes, it is."

She pushed through the swinging door. Gansey stood in the dim, root-vegetable-scented kitchen until the door had stopped. Then he called Ronan's number.

"Dick," Kavinsky said. "Gansey."

Pulling the phone back from his head, Gansey confirmed he had actually dialed the correct number. The screen read *RONAN LYNCH*. He couldn't quite understand how Ronan's phone had ended up in Kavinsky's hands, but stranger things had happened. At least now the text messages made sense.

"Dick-Three," Kavinsky said. "You there?"

"Joseph," Gansey said pleasantly.

"Funny I should hear from you. Saw your car running around last night. It's got half a face now. Poor bastard."

Gansey closed his eyes and let out a whisper of a sigh.

"Sorry, I didn't hear you," Kavinsky said. "Come again? I know, I know — that's what Lynch says."

Gansey set his teeth in a very straight line. Gansey's father, Richard Campbell Gansey II, had also gone to a boarding school, the now defunct Rochester Hall. His father, collector of things, collector of words, collector of money, offered tantalizing stories. In them, Gansey caught glimpses of a utopian community of peers intent on learning, keen with the pursuit of wisdom. This was a school that didn't just teach history — no, it wore the past like a comfortable jacket, beloved for all of its frayed ends. Gansey II described students — comrades, really — forming bonds of brotherhood that would last for the rest of their lives. It was C. S. Lewis and the Inklings, Yeats and the Abbey Theatre, Tolkien and his Kolbítar, Glendower and his poet Iolo Goch, Arthur and his knights. It was a community of scholars just outside of adolescence, a sort of Marvel comic where every hero represented a different arm of the humanities.

It was not toilet-papered trees and whispered bribes, front-lawn hacky sack and faculty affairs, gifted vodka and stolen cars.

It was not Aglionby Academy.

Sometimes, the difference between that utopia and reality exhausted Gansey.

"All right, now," Gansey said. "This was great. You giving this phone back to Ronan at any point?"

There was silence. It was a *slick* sort of silence, the sort that would make bystanders turn their heads to note it, same as a loud laugh.

Gansey didn't quite care for it.

"He's going to have to try harder," Kavinsky said.

"I beg your pardon?"

"That's what Lynch says, too."

Gansey could hear the crooked smile in Kavinsky's voice. He asked, "Do you ever think your humor veers too much on the side of prurient?"

"Man, don't SAT at me. Here's what's up. The Ronan you know is no more. He's having a coming-of-age moment. A — a — bildungsroman. Goddamn me! SAT *that*, Dick-dick-dick."

"Kavinsky," Gansey said evenly. "Where's Ronan?"

"Right here. *WAKE UP, FUCKWEASEL, IT'S YOUR GIRLFRIEND!*" Kavinsky said. "Sorry. He's totally pissed. Can I take a message?"

Gansey had to take a very long minute to compose himself. He discovered, on the other side of the minute, that he was still too angry to speak.

"Dickie. You still there?"

"I'm here. What do you want?"

Kavinsky said, "Same thing I always want. To be entertained."

The phone went dead.

As Gansey stood there, he suddenly recalled a story about Glendower, one that had always bothered him. Glendower was a legend in most ways. He'd risen in rebellion against the English when every other medieval man his age was giving old age and death the stink eye. He'd united the people, defeated impossible odds, and ridden across Wales on rumors of his magical powers. A lawyer, a soldier, a father. A mystical giant who'd left a permanent footprint.

But this story . . . some of the Welsh weren't convinced that throwing sticks at their English neighbors would improve Wales's dire straits. In particular, one of Glendower's cousins, a man named Hywel, thought Glendower was out of his lawyerly mind. In the way of most families, he expressed his difference of opinion by raising a small army. This might have put off most princes, but not Glendower. He was a lawyer and — like Gansey — a believer in the power of words. He arranged to meet Hywel alone in a deer park to talk it all over.

Gansey was untroubled with the story up to this point. This was the Glendower he'd follow anywhere.

Then, the two men spotted a deer. Hywel lifted his bow. But instead of shooting the animal, he let the arrow fly at Glendower . . . who had cleverly worn chain mail beneath his tunic.

Gansey would've preferred the story to end here.

But it didn't. Instead, unharmed by the arrow and enraged by the betrayal, Glendower pursued Hywel, stabbed him, and finally stuffed Hywel's body inside an oak tree.

All the stabbing and stuffing and utter loss of temper seemed rather ignoble. Gansey wished he hadn't ever found the story. There was no unreading it. But now, after hearing Kavinsky's slow laugh on the other end of the line, imagining Ronan drunk in his absence from Henrietta, picturing the Camaro in any state other than how he'd left it, Gansey thought he finally glimpsed understanding.

He was at once closer and farther from Glendower than he'd been before.

41

Ronan woke up in a movie theater seat.

Of course, it wasn't really a movie theater; it was just a basement home theater in a big, flimsy suburban mansion. In the light of day, he could see that it was done up with the works. Real movie seats, popcorn machine, ceiling projector, shelf full of action flicks and porn with uninventive titles. He vaguely recalled, with less acuity than a dream, watching an endless video of Saudi Arabian street racing on the big pull-down screen last night. What was he doing? He had no idea what he was doing. He couldn't focus on anything except one hundred white Mitsubishis in a field.

"You didn't throw up," Kavinsky noted, from his perch two seats away. He held Ronan's phone. "Most people throw up after drinking that much."

Ronan didn't say the truth, which was that he was not a stranger to drinking himself senseless. He didn't say anything at all. He just stared at Kavinsky, doing the math: *One hundred white Mitsubishis. Two dozen fake IDs. Five leather bracelets. Two of us.*

"Say something, Rain Man," said Kavinsky.

"Are there others?"

Kavinsky shrugged. "Hell if I know."

"Is your father one?"

"Is *your* father one?"

Ronan got up. Kavinsky watched him try all three of the insubstantial white doors until he found the bathroom. He shut the door behind himself and peed and splashed water on his face and stared at himself.

One hundred white Mitsubishis.

On the other side of the door, Kavinsky said, "I'm getting bored, man. You want a line?"

Ronan didn't answer. He dried his trembling hands, got himself together, and stepped out. He sat against the wall and watched Kavinsky do a line off the top of the popcorn machine. Shook his head when Kavinsky raised an eyebrow, an offering.

"You always this talkative after you drink?" Kavinsky asked.

"What were you doing with my phone?"

"Calling your mother."

"Say something else about my mother," Ronan said easily, "and I'll smash your face in. How do you do it?"

He expected Kavinsky to crack another lewd joke about his mom, but instead, he just fixed a gaze on Ronan, his pupils cocaine-huge.

"So violent. Such a PTSD poster boy. You know how to do it," Kavinsky said. "I saw you do it."

Ronan's heart twitched convulsively. It couldn't seem to get used to this secret being the opposite of one. "What are you talking about?"

Kavinsky leapt to his feet. "Your 'suicide attempt,' man. I saw it happen. The gate's right by Proko's window. I saw you wake up and the blood appear. I knew what you were."

That had been months and months and months ago. Before the street racing had even begun. All this time. Kavinsky had known all this time.

"You don't know a damn thing about me," Ronan said.

Kavinsky jumped to stand on one of the theater seats. As the furniture rocked beneath him, it sang a little — just a little scrap of a pop song that had been overplayed two years before — and Ronan realized it must be a dream thing, too. "Come on, man."

"Tell me how you do it," Ronan said. "I don't mean just the dreaming. The cars. The IDs. The —" He lifted his wrist to indicate the bracelets. The list could've gone on and on. The fireworks. The drugs.

"You have to go after what you want," Kavinsky said. "You have to know what you want."

Ronan said nothing. Under those parameters, it would be impossible for him. What he wanted was to know what he wanted.

Kavinsky's smile was wide. "I'll teach you."

42

Adam was gone.

At two P.M., Gansey thought he'd waited long enough for Adam. Bracing himself, he knocked on the bedroom door. Then he pushed it open and found the room empty and sterile. Afternoon sun washed over the unfinished silhouettes of old models. He leaned toward the bathroom and called Adam's name, but it was clear there was no one in either room.

Gansey's first thought was only mild irritation; he didn't blame Adam for avoiding everything having to do with the tea party, nor was he surprised he was lying low after last night's argument. But now he *needed* him. If he didn't tell someone about Ronan breaking parts off the car, he was going to self-immolate.

But Adam wasn't there. It turned out that Adam wasn't anywhere.

He was not in the onion-scented kitchen or the brick-floored library or the small, moldy mudroom. Not stretched on the stiff sofas in the formal living room, nor the voluminous corner couches in the casual family room. He was not holed up in the basement bar nor wandering in the humid garden outside.

Gansey replayed the argument from the night before. It felt worse this time around.

"I can't find Adam," Gansey told Helen. She'd been dozing in an armchair in the upstairs study, but when she saw his face, she sat up without complaint.

"Does he have a cell phone?" Helen asked.

Gansey shook his head and said, in a smaller voice, "We fought." He didn't want to have to explain further.

Helen nodded. He didn't say anything else.

She helped him look in the trickier places: the cars in the garage, the attic crawl space, the rooftop patio on the east wing.

There was no place for him to have gone. This wasn't a walking neighborhood; the closest coffee shop or retail area or congregation of women in yoga pants was three miles away, accessed by busy four- and six-lane northern Virginia streets. They were two hours from Henrietta by car.

He had to be here, but he wasn't.

The entire day felt imaginary: the Camaro news this morning, Adam lost this afternoon. This wasn't happening.

"Dick," Helen said, "do you have any ideas?"

"He doesn't disappear," Gansey replied.

"Don't panic."

"I'm not panicking."

Helen looked at her brother. "Yes, you are."

He called Ronan (*Pick up, pick up, for once pick up*) and he called 300 Fox Way (*Is Blue there? No? Has Adam — Coca-Cola T-shirt — called?*).

After that, it was no longer only Gansey and Helen. It was Gansey and Helen, Mr. Gansey and Mrs. Gansey, Margo the housekeeper and Delano the neighborhood gateman. It was a discreet call placed to Richard Gansey II's friend at the police department. It was evening plans silently shunted aside. It was a small force of private vehicles canvassing the nearby shaded streets and crowded shopping districts.

His father drove a '59 Tatra, a Czech specimen rumored to have once belonged to Fidel Castro, while Gansey cradled his phone in the passenger seat. Despite the air-conditioning, his palms sweated. The true Gansey huddled deep inside his body so that he could keep his face composed.

He left. He left. He left.

At seven P.M., as the thunderheads began to build over the suburbs and as Richard Gansey II once more circled the beautiful, green streets of Georgetown, Gansey's phone rang — an unfamiliar northern Virginia number.

He snatched it up. "Hello?"

"Gansey?"

And with that, relief melted through him, liquefying his joints. "Jesus, Adam."

Gansey's father was looking at him, so he nodded, once. Immediately, his father started looking for a place to pull over.

"I couldn't remember your number," Adam said miserably. He was trying so hard to make his voice sound ordinary that it sounded dreadful. He either didn't or couldn't suppress his Henrietta accent.

It's going to be all right.

"Where are you?"

"I don't know." Then, a little quieter, to someone else, "Where am I?"

The phone was passed to the other person; Gansey heard the sound of cars rushing by in the background. A woman's voice asked, "Hello? Are you a friend of this kid?"

"Yes."

The woman on the other end of the phone explained how she and her husband had stopped by the side of the interstate. "It looked like there was a body. No one else was stopping. Are you close by? Can you come get him? We're near exit seven on 395 south."

Gansey's mind shifted abruptly to adjust his image of Adam's surroundings. They had been nowhere close. It hadn't even occurred to him to look that far away.

Richard Gansey II had overheard. "That's south of the Pentagon! That's got to be fifteen miles from here."

Gansey pointed to the road, but his father was already checking the traffic to make a U-turn. When he turned, the evening sun suddenly came full in the windshield, blinding both of them momentarily. As one, they both threw up a hand to block the light.

"We're coming," Gansey told the phone.

It's going to be all right.

"He might need a doctor."

"Is he hurt?"

The woman paused. "I don't know."

But it wasn't all right. Adam said absolutely nothing to Gansey. Not while curled in the backseat of the car. Not while sitting at the kitchen table as Margo brought him coffee. Not after standing by the sofa with the phone clutched to his ear, talking to a doctor, one of the Ganseys' old family friends.

Nothing.

He'd always been able to fight for so much longer than anyone else.

Finally, he stood in front of Gansey's parents, chin lifted but eyes faraway, and said, "I'm very sorry for all the trouble."

Later, he fell asleep sitting up on the end of that same sofa. Without any particular discussion, the Gansey family in its entirety moved the conversation to the upstairs study, out of earshot. Although several engagements had been canceled and Helen had missed a flight to Colorado that evening, no one had mentioned the inconvenience. And they never would. It was the Gansey way.

"What did the doctor call it?" Mrs. Gansey asked, sitting in the armchair Helen had slept in earlier. In the green light through the verdant lampshade beside her, she looked like Helen, which was to say she looked like Gansey, and also to say she looked a little bit like her husband. All of the Ganseys sort of looked like one another, like a dog that begins to look like its owner, or vice versa.

"Transient global amnesia," Helen replied. She had listened to the phone conversation and following discussion with great interest. Helen very much enjoyed climbing down into other people's lives and muddling about there with a pail and a shovel and possibly one of those old-fashioned striped bathing suits with the legs and arms. "Two- to six-hour episodes. Can't remember anything past the last minute. But the victims — that was Foz's word, not mine — apparently know they're losing time while it's happening."

"That sounds dreadful," said Mrs. Gansey. "Does it get worse?"

Helen doodled on the desk blotter with a two-inch pencil. "Apparently not. Some people only have one episode. Some people get them all the time, like migraines."

"And it's stress related?" Richard Gansey II broke in. Although he didn't know Adam well, his concern ran deep and genuine. Adam was his son's friend, and so he had inherent worth. "Dick, do you know what he might be stressed about?"

It was clear this was a problem that all of the Ganseys were intent on solving before Gansey returned to Henrietta with Adam.

"He just moved out of his parents' house," Gansey said. He had started to say *trailer*, but he didn't like to think of what his own parents would do with that visual. He thought for a moment and then added, "His father beat him."

"Jesus Christ," his father remarked. Then: "Why do they let these people breed?"

Gansey just looked at his father. For a long moment, nothing was said.

"Richard," his mother chastised.

"Where is he staying now?" his father asked. "With you?"

He couldn't know how much or why this question smarted. Gansey shook his head. "I tried. He's staying at a room that belongs to St. Agnes — a local church."

"Is it legal? Does he have a car?"

"He'll be eighteen in a few months. And no."

"It would be better if he stayed with you," Richard Gansey II observed.

"He won't. He just won't. Adam has to do everything himself. He won't take anything that looks like a handout. He's paying his own way through school. He works three jobs."

The other Gansey faces were approving. The family as a whole enjoyed charm and pluck, and this idea of Adam Parrish, self-made man, appealed to them immensely.

"But he has to have a car," Mrs. Gansey said. "That would surely help. Can we not give him a little something to help him get one?"

"He won't take it."

"Oh, surely if we say —"

"He won't take it. I promise you, he will not take it."

They thought for a long moment, during which Helen drew her name in large letters and his father paged through *A Brief Encyclopedia of World Pottery* and his mother discreetly looked up *transient global amnesia* on her phone and Gansey contemplated just throwing everything he possessed into the Suburban and driving away as fast as he could. A very small, very selfish voice inside Gansey whispered, *What if you left him here, what if you made him find his own way back; what if he had to call you and apologize for once?*

Finally, Helen said, "What if I gave him my old college car? The crappy one I'm going to donate to that broken-car charity if he doesn't want it. He'd be saving me the trouble of arranging the tow!"

Gansey frowned. "Which crappy car?"

"Obviously, I would *obtain* one," Helen replied, drawing a fifty-eight-foot yacht on the blotter. "And say it was mine."

The older Ganseys adored the idea. Mrs. Gansey was already on the phone. The collective mood had buoyed with the implementation of this plan. Gansey felt it would take more than a car to relieve Adam's stress, but the truth was that he *did* need a vehicle. And if Adam really did buy Helen's story, it wouldn't hurt a damn thing.

Gansey couldn't shake the image of Adam by the side of the interstate, walking, walking, walking. Knowing he was forgetting what he was doing, but unable to stop. Unable to remember Gansey's number, even when people *did* stop to help.

I don't need your wisdom, Gansey.

So there was nothing he could do about it.

43

"Okay, Princess," Kavinsky said, presenting a six-pack to Ronan. "Show me what you can do."

They were back in the clearing near the fairgrounds. It was hazy, shimmering, dazed in the heat. This was a place for more dream math. One hundred white Mitsubishis. Two dozen fake licenses. Two of them.

One day.

Two? Three?

Time had no meaning. Days were irrelevant. They marked time with dreams.

The first one had been just a pen. Ronan woke in the frosty air-conditioning of the passenger seat, his fingers motionless over a slender plastic pen balanced on his chest. As always, he hovered above himself, a paralyzed non-participant in his own life. The speaker thumped out something that sounded good-natured, offensive, and Bulgarian. Biting flies clung hopefully to the exterior of the windshield. Kavinsky wore his white sunglasses, because he was awake.

"Wow, man, this is . . . a pen." Taking the pen from beneath Ronan's unprotesting fingers, Kavinsky tried it out on the dashboard. There was something dazzling about his total disregard for his own property. "What's this shit, man? Looks like the Declaration of Independence."

Just as in the dream, the pen wrote everything in a dainty

cursive, no matter how the user held it. Kavinsky quickly bored of its single-minded magic. He tapped the pen on Ronan's teeth along with the Bulgarian beat until feeling came back to Ronan's hands and he was able to knock it away.

Ronan thought it wasn't bad for a dream object produced on command. But Kavinsky regarded the pen scornfully.

"Watch this." Producing a green pill, he flicked it into his mouth and washed it down with some beer. Pulling off his sunglasses, he pressed his knuckles into one of his eyes, grimacing. Then he was asleep.

Ronan watched him sleep, head thrown to the side, tapping pulse visible through the skin of his neck.

Kavinsky's pulse stopped.

And then, with a violent start, Kavinsky jerked awake, one of his hands fisted. His mouth cracked into a grin at Ronan's surprise. With a theatric twist of his hand, he presented his dream object. A pen cap. He twitched his fingers until Ronan handed over the dream-pen.

The cap, of course, fit perfectly. Right size, right color, right sheen to the plastic. And why shouldn't it be perfect? Kavinsky was known for his forgery.

"Amateur," Kavinsky said. "*This* is the way to dream back Gansey's balls for him."

"Is this going to be a thing?" Ronan demanded. He was angry, but not as angry as he would've been before he started drinking. He put his fingers on the door handle, ready to get out. "Like, is this going to be what's funny to you? Because I don't want this that bad. I can figure it out myself."

"Sure you can," Kavinsky said. He cocked a finger at him. "Give him that pen. Write him a little note with it. In fucking

George Washington letters, 'Dear Dick, drive *this*, ex-oh-ex-oh. Ronan Lynch.'"

Ronan wasn't sure if it was Kavinsky using his real name or the refreshed memory of the ruined Pig that did it, but he dropped his hand from the door. "Leave Gansey out of this."

Kavinsky made a *whoo* shape with his mouth. "Gladly, Lynch. Here's the deal. You get your stuff from the same place every time, right?"

The forest. "Mostly."

"Go back there. Don't go anywhere else. Why would you want to go anywhere else? You wanna go where your shit's at. That's where you go. You're thinking of what you want before you go to sleep, right? You know it's gonna be there, in that place. Don't let it know you're there. It'll change on you if you do. You've gotta be in and out, Lynch."

"In and out," Ronan repeated. It didn't sound like a dream he'd ever had.

"Like a motherfucking thief."

Kavinsky revealed another two green pills in his hand. One he kept for himself. The other he offered to Ronan.

"See you on the other side?"

Fall asleep. Yes, you fall asleep. You are awake and then you close your eyes and thoughts press in and lucidity invades but then, eventually, you teeter on the edge of slumber and fall.

Ronan did not fall asleep. He swallowed the green pill and he was thrown into sleep. Hurled into it. Dashed, wrecked, destroyed into sleep. He rolled onto that shore a crushed version of himself, his legs gone beneath him. The trees leaned over him. The air grinned. Thief? *He* had been robbed.

In

Out

There was the object he had planned to take. Was it? He couldn't tell what it was. The trees wrapped their branches around it. Orphan Girl tugged and tugged.

In

Out

Kavinsky's voice, very clear: "Dying's a boring side effect."

Ronan snatched the metal of the thing. Inside him, a ventricle jerked restlessly. Blood poured into the empty atria of his heart.

"GET OUT!" screamed Orphan Girl.

His eyelids flashed open.

"Welcome back to the land of the living, sailor." Kavinsky leaned over him. "Remember: You take the pill, or it'll take you."

Ronan couldn't move. Kavinsky gave his chest a supportive thump of the fist.

"You're all right," he said amiably. He poured some beer into Ronan's unprotesting lips and finished it himself. The sun looked strange outside the windshield, like time had passed, or the car had moved. "What the hell do you even have there?"

Ronan's arms regained sensation. He held a metal cage with a tiny glass Camaro in it. It bore no resemblance to the boom box he'd planned to take out. It bore only a slightly better resemblance to the actual Camaro. Inside the glass car was an anonymous driver, his facial expression vaguely shocked.

"Dear Dick," Kavinsky said. "Drive *this!*"

This time, Ronan laughed. Kavinsky showed him his own prize: a silver gun with the words *DREAM KILLER* engraved on the muzzle.

"You didn't sneak in, did you?" he said accusingly. "Sneak in, sneak out. Get your stuff, get out. Before the place notices."

"Fucking pill," Ronan said.

"It's a wonder drug. My mom loves the hell out of these, man. When she starts breaking shit in the house, I grind one of these for her. Put it in her smoothie. You can make a joke there, man. It's easy. Go on. I left it wide open for you."

"What is your place?"

Kavinsky set two more green pills on the dash; they danced and jittered along to the beat of the speakers. The song slyly told Ronan: Ape махай се, ape махай се, ape махай се. Kavinsky handed him a beer.

"My secret place? You want into my secret place?" Kavinsky howled a laugh. "I knew it."

"Fine. Don't tell me. You put pills in your mom's drink?"

"Only when she steals my stuff. She wasn't such a bitch back in Jersey."

Ronan didn't know much about Kavinsky's home life, other than the legend everyone knew: His father, rich and powerful and Bulgarian, lived in Jersey where he was possibly a mobster. His mother, tanned and fit and made of non-factory-standard parts, lived in the suburban mansion with Kavinsky. This was the story Kavinsky told. That was the legend. The *rumor* was his mother's nasal septum had been eaten away by cocaine and his father's patriarchal instinct had died when Kavinsky tried to kill him.

With Kavinsky, it had always been hard to say what was real. Now, looking at him holding a fraudulently perfect chrome firearm, it was even harder.

"Is it true you tried to kill your father?" Ronan asked. He looked right at Kavinsky when he said it. His unflinching gaze was his second finest weapon, after his silence.

Kavinsky didn't look away. "I never *try* to do anything, man. I do what I mean to."

"Rumor has it that's why you're here and not Jersey."

"He tried to kill *me*," Kavinsky replied. His eyes glittered. He had no irises. Just black and white. The line of his smile was ugly and lascivious. "And he doesn't always do what he means to. And anyway, I'm harder to kill than that. You kill your old man?"

"No," Ronan said. "This killed him."

"Like father, like son," Kavinsky noted. "You ready to go again?"

Ronan was.

Pills on tongue. Chase it with beer.

This time, he saw the ground coming. Like being spat from the air. He had time to hold his thought, hold his breath, curl his body. He rolled into the dream. Fast. Tossed from a moving vehicle.

Soundlessly, he rolled into the trees.

They watched each other. A strange bird screamed. Orphan Girl was nowhere to be seen.

Ronan ducked low. He was quiet as rain under a root. He thought:

bomb

And there it was, a Molotov cocktail, not very different from the one he'd thrown into the Mitsubishi. Three rocks jutted from the damp forest floor, only the tips visible, eroded teeth, mossy gums. The bottle was tipped between them.

Ronan crept forward. Closed his fingers around the dew-covered neck of the bottle.

Te vidimus, Greywaren, whispered one of the trees.

(We see you, Greywaren.)

He clenched his hand around the bomb. He felt the dream shifting, shifting —

He exploded awake.

Kavinsky was already back, doing a line of coke off the dash. The light outside was dull and dead, past twilight. His neck and chin were lit like a garden feature by the dash lights below. He wiped his nose. His already keen expression sharpened when he saw Ronan's dream object.

Ronan was paralyzed as usual, but he could see perfectly well what he'd just produced: a Molotov cocktail identical to those at the substance party — a T-shirt twisted and stuffed into a beer bottle full of gasoline. It looked just as it had in the dream.

Only now it was burning.

The flame, beautiful and voracious, had chewed well down into the glass. The gasoline was slicked up the side, reaching for demolition.

With a wild laugh, Kavinsky hit the window button with his elbow and seized the bomb. He hurled it into the dusk. The bottle only made it two yards before it exploded, shivering glass against the side of the Mitsubishi and in through the open window. The smell was terrific, an aerial battle, and the sound sucked all of the hearing out of Ronan's ears.

Hanging his arm out the window and looking profoundly unconcerned, Kavinsky shook glass shards off his skin and into the grass. Two seconds later, and he wouldn't have had any arms to worry about. Ronan wouldn't have had a face.

"Hey," Ronan said. "Don't touch my stuff."

Kavinsky turned his heavy-lidded eyes to Ronan, eyebrows raised. "Check it."

He lifted his dream thing: a framed diploma. Joseph Kavinsky, graduated from Aglionby Academy with honors. Ronan hadn't seen one to know if the creamy paper was correct, or if the wording was accurate. But he recognized the spattered signature from Aglionby correspondence. President Bell's artistic scrawl was unmistakable.

It was badly against Ronan's code to be impressed, much less show it, but the accuracy and detail was striking.

"You're too emotional, Lynch," Kavinsky said. "It's okay. I get it. If you had balls, it'd be different." He tapped his temple. "This is a Walmart. Just go to electronics, swipe some TVs, get out of there. Don't wallow around in there. This would help."

He gestured to the powder still dusting the dash. Barely there. A fine memory of powder. Ronan shook his head. He could feel Gansey's eyes on him.

"Suit yourself." Kavinsky retrieved another six-pack from the backseat. "Ready to go?"

And they dreamt. They dreamt and dreamt, and the stars wheeled overhead and away and the moon hid in the trees and the sun moved around the car. The car filled with impossible gadgets and stinging plants, singing stones and lacy bras. As the noon boiled down, they climbed out and stripped their sweaty shirts and dreamt in the heat instead. Things too big to be contained in a car. Again and again Ronan punched into the forest in his fraying dreams, snuck between the trees, stole something. He was beginning to understand what Kavinsky meant. The dream was a byproduct in all of this; sleep was irrelevant. The trees were just obstacles, a sort of faulty alarm system. Once he short-circuited that, he could take things from his mind without worrying about the dream itself corrupting them.

The light stretched long and thin, nearly to breaking, and then there was night with its tantalizing reflections off one hundred white cars. Ronan didn't know if it had been days or if this was the same night as before. How long ago had he wrecked the Pig? When was his last nightmare?

Then it was a morning. He didn't know if they'd already done a morning, or if this was a brand-new one. The grass was wet and the Mitsubishis' hoods were beaded sweatily, but it was hard to tell if it had rained or if it was merely dew.

Ronan sat against the rear fender of one of the Mitsubishis, the smooth surface cool against his bare back, and wolfed Twizzlers. They felt as if they floated in alcohol inside him. Kavinsky was inspecting Ronan's latest piece of work — a chain saw. After he'd satisfied himself it worked by mutilating some of the tires on the other Mitsubishis, he rejoined Ronan and accepted a single Twizzler. He was too high for food to be very interesting as anything besides a concept.

"Well?" Ronan asked.

Chainsawing had blasted little flecks of rubber across Kavinsky's face and bare chest. He said, "Now you dream the Camaro."

44

Now it seemed simple.

Pill. Beer. Dream.

A Camaro sat among the trees of the dream forest: no more difficult to imagine than any of the other dream objects Ronan had pursued. Just larger.

In

Out

Silently, he put his hand on the door handle. The leaves of the trees shivered above; a bird sobbed distantly.

Orphan Girl watched from the other side of the car. She shook her head. He put his finger to his lips.

Awake.

He opened his eyes on the morning sky, and there it was. A glory-red Camaro. Not perfect, but perfectly imperfect, smudged and scuffed as the Pig. Down to the scratch on the door where Gansey had backed it into an azalea bush.

The first sensation wasn't joy but relief. He had not ruined things — he had the Pig back, he could return to Monmouth without begging. And then the joy hit. It was worse than Kavinsky's green pills. He was hurled into the emotion. It pummeled and thrilled him. He'd been so proud of the puzzle box, of the sunglasses, the keys. How stupid he'd been then, like a kid in love with his crayon drawings.

This was a car. An entire car. It hadn't been there, and now it was.

An entire world.

Now it would be all right. Everything would be all right.

From the front of the car, Kavinsky sounded unimpressed. He'd lifted the hood. "I thought you said you fucking knew this car, man."

After Ronan's limbs had feeling in them again, he joined Kavinsky by the open hood. The defect was immediately apparent. There was no engine. Ronan could see all the way to the stubbled grass. It would probably run, of course. If it worked in the dream, it worked in real life. But that was no comfort.

"I didn't think of it," he said. "The engine."

The joy was fading as quickly as it had appeared. How could Ronan hope to hold all of the Pig's foibles in his head? Gansey wouldn't want a perfect Pig, a Pig that ran sans engine. He would want *his* Pig. He loved the Camaro *because* it broke down, not despite it. Despair rang in Ronan's thoughts. It was too complicated.

Kavinsky abruptly punched the side of Ronan's head. "Think? There's no thinking, fool! We're not professors. Kill your brain." He surveyed the empty engine compartment again. "I guess Dick can use this as a planter. Put his petunias and shit in here."

Irritated, Ronan slammed the hood shut. He climbed onto it — no point to sparing the paint from scratches — and flicked his fingers against his knee while he tried to get his mind back together. *No thinking.* Ronan didn't know a better way to get the car from his dreams. He didn't understand how to hold the concept inside him as he was thrust into sleep. He was weary of his dreams. They felt as tattered as the night horror's wings.

"Hey, man, I'm sure he'll like this one," Kavinsky said. "And if he doesn't, fuck him."

Ronan merely leveled his heaviest gaze. Kavinsky was not Gansey, so maybe he didn't understand its meaning. There would be no fucking of Gansey. Ronan hadn't intended to wreck the Camaro when he'd first taken it, but he had. He wasn't going to add insult to injury by bringing back this impostor. This car was not a truth. This car was a very pretty lie.

"This," Ronan said, pressing his hands flat against the warm metal of the car, "is a very shitty goldfish."

"Whose fault is that?"

"Yours."

Kavinsky had said he'd teach him. He was not taught.

"*Yours.* I practiced, man!" Kavinsky gestured broadly to the field of Mitsubishis. "You see all these losers? It took me months to get it right. Look at that bitch!"

He pointed to one with a single axle, right in the middle. The car rested sleepily on its front bumper. "I get it wrong, try it again, wait for my dream place to get its juice back, do it again, get it wrong, do it again."

Ronan repeated, "What do you mean, get your juice back?"

"The dream place runs out," Kavinsky said. "Walmart can't keep making TVs all night long! It's getting low now. Can't you feel it?"

Was that what he felt? The fraying around the edges? Right now, he could only feel anxiety, dulled to stupidity by beer.

"I don't have time to practice. I need it now or I can't go back."

Kavinsky said, "You don't have to go back."

This was the most nonsensical thing he'd said since this entire experience had begun. Ronan didn't even acknowledge it. He said, "I'm doing it again. I'm doing it right this time."

"Hell yeah, you are." Kavinsky retrieved yet more alcohol — maybe he'd been dreaming *that*, too — and joined Ronan on the hood of the faulty Camaro. They drank in silence for several minutes. Kavinsky poured a handful of green pills into Ronan's palm; Ronan pocketed them. He wished passionately for something besides Twizzlers. He was wasted on dreams.

If Gansey saw him now . . . the thought twisted and blackened in him, curled like burned paper.

"Bonus round," Kavinsky said. Then: "Open."

He put an impossibly red pill on Ronan's tongue. Ronan tasted just an instant of sweat and rubber and gasoline on his fingertips. Then the pill hit his stomach.

"What's this one do?" Ronan asked.

Kavinsky said, "Dying's a boring side effect."

It took only a moment.

Ronan thought, *Wait, I changed my mind.*

But there wasn't any going back.

Ronan was a stranger in his own body. The sunset cut into his gaze, slantwise and insistent. As his muscles twitched, he lowered himself onto his chest and then rested his cheek against the hood, the heat of the metal not quite painful enough to be unbearable. He closed his eyes. This wasn't the hurtling-to-sleep pill of before. This was a liquid fatality. He could feel his brain shutting down.

After a moment, he heard the hood groan as Kavinsky leaned over him. Then he felt the ridged callus of a finger drag slowly over the skin on his back. A slow arc between his shoulder blades, drawing the pattern of his tattoo. Then sliding down his spine, tensing every muscle it moved over.

The fuse inside him was burning to nothing, nothing at all.

Ronan didn't move. If he moved, the touch on his spine would stab him — a wound like this pill. No coming back.

But when his eyes slitted, battling sleep, Kavinsky was just doing another line of coke off the roof, body stretched over the windshield.

He might have imagined it. What was real?

Again the Camaro was parked in the dreaming trees. Again Orphan Girl crouched on the other side of it, eyes sad. The leaves quivered and faded.

He felt this place's power dissipating.

He crept toward the car.

In

Out

"Ronan," whispered Orphan Girl. *"Quid furantur a nos?"*
(Why do you steal from us?)

She was faded as Noah, smudgy as the dead.

Ronan whispered, "Just one more. Please." She stared at him. *"Unum. Amabo te.* It's not for me."

In

Out

But he didn't hide this time. He wasn't a thief. Instead, he stood, rising from his hiding place. The dream, suddenly aware, shuddered around him. Flickered. The trees leaned away.

He hadn't stolen Chainsaw, the truest thing he'd ever taken from a dream.

He wasn't going to steal the car. Not this time.

"Please," Ronan said again. "Let me take it."

He ran his hand across the elegant line of the roof. When he lifted his palm, it was dusted green. His heart thudded as he rubbed pollen-covered fingertips against one another. The air was suddenly hot, sweat sticky in the crease of his elbows, gasoline pricking his nostrils. This was a memory, not a dream.

He pulled open the door. When he got in, the seat burned his bare skin. He was aware of everything around him, down to the scuffed vinyl beneath the improperly restored window cranks.

He was lost in time. Was he sleeping?

"Call it by name," said Orphan Girl.

"Camaro," Ronan said. "Pig. Gansey's. Cabeswater, *please*."

He turned the key. The engine turned, turned, turned, finicky as it had always been. It was as real as anything had ever been.

When it caught, he woke up.

Kavinsky grinned in the windshield at him. Ronan sat in the driver's seat of the Pig.

Air sputtered in the air-conditioning vents, scented with gasoline and exhaust. Ronan didn't have to look under the hood to know that the thundering he felt in his feet came from a proper engine.

Yes-yes-yes.

Also, he thought he knew why Cabeswater had disappeared. Which meant he might know how to get it back. Which meant he might get his mother back. Which meant he might make Matthew smile for a little while longer. Which meant he had something besides a restored car to bring back to Gansey.

He rolled down the window. "I'm going."

For a moment, Kavinsky's face was perfectly blank, and then *Kavinsky* flickered back onto it. He said, "You're shitting me."

"I'll send flowers." Ronan revved the engine. Exhaust and dust swirled in a wild torment behind the Camaro. It coughed at twenty-eight-hundred rpm. Just like the Pig. Everything was back the way it was.

"Running back to your master?"

"This was fun," Ronan said. "Time for big-boy games now, though."

"You're a player in his life, Lynch."

The difference between us and Kavinsky, Gansey whispered in Ronan's head, *is we matter.*

"You don't fucking *need* him," Kavinsky said.

Ronan released the parking brake.

Kavinsky threw up a hand like he was going to hit something, but there was nothing but air. "You are *shitting me.*"

"I never lie," Ronan said. He frowned disbelievingly. This felt like a more bizarre scenario than anything that had happened to this point. "Wait. You thought — it was never gonna be you and me. Is that what you thought?"

Kavinsky's expression was scorched. "There's only with me or against me."

Which was ludicrous. It had always been Ronan against Kavinsky. There was never any possibility of *with.* "It was never going to be you and me."

"I will burn you down," Kavinsky said.

Ronan's smile was sharp as a knife. He had already been burned to nothing. "You wish."

Kavinsky made a gun of his thumb and finger and put it to Ronan's temple.

"Bang," he said softly, withdrawing the fake gun. "See you on the streets."

45

So now Adam had a car.

The vehicle was but one of three objects Adam had acquired that morning. As each of the other Ganseys had gone out the door, they'd all bestowed a gift, eccentric fairy godmothers. Richard Gansey II checked his tie in a hallway mirror and handed Adam a checked vest.

"I'm not as thin as I used to be," he told Adam. "I was going to give this to Dick, but it will suit you better, I think. Here, put it on."

It was not even a gift; it was an order.

Next was Mrs. Gansey, peering out the window to verify that her driver was out front before saying, "Dick, I've gotten you another mint plant to take back. Don't forget it. Adam, I picked you up a rubber plant, too. You boys never think about feng shui."

He knew it was because they had retrieved him pathetically from the side of an interstate, but he didn't feel he could refuse. It was a plant. And he had ruined their Saturday.

Gone, he thought. He'd ruined their Saturday, but he'd *entirely* lost *his* Saturday. Whatever made him Adam had just vanished while his body shambled on.

If he let himself think about it, the terror just —

It wouldn't happen again. It couldn't.

As the boys were headed out the door, Gansey holding his tiny mint plant and Adam struggling beneath a five-gallon pot of rubber tree, Helen came down dragging a tiny black wheeled suitcase.

"Dick," she said, "those guys from the tow place said they couldn't come this morning. Could you *please* take care of it before you go? I'm going to miss my flight."

Gansey, who'd already looked terse, increased the irritation on his face to officially harassed. "Does it run? Can we just drop it off?"

"It runs. I guess. But it's in Herndon, the drop-off."

"Herndon!"

"I know. That's why I was having it towed. It's costing me more to get it there than I'm getting to donate it. Hey, do you have any need for it? Adam, you want a piece-of-shit car? Save me the tow."

The offer felt imaginary. Consciousness was being played on a movie screen.

Three Ganseys, three gifts, and three hours back to Henrietta.

Don't let me lose control on the way home, Adam thought. *Just get me back, that's all I ask.*

His new car was of uncertain make and model year. It was a two-door something and smelled of automotive body fluids. The hood, passenger-side door, and right rear fender were clearly from three entirely different cars. It was a stick shift. Adam was in the peculiar position of knowing how to rebuild a clutch better than how to operate one. But he'd get better, with practice.

It was nothing, but it was Adam Parrish's nothing.

This day — this place — this life —

It felt like he'd always been here in D.C., born in the simmering asphalt petri dish of the city. He'd dreamt Henrietta and Aglionby. It was taking everything in him to remember that there was a future beyond this immediate moment.

Just get back, he thought. *Get back so you can find out . . .*

"Look, just flash your lights if something goes wrong," Gansey said, standing before the open door of his black Suburban. He ordinarily kept it here, but no one really trusted Adam's new vehicle to make the drive across the state. Gansey rocked the driver's side door a little. Adam could tell that he wanted nothing more than to ask, *Are you all right?* or *What do you* need, *Adam?* The mint plant, placed on the dash, peered anxiously around Gansey's shoulder.

"Don't," Adam warned.

A frown, angrier than the night before last. "You don't even know what I was going to say."

"It's possible I did."

Gansey swung the door another time. The Suburban was huge behind him. Adam's new car *and* the Pig would fit inside it, with room for a bicycle or two. Adam remembered how breathtaking its existence had been when he first learned of it. *Rich enough for two cars?*

"What was I going to say, then?"

The power lines shivered above Adam. Something was singing and shaking inside him. He needed to get back. Soon. That was all he knew.

Adam said, "I don't think we should do this now."

"*Are* we doing something now? I thought what was happening was that *you* were being —" With visible effort, Gansey checked himself. "Are you coming back to Monmouth or . . ."

No time. No time for that. He needed to stop waiting and start acting. He was no better than Gansey hoping for someone else to wake the ley line. He needed to move.

"I'm going to Fox Way to ask for advice," Adam replied.

Gansey opened his mouth. There were a hundred things he

could say, and ninety-nine of them would only make Adam angry. Gansey seemed to intuit this, because he took his time before he said, "I'll check up on Ronan, then."

Adam sank into the worn and dusty seat of his new old car. Whispers escaped from the air vents. *Fine, I'm coming, I'm coming.*

Gansey was still staring at Adam, but what did he want him to say? It was taking everything in him to remember who he was.

"Just flash your lights," Gansey said finally, "if something goes wrong."

46

When Maura opened the door of 300 Fox Way, she found the Gray Man standing pensively on the other side. He had brought her two things: a daisy-chain crown, which he somberly placed on her head, and a pink switchblade, which he handed to her. Both had taken some effort to procure. The first because the Gray Man had forgotten how to efficiently link daisies and the second because switchblades were illegal in Virginia, even if they were pink.

"I've been looking for something," the Gray Man said.

"I know."

"I thought it was a box."

"I know."

"It's not, is it?"

Maura shook her head. She stepped back to let him in. "Drink?"

The Gray Man didn't immediately step inside. "Is it a person?"

She held his gaze. She repeated, "Drink?"

With a sigh, he followed her in. She led him down the main hallway to the kitchen, where she (badly) made him a drink and then let him onto the back patio. Calla and Persephone were already positioned in chairs arranged where the shaggy lawn gave way to new puddles and old bricks. They looked ethereal and pleased in the long golden afternoon sunshine that had emerged after the storm. Persephone's hair was a white cloud. Calla's was three different colors of purple.

"Mr. Gray," Calla said, expansive and scathing. She assassinated a mosquito on her calf and then eyed the glass in Maura's hand. "I can tell already that drink's shit."

Maura looked at it sadly. "How can you tell?"

"Because you made it."

Straightening the daisy chain on her head, Maura patted the remaining chair and sat on the bricks beside it. The Gray Man sagged into it.

"Oh, dear," Persephone said, observing this bonelessness of the Gray Man. "So you found out, did you?"

By way of response, he drained his glass. The readings had taken him to a clearing with one hundred white Mitsubishi Evolutions and two drunk boys manifesting their dreams. He had watched them for hours. Each minute, each impossible dream, each overheard snatch of conversation had hammered in the truth.

"What happens now?" Maura asked.

The Gray Man said, "I'm a hit man, not a kidnapper."

Maura frowned. "But you think your employer might be."

The Gray Man was not sure what he thought Greenmantle might be. He knew that Greenmantle didn't like to lose, and he knew that he had been obsessed with the Greywaren for at least five years. He also knew he himself had bludgeoned the last Greywaren to death with a tire iron. Although the Gray Man had killed quite a few people, he had never destroyed any of the artifacts he'd been sent to collect.

This was all more complicated than he'd expected.

"It's definitely those two boys, isn't it." It wasn't a question, though. The Gray Man tried to imagine bringing one of them back to Greenmantle. He was unaccustomed to transporting *live* victims for any distance. It struck him as oddly distasteful, a different animal from outright killing.

"Two?" Calla echoed. She and Persephone looked at each other.

"*Well*," Persephone said in her small voice. She used a cocktail umbrella to rescue a gnat in her drink. "That makes more sense."

"It's not a thing," Maura said. "That's what's important. It's not a thing any more than . . . conjunctivitis is a thing."

Rubbing her eye, Persephone murmured, "That's a strangely unpleasant metaphor, Maura."

"It's nothing you can take back," Maura clarified. She added pointedly, "And we know at least one of the boys. We'd be very angry if you took him. *I'd* be very angry with you."

"He's not a very kind man," the Gray Man said. It hadn't gotten in the way of their relationship before; kindness had, until then, been largely lost on the Gray Man.

"So you couldn't explain what nice boys they are?" Persephone asked.

Calla growled, "They are not nice boys. Well, at least one of them isn't."

The Gray Man said, "I don't expect it would make a difference to him anyway."

With a deep sigh, he leaned his head far back and closed his eyes, as defenseless as he'd ever been. The afternoon sun lit his face and neck and muscled biceps, and also lit Maura looking at them.

They all took a drink, except for the Gray Man, who had already finished his. He didn't want to kidnap a boy, he didn't want to anger Maura, he wanted . . . he just wanted. Cicadas sang madly from the trees. It was so impossibly summer.

He wanted to stay.

"Well," Calla said, checking her watch and standing. "I don't envy you. I've got my boxing. Must run. Ta. Ta. Maura, don't get murdered."

Maura waved the switchblade.

Persephone, standing as well, said, "I'd give that to Blue, if I were you. I'm going to go work on my thing. My stuff. My PhD. You know."

The Gray Man opened his eyes, and now Persephone stopped in front of him, her hands folded around her empty glass. She looked very small and delicate and not-really-there in comparison to his knotted presence. She removed one hand from her glass to gently pat his knee. "I know you'll do the right thing, Mr. Gray."

She and Calla slid the door shut behind themselves. Maura scooted her butt a few inches closer and leaned against his leg. It struck the Gray Man as a very trusting gesture, putting her back to a hit man. His previously lifeless heart flopped hopefully. He carefully rearranged the daisy chain in her hair, and then he took out his phone.

Greenmantle answered at once. "Give me good news."

The Gray Man said, "It's not here."

There was a long pause. "Sorry, the connection is bad. Say it again?"

The Gray Man didn't like repeating himself unnecessarily. He said, "All of the readings are because of an old fault line that runs along these mountains. They're pointing you to a place, not a thing."

Another pause, uglier in quality than the first. Greenmantle said, "So, who got to you? Was it one of Laumonier's? What did he say he'd pay you? You know what — goddamn, this is not the day you want to mess with me. Today of all days."

The Gray Man said, "I'm not angling for more money."

"So you're keeping it for yourself? I feel like that should make me feel better, but it doesn't." Usually, it took Greenmantle a few minutes to work himself up to a frenzy, but it was clear the Gray Man had interrupted one already in progress. "All these years I've trusted you, you creepy, sick bastard, and now —"

"I don't have it," the Gray Man interrupted. "I'm not cheating you."

Beside him, Maura ducked her head and shook it a little. Even without knowing Greenmantle, she'd already guessed what the Gray Man knew: This wasn't going to work.

"Have I ever lied to you?" Greenmantle demanded. "No! I haven't lied to anybody, and yet, today, *everybody* is just insistent on — you know, why didn't you just wait four months and tell me you couldn't find it? Why didn't you make a better lie?"

The Gray Man said, "I prefer the truth. The energy anomalies follow the course of the fault and escape through the established bedrock in certain areas. I've photographed some of the abnormalities in plant growth these energy leakages have caused. The power company has been battling surges connected to the leakages for quite some time. And activity has only intensified because of an earthquake that happened earlier this year. There's full documentation of that available on online newspapers. I can walk you through it when I return the electronics."

He stopped. He waited.

There was a brief moment where he thought: *He will believe me.*

Greenmantle hung up on him.

The Gray Man and Maura sat quietly and looked at the large, spreading beech tree that took up most of the backyard. A mourning dove called from it, persistent and dolorous. The Gray Man's hand hung down and Maura stroked it.

"This is the ten of swords," he guessed.

Maura kissed the back of his hand. "You're going to have to be brave."

The Gray Man said, "I'm always brave."

She said, "Braver than that."

47

Gansey had only a few seconds of warning before the Camaro hit him.

He was sitting at a stoplight near Monmouth Manufacturing when he heard the familiar, anemic sound of the Pig's horn honking. Possibly he had imagined it. As he blinked out the windows and the rearview mirror, the Suburban shook slightly.

Something had pushed it from behind.

The Pig's horn quacked again. Rolling down the window, Gansey craned his head out to see behind the Suburban.

He heard Ronan's hysterical laugh before he managed to glimpse the Pig. And then the engine revved up and Ronan nudged the Camaro into the Suburban's rear bumper again.

It was about the sort of homecoming he should have expected after the disastrous weekend.

"HEY, OLD MAN!"

"*Ronan!*" shouted Gansey. He had no other words. *Wrecked.* The quarter panel he could see looked fine; he didn't want to see the rest. He wanted to preserve the idea of the Camaro, whole and entire, for a few moments longer.

"Pull over!" Ronan howled back. There was still rather a lot of a laugh to his voice. "Mennonites! Now!"

"I don't want to see it!" Gansey shouted back. The light turned green above him. He didn't move.

"Oh, *you really do!*"

He really didn't, but he still did as Ronan asked, pulling through the light and making the next right into Henrietta Farm and Garden (and Home), a complex of shops largely staffed by Mennonites. It was a fine one-stop destination for vegetables, antiques, doghouses, Western wear, military surplus, Civil War bullets, chili dogs, and custom chandeliers. He was aware of eyes from the outdoor vegetable stands as he parked the Suburban as far away from the buildings as possible. As he climbed out, the Pig thundered into the spot next to him.

And there wasn't a thing wrong with it.

Gansey pressed a finger to his temple, struggling to reconcile the texts from earlier with what he was seeing. It was possible Kavinsky had just been jerking his chain.

But still, here was Ronan, climbing from the driver's seat, which was impossible. The keys remained in Gansey's bag.

Ronan leapt from the car.

And this, too, was bewildering. Because he was grinning. Euphoric. It wasn't that Gansey hadn't seen Ronan happy since Niall Lynch died. It was just that there had always been something cruel and conditional about it.

Not this Ronan.

He seized Gansey's arm. "Look at it, man! *Look at it!*"

Gansey was looking. He was staring, first at the Camaro and then at Ronan. Then back again. He kept rinsing and repeating and nothing made any more sense. He stepped slowly around the car, looking for a hammered-out dent or a scratch. "What's going on? I thought it was wrecked —"

"It was," Ronan said. "It totally was." He released Gansey's arm, but only to punch it. "I'm sorry, man. It was a shitty thing for me to do."

Gansey's eyes were wide. He hadn't thought he would live

long enough to hear Ronan apologize for anything. He realized, belatedly, that Ronan was still talking. "What? What did you say?"

"I said," Ronan said, and now he grabbed Gansey's shoulders, both of them, and shook them theatrically, "I *said* I dreamt this car. I did this! *That's* from my head. It's *exactly* the same, man. I did it. I know how my dad got everything he wanted and I know how to control my dreams and I know what's wrong with Cabeswater."

Gansey covered both his eyes with his hands. He thought his brain was going to melt.

Ronan, however, was in no mood for introspection, his or anyone else's. He ripped Gansey's hands from his face. "Sit in it! Tell me it's any different!"

He pushed Gansey down into the driver's seat and draped Gansey's lifeless arms over the steering wheel. He considered the image before him as if analyzing a museum piece. Then he reached in over the steering wheel and snatched a pair of sunglasses that were sitting on the dash.

White, plastic, lenses dark as hell. Joseph Kavinsky's — or maybe a copy. Who was to say what was real anymore?

Ronan put the white sunglasses onto Gansey's face and regarded him once more. His face went somber for half a second, and then it dissolved into an absolutely wonderful and fearless laugh. The old Ronan Lynch's laugh. No, it was better than that one, because this new one had just a hint of darkness beneath it. This Ronan knew there was crap in the world, but he was laughing anyway.

Gansey couldn't help laughing along, rather more breathless. Somehow he had gone from such a terrible place to such a joyful one. He wasn't sure that the feeling would be so profound if he hadn't braced every bone in his body for an argument with Ronan. "Okay," he said. "Okay, tell me."

Ronan told him.

"Kavinsky?"

Ronan explained.

Gansey rested his cheek against the hot steering wheel. That, too, was comforting. He should have never gone without this car. He was never getting out of it again.

Joseph Kavinsky. Unbelievable.

"And what's wrong with Cabeswater?"

Ronan shielded his eyes. "Me. Well, Kavinsky, actually. We're taking all the energy from the line when we dream."

"Solution?"

"Stop Kavinsky."

They eyed each other.

"I don't suppose," Gansey said slowly, "that we could just ask him nicely."

"Hey, Churchill tried to negotiate with Hitler."

Gansey frowned. "Did he?"

"Probably."

Letting out a huge breath, Gansey closed his eyes and let the steering wheel cook his face. This was home: Henrietta, the Pig, Ronan. Nearly. His thoughts darted toward Adam, toward Blue, and rabbited away.

"How was your party, man?" Ronan asked, kicking Gansey's knee through the open door. "How'd Parrish do?"

Gansey opened his eyes. "Oh, he brought down the house."

48

At about the same time that Gansey was donning a pair of white sunglasses, Blue biked two neighborhoods over from her house. She carried the Camaro wheel, the shield boss, and a small pink switchblade.

She was decidedly uncomfortable with the switchblade. Although she very much liked the *idea* of it — Blue Sargent, desperado; Blue Sargent, superhero; Blue Sargent, badass — she suspected that the only thing she would cut the first time she opened it was herself. But Maura had insisted.

"Switchblades are illegal," Blue protested.

"So's crime," Maura replied.

Crime was all the papers — yes, papers, plural, because against all reason, Henrietta had two of them — could talk about. All over town, increasingly fearful citizens reported break-ins. The accounts were conflicting, however — some said they had seen a single man, others two men, and still others said gangs of five or six.

"That means none of them are true," Blue said scathingly. She was skeptical of mainstream journalism.

"Or all of them," Maura replied.

"Did your hit-man boyfriend tell you that?"

Maura said, "He's not my boyfriend."

By the time Blue parked her bike outside the rambler where Calla took boxing lessons, she was feeling sticky and unappealing. The shaded lawn had no effect at all as she trudged across it to the door and rang the bell with her elbow.

"Hello, lady," said Mike, the enormous man who taught Calla. He was as wide as Blue was tall — which, in all fairness, was not very wide. "Is that off a Corvette?"

Blue readjusted the pitted wheel beneath her arm. "Camaro."

"What year?"

"Uh, 1973."

"Ooh. Big block? 350?"

"Sure?"

"Nice, lady! Where's the rest of it?"

"Out having a grand old time without me. Is Calla still here?"

Mike opened the door wider to admit Blue. "She's just cooling down in the basement."

Blue found Calla lying on the worn gray carpet in the basement, a generous and out-of-breath mountain of psychic. There were an astonishing number of punching bags hanging and stacked. Blue placed the Camaro wheel on Calla's heaving stomach.

"Do your magic trick," she ordered.

"How rude!" But Calla reached up to fold her hands over the top of the pocked metal. Her eyes were closed, so she couldn't know what it was, but she said, "He's not alone when he leaves the car behind."

There was something chilling about the phrase. *Leaves behind.* It could have just meant "parked the car." But it didn't sound like that when Calla said it. It sounded like a synonym for *abandon.* And it seemed like it would take something pretty momentous to make Gansey abandon the Pig.

"When does it happen?"

"It already has," Calla replied. Her eyes opened and fixed on Blue. "And it hasn't yet. Time's circular, chicken. We use the same parts of it over and over. Some of us more than others."

"Wouldn't we remember that?"

"I said *time* was circular," Calla replied. "I didn't say memories were."

"You're being creepy," Blue said. "Maybe you mean to be, but in case you're just being accidentally creepy, I thought I'd let you know."

"You're the one dealing with creepy things. Running with people who use time more than once."

Blue thought about how Gansey had cheated death on the ley line, and how he seemed to be old and young at the same time. "Gansey?"

"Glendower! Hand me that other thing you've got there."

Blue traded the wheel for the shield boss. Calla held it for a long while. Then she sat up and reached for Blue's hand. She began to hum a little as she ran her fingers over the ravens on the boss. It was an archaic, haunted sort of tune, and it made Blue clasp her free arm around herself.

"They were dragging him at this point," Calla said. "The horses had died. The men were very weak. It wouldn't stop raining. They meant to bury this with him, but it was too heavy. They left it behind."

Left it behind.

The echo felt deliberate. Gansey would not abandon the Camaro unless he was under duress; Glendower's men wouldn't abandon his shield without similar distress.

"But it is Glendower's? Is he close?" Blue felt a little kick to her heart.

"*Close* and *far* is like *already happened* and *not happened yet*," Calla replied.

Blue tired of the enigmatic psychic talk. She insisted, "But they had no horses. So it's only as far as they could go on foot."

"People," Calla said, "can walk a long way if they have to."

She got up and returned the shield boss to Blue. She smelled like she'd been boxing. She sighed very noisily.

"Calla?" Blue asked suddenly. "Are you one of those people who reuses time? You and Mom and Persephone?"

By way of answer, Calla answered, "Have you ever felt like there is something different about you? Like there is *something more*?"

Blue's heart jumped inside her again. *"Yes!"*

Calla removed the keys to the Fox Way car from her pocket. "Good. Everyone should feel that way. Here. Take these. You're driving home. You need the practice."

Blue could get nothing more out of her. They bade Mike farewell (*Don't drive that wheel too fast, now!*), put Blue's bike in the trunk, and drove rather slowly home. As Blue attempted to park in front of the house without hitting a small three-colored car already parked on the curb, Calla clucked.

"Well," she remarked. "Trouble looks good today."

This was because Adam Parrish was waiting on their front step.

49

Adam sat awkwardly on the edge of Blue's bed. It felt strange to have so easily gained access to a girl's bedroom. If you knew Blue at all, the room was unsurprising — canvas silhouettes of trees stuck to the walls, leaves hanging in chains from the ceiling fan, a bird with a talk bubble reading WORMS FOR ALL painted above a shelf cluttered with buttons and about nine different pairs of scissors. Against the wall, Blue self-consciously taped up the drooping branch on one of the trees.

No time, no time.

He squeezed his eyes shut for just a second. He waited for her to stop messing over the trees so they could talk. She kept fiddling. He felt his pulse simmering inside him.

He stood up. He couldn't sit any longer.

Blue stopped abruptly. She leaned on her hands against the wall, expression watchful.

Adam had intended to begin the conversation with a persuasive statement on why Gansey's conservative approach to the quest was wrong, but that wasn't what he said. Instead, he said, "I want to know why you won't kiss me, and I don't want a lie this time."

There was silence. A rotating fan in the corner moved over both of them. The tips of the branches fluttered. The leaves spiraled.

Blue demanded, "That's what you came here for?"

She was mad. Adam was glad of it. It was worse to be the only person angry.

When he didn't answer, she kept going, voice ever angrier, "That's the first conversation you want to have after coming back from D.C.?"

"What does it matter where I came from?"

"Because if I was Ronan or Noah, we'd be talking about — about how the party went. We'd be talking about where you disappeared to and what you wanted to do about that and I don't know, real *things*. Not whether or not you got to kiss me!"

Adam thought it was the most irrelevant response ever, and she still hadn't answered his question. "Ronan and Noah aren't my girlfriend."

"Girlfriend!" Blue repeated, and he felt a disconnected thrill to hear her say the word. "How about *friend-friend*?"

"I thought we were friend-friends."

"Are we? Friends talk. You go walking to the Pentagon and I find out from Gansey! Your dad's a jerk and I find out from Gansey! Noah knows everything. Ronan knows everything."

"They don't know everything. They know what they were there for. Gansey knows because he was there."

"Yeah, and why wasn't I?"

"Why would you be?"

"Because you'd invited me," Blue said.

The world tilted. He blinked; it straightened. "But there wasn't any reason for you to be there."

"Right, sure. Because there's no girls in politics! I have no interest. Voting? What? I forgot my apron. I think I ought to be in the kitchen right now, actually. My rolling pin —"

"I didn't know that you —"

"That's my point! Did it even occur to you?"

It had not.

"You wouldn't have gone someplace without Gansey, though," Blue snapped. "You two make a grand couple! Kiss him!"

Adam cocked his head witheringly.

"Well, I don't want to be just someone to kiss. I want to be a real friend, too. Not just someone who's fun to have around because — because I have breasts!"

She didn't generally swear, but *breasts* felt as close to swearing as Adam could imagine at that moment. The combination of *breasts* and the morphing of the conversation annoyed him. "Nice, Blue. Gansey was right. You really can be a raging feminist."

Blue sealed her mouth. Her shoulders trembled slightly: not like fear, but like the tremors before an earthquake.

He shot out, "You still didn't answer my question. Nothing of what you just said actually has any bearing on *us*."

Her lips made a sour shape. "You want the truth?"

"It's what I wanted at the beginning of all this," Adam said, even though he didn't actually know what he wanted from her anymore. He wanted this fight to be done. He wished he hadn't come. He wished he'd asked her about Glendower instead. He wished he'd thought to ask her to the party. How could he have? His head was too full, too empty, too askew. He'd walked too far out, right past solid ground, but he couldn't seem to turn around.

"Right. The truth." She balled her fists and crossed her arms. "Here it is. I've been told by psychics my whole life that if I kiss my true love, I'll kill him. There it is. Are you happy? I didn't tell you right away because I didn't want to say *true love* and scare you off."

The trees wobbled behind her. Another vision was trying to manifest. He tried to untangle himself from it to sift his memories, trying to coordinate their near-kisses with her confession of this deadly prophecy. It didn't feel real, but nothing did.

"And now?"

"I don't *know* you, Adam."

That's not your fault, whispered the air. *You are unknowable.*

"And now?"

"Now? Now —" Finally, Blue's voice shook a little. "I didn't tell you until just now because I realized it didn't matter. Because it's not gonna be you."

He felt it like one of his father's punches. A moment of deadness and then blood rushing to the point of contact. And then it wasn't sadness, but the now-familiar heat. It tore through him like an explosion, busting windows and devouring everything in an instantaneous blast.

In slow motion he could imagine the swing of his hand.

No.

No, he'd done this before with her, and he wasn't doing it again.

He spun away, one fist on his forehead. With the other, he struck the wall, but not hard. Just like he was grounding himself, discharging. He tore apart the anger, limb from limb. Focused on the burning, terrible fire in his chest until it went out.

It's not gonna be you.

And at the end, all that was left was this: *I want to leave.*

There had to be some other place he hadn't been yet, some soil where this emotion wouldn't thrive.

When he turned back around, she was motionless, watching him. When she blinked, two tears appeared like magic on her cheeks. The fast tears. The ones that were in your eyes and down your chin before you realized you were crying. Adam knew about those.

"Is that the truth?" he asked. He asked it so quietly that the words came out gravelly, like a violin played too softly.

Two more tears had queued up, but when she blinked, they remained in her eyes. Shining little lakes.

Not you.

Not him with his shabby anger, his long silences, his brokenness.

Not you.

Look at you, Adam, Gansey's voice said. *Just* look.

Not you.

"Prove it," he whispered.

"What?"

Louder: "Prove it."

She started shaking her head.

"If it's not me, it's not going to do anything, is it?"

She shook her head harder. "No, Adam."

Louder. "If it's not gonna be me, Blue, it doesn't matter, does it? That's what you said. It's never gonna be me."

Miserably, she said, "I don't want to hurt you, Adam."

"Either it's the truth or it's not."

Blue put a hand on his chest and pressed. "I don't *want* to kiss you. It's not going to be you and me."

Not you.

Since the last time his father had hit him, Adam's left ear had been dead and unresponsive. No hissing, no static. Just the absence of sensation.

That was how his entire body felt now.

"Okay," he said, voice colorless.

Blue wiped her eyes with the back of her hand. "I'm sorry. I really am."

"Okay."

Feeling was coming back, but it was unfocused and dull. Shimmering and fuzzy. It wasn't going to be him and her. It wasn't going to be him and Gansey. There was no more *not here, not now.* It was here. It was now. It was just going to be him and Cabeswater.

I am unknowable.

He was going down the stairs, though he didn't remember leaving Blue's room. Had he said anything? He was just going. He didn't know where. Voices and images flickered around him, pressing crookedly.

One voice cut through the dissonance. It was the quietest in the house.

"Adam," Persephone said, catching his sleeve as he opened the front door, "it's time for us to talk."

50

ersephone gave him pie. It was pecan and she had made it and his taking it wasn't presented as an option.

Maura frowned at him. "Are you sure this is the right way, P? I guess you know best . . ."

"Sometimes," Persephone admitted. "Come on, Adam. We're going to the reading room. Blue can come in with you. But it will be very personal."

He hadn't realized Blue was there. He kept his head down. There was a scuff on his hand from his walk down the interstate, and he worried silently at the skin at the edges.

Blue said, "What's happening?"

Persephone flapped a hand as if it was too difficult for her to explain.

Maura said, "She's balancing his insides with his outsides. Making peace with Cabeswater, yes?"

Persephone nodded. "Close enough."

Blue said, "I'll come with, if you want me to."

All faces swung toward him.

If he went in by himself, it was nothing but this: Adam Parrish.

In a way, it had always been that. Sometimes the scenery changed. Sometimes the weather was better.

But in the end, all he had was this: Adam Parrish.

He made it easier to accept by telling himself again: *It's just the reading room.*

He knew it was not the truth. But it was shaped like the truth.

"I'd like to do it by myself," he said in a low voice. He didn't look at her.

Persephone stood up. "Bring your pie."

Adam brought his pie.

The reading room was darker than the rest of the house, lit only by blocky candles congregated in the center of the reading table. Adam set the plate on the table.

Persephone closed the doors behind her. "Take a bite of pie."

Adam took a bite of pie.

The world focused, just a little bit.

With the doors shut, the room smelled like roses after dark and a match just blown out. And with the lights off, it was strangely difficult to tell how large the room was. Even though Adam knew full well the tiny dimensions of the room, it felt massive now, like an underground cavern. The walls seemed distant and uneven, the space swallowing the sounds of their breathing and the movement of the cards.

Adam thought: *I could stop now.*

But it was only the reading room. This was only a room that should have been a dining room. Nothing was going to change in here.

Adam knew that none of these things was true, but it was easier to pretend that they were.

Persephone selected a frame from the wall. Adam just had time to see that it was a photograph of a standing stone in a ragged field, and then she set it glass-up on the table in front of him. In the dark and candlelight, the image disappeared. All that was visible was the reflection off the glass; it was suddenly a rectangle pool or mirror. The candlelight twirled and spun in the glass, not quite like the candlelight in reality. His stomach surged.

"You must feel it," Persephone said, on the other side of the table. She did not sit. "How out of balance you are."

It was too obvious to agree to. He pointed to the glass with its faulty reflections. "What is that for?"

"Scrying," she replied. "It's a way of looking other places. Places that are too far away to see, or places that only sort of exist, or places that don't want to be seen."

Adam thought he saw smoke spiral up against the glass. He blinked. Gone. His hand smarted. "Where are we looking?"

"Someplace very far away," Persephone said. She smiled at him. It was a tiny, secretive thing, like a bird peering from branches. "Inside you."

"Is it safe?"

"It is the opposite of safe," Persephone said. "In fact, you'd better have another bite of pie."

Adam took a bite of pie. "What will happen if I don't do it?"

"What you're feeling will only get worse. You can't really do the edge pieces first on this puzzle."

"But if I do it," Adam started — then stopped, because the truth bit and burrowed and *fit* inside him, "I'll be changed forever?"

She tilted her head sympathetically. "You've already changed yourself. When you made the sacrifice. This is just the end part of that."

Then there was no point *not* doing it.

"Tell me how to do it, then."

Persephone leaned forward, but she still didn't sit. "You have to stop giving things away. You didn't sacrifice your mind. Start choosing to keep your thoughts your own. And remember your sacrifice, too. You need to mean it."

"I *did* mean it," Adam said, anger rushing up, sudden and singing and pure. It was an undying enemy.

She just blinked at him with her pure black eyes. His fury shriveled.

"You promised to be Cabeswater's hands and eyes, but have you been listening to what it's asked you for?"

"It hasn't said anything."

Persephone's expression was knowing. Of course, it had. All at once, he knew that that was the cause of the apparitions and half-visions. Cabeswater *had* been trying to get his attention, the only way it could. All of this noise, this sound, this chaos inside him.

"I couldn't understand."

"It's out of balance, too," she said. "But that's a different ritual for a different problem. Now, look inside yourself, but know there are things in there that are hurtful. Scrying is never safe. You never know who you will meet."

He asked, "Will you help me if something goes wrong?"

Her black eyes held his. He understood. He'd left his only help outside in the kitchen.

"Beware of anyone promising you help now," Persephone said. "Inside yourself, it's only you who can help you."

They began.

At first he was aware only of the candles. The thin, high flicker of the true candles, and the twisted, circuitous burning of the candles in the mirrored glass. Then, a drop of water seemed to plunge from the darkness above him. It should have splashed on the glass, but instead it pierced the surface easily.

It landed in a tumbler of water. One of the chunky, cheap ones that used to fill his mother's cabinets. This one was in Adam's hand. Just as he was about to drink, he caught a flash of movement. He had no time to brace himself before light — sound —

His father hit him.

"Wait —!" Adam said, explaining, always about to explain, as he struck the faded counter of their kitchen.

It should have been done by now, the punch, but he seemed to be trapped *inside* it. He was the boy, the blow, the counter, the flaring anger that drove it all.

This lived in him. This punch, the first time his father had ever hit him, was always being thrown somewhere in his head.

Cabeswater, Adam thought.

He was released from the punch. As the tumbler crashed on the floor, too sturdy to smash, the drop of water slid out and began to fall again. This time it plummeted into a still, mirrored pool surrounded by trees. Blackness crept between the trees, lush and dark and living.

Adam had been here before.

Cabeswater.

Was he really here, or was it a dream? Did it make a difference to Cabeswater?

This place — he smelled the damp earth beneath fallen branches, heard the sound of insects working themselves under rotting bark, felt the same breeze touch his hair that breathed on the leaves overhead.

In the night water at Adam's feet, red fish circled. They mouthed the ripples where the droplet had broken the surface. The movement drew his eye to the dreaming tree on the opposite shore. It looked just as it had before: a massive old oak with a rotted cavern inside it, big enough to admit a person. Months ago, Adam had stood inside the tree and had a terrible vision of the future. Gansey, dying because of him.

Adam heard a groan. It was the woman he'd seen in his apartment, the very first spirit. She wore a pale, old-fashioned dress.

"Do you know what Cabeswater wants?" he asked.

Leaning against the rugged bark of the dreaming tree, the woman pressed the back of her hand against her forehead in distress. *"Auli! Greywaren furis al. Lovi ne . . ."*

It wasn't Latin. Adam said, "I don't understand."

Beside her, suddenly, was the man with the bowler hat, the one Adam had glimpsed at the Gansey mansion. The man begged, *"E me! Greywaren furis al."*

"I'm sorry," Adam said.

Another spirit appeared, hand outstretched to him. And another. And another. All of the flashes he had seen, a dozen figures. Incomprehensible.

A small voice at his elbow said, "I will translate for you."

He turned to see a small girl in a black frock. She was not unlike a miniature Persephone: mountainous white hair spun like cotton candy, narrow face, black eyes. She took his hand. Hers was very cold, and a little damp.

He shivered warily. "Will you translate truthfully?"

Her tiny fingers were tight on his. He had not seen her before, he was certain. Of all of the flashes and visions he'd had since making the sacrifice, she'd not been one of them. She was so like Persephone, but twisted.

"No," he said. "I can only help myself."

She tipped her head back, angry. "You're already dead in here." Before he could pull away, she clawed her other hand down his wrist. Three sharp lines of blood welled up. He could taste it, like she had torn his tongue instead.

It was like a bad dream.

No. If this was like a dream, if Cabeswater was like a dream, it meant it was all in his control, if he chose it. Adam shook himself free. He wasn't going to give his mind away.

"Cabeswater," he said out loud. "Tell me what you need."

He reached into the pool. It was cold and insubstantial, like sliding his hand against sheets. Carefully, he scooped out the single drop of water he'd followed into the vision. It tipped back and forth in his palm, rolling along his life line.

He hesitated. On the other side of this moment, he knew, there was something that would separate him from the others forever. How much, he didn't know. But he would have been somewhere they hadn't. He would be something they weren't.

But he already was.

And then he was in the drop of water. No longer did Cabeswater need to reach out to him through apparitions. He didn't need the clumsy flickers in his vision. No desperate pleas for his attention.

He was Cabeswater, and he was the dreaming tree, and he was every oak with roots digging through rocks, looking for energy and hope. He felt the suck and pulse of the ley line through him — what a crass, mundane term for it, *ley line*, now that he'd felt it. He could remember every other name for it now, and they all seemed more fitting. *Fairy roads. Spirit paths. Song lines. The old tracks. Dragon lines. Dream paths.*

The corpse roads.

The energy flickered and sputtered through him, less like electricity and more like remembering a secret. It was strong, all-encompassing, and then fading, waiting. Sometimes he was nothing but it, and sometimes, it was nearly forgotten.

And beneath it all, he felt the oldness of Cabeswater. The strangeness. There was something true and inhuman at its core. It had been there so many centuries before him, and it would exist for centuries after. In the relative scheme of things, Adam Parrish was irrelevant. He was such a small thing, just a whorl in the fingerprint of a massive being —

I didn't agree to give my thoughts away.

He would be Cabeswater's hands and Cabeswater's eyes, but he wouldn't be Cabeswater.

He would be Adam Parrish.

He sat back.

He was in the reading room. A drop of water sat on top of the framed photograph. Across from him, Persephone dabbed three bloody scratches on her wrist; her sleeve had been ripped through.

Everything in the room looked different to Adam. He just wasn't sure how. It was like — like he'd adjusted the aspect on his television, from wide screen to normal.

He didn't know how he'd thought before that Persephone's eyes were black. Every color combined to make black.

"They won't understand," Persephone said. She laid her deck of tarot cards on the table in front of him. "They didn't when I came back."

"Am I different?" he asked.

"You were different before," Persephone replied. "But now they won't be able to stop noticing."

Adam touched the tarot cards. It seemed a very long time ago that he'd looked at the deck on the table. "What am I supposed to do with them?"

"Knock on them," she whispered. "Three times. They like that. Then shuffle them. And then hold them to your heart."

He softly rapped his knuckles on the deck, shuffled the cards, and then grasped the oversized deck. When he held it to his chest, the cards felt warm, like a living creature. They hadn't felt like *that* before.

"Now ask them a question."

Adam closed his eyes.

What now?

"Put down four of them," Persephone said. "No, three. Three. Past, present, future. Faceup."

Carefully, Adam laid three cards on the table. The art in Persephone's deck was dark, smudgy, barely visible in this dim light. The figures on them seemed to move. He read the words at the bottom of each:

The Tower. The Hanged Man. Nine of swords.

Persephone pursed her lips.

Adam's eyes drifted from the first card, where men fell from a burning tower, to the second, where a man hung upside down from a tree. And then to the last, where a man wept into his hands. That third card, that utter despair. He couldn't take his gaze from it.

Adam said, "It looks like he's woken from a nightmare."

It looks, he thought, *like I will, if the vision from the dreaming tree comes true.*

When Adam lifted his eyes to Persephone, he was certain she was seeing the same things he was seeing. He could tell from the flattening of her lips, the remorse in her eyes. The room stretched out around them, black and limitless. A cave or an old forest or a flat, mirror-black lake. The future kept being a something Adam was thrown into: a quest, a sacrifice, the dead face of a best friend.

"No," Adam said softly.

Persephone echoed, "No?"

"No." He shook his head. "Maybe this *is* the future. But it's not the end."

Persephone said, "Are you sure?"

There was a note to her voice that hadn't been there before. Adam thought about it. He thought about the warm feeling to the deck of cards, and how he'd asked that question *what now* and they had given him this terrible answer. He thought about how he could still hear the sound of Persephone's voice echoing all around him, although it should have disappeared into the close walls of this reading room. He thought about how he had been Cabeswater and felt the corpse road snaking through him.

He said, "I am. I'm — I'm pulling another card."

He hesitated, waiting for her to tell him it wasn't allowed. But she just waited. Adam cut the deck, laid his hand on each stack. He took the card that felt warmer.

Flipping it, he placed the card beside the nine of swords.

A robed figure stood before a coin, a cup, a sword, a wand — all of the symbols of all the tarot suits. An infinity symbol floated above his head; one arm was lifted in a posture of power. *Yes*, thought Adam. Understanding prickled and then evaded him.

He read the words at the bottom of the card.

The Magician.

Persephone let out a long, long breath and began to laugh. It was a relieved laugh that sounded as if she'd been running.

"Adam," she said, "finish your pie."

51

Blue had indeed cut herself.

After Adam had gone into the reading room, she'd experimentally opened the switchblade and it had obligingly attacked her. It was just a scratch, really. It barely warranted a Band-Aid, but she put one on anyway.

She did not feel like Blue Sargent, superhero, or Blue Sargent, desperado, or Blue Sargent, badass.

Maybe she shouldn't have told the truth.

Even though it had been hours since the fight, her heart still felt jittery. Like it wasn't attached to anything and every time it beat, it rattled around in her chest cavity. She kept replaying their words. She shouldn't have lost her temper; she should have told him at the very beginning; she should have —

Anything but how it happened.

Why couldn't I have fallen in love with him?

He was sleeping now, thrown across the couch, lips parted in unselfconscious exhaustion. Persephone had informed Blue that she expected him to sleep for sixteen to eighteen hours after the ritual, and that he might experience light nausea or vomiting once he woke. Maura, Persephone, and Calla sat at the kitchen table, heads together, debating. Every so often, Blue heard snatches of conversation: *should have done it sooner* and *but he needed to accept it!*

She looked at him again. He was handsome and he liked her and if she hadn't told him the truth, she could have dated him like a normal girl and even kissed him without worrying about killing him.

Blue stood by the front door, her head leaning against the wall. But she didn't want that. She wanted *something more*.

Maybe there is nothing else!

Maybe she'd go for a walk, just her and the pink switchblade. They were a good pair. Both incapable of opening up without cutting someone. She didn't know where she'd go, though.

She crept up to the reading room, quietly, so that she wouldn't wake Adam or alert Orla. Picking up the phone, she listened to make sure no one was having a psychic experience on the other end. Dial tone.

She called Gansey.

"Blue?" he said.

Just his voice. Her heart tethered itself. Not completely, but enough to stop quivering so much. She closed her eyes.

"Take me somewhere?"

They took the newly minted Pig, which indeed seemed identical to the last one, down to the odor of gasoline and the coughing start of the engine. The passenger seat was the same busted vinyl bucket it had been before. And the headlights on the road ahead were the same twin beams of weak golden light.

But Gansey was different. Though he wore his usual khakis and stupid Top-Siders, he was wearing a white, collarless T-shirt and his wireframe glasses. This was her favorite Gansey, the scholar Gansey, not a hint of Aglionby about him. There was something terrible about how this Gansey made her feel at the moment, though.

When she got in, he asked, "What happened, Jane?"

"Adam and I fought," she said. "I told him. I don't want to talk about it."

He put the car in gear. "Do you want to talk at all?"

"Only if it isn't about him."

"Do you know where you want to go?"

"Someplace that isn't here."

So he drove them out of town and he told her about Ronan and Kavinsky. When he'd done with that, he kept driving into the mountains, onto ever more narrow roads, and he told her about the party and the book club and organic cucumber sandwiches.

The Camaro's engine growled, echoing up the steep bank beside the road. The headlights only illuminated as far as the next turn. Blue pulled her legs up and wrapped her arms around them. Resting her cheek on her knees, she watched Gansey switch gears and glance in his rearview mirror and then at her.

He told her about the pigeons and he told her about Helen. He told her about everything except for Adam. It was like describing a circle without ever saying the word.

"Okay," she said finally. "You can talk about him now."

There was silence in the car — well, less sound. The engine roared and the anemic air-conditioning blew fitful breaths over them both.

"Oh, Jane," he said suddenly. "If you'd been there when we got the call about him walking on the interstate, you would've . . ." He trailed off before she found out what she would've done. And then, all of a sudden, he pulled himself together. "Ha! Adam's communing with trees and Noah keeps reenacting being murdered and Ronan's wrecking and then making me new cars. What's new with you? Something terrible, I trust?"

"You know me," Blue said. "Ever sensible."

"Like myself," Gansey agreed grandly, and she laughed delightedly. "A creature of simple delights."

Blue touched the radio knob, but she didn't turn it. She dropped her fingers. "I feel terrible about what I said to him."

Gansey guided the Pig up an even more narrow road. It might have been someone's driveway. It was difficult to tell in these mountains, especially after dark. The insects in the close-pressed trees trilled even louder than the engine.

"Adam has killed himself for Aglionby," he said suddenly. "And for what? Education?"

No one went to Aglionby for education. "Not just that," she said. "Prestige? Opportunity?"

"But maybe he never had a chance. Maybe success is in your genes."

Something more. "This really isn't a conversation I feel like having right now."

"What? Oh — that is *not* what I meant. I mean that I'm rich —"

"Not helping."

"I'm rich in *support.* So are you. You grew up *loved,* didn't you?"

She didn't even have to think before she nodded.

"Me too," Gansey said. "I never doubted it. I never even thought to doubt it. And even Ronan grew up with that, too, back when it mattered, when he was becoming the person he was. The age of reason, or whatever. I wish you could have met him before. But growing up being told you can do anything . . . I used to think, before I met you, that it was about the money. Like, I thought Adam's family was too poor for love."

"Oh, but since *we're* poor but happy —" started Blue hotly. "The cheerful peasants —"

"Don't, please, Jane," he interrupted. "You know what I mean. I'm telling you I was stupid over it. I thought it was about trying so hard to survive that you didn't have the time to be a good parent. Obviously, that's not it. Because you and I, we're both . . . wealthy in love."

"I suppose," Blue said. "But that's not going to get me into community college."

"Community college!" Gansey echoed. His shocked emphasis on *community* hurt Blue more than she could admit out loud. She sat quietly and miserably in the passenger seat until he glanced over. "Surely you can get scholarships."

"They don't cover books."

"That's only a few hundred dollars a semester. Right?"

"Just how much do you think I make at a shift at Nino's, Gansey?"

"Don't they make grants to cover that?"

Frustration welled in her. Everything that had happened that day felt ready to explode out of her. "Either I'm an idiot or I'm not, Gansey — make up your mind! Either I'm clever enough to have researched this myself and be eligible for a scholarship, or I am too stupid to have considered the options and I can't get a scholarship anyway!"

"Please don't be angry."

She rested her head on the door. "Sorry."

"Jesus," Gansey said. "I wish this week was over."

For a few minutes, they drove in silence: up, up, up.

Blue asked, "Did you ever meet his parents?"

In a low, unfamiliar voice, he said, "I *hate* them." And a little bit later, "The bruises he'd come to school with. Who has he ever had to love him? Ever?"

In her mind, Adam pressed that fist against her bedroom wall. So gently. Though every muscle was knotted, wanting to destroy it.

She said, "Look there."

Gansey followed her gaze. The trees on one side of the road had fallen away, and suddenly they could see that the little gravel track they were on clung to the very side of the mountain, winding up like tinsel. All of the valley suddenly spread out below. Though hundreds of stars were already visible, the sky was still a deep blue, a whimsical touch from an idealistic painter. The mountains on the other side of the valley, however, were night-black, everything the sky was not. Dark and cool and silent. And between them, at the mountains' feet, was Henrietta itself, studded with yellow and white lights.

Gansey let the Pig slide to a stop. He stepped on the parking brake. They both gazed out the driver's side window.

It was a sort of ferocious, quiet beauty, the sort that wouldn't let you admire it. The sort of beauty that just always hurt.

Gansey sighed, small and quiet and ragged, like he hadn't meant to let it escape. She shifted her gaze from the window to the side of his head, watching him watch instead. He pressed his thumb against his lower lip — this was Gansey, that gesture — and then he swallowed. It was, she thought, just as she felt when she looked at the stars, when she walked in Cabeswater.

"What are you thinking?" Blue asked.

He didn't answer right away. Then, when he did, he kept his eyes trained on the view. "I've been all over the world. More than one country for every year that I'm alive. Europe and South America and — the highest mountains and the widest rivers and the prettiest villages. I'm not saying that to show off. I'm just saying it because I'm trying to understand how I could have been so many places and yet this is the only place that feels like home. This is the only place I *belong*. And because I'm trying to understand how, if I belong here, it . . ."

"— hurts so much," Blue finished.

Gansey turned to her, his eyes bright. He just nodded.

Why, she thought, agonized, *couldn't it have been Adam?*

She said, "If you find out, will you tell me?"

He's going to die, Blue, don't —

"I don't know if we're meant to find out," he said.

"Oh, we're finding out," Blue said with extra ferocity, trying to tamp down the feeling rising in her. "If you're not going to, I'll do it myself."

He said, "If you find out first, will you tell *me*?"

"Sure thing."

"Jane, in this light," he started, "you . . . *Jesus.* Jesus. I've got to get my head straight."

He suddenly threw open the door and got out, seizing the roof to pull himself out faster. He slammed the door and then walked around the back of the car; one hand scrubbed through his hair.

The car was utterly quiet. She heard the buzzing of night insects and singing of frogs and slow chirps of birds who should have known better. Every so often, the cooling engine let out a little sigh like a breath. Gansey didn't return.

Fumbling in the dark, she pushed open her door. She found him leaning against the back of the car, arms crossed over his chest.

"I'm sorry," Gansey said, not looking at her as she leaned on the car beside him. "That was very rude."

Blue thought of a few things to reply, but couldn't say any of them out loud. She felt like one of the night birds had gotten inside her. It tumbled and fumbled every time she breathed.

He's going to die; this is going to hurt —

But she touched his neck, right where his hair was cut evenly above the collar of his shirt. He was very still. His skin was hot, and she could very, very faintly feel his pulse beneath her thumb. It wasn't like when she was with Adam. She didn't have to guess what to do with her hands. They knew. This was what it *should* have felt like with Adam. Less like playacting and more like a foregone conclusion.

He closed his eyes and leaned, just a little, so that her palm was flat on his neck, fingers sprawled from his ear to his shoulder.

Everything in Blue was charged. *Say something. Say something.*

Gansey lifted her hand gently from his skin, holding it as formally as a dance. He put it against his mouth.

Blue froze. Absolutely still. Her heart didn't beat. She didn't blink. She couldn't say *don't kiss me.* She couldn't even form *don't.*

He just leaned his cheek and the edge of his mouth against her knuckles and then set her hand back.

"I know," he said. "I wouldn't."

Her skin burned with the memory of his mouth. The thrashing bird of her heart shivered and shivered again. "Thanks for remembering."

He looked back over the valley. "Oh, Jane."

"Oh, Jane, what?"

"He didn't want me to, did you know? He told me not to try to get you to come to the table that night at Nino's. I had to talk *him* into it. And then I made such an idiot of myself —" He turned back to her. "What are you *thinking*?"

She just looked at him. *That I went out with the wrong boy. That I* destroyed Adam tonight for no reason at all. That I am not sensible at all —

"I thought you were an asshole."

Gallantly, he said, "Thank God for past tense." Then: "I can't — we can't do this to him."

It was jagged inside her. "I'm not a thing. To *have*."

"No. Jesus. Of course you're not. But you know what I mean."

She did. And he was right. They couldn't do this to him. She shouldn't do it to herself, anyway. But how it made a disaster of her chest and her mouth and her head.

"I wish you could be kissed, Jane," he said. "Because I would beg just one off you. Under all this." He flailed an arm toward the stars. "And then we'd never say anything about it again."

That could've been the end of it.

I want something more.

She said, "We can pretend. Just once. And then we'll never say anything about it again."

What a strange, shifting person he was. The Gansey who turned to her now was a world away from the lofty boy she'd first met. Without any hesitation, she stretched her arms around his neck. Who was this Blue? She felt bigger than her body. High as the stars. He leaned toward her — her heart spun again — and pressed his cheek against hers. His lips didn't touch her skin, but she felt his breath, hot and uneven, on her face. His fingers splayed on either side of her spine. Her lips were so close to his jaw that she felt his hint of stubble at the end of them. It was mint and memories and the past and the future and she felt as if she'd done this before and already she longed to do it again.

Oh, help, she thought. *Help, help, help.*

He pulled away. He said, "And now we never speak of it again."

52

That night, after Gansey had gone to meet Blue, Ronan retrieved one of Kavinsky's green pills from his still-unwashed pair of jeans and returned to bed. Propped up in the corner, he stretched out his hand to Chainsaw, but she ignored him. She had stolen a cheese cracker and now was very busily stacking things on top of it to make sure Ronan would never take it back. Although she kept glancing back at his out-stretched hand, she pretended not to see it as she added a bottle cap, an envelope, and a sock to the pile hiding the cracker.

"Chainsaw," he said. Not sharply, but like he meant it. Recognizing his tone, she soared to the bed. She didn't generally enjoy petting, but she turned her head left and right as Ronan softly traced the small feathers on either side of her beak. How much energy had it taken from the ley line to create her? he wondered. Was it more to take out a person? A car?

Ronan's phone buzzed. He tilted it to read the incoming text:

your mom calls me after we spend the day together

Ronan let the phone fall back to the bedspread. Ordinarily, seeing Kavinsky's name light up his phone gave him a strange sense of urgency, but not tonight. Not after spending so many hours with him. Not after dreaming the Camaro. He needed to process all of this first.

ask me what my first dream was

Chainsaw pecked irritably at the buzzing phone. She'd learned a lot from Ronan. He rolled the green pill in his hand.

He wouldn't take anything out of his dreams tonight. Not knowing what they were doing to the ley line. But it didn't mean he couldn't still choose what to dream of.

my favorite forgery is Prokopenko

Ronan put the pill back in his pocket. He felt warm and sleepy and just — fine. For once, he felt fine. Sleep didn't feel like a weapon tucked inside his brain. He knew he could choose to dream of the Barns now, if he tried, but he didn't want to dream of something that existed in this world.

I'm going to eat you alive man

Ronan closed his eyes. He thought: *My father. My father. My father.*

And when he opened his eyes again, the old trees roamed upward all around him. The sky was black and star-full overhead. Everything smelled of hickory smoke and boxwood, grass seed and lemon cleaner.

And there was his father, sitting in the charcoal BMW he had dreamt all those years ago. He was an image of Ronan, and also of Declan, and also of Matthew. A handsome devil with one eye the color of a promise and the other the color of a secret. When he saw Ronan, he rolled down the window.

"Ronan," he said.

It sounded like he meant to say *Finally.*

"Dad," Ronan said.

He was going to say *I missed you.* But he had been missing Niall Lynch for as long as he knew him.

A grin cracked over his father's face. He had the widest smile in the world, and he'd given it to his youngest son. "You figured it out," he said. He held a finger to his lips. "Remember?"

Music wafted out the open window of the BMW that had been Niall Lynch's but was now Ronan's. A soaring bit of tune played by the uilleann pipes, dissipating into the trees.

"I know," Ronan replied. "Tell me what you meant in the will."

His father said, *"T'Libre vero-e ber nivo libre n'acrea."*

This Will stands as fact unless a newer document is created.

"It's a loophole," his father said. "A loophole for thieves."

"Is that a lie?" Ronan asked.

Because Niall Lynch was the biggest liar of them all, and he'd stuffed all of that into his eldest son. There was not much difference between a lie and a secret.

"I never lie to *you*."

His father started the BMW and flashed his slow smile at Ronan. What a grin he had, what ferocious eyes, what a creature he was. He had dreamt himself an entire life and death.

Ronan said, "I want to go back."

"Then take it," said his father. "You know how now."

And Ronan did. Because Niall Lynch was a forest fire, a rising sea, a car crash, a closing curtain, a blistering symphony, a catalyst with planets inside him.

And he had given all of that to his middle son.

Niall Lynch reached his hand out. He clasped Ronan's in his own. The engine was revving; even while holding Ronan's hand, his foot was already on the gas pedal, on the way to the next place.

"Ronan," he said.

And it sounded like he meant to say

Wake up

After the house had gone quiet, Blue got into bed and pulled the blanket over her face. Sleep was nowhere. Her mind was full of Adam's dull expression, Ronan's invented Camaro, and Gansey's breath on her cheek.

Her mind took the memory of mint and spun it into a related memory of him, one that Gansey didn't have yet: the first time she had ever seen him. Not at Nino's when he asked her out on Adam's behalf. But that night in the churchyard when all of the spirits of the future dead walked past. One year — that was the longest that any of those spirits had. They would all be dead before the next St. Mark's Eve.

She had seen her first spirit: a boy in an Aglionby sweater, the shoulders of it spattered darkly with rain.

"What's your name?"

"Gansey."

She couldn't make it untrue.

Downstairs, Calla's voice suddenly swelled angrily. "Well, I will break the damn thing myself if I find you using it again."

"Tyrant!" Maura shot back.

Persephone's voice murmured amiably, too low for eaves-dropping.

Blue closed her eyes, tight. She saw Gansey's spirit. One hand braced in the dirt. She felt his breath. His hands pressed into her back.

Sleep didn't come.

A few amorphous minutes later, Maura knocked the pads of her fingers on Blue's open door. "Sleeping?"

"Always," Blue replied.

Her mother climbed into Blue's narrow bed. She jerked at the pillow until Blue allowed her a few inches of it. Then she lay down behind Blue, mother and daughter like spoons in a drawer. Blue closed her eyes again, inhaling the soft clove scent of her mother and the fading mint of Gansey.

After a moment, Maura asked, "Are you crying?"

"Only a little."

"Why?"

"Generalized sadness."

"Are you *sad*? Did something bad happen?"

"Not yet."

"Ah, Blue." Her mother wrapped her arms around her and breathed into the hair at the base of Blue's neck. Blue thought about what Gansey had said, about being wealthy in love. And she thought about Adam, still collapsed on their sofa downstairs. If he had no one to wrap their arms around him when he was sad, could he be forgiven for letting his anger lead him?

Blue asked, "Are *you* crying?"

"Only a little," her mother said, and inhaled snottily and unbecomingly.

"Why?"

"Generalized sadness."

"Are you *sad*? Did something bad happen?"

"Not yet. A long time ago."

"Those are the opposite," Blue said.

Maura sniffed again. "Not really."

Blue wiped her eyes with her pillowcase. "Tears don't become us."

Her mother wiped her eyes on the shoulder of Blue's T-shirt. "You're right. What becomes us?"

"Action."

Maura laughed softly under her breath.

How terrible it would be, Blue thought, her mind on Adam again, *to not have a mother who loved you?*

"Yes," she agreed. "How wise you are, Blue."

On the other side of Henrietta, the Gray Man answered his phone. It was Greenmantle.

Without any particular preamble, he said, "Dean Allen."

The Gray Man, phone in one hand, book in the other, didn't immediately respond. He set his tattered edition of Anglo-Saxon riddles facedown on the side table. The television prattled in the background; one spy met another on a bridge. They were exchanging hostages. They'd been told to come alone. They hadn't come alone.

It was taking an unexpectedly long period of time for the Gray Man to register the meaning of Greenmantle's words. Then, once that had sunk in, it took him even longer to understand why Greenmantle was saying them.

"That's right," Greenmantle said. "The mystery's gone. It wasn't that hard to figure out who you were. Turns out Anglo-Saxon poetry is a very small field. Even at the undergrad level. And you know how well I do with undergrads."

The Gray Man hadn't been Dean Allen for a very long time. It was harder than one might expect to abandon an identity, but the Gray Man was more patient and devoted than most. Usually, one traded one identity for another, but the Gray Man wanted to be no one. Nowhere.

He touched the weathered spine of the riddle book.

ic eom wrætlic wiht on gewin sceapen

Greenmantle added, "So, I want it."

(I am a beautiful thing, shaped for fighting)

"I don't have it."

"Sure, Dean, sure."

"Don't call me that."

nelle ic unbunden ænigum hyran

nymþe searosæled

"Why not? It's your name, isn't it?"

(Unstrung I obey no man; only when skillfully tied —)

The Gray Man said nothing.

"So you're not going to change your story, Dean?" Greenmantle asked. "And yet you're going to keep taking my calls. So that means you know where it is, but you don't have it yet."

For so many years he'd buried that name. Dean Allen wasn't supposed to exist. There was a *reason* he'd given it up.

"Tell you what," Greenmantle said. "I *tell you what*. You get the Greywaren and call me by the Fourth of July with your flight confirmation number back here. Or I tell your brother where you are."

Hold still, Dean.

Logic swam away from the Gray Man. Very quietly, he said, "I told you about him in confidence."

"I paid you in confidence. Turns out he's eager to know where you are," Greenmantle said. "We had a chat, Dean. Says he lost touch with you in the middle of a conversation he's been wanting to finish."

The Gray Man turned off the television, but voices still hummed in the background.

"Dean," Greenmantle said. "You there?"

No. Not really. Color was draining from the walls.

"Do we have an agreement?"

No. Not really. A weapon didn't come to an agreement with the hand that held it.

"Two days is plenty of time, Dean," Greenmantle said. "See you on the other side."

53

For twenty-one hours, Adam Parrish and the Gray Man slept. While they slept without dreaming, Henrietta prepared for the Fourth of July. Flags climbed poles over car dealerships. Parade signs warned would-be parallel parkers to rethink their choices. In the suburbs, fireworks were bought and dreamt. Doors were locked and, later, busted open. At 300 Fox Way, Adam quietly turned eighteen. Calla was called into her office to make certain nothing important had been stolen during a break-in. At Monmouth Manufacturing, a white Mitsubishi with a set of keys in the ignition and a knife graphic on the side appeared in the parking lot overnight. It bore a note that read, *This one's for you. Just the way you like it: fast and anonymous.*

Gansey frowned at the disordered handwriting. "I think he needs to come to terms with his sexuality."

Ronan, chewing his leather bracelets, dropped them from his teeth and said, "There is no coming to terms with having three balls."

It was the sort of joke he normally made for Noah. But Noah wasn't there.

Back at the psychics' house, Adam woke up. According to Maura, he swung his legs over the sofa, walked into the kitchen where he drank four glasses of pomegranate juice and three cups of one of the more noxious healing teas, thanked Maura for the use of her couch, and then got into his tri-colored car and drove away, all within the space of ten minutes.

Fifteen minutes after that, Maura reported, Persephone came downstairs with a butterfly-shaped handbag and a pair of sensible boots with three-inch heels and laces all the way up her thighs. A taxi arrived and she climbed into it. It drove away in the same direction as the tri-colored car.

Twelve minutes after that, Kavinsky texted Ronan: *ballsack.* Ronan replied: *shitstack.* Kavinsky: *coming to 4th of July?* Ronan: *would you stop if you knew it was destroying the world?* Kavinsky: *god that would be awesome*

"Well?" Gansey asked.

Ronan said, "Wouldn't bet on the negotiations."

Seven minutes after that, Maura, Calla, and Blue climbed into the fatigued Ford, drove to get Ronan and Gansey, and headed into the simmering day.

Gansey looked like a king, even sitting in the shabby backseat of the shared Fox Way vehicle. Perhaps especially when sitting in the backseat of a shabby vehicle. He asked, "What is it we're doing?"

Maura replied, "Action."

54

"hy are we here, man?" Ronan asked. His eyes followed Chainsaw as she cantered anxiously across the counter. He'd brought her to enough places that new locations didn't generally faze her for long, but she wouldn't be truly happy until she'd done a perimeter search. She paused to tap her beak on an absolutely darling bird-themed cookie jar. "There are more goddamn roosters than a Hitchcock movie."

"Are you referring to *The Birds*?" Gansey asked. "Because I don't recall any chickens in it. It's been a long time, though."

They stood in a homey, belowground kitchen in the basement of the Pleasant Valley Bed and Breakfast. Calla searched the cupboards and drawers; her version of Chainsaw's room check, possibly. She'd already discovered a waffle maker and a gun, and had placed both on the round breakfast table. Blue stood at the far doorway, peering around to where her mother had gone. Ronan assumed she and Gansey must have fought; she was as far away from him as she could get. Next to Ronan, Gansey reached up to brush one of the dark, exposed beams with his fingertips. He was clearly discomfited by what Maura had told him about Adam on the ride over. Ganseys were creatures of habit, and he wanted Adam here, and he wanted Noah here, and he wanted everyone to like him, and he wanted to be in charge.

Ronan had no idea what he wanted. He checked his phone.

He wondered if Kavinsky really did have three balls. He wondered if Kavinsky was gay. He wondered if he should go to the Fourth of July party. He wondered where Adam had gone.

"Lynch," Gansey said. "Are you even listening?"

He glanced up. "No."

On the counter, Chainsaw tore shreds from a roll of paper towels. Ronan snapped his fingers at her and, with an insolent gurgle, she flapped from the counter to the table, claws making a substantial scratch-click as she landed. Ronan was abruptly satisfied with her as a dream creature. He hadn't even asked for her. His subconscious had just, for once, sent him something nice instead of something homicidal.

Gansey asked Calla, "Why *are* we here?"

Calla echoed, "Yes, Maura, why are we here?"

Maura had entered from the other room; behind her Ronan glimpsed the corner of a bed, a gray suitcase. There was a sound like pipes clanging, a tap running. She dusted off her palms and joined them in the kitchen. "Because when Mr. Gray comes out here, I want *you* to look him in the eye and convince him not to kidnap you."

Gansey elbowed Ronan.

Ronan looked up sharply. "What, me?"

"Yes, you," Maura said. "Mr. Gray was sent here to retrieve an object that lets the owner take things from dreams. The Greywaren. As you know, that's you."

He felt a little thrill at the word *Greywaren*.

Yes, that's me.

Calla added, "And, unbelievably, it falls to *your* charm to convince him to have mercy on you."

He smiled nastily at her. She smiled nastily back. Both smiles said, *I've got your number.*

There was no part of Ronan that was surprised by this news. Part of him, he realized, was surprised it had taken so long. He felt he must have prompted it: He had been told not to go back to the Barns, and he had. His father had told him not to tell anyone about his dreams, and he had. One by one, he was violating every rule in his life.

Of course someone was looking. Of course they had found him.

"He's not the only one looking," Blue said suddenly. "Is he? That's what all of these break-ins are." Quite impossibly, she produced a pink switchblade to punctuate this statement. That little knife was the most shocking thing about the conversation so far.

"I'm afraid so," Maura replied.

Burglars, Ronan thought, all at once.

Gansey said, "Are the —"

Ronan interrupted, "Is he the one who beat up my brother? I should buy him a card if he is."

"Does it matter?" Maura asked, at about the same time that Calla asked, "Do you think your brother told anybody anything?"

"I'm sure he did," Ronan said darkly. "But don't worry — none of it was true."

Gansey took control. In his voice, Ronan could hear the relief that he knew enough about the situation to actually do so. He asked whether Mr. Gray really wanted to kidnap Ronan, whether his employer knew that the Greywaren was definitely in Henrietta, whether the others wandering about knew. Finally, he asked, "What happens to Mr. Gray if he doesn't come back with something?"

Maura pursed her lips. "Let's just use *death* as a short version of the consequences."

Calla added, "But for decision-making purposes, assume it's worse than that."

Blue muttered, "He can take Joseph Kavinsky."

"If they take that other boy," Calla said, "they'll be back for the snake." This was said with a jerk of her chin toward Ronan. Then her eyes flickered up to Maura.

The Gray Man stood in the doorway behind Maura, his gray suitcase in one hand and a gray jacket slung over the other. He set them both down and straightened.

There was that heavy silence that sometimes happens when a hit man enters a room.

It was against Ronan's nature to appear overly interested in anything, but he couldn't help staring at the Gray Man. It was the man from the Barns, the man who'd taken the puzzle box. He would have never put the words *hit man* to him. To him, a hit man was something else. A bouncer. A bodybuilder. An action hero. This wary predator was none of those things. His build was unassuming, all sly kinetics, but his eyes —

Ronan was suddenly afraid of him. He was afraid of him in the same way that he was afraid of the night horrors. Because they had killed him before, and they would kill him again, and he precisely remembered the pain of each death. He felt the fear in his chest, and in his face, and in the back of his head. Sharp and stinging, like a tire iron.

Chainsaw scrambled to Ronan's shoulder and ducked low, eyes on the Gray Man. She cawed stridently, just once.

For his part, the Gray Man stared back, his expression guarded. The longer he looked at Ronan and Chainsaw, the more his eyebrows furrowed. And the longer he looked, the closer Gansey edged to Ronan, nearly imperceptible. At some point it became the Gray Man watching the space between the two of them instead of Ronan.

Finally, the Gray Man said, "If I don't return with the Greywaren on the Fourth of July, they're telling my brother where I am, and he will kill me. He will do it very slowly."

Ronan believed him in a way that he didn't believe most things in life. It was real like a memory: This strange man would be tormented in the bathroom of one of the Henrietta motels and then he would be discarded and no one would ever look for him.

The Gray Man didn't have to tell any of them how much easier it would be to merely take Ronan to his employer. He also didn't have to tell any of them how simple it would be to do it against Ronan's will. Though Calla stood beside the gun of his that she'd retrieved from the cabinet — now Ronan saw why — Ronan didn't believe in it. If it came down to them versus Mr. Gray, he thought Mr. Gray would win.

It was like hearing the night horrors coming in his dreams. The inevitability of it.

Gansey, very softly, said, "Please."

Maura sighed.

"Brothers," said the Gray Man. He did not mean Declan or Matthew. At once the power went out of him. "I don't care for birds."

Then, after a moment, "I'm not a kidnapper."

Maura shot a rather meaningful look at Calla, who pretended not to see it.

"Are you sure your brother will be able to find you?" Gansey asked.

"I'm certain I won't be able to go home again," the Gray Man said. "I don't have many things there, but my books. . . . I would have to stay on the move for quite a while. It took me years to lose him before. And even if I leave, it won't stop the others. They're tracking the energy abnormalities, above and beyond what runs through Henrietta, and right now, they point right at him." He looked at Ronan.

Gansey, who had looked aghast at the idea of the Gray Man having to abandon his books, frowned even deeper.

"Could you dream a Greywaren?" Blue asked Ronan.

"I'm not giving this to anyone else," Ronan growled. He knew he should be kinder; they were trying to help him, after all. "It's killing the ley line as it is. You want to see Noah again? *I'm* stopping."

But Kavinsky's not. It would be like standing next to a giant bull's-eye.

"You could lie," Calla suggested. "Give them something and tell them it's the Greywaren and let them think they aren't clever enough to figure out how to work it."

"My employer," said the Gray Man, "is not an understanding man. If he ever discovered or suspected a ruse, it would be very ugly for all of us."

"What would they do to me?" Ronan asked. *To Kavinsky?* "If you turned me in?"

"No," Gansey said, as if replying to an entirely different question.

"No," the Gray Man agreed.

"Don't say *no*," Ronan insisted. "Fucking tell me. I didn't say I'd do it. I just want to know."

The Gray Man took his suitcase to the table, opened it, and laid the gun inside on top of the neatly folded slacks. He closed it. "He is not interested in people. He is interested in things. He will find the thing that makes you work, and he will remove it.

He will put it in a glass box with a label and when his guests have had enough wine, he will take them down to where you are and show them that thing that was inside you. And then they will admire the other things in the other cases beside you."

When Ronan didn't flinch — the Gray Man couldn't know that Ronan would rather do most anything than flinch — he continued, "It's possible he would make an exception for you. But it would only be that he'd put all of you in the glass box. He is a curator. He will do what he needs to do for his collection."

Ronan still didn't flinch.

The Gray Man said, "He told me to kill your father as messily as I could and leave the body where your older brother would find it. So that he would confess to where the Greywaren was."

For one moment, Ronan didn't move. It took him that long to realize that the Gray Man was saying he had killed Niall Lynch. Ronan's mind went perfectly blank. Then he did what had to be done: He hurled himself at the Gray Man. Chainsaw blasted into the air.

"Ronan!" howled approximately three voices at once.

The Gray Man let out a small *oof* with the ferocity of the hit. Three or four punches landed on his person. It was difficult to tell if it was through skill on Ronan's part or permissiveness on the Gray Man's. Then the Gray Man gently threw Ronan across the breakfast table.

"*Mr. — Gray!*" shouted Maura, forgetting his fake name in the heat of the moment.

Chainsaw cannonballed toward the Gray Man's face. As he ducked his eyes against her, Ronan slammed into the Gray Man's stomach. He somehow managed to include several swear words in the blow. The Gray Man, searching for footing, smacked the back of his head against the doorjamb behind him.

"You *must* be joking!" This was Calla. "You! *Pretty one!*" She forgot Gansey's real name in the heat of the moment. "Stop him!"

"I think this is justified," Gansey replied.

The Gray Man had Ronan in an indifferent headlock. "I understand," he told Ronan. "But it wasn't personal."

"It. Was. To. Me."

Ronan slammed one fist into one of the Gray Man's knee-caps and the other tidily into his crotch. The Gray Man dropped him. The floor rose up to tap Ronan's temple quite abruptly.

There was a pause, filled only with the sound of two people gasping for air.

Voice muffled by the tile pressed against his cheek, Ronan said, "No matter how much you do for me, I'll never forgive you."

The Gray Man, buckled over, braced himself on the door-jamb. He panted, "They never do."

Ronan heaved himself up. Blue handed him Chainsaw. The Gray Man stood up. Maura handed him his jacket.

The Gray Man wiped a palm on his slacks. He eyed Chainsaw, and then he said, "On the Fourth, unless I think of a better idea, I will call my employer and tell him that I have the Greywaren."

They all looked at him.

"And then," the Gray Man said, "I'll tell him I'm keeping it for myself and he can't have it."

There was a long, long pause.

"And then what?" Maura asked.

The Gray Man looked at her. "I run."

55

Adam drove the tri-colored car as close as he could get to the field where Cabeswater used to be, and when he could drive it no farther, he parked it in the grass and began to walk. Before, when he'd been with the others, they'd used the GPS and the EMF reader to find Cabeswater. He didn't need that now. *He* was the detector. If he focused, he could feel the line far below him. It sputtered and flickered, deprived and uneven. Holding his hands out, palms down, he walked slowly through the tall grass, following the trembling energy. Grasshoppers catapulted out of his way. He watched his feet for snakes. Overhead, the smoldering sky gave way to storm clouds on the western horizon. He wasn't worried about the rain, but lightning — *lightning*.

Actually, lightning might be useful. He made a note to remember that, later.

He glanced up at the tree line to his right. They hadn't yet begun to flip their leaves. He had hours before the storm, anyway. He ran his fingers through the stalks.

It had been so long since he had felt like this — like he could devote his thoughts to something other than when he might get to sleep. Like his mind was huge and whirring and hungry. Like anything was possible, if he only threw himself into it hard enough. This had been how he felt before he decided to go to Aglionby.

World, I'm coming.

He wished he had thought to bring a set of tarot cards from 300 Fox Way. Something that Cabeswater could use to more easily communicate with him. Maybe later he could return for them. Now — it seemed more urgent to return to this place where the ley line was the strongest.

I will be your hands. I will be your eyes.

This was the bargain he had made. And in return, he could feel Cabeswater in him. Cabeswater couldn't offer him eyes or hands. But it was something else. Something he wanted to name *life* or *soul* or *knowledge.*

It was an old sort of power.

Adam walked out and out beneath the growing purple thunderheads. Something in him said *ahhh* and *ahhh* and *ahhh* again, relieved over and over that he was himself again, himself and something more, that he was alone and didn't have to worry about hurting or wanting anyone else.

He walked to the tiny stream that used to lead into Cabeswater and now led only to more field. Kneeling, he hovered his hands over the trickle of water. There was no one to see him, but he smiled anyway, bigger and bigger. Because the first time they'd been at this stream, Gansey had been holding an EMF reader over the water and watching the flashing red lights. He'd been so excited by those lights — they'd found something, the machine told them they'd found something!

And now Adam felt it in his hands. He felt it in his spine. He could *see* it mapped in his brain. The ley line traveled beneath him, waves of energy, but it detoured here, snagged and conducted through the water, traveling upward to the surface. It was only a small stream, only a small crack in the bedrock, so this was only a small leak.

Thunder rumbled, reminding Adam of time's passage. He straightened and followed the stream upward through the rising field. The ley line strengthened inside him, tripping his heart, but he kept going. Cabeswater was not here now, but his memory of walking through it the first time was nearly as clear as experiencing it again. Here was where they'd had to climb between two rocks to follow the stream. Here was where the trees had begun to grow larger in diameter, big knuckles of roots bursting from the forest floor. Here the moss furred the trunks.

And here was the pool and the dreaming tree. The first place Cabeswater had changed itself for Gansey, and the first place magic had truly revealed itself to all of them.

He hesitated. His vision in the dreaming tree pressed into his mind. Gansey on the ground, dying. Ronan, furious with grief, spitting at Adam, *"Are you happy now, Adam? This is what you wanted, wasn't it?"*

That wasn't going to happen now. He'd changed his future. He'd chosen a different way.

Thunder guttered and popped distantly. With a deep breath to steel himself, Adam waded through the grass to where the dreaming tree had been — would be — was still? No vision overcame him, but he felt the surge of the ley line beneath his feet.

Yes, this was where he needed to be. Crouching, he parted the grass and pressed his palms to the soil. It was hot, like a living body. He closed his eyes.

He felt the course of the ley line stretching out on either side of him. Hundreds of miles one way, hundreds of miles the other. There were distant starbursts where the line intersected with other lines, and for a moment, he was dazzled by them. By the possibility of endless wonders. Glendower was miracle enough, but if there was a miracle on each line that he felt, it was enough miracles for a lifetime, if only you had the patience to look.

Oh, Gansey, he thought suddenly. Because Gansey had the patience to look. And because things wanted Gansey to find them. He should have been here, now.

No. It wouldn't work like this if he was here. You have to be alone for this.

Adam pulled his mind away from Gansey and from those intersections, focusing instead on only the ley line beneath him. He raced along it, following the peaks and valleys of energy. Here it spurted up through an underground river. Escaped through an earthquake-shocked bedrock. Burst up through a well. Exploded through a transformer.

No wonder it was so drained by the dreaming. It was a frayed wire, energy leaking at a hundred different points.

"I feel it," he whispered.

The wind hissed through the grass around him. He opened his eyes.

If he could repair those points, like electrician's tape on a wire, he might be able to make it strong enough to bring Cabeswater back.

Adam stood up. It felt good to have identified the problem. That had always been the hardest part. With an engine, with school, with life. Solutions were easy, once you knew what was in your way.

Cabeswater murmured urgently. The voices tickled inside him and crackled in the corners of his eyes.

Wait, he thought. He wished he had the cards. Something to focus his thoughts on what Cabeswater was trying to say. *I won't be able to understand you. Wait until I can understand you.*

As he looked back down the hill, he saw a woman approaching. He shielded his eyes with his hand. At first he thought she was one of Cabeswater's manifestations. Certainly she seemed whimsical and imaginary from this distance — a great cumulo-nimbus of hair, a gray frock, boots up her entire leg.

But then he saw that she had a shadow and form and mass, and that she was a little out of breath.

Persephone climbed up to meet him and then stood with her hands on her hips. She turned in a slow circle, looking at the view, blowing out her breath.

"Why are you here?" he asked her. Was she here to bring him back? To tell him he was wrong to be so sure?

She grinned at him, a strangely impish, child-like expression. He thought of what a cruel mockery that mirror-version of her had been, the terrible child-creature from his ritual before. Nothing like this airy whisper of a person in front of him now. Unzipping her butterfly handbag, she retrieved a black silk bag from inside. It was the sort of fabric that you wanted to touch, smooth and shimmery and floaty. It seemed to be the only thing inside the handbag.

"You left, Adam, before I could give you these," she said, offering the smaller silk bag.

Adam accepted it, feeling its weight. Whatever was inside was vaguely warm, as if it, like the hill, were alive. "What is it?"

After he asked, he thought suddenly about how she had taken care to say his name just before. It could have been nothing. But it felt as if she were reminding him of what it was.

Adam. Adam Parrish.

He slid the contents of the bag into his other hand. A word leapt out at him.

Magician.

Persephone said, "My tarot cards."

56

hey Lynch I didn't leave that car for it to just sit while you blow III

57

The Gray Man checked out of Pleasant Valley Bed and Breakfast and placed his suitcase just inside the door of Maura's bedroom. He didn't unpack it. It was not that long until the Fourth. There was no point.

Calla said, "Give me some poetry, and I'll make you a drink."

The Gray Man said, "'Our hearts must grow resolute, our courage more valiant, our spirits must be great, though our strength grows less.'"

Then he did it in the original Old English.

Calla made him a drink.

Then Maura made something with butter and Calla made something with bacon and Blue steamed broccoli in self-defense. In the rest of the house, Jimi got ready for her night shift and Orla answered the ever-ringing psychic hotline. The Gray Man got underfoot trying to be helpful. He understood that this was an ordinary night at 300 Fox Way, all of this noise and commotion and disorder. It was a senseless sort of dance, artful and confused. Blue and Maura had their own orbit; Maura and Calla another. He watched Maura's bare feet circle on the kitchen floor.

It was the opposite of everything he had cultivated for the past five years.

How he wanted to stay.

This isn't a life for what you are, he told himself.

But for tonight, he would pretend.

At dinner, Calla said, "So, what's next?" She was only eating the foods with bacon in them.

Blue, who was only eating broccoli, answered, "I guess we have to find a way to make Joseph Kavinsky stop dreaming."

"Well," Maura asked. "What does he want?"

Blue shrugged from behind her mountain of broccoli. "What does a drug addict want? Nothing."

Maura frowned over her plate of butter. "Sometimes everything."

"Either way," Blue replied, "I can't see how we can offer that."

The Gray Man politely interjected, "I could talk to him this evening for you."

Blue stabbed a piece of broccoli. "Sounds great."

Maura gave her a look. "What she means to say is, no thanks."

"No," Blue said, brows beetled, "I meant to say, and can you make him feel worthless while you do?"

"Blue Sargent!" Maura looked shocked. "I didn't raise you to be violent!"

Calla, who'd inhaled some bacon while laughing, clutched the table until she stopped choking.

"No," Blue said dangerously. "But sometimes bad things happen to good children."

The Gray Man was amused. "The offer stands until I go."

The phone rang. Upstairs, they heard the sound of Orla scrambling desperately for it. With a pleasant smile, Maura snatched the downstairs extension and listened for a moment.

"What an excellent idea. It *will* be harder to trace," Maura told the phone. To the table, she said, "Gansey has a Mitsubishi that Mr. Gray can take instead of his rental. Oh, he says it was actually Ronan's idea."

The gesture warmed the Gray Man considerably. The reality of his escape was far more difficult than he'd admitted to any of them. There was a car to worry about, money for food, money for gas. He had left a dirty pot in the sink at his home back in Massachusetts, and he would think about it forever.

It would help if he didn't have to steal the Champagne Disappointment. He was gifted at car theft, but he longed for simplicity.

To the phone, Maura said: "No — no, Adam's not here. He's with Persephone, I believe. I'm sure he's all right. Would you like to talk to Blue? No —?"

Blue's head ducked to her plate. She stabbed another piece of broccoli.

Maura hung up the phone. She looked narrowly at Blue. "Did you two fight again?"

Blue muttered, "Yep. Definitely."

"I can have a talk with him as well," the Gray Man offered.

"I'm good," she replied. "But thanks. My mother didn't raise me to be violent."

"Neither," observed the Gray Man, "did mine."

He ate his broccoli and butter and bacon, and Maura ate her butter, and Calla ate her bacon.

It was another frenzied dance to clean up after dinner and fight for showers and television and who got which chair. Maura gently took the Gray Man's hand and led him to the backyard instead. Under the black, spreading branches of the beech tree, they kissed until the mosquitos became relentless and the rain began to fall.

Later, as they lay in her bed, his phone buzzed a call, and this time it went to voicemail. Somehow, he always knew it would end this way.

"Hey, Dean," said his brother. His voice was slow, easy, patient. The Allen brothers were alike, that way. "Henrietta is a pretty little place, isn't it?"

58

Hurry."

Persephone and Adam didn't speak much through that night, or as the pugilistic sun rose the next morning, and when they did, it was usually that word: *hurry*. They had already driven to a dozen other locations to repair the ley line, some as far as two hours away, and now they pushed their way back into Henrietta.

Now, Adam knelt beside a diseased rose in another backyard. His already grubby hands pressed against the dirt, digging to find the stone he knew was hidden somewhere beneath. Persephone, standing watch, glanced at the rambler on the other side of the yard.

"Hurry," she said once more. Fourth of July was already hot and unforgiving. A bank of clouds moved slowly behind the mountains, and already Adam knew how the day would go: The heat would build and build, until it snapped in another cacophonous summer thunderstorm.

Lightning.

Adam's fingers found the stone. It was the same at every fray in the line: a stone or a body of water that confused and diffused the ley line's direction. Sometimes Adam had only to turn a stone to feel the ley line immediately snap into place, clean as a light switch. Other times, though, he had to experiment by moving more stones into the area, or removing a stone entirely, or digging a trench to redirect a stream. Sometimes neither he nor

Persephone could understand what they needed to do, and then they would draw out one or two of the tarot cards. Persephone helped him see what the cards were trying to say. *Three of wands:* build a bridge across the stream with these three stones. *Seven of swords:* Just dig out the biggest of the stones and put it in the tricolored car.

Using the tarot cards was like when he had begun learning Latin. He danced ever closer to that moment when he would understand the sentences without having to translate each word.

He was exhausted and awake, euphoric and anxious.

Hurry.

What was it that made these stones special? He didn't know. Not yet. Somehow, they were like the rocks at Stonehenge and Castlerigg. Something about them conducted the ley line's force and dragged the energy out of line.

"Adam," Persephone said again. There was no sign of a car, but she frowned at the road. Her fingers were as dirty as his; her delicate gray frock was stained. She looked like a doll dug from a landfill. "Hurry."

This stone was larger than he expected. Twelve inches across, maybe, and who knew how deep. There was no way to get to it without digging up the rose. Hurriedly, he snatched a spade lying beside him. He spiked the dirt, twisted out the deformed rose, tossed it aside. His palms sweated.

"Sorry," Persephone suggested.

"Pardon?"

She murmured, "You should say sorry when you kill something."

It took him a moment to realize she meant the rose. "It was dying anyway."

"*Dying* and *dead* are different words."

Shamed, Adam muttered an apology before sticking the tip of the spade beneath the stone. It came free. Persephone turned a questioning look to him.

"We take this one," he said immediately. She nodded. It went in the backseat with the others.

They had only just headed back down the street when another car pulled into the driveway they'd just abandoned.

Close.

Multiple stones were stacked in the tri-colored car now, but this latest one pressed into Adam's consciousness more than the others. It would be useful, with the lightning, he thought. For . . . something. For concentrating the ley line into Cabeswater. For . . . making a gate.

Hurry.

"Why now?" he asked her. "Why are all these parts frayed?"

She didn't look up from her task, which was laying cards on the dashboard. The smudgy, inked art looked like thoughts instead of images. "It's not just fraying now. It's only that it's more obvious with the greater current running through it. Like a wire. In the past, priestesses would've taken care of the line. Maintained it. Just like we're doing now."

"Like Stonehenge," he said.

"That's a very large and cliché example, yes," she answered softly. She glanced up at the sky. The clouds at the horizon had gotten just a little closer since he'd last looked; they were still white, but they were beginning to pile on top of one another.

"I wonder," he said, more to himself than to her, "what it would be like if all the ley lines were repaired."

She replied, "I expect that would be a very different world with very different priorities."

"Bad?" he asked. "A bad world?"

She looked at him.

"Different isn't bad, right?" he asked.

Persephone turned back to her cards. *Swick.* She turned over a second one.

I should call work, Adam thought. He was supposed to come in tonight. He hadn't called in sick before. *I should call Gansey.*

But there was no time. They had so many more places to go before — before —

Hurry.

As they pulled onto the interstate, Adam's attention was snagged by a white Mitsubishi screaming in the opposite direction on the other side of the median. Kavinsky.

But was that Kavinsky behind the wheel? Adam craned his head to look in the mirror, but the other car was already a diminishing speck on the horizon.

Persephone turned over a card. *The Devil.*

All of a sudden, Adam was quite certain of why they were hurrying. He'd known since the night before that he needed to hone the line's energy in order for Cabeswater to reappear. An important task, certainly, but not life-or-death.

But now, he knew all at once what he was hurrying for. They were restoring the ley line for Cabeswater. They were restoring it *now* because Ronan was going to need it. Tonight.

Hurry.

59

The first thing Ronan noticed at church on the Fourth was that the priest had a black eye. The second thing he noticed was that Matthew wasn't there. The third thing he noticed was that there was space for two people on the pew beside Declan. Everyone at St. Agnes knew the Lynch brothers didn't come to church alone.

It was an oddly discomfiting image. For the first few weeks after Niall had died, the boys had always left room for their mother, as if she would magically arrive partway through the service.

I'm working on that, Ronan thought, and then pushed it out of his head.

He was quite late to the special Mass; it looked like insolence. By the time he slid into the pew beside Declan, a small crumpled woman had already begun to intone the first reading. It was a passage Ronan used to love as a child — *of this one I am proud.* Really, Ronan's tardiness was because he had gone with Gansey to pick up the Gray Man from the car rental office. The boys had given him the Mitsubishi and, in return, Ronan had gotten the puzzle box back. It seemed a fair trade. A dream thing for a dream thing.

Declan looked sharply to Ronan. He hissed, "Where's Matthew?"

"You tell me."

The churchgoers in the pew behind them rustled meaning-fully.

"You weren't here on Sunday." Declan's voice held the weight of an accusation. "And Matthew says you didn't ever explain."

Ronan had to guiltily admit to himself that this was true. He'd been lying on the hood of an invented Camaro and he hadn't given a second's thought to what day it was. Then he realized what Declan was hinting at — that possibly, Matthew was taking revenge on Ronan with an unannounced disappearance of his own. While it was true that tricking Ronan into a solo church visit with Declan would have been an excellent punishment, it didn't feel like Matthew's handiwork at all.

"Oh, please," Ronan whispered. "He's not that clever."

Declan looked shocked and poisonous. He was always so alarmed by the truth.

"Have you called him?" Ronan asked.

"Not picking up." Declan narrowed his eyes as if this failure to answer his phone was an infection his youngest brother had picked up from Ronan.

"You saw him this morning?"

"Yeah."

Ronan shrugged.

"He doesn't skip." The inverse statement was implied: *unlike you.*

"Until he does."

"This is all your fault," Declan said, hushed. His eyes darted to the empty pew beside Ronan and then to the priest. "I told you to keep your mouth shut. I told you to keep your head down. Why can't you just do what you're told for once?"

Someone kicked the back of their pew. It struck Ronan as an extremely un-Catholic action. He looked over his shoulder, elegant and dangerous, and raised an eyebrow at the middle-aged man sitting behind him. He waited. The man dropped his eyes.

Declan flicked Ronan's arm. "Ronan."

"Stop acting like you know everything."

"Oh, I know enough. I know exactly what you are."

There was a time when this statement would've trickled through Ronan like venom. Now, he didn't have time for it. In the relative scheme of things, his older brother's opinion ranked very low. In fact, Ronan was only here because of Matthew, and without Matthew here, there was no reason to stay. He slid out of the pew.

"Ronan," whispered Declan ferociously. "Where are you going?"

Ronan put a finger to his lips. A smile snaked out on either side of it.

Declan just shook his head, lifting a hand like he was simply *done* with Ronan. And that, of course, was another lie, because he was never done with Ronan. But at the moment, eighteen and freedom seemed a lot closer than it had before, and it didn't matter.

As Ronan pushed through the great, heavy doors of the church — the same doors he'd walked through with the newly dreamt Chainsaw — he pulled out his phone and called Matthew.

It went to voicemail.

Ronan didn't believe it. He got into the BMW to head back to Monmouth and called again.

Voicemail.

He couldn't let it go. He didn't know why. It wasn't that Matthew never abandoned his phone. And it wasn't quite that Matthew never abandoned church, especially not an additional holiday Mass.

It was the Gray Man's face and the beaten-up priest and the world turned on its ear.

He put the car in gear and headed out of the smoldering downtown. He steered with his knee. Called again. Voicemail.

This didn't feel right.

As he pulled into the lot outside of Monmouth, a text buzzed in from Matthew's number.

Finally.

Ronan pulled up the parking brake, turned the car off, and looked at the screen.

what's up mofo

This wasn't what he generally expected from his younger brother. Before he had time to consider a reply, a text buzzed in from Kavinsky's number as well.

what's up mofo

Something ill turned over inside Ronan.

A moment later, Kavinsky texted again.

bring something fun to fourth of july or we'll see which pill works the best on your brother

Without pause, Ronan snatched up his phone and called Kavinsky.

Kavinsky picked up at once. "Lynch, fancy hearing from you."

Ronan demanded, "Where is he?"

"You know, I asked nice the first few times. Are you coming to Fourth? Are you coming? Are you coming? Here, have a moth-erfucking car. Are you coming? *You* made it ugly. Bring something impressive tonight."

"I'm not doing this," Ronan said.

One thousand nightmares of Matthew dead. Blood in his curls, blood in his teeth, flies in his eyes, flies in his guts.

"Oh," Kavinsky said, with that slow, despicable laugh in his voice. "I think you are. Or I'll keep trying different things on him. He can be my finale tonight. *Boom!* You want to see something explode. . . ."

Ronan turned the key, threw down the parking brake. The door to Monmouth had opened and Gansey stood there, one hand up, asking a question.

"You won't get away with this."

"I got away with dear old dad," Kavinsky observed. "And Prokopenko. And no offense to your brother, but they were a lot more complicated."

"This was the wrong play. I will destroy you."

"Don't let me down, Lynch."

60

Gansey blasted into 300 Fox Way well in advance of the thunderstorm. He didn't knock. He just suddenly burst in as Blue was unlacing her shoes from her part-time dog-walking gig.

"Jane?" he called. Her stomach twisted. *"Blue!"*

This was how Blue knew something was really wrong.

Ronan exploded in behind him, and if she hadn't been able to tell from Gansey, she would've known it from Ronan. He was wild-eyed as a trapped animal. When he stopped, he rested his hand on the doorjamb and his fingers crawled up it.

"What's happened?" she asked.

They told her.

Immediately, she accompanied them to the Fourth of July parade, where they searched unsuccessfully for Maura or Calla. They drove by Kavinsky's house and found it empty. Then, as the afternoon wore on, Blue directed them to the Henrietta drag strip — the annual location of Kavinsky's Fourth of July party. It seemed impossible that neither Gansey nor Ronan had ever been to it. Impossible that Blue, a student at ordinary old Mountain View High School, should have special knowledge about Kavinsky that they didn't. But maybe this part of Joseph Kavinsky wasn't very Aglionby at all.

Kavinsky's Fourth of July party was infamous.

Two years before, he had supposedly had an actual tank for his fireworks finale. As in a full-size, olive drab tank with

Russian characters painted on the side. It was rumor, of course, and stayed rumor, because the end of the story was that he blew up the tank itself. Blue knew a senior who claimed to have a metal strip off it.

Three years before, a junior from a school three counties over had overdosed on something the hospital hadn't seen before. It wasn't the overdose that impressed people, though. It was that fifteen-year-old Kavinsky was already capable of pulling in kids from forty-five minutes away. Statistically, you probably weren't going to die at Kavinsky's party.

Every year, there were dozens of cars waiting to be flogged on the drag strip. No one knew who provided them or where they went afterward. It didn't matter if you had a license. All you needed was to know how to hit a gas pedal.

Last year, Kavinsky had supposedly sent a firework so far into the air that the CIA had come to his house to question him. Blue found this story rather suspect. Surely it would've been the Department of Homeland Security instead.

This year, two ambulances and four cops parked half a mile from the drag strip. Close enough to be there in time. Not close enough to watch.

Kavinsky was untouchable.

The drag strip — a long, dusty field cut into the hills around it — was already packed when they got there. Music blared from somewhere, benevolent and upbeat. Barbecue grills scented the air with charcoal and neglected hot dogs. There was no sign of alcohol. Nor of the infamous cars that supposedly populated the drag strip later. There was an old Mustang and a Pontiac facing off down the strip, throwing up rubber and dust while onlookers cheered them on, but the matches seemed awfully playful and easygoing. There were adults here, and young kids. Ronan stared at a girl holding a balloon as if she were a bewildering creature.

This wasn't really what any of them had expected.

Gansey stood in the dirt and glanced around, dubious. "Are you sure this is Kavinksy's?"

"It's early," Blue said. She glanced around herself. She was torn between wanting to be recognized by someone from school and wanting to not be seen running with Aglionby boys.

"He can't be here," Ronan said. "You have to be wrong."

"I don't know if he's here yet," Blue snapped, "but this is the place. This is always the place."

Ronan glared at one of the speakers. It was playing something Blue thought was called "yacht rock." He was more wound up by the moment. People were dragging their younger kids out of his way.

"Jane says this is the place," Gansey insisted. "So it's the place. Let's do a study."

They did a study. As the afternoon shadows grew longer, they pushed through the crowd and asked after Kavinsky and looked behind the buildings at the edge of the strip. They didn't find him, but as the evening graded into night, the character of the party subtly changed. The young kids were the first to disappear. Then the adults started to go, replaced by either seniors or college kids. Red plastic cups started to appear. The yacht rock got darker, deeper, filthier.

The Mustang and the Pontiac were gone. A girl offered Blue a pill.

"I've got extras," she told Blue.

Nerves, sudden and searing, burned along Blue's skin. She shook her head. "No thanks."

When the girl asked Gansey, he just gazed at her for a minute too long, not realizing he was being rude until too late. This was so far from Richard Gansey's scene that he had no words at all.

And then Ronan flicked the pill out of the girl's hand onto the ground. She spit in his face and stalked off.

Ronan turned in a slow circle. "Where are you, you bastard?"

The floodlights came on.

The crowd whooped.

Overhead, the speakers spat in Spanish. The bass thundered through Blue's boots. Real thunder groaned overhead.

Engines revved high, and the crowd pressed back to admit the cars. Every hand was up in the air, jumping, dancing, celebrating. Someone shouted:

"God bless *AMERICA*!"

Ten white Mitsubishis drove onto the drag strip. They were identical: black yawning mouths, shredded knife graphic carved down the sides, giant spoilers. But one tore down the strip in front of the others, and then jerked sideways to skid before a massive boom of dust. It was hidden in the cloud, nothing visible but the headlights cutting through the dirt.

The crowd went wild.

"That's him," Ronan said, already shoving his way through the teens.

"Lynch," Gansey said. "*Ronan!* Hold up!"

But Ronan was already several feet away, heading straight for the lone car. The dust had cleared and Kavinsky was visible, standing on its roof.

"Let's burn something!" Kavinsky howled. He snapped his fingers, pointing. There was a hiss and a whine, and suddenly the

first firework of the night spiraled up into the chaotic blue, high above the floodlights. He laughed, loud and wild. "Fuck you all!" He said something else, but it was lost in the ascending music. The bass buffeted them.

"I don't like this," Gansey shouted in Blue's ear.

But there was no other way.

They caught up to Ronan just as he reached Kavinsky, who now stood next to the open door of the car. Whatever the opening volley had been, it had been unpleasant.

"Oh, hey," Kavinsky sneered. His eyes had found Blue and Gansey. "It's Daddy. Dick, that's a strangely hetero partner you have there tonight. Lynch having performance issues?"

Ronan grabbed Kavinsky's throat, and for once, Blue wasn't displeased. Another firework screamed into the black overhead. Lightning arced past it.

"Where is he?" Ronan snarled. It was barely words.

Kavinsky seemed fairly unconcerned. He gestured toward the car behind him, and then toward one of the others, and then another. In a slightly strangled tone, he said, "In that car. Or that one. Or that one. Or that one. You know these things. They all look alike."

He kneed Ronan in the stomach. With a gasp, Ronan dropped him.

"Here's the thing, Lynch," Kavinsky said. "When I said *with me* or *against me*, I didn't really think you'd pick against me."

Blue leapt forward as one of the Mitsubishis tore by behind her, the engine wailing high, smoke swirling. Already she was thinking about what they'd have to do to search them all. To keep track of the ones they'd already stopped and checked. All of the cars were identical, with the same Virginia license plate: THIEF.

"But in a way," Kavinsky added, "it's better this way. You know how I like things to explode."

Ronan said, "I want my brother."

"First," Kavinsky said, opening his palm, revealing a green pill, "save your life. I'll be right back, sweetie."

He dropped it on his tongue.

He was down in a second, on his knees, then slumped against the car. Blue and Gansey just stared at Kavinsky's prone form, uncomprehending. His veins were raised roads up his arms, the pulse in his jaw pounding out the bass.

"Shit," said Ronan, diving into the car, throwing open the center console and digging in the contents. He found what he was looking for — another one of the green pills. "Shit, shit."

"What's happening?" Blue demanded.

"He's dreaming," Ronan said. "Who knows what he's gone to get. Nothing good. *Shit*, Kavinsky!"

"Can we stop him?" Gansey asked.

"Only if you kill him," Ronan replied. He stuffed the pill in his mouth. "Get Matthew. And get the hell out of here."

61

Ronan hurtled into the dream. When he landed, elbows scuffing blood on the dirt, Kavinsky was already there, sunk down in the briars, covering his face. The trees Ronan knew so well were attacking him, claws of branches. Something about Kavinsky was the wrong color, or something, in comparison to the woods around him. It was as if the dream painted him a usurper.

"Guess our secret place is the same," Kavinsky said. He grinned. His face was striated with fine scratches from the thorns.

Ronan replied, "Not such a thief tonight."

"Some nights," Kavinsky said, all teeth, "you just take it. Consent is overrated."

The branches shook over them both. Thunder grumbled and smashed, close and real, real, real.

"You don't have to do this," Ronan said.

"There isn't anything else, man."

"There's reality."

Kavinsky laughed the word. "Reality! Reality's what other people dream for you."

"Reality's where other people are," Ronan replied. He stretched out his arms. "What's here, K? Nothing! No one!"

"Just us."

There was a heavy understanding in that statement, amplified by the dream. *I know what you are,* Kavinsky had said.

"That's not enough," Ronan replied.

"Don't say Dick Gansey, man. Do not say it. He is never going to be with you. And don't tell me you don't swing that way, man. I'm in your head."

"That's not what Gansey is to me," Ronan said.

"You didn't say you don't swing that way."

Ronan was silent. Thunder growled under his feet. "No, I didn't."

"That makes it worse, man. You really are just his lapdog."

There wasn't even a tiny part of Ronan that was stung by this statement. When Ronan thought of Gansey, he thought of moving into Monmouth Manufacturing, of nights spent in companionable insomnia, of a summer searching for a king, of Gansey asking the Gray Man for his life. *Brothers.*

Ronan said, "Life isn't just sex and drugs and cars."

Kavinsky stood up. The thorns whipped at his legs, sinking into his cargo pants. His heavy-lidded eyes held Ronan's, and Ronan thought of all of the times he had looked through the window of his BMW and seen Kavinsky looking back. The illicit thrill of it. The certainty that Kavinsky didn't let anyone tell him who he was.

Kavinsky said, "Mine is."

He looked to the woods. Holding out his hand, he snapped his fingers, just as he had to queue the first firework.

The forest screamed.

Or whatever Kavinsky had manifested had screamed. The sound tore Ronan to his spine. There was a sound like someone clapping their hand over your ear. A beat of air. Whatever was coming was huge.

The trees shimmered and wept, sagged and flickered. The already sapped ley line guttered and blackened. There was nothing left. Kavinsky was taking it all to create his dream beast.

"You don't have to do this," Ronan said again.

It was a ball of fire. An explosion in flight. It was a dragon and a bonfire and an inferno and teeth. It was the destruction of the Mitsubishi made into a living creature.

As it descended, it opened its maw wide and screamed at Ronan. It wasn't the sound Ronan had heard before. It was the roaring hiss of a fire dampened with water. Sparks rained onto Ronan's shoulders.

He could feel how it hated him. How it hated Kavinsky, too. How it hated the world.

It was so hungry.

Kavinsky looked at Ronan, his eyes dead. "Try to keep up, Lynch."

Then both he and the dragon vanished.

He'd woken up, and taken it with him.

Hurry.

If Adam and Persephone had not already been at the final energy fray point, they wouldn't have found it. Because as they stood there in the dark, staring at the great, flat, man-made lake, the ley line went dead inside Adam.

Kavinsky, Adam thought immediately. He knew it in the way that a dropped body knew it was falling. Both intellectually and physically. The same way he'd been so certain, earlier, that Ronan was the reason for their urgency.

And here it was.

Ronan needed the ley line. He needed it *now*. There was no more time.

But the ley line was dead and Cabeswater had no voice inside Adam. All he had was this flat black mirror of a lake and a car full of stones and a bag of cards that no longer said anything to him.

"What do we do?" he asked Persephone. Fireworks whined distantly, as threatening as bombs.

"Well, *I* don't know."

He threw a hand toward the cards. "You're psychic! Can't you look at the cards? They don't mean anything to me without the ley line!"

Thunder boomed overhead; lightning darted from cloud to cloud. The ley line didn't even flutter beneath Adam. Kavinsky had just dreamt something huge, and Ronan had nothing to work with.

Persephone said, "Are you the Magician or aren't you?"

"I'm not!" Adam replied immediately. There was nothing inside him. The line was dead, and so was everything *other* inside him. "Cabeswater makes me that way."

Persephone's eyes mirrored the motionless water beside them. "Your power, Adam, isn't about other people. It isn't about other *things.*"

Adam had never been powerful in his life.

"Being the Magician isn't about being powerful when you have things and useless when you don't," Persephone said. "The Magician sees what is out there and finds connections. The Magician can make anything magical."

He wished fervently for the line to sputter to life beneath him. If he could grab even a hint of it, he might be able to gather clues for how to fix this last section. But there was nothing in the ley line. Nothing.

"Now," Persephone said, and her voice was very small and soft. "Are you the Magician? Or aren't you?"

Adam closed his eyes.

Connections.

His mind darted to the stones, the lake, the thunderheads. Lightning.

He thought, bizarrely, of the Camaro. Needing the battery just to get them home.

In indiget homo battery.

Yes.

He opened his eyes.

"I need the stone from the car," he said. "The one from the garden."

Hurry.

"Adam?" Ronan demanded. "Is it really you?"

Because suddenly, the landscape had shifted. The trees had moved and shivered to the side, and now there was the ugly man-made lake they had discovered with Gansey. Adam crouched beside the shore, laying out stones in a complicated pattern. Was it the real Adam? Or was it a dream Adam?

This Adam looked up sharply. He was himself, and he was something else. "Lynch. What did Kavinsky just dream?"

"A fire fucker," Ronan said. He should wake up. He didn't stand a chance lying on the ground back at the party.

Adam looked behind him and gestured wildly to someone. "What are you dreaming to take it down?"

Ronan tested the dream, cautiously. It felt stretched thin as a string of caramel. He wouldn't be able to take a thing from it.

"Nothing. There's nothing here."

Persephone ran up to Adam, a large, flat rock in her arms.

"What are you doing?" Ronan demanded.

"Fixing it," Adam said. "Start making something. I'll try to have it up by the time you're done."

Ronan heard a scream, far away. It was from outside his dream. Sleep was collapsing around him.

"Hurry," Persephone advised.

Adam looked up at Ronan. "I know it was you," he said. "I figured it out. The rent."

He held Ronan's gaze for just a moment longer, until something inside Ronan unwound and he almost said something. And then Adam leapt up, snatched the rock from Persephone, and sprinted toward the opposite side of the shore.

"Now," Persephone said.

Ronan turned to the failing trees. "Cabeswater," he said, "I need your help. You need my help."

Raptor, hissed the trees.

Plunderer.

There was no time for this. "I'm not here to steal! Do you want to save yourself?"

Nothing.

Damn Kavinsky.

Ronan shouted, "I'm not him, all right? I'm not like him. Damn it, you *know* me. Haven't you always? Didn't you know my father? We're both Greywarens."

There was Orphan Girl, finally. *Yes.* She peered out from behind one of the trunks. If she would help him, he could bring out something, anything. He stretched out his hand to her, but she shook her head. *"Vos estis unum tantum."*

(You are the only one.)

In English, she added, "Many thieves. One Greywaren."

In the way of a dream, knowledge flooded through him. How many could make their dreams real, but how few could speak to the dream. How he was meant to be Cabeswater's right hand. Didn't he know? asked Cabeswater — but not with words. Hadn't he known it all along?

"Look, I'm sorry," he said. "I didn't know. I didn't know anything. I had to figure everything out myself, and it took a fucking long time, okay? Please. I can't do it without you."

In his hands, suddenly, was the puzzle box. It didn't feel like a dream. It felt weighty and cool and real. He flipped the dials and wheels until it read *please* on the English side. He turned it to the side with the mysterious language on it. This, he knew now, was not a language of men. This was a language of trees. He read, *"T'implora?"*

The effect was instantaneous. He could hear leaves moving and shifting in a wind he didn't feel, and only now did he realize how many trees *hadn't* been speaking before. Muttering and whispering and hissing in three different languages, they all agreed: They would help him.

He closed his eyes in relief.

It would be all right. They would give him a weapon, and he would wake and destroy this dragon of Kavinsky's before anything else happened.

In the blackness of his closed lids, he heard: *tck-tck-tck-tck.*

No, thought Ronan. *Not night horrors.*

But there was the rattle of their claws. The chatter of their beaks.

Dream to nightmare, just like that.

There was no real fear, just dread. Anticipation. It took so long to kill him in a dream.

"This won't help," he told the trees. He knelt down, bracing his fingers in the soft soil. Even though he knew he couldn't save himself, he couldn't ever seem to convince himself to stop fighting. "This won't save anyone."

The trees whispered, *Quemadmodum gladius neminem occidit; occidentis telum est.*

(*A sword is never a killer; it is a tool in the killer's hand.*)

But the night horrors were not a weapon Ronan could wield.

"I can't control them!" he shouted. "They only want to hurt me!"

A night horror appeared. It surged over the trees, blocking out the sky. It was like nothing he had dreamt before. Three times the size of the others. Reeking of ammonia. Glacially white. The claws were yellowed and translucent, darkening to red tips. Pink veins stood out on the tattered rag wings. Its red albino eyes were tiny and furious in its wrinkled head. And instead of one ferocious beak, there were two, side by side, screaming in unison.

On the other side of the lake, Adam held up his hands, pointing at the sky. He was an alien version of himself. A dream version of himself. Lightning struck the stone beside him.

Like a heart, the ley line jerked and spasmed to life.

Cabeswater was alive.

"Now!" Adam shouted. "Ronan, now!"

The night horror hissed a scream.

"It's only you," whispered Orphan Girl. She was holding his hand, crouched down next to him. "Why do you hate you?"

Ronan thought about it.

The albino night horror swept in, talons opening.

Ronan stood up, stretching out his arm like he would to Chainsaw.

"I don't," he said.

And he woke up.

62

Apart from ruining the Gray Man's life, the Gray Man's plan to lead the others out of Henrietta had been going exceptionally well. Greenmantle must not have ever really trusted him, because he had immediately accepted the Gray Man's confession of theft. He'd sworn and threatened, but really, Greenmantle had already done the worst thing he could manage, so his words lacked force.

And news had spread fast, apparently. Those headlights there were the two men who had, he'd discovered, trashed the Pleasant Valley Bed and Breakfast. And those headlights behind that, calculating and inexorable, were his brother's.

Follow me, follow me.

For a mile, two miles, three miles, fifteen miles, the Gray Man played crack the whip with the other two cars. The car containing the other treasure seekers tried to be discreet, but the car in back didn't. That was how he knew it was his brother. His brother always wanted Dean to know. That was part of the game.

My brother. My brother. My brother.

It had been paralyzing, at first, knowing that his brother was so close. At first, the only way the Gray Man could focus on driving was by thinking of everything he had become as the Gray Man instead of everything he had been as Dean Allen. Because Dean Allen kept telling him to just pull over and get it over with. *It will only be worse,* whispered Dean Allen in a small voice, *if you make him come looking for you.*

The Gray Man, on the other hand, said: *He is a thirty-nine-year-old investment manager, and for efficiency, he should probably just be shot twice in the head and returned to his office with an ambiguous note.*

And there was a third part of him, now, that was neither the Gray Man nor Dean Allen, that wasn't thinking about his brother at all. This part — perhaps it was Mr. Gray — couldn't stop thinking about everything he was leaving behind. The faded and beautiful crevices of the little town, the unapologetic spread of Maura's smile, the new thunder of his suddenly operating heart. This part of him even missed the Champagne Killjoy.

The Gray Man's eyes drifted down to the note still stuck to the steering wheel:

This one's for you. Just the way you like it: fast and anonymous.

It was such a brilliant little plan, slick and simple. All he'd had to do was give up everything. And it was working so very well.

But then something happened.

There was nothing around them but trees and highway and blackness, but suddenly the lights on the dormant machines in the passenger seat exploded.

Not a flicker. Not a hint.

A blasted shout into the night. The headlights behind him dipped as the cars slammed on their brakes, their meters undoubtedly howling the same as his.

No, the Gray Man thought. One of those stupid boys had dreamt back in Henrietta and ruined everything.

But that wasn't it.

Because the readings were solid and screaming. Ordinarily, the energy spiked at the moment of the dream object's creation, and then fell off abruptly. But the meters were still pegged. And remained so, despite the fact that the Gray Man was headed away from Henrietta at seventy miles an hour.

Behind the Gray Man, the first car had faltered. They doubted the Gray Man's story, perhaps. Assuming, like the Gray Man, that someone elsewhere was using the Greywaren.

But the longer the flashing lights and wailing alerts went on, the more obvious it was that this was not the Greywaren's doing. Not only were the readings constant, but they were coming from everywhere. It had to be the line Maura had talked about. Something had happened to it, and now it was alive, blasting these energy readings through the roof.

The car behind him was still following, but slowly. They had access to the same readings as the Gray Man — and they were confused.

A realization gradually occurred to the Gray Man. As long as the ley line was creating such dramatic readings, the Greywaren was invisible. An energy spike wouldn't be noticed in this already existing riot.

Which meant Henrietta didn't have to worry about any new hunters coming after the Greywaren. No one could use these readings to pinpoint anything but the location of the line. It meant that if the Gray Man could somehow get rid of this car-load of treasure seekers, there was only one reason for the Gray Man to run from Henrietta.

His brother.

Ronan had created this night horror to fight Kavinksy's dragon, and fight they did.

Up through the black the creatures climbed, snarled around each other. Fireworks burst past them, illuminating their scales.

The crowd, drunk and high and gullible and desirous of wonders, screamed their support.

Down on the ground, Ronan and Kavinsky leaned their heads back, too, watching what they had made.

The creatures were beautiful and terrible. Sparks cascaded from them as claws and fire met. A wheeling scream like a firework escaped from the night horror.

Up, up, up, into the black. Ronan's eyes darted through the crowd. Gansey and Blue had gone separate ways and he saw them now tearing open the doors on Mitsubishis, looking for Matthew. The cars were all stopped as everyone watched the dragons. There weren't that many cars. Gansey and Blue would find him. It would be all right.

But then Kavinsky's fire dragon broke off from the night horror. It tucked its gaseous forearms and dove. With a hissing blast of noise, it collided with one of the flood lamps. The impact had no effect on the dragon, but the lamp capsized. Shocked screams punctuated the air; the lamp tumbled like a tree.

Kavinsky's face was alight. He'd leapt to his feet as the fire dragon hurled itself at another one of the lamps. Flames burst and dissipated. The bulb exploded.

Ronan's night horror plummeted from the sky, snatching at the fire dragon. For a moment, the two hit the ground, rolling across the dirt, and then they were aloft again.

No one was really afraid. Why weren't they afraid?

It was magic, but nobody believed it was.

The music was still blaring. The cars were still wheeling. There were dragons fighting above them, and it was just another party.

The fire dragon screamed, the same horrible scream as before. It sped toward where Kavinsky and Ronan stood by the car.

"Stop it," Ronan said.

Kavinsky's eyes were still on it. "No stopping it now, Lynch."

His furious dragon spun, wings outstretched. Tearing along the drag strip, it pulled a stretch of flames along the dirt behind it. It sprang off the roof of one of the Mitsubishis at the end. As its claws shrieked on the metal, the car burst into flame. The dragon charged into the air. The movement flipped the car behind it, easy as a toy.

Matthew?

On the other side of the strip, Gansey waved his arms above his head, shaking his head, catching Ronan's eye. Not in that one.

"Tell me which car my brother's in," Ronan said.

"A white one."

The dragon gathered itself up. It was obviously preparing to plummet down once more. It was curious, really, how clearly he could see its eyes from that great height. It had terrible eyes. It was not that they were empty, but rather that when you looked past all the flame and smoke and more flames, you could see that deep down inside the eyes was really just more smoke and flames.

There was a silence in the crowd.

In that silence, Kavinsky's laugh was louder than anything.

A single scream erupted from the crowd. It was a sort of experimental sound, trying to decide if now, finally, fear was the correct response.

As Ronan's night horror flapped toward the fire dragon, Kavinsky's monster pinned its vaporous legs to its body. Sulfur clouded from its mouth. It was deadly like a cancer. Like radiation. It had teeth, but those were irrelevant.

Kavinsky snapped his fingers. Another firework shot up, smearing a glowing path between the two creatures. It exploded above them all like a toxic flower.

The night horror slammed into the fire dragon. The two of them crashed into the ground, rolling into the crowd. Now there was screaming as people leapt out of the way. The two creatures clawed their way over another of the Mitsubishis. Into the air. Back down again.

"Ronan!" Blue's voice carried, high and thin. She had looked in another Mitsubishi — still no Matthew. The crowd was still scattering — somewhere, a siren howled. There was so much fire. It was as if Kavinsky's dragon were slowly remaking the world in its own image. Most of the flood lamps were out, but the drag strip was brighter than before. Every car a lantern.

The fire dragon pitched toward Gansey and Blue.

Ronan didn't have to shout to his night horror. It knew what Ronan wanted. It wanted exactly what Ronan wanted.

Save them.

The night horror tangled in the fire dragon's wings. The two creatures sailed narrowly past Gansey and Blue.

Gansey shouted, *"Do something!"*

Ronan could kill Kavinsky. If he stopped Kavinsky, the dragon stopped. But it was one thing to know this solution. It was a very different thing to look at Kavinsky, his arms stretched over his head, fire in his eyes, and think: *I could kill him.*

And most important, it wasn't *true.*

Ronan couldn't kill him.

"Okay," he snarled, grabbing Kavinsky's arm, "we're done. Where is my brother? No *more.* Where is he?"

Kavinsky threw his free hand out toward the Mitsubishi beside them. "He's all yours! You missed my *point,* man. All I wanted was *this* —"

He gestured now at the tumbling dragon and night horror.

Releasing him, Ronan scrambled to the car. He pulled open the back door. It was empty.

"He's not in here!"

"Boom!" shouted Kavinsky. Another car had just gone up. The flames were glorious and rolling, bubbling out of the car like thunderclouds. As Ronan slammed the door shut, Kavinsky scrambled up onto the hood of the Mitsubishi. He was shaking and ecstatic.

Pressing one hand to his concave chest, he fetched his white sunglasses from his back pocket with the other. He put them on, hiding his eyes. The lenses mirrored the furnace around them.

On the opposite end of the strip, the fire dragon screamed its dreadful scream again. It tore free of the night horror.

The creature turned directly toward them.

And suddenly, Ronan saw it. He saw how every car but this one burned. How the dragon had destroyed each of Kavinsky's dream things here at the strip. How now it came at them, a frenzy of destruction. The night horror flew after it, less graceful, a bit of ash tossed in a nuclear wind.

He heard thumping, barely audible over the chaos.

Matthew was in the trunk.

Ronan bolted around the back of the car — no, no, that wasn't right, he needed to open the trunk from inside the car. He darted a look at the dragon. It was flying directly for them, purposeful and malevolent.

Fumbling along the driver's side door, he popped the trunk. As he tore around the car, he saw Matthew kick the trunk open the rest of the way. Rolling out, his younger brother stumbled drunkenly, clambering up, hand pressed against the car for support.

Ronan could smell the fire dragon, all carbon and sulfur.

Ronan dove for his brother. He dragged him away from the car. He shouted to Kavinsky, "Get down!"

But Kavinsky didn't look away from the two creatures. He said, "The world's a nightmare."

Horror clawed its way up inside Ronan. It was precisely the feeling he'd had when he realized Kavinsky was going to blow up the Mitsubishi at the substance party.

Dust swirled up from the dragon's wings.

Furious, Ronan shouted, "Come down, you bastard!"

Kavinsky didn't answer.

There was that *whoof* he'd heard in the dream, that clap of wings against air. Like an explosion taking all the oxygen from a room.

Ronan wrapped his arms around Matthew and ducked his head.

A second later, the fire dragon exploded into Kavinsky. It went straight through him, around him, flame around an object. Kavinsky fell. Not as if he was struck, though. Just like when he'd taken the green pill. He crumpled to his knees and then slumped gracelessly off the car.

A few feet away, the fire dragon careened into the dirt, limp.

Non mortem, somni fratrem.

Across the dirt track, one of the Mitsubishis, still smoldering, crashed resoundingly into one of the buildings. Ronan didn't have to see the driver to know it was Prokopenko. Asleep.

Which meant that Kavinsky was dead.

But he had been dying since Ronan met him. They both had been.

Dying's a boring side effect.

The pair of white sunglasses lay in the dust beside Ronan's toe. He didn't take them. He just held Matthew tightly, unwilling to let him go yet. His brain kept replaying the image of Matthew climbing out of the trunk, fire hitting the car, Kavinsky falling —

He'd had so many nightmares of something happening to him.

Overhead, the albino night horror flapped. Both Matthew and Ronan looked up at it.

Tck-tck-tck-tck.

Both beaks chattered. It was a dreadful thing, this night horror, impossible to understand, but Ronan was done being afraid. There was no fear left.

With a shudder, Matthew pressed his face into his older brother's shoulder, trusting as a child. He whispered, voice slurred, "What is it?"

The night horror barely checked itself as it regarded its creator. It flapped upward, spinning two or three times as it did. It was headed into the night — where, it was impossible to say.

"It's all right," Ronan said.

Matthew believed him; why shouldn't he? Ronan had never lied. He looked up over Matthew's head as Gansey and Blue began to head toward them. Sirens wailed from close by; blue and red lights strobed through the dust like lights at a club. Ronan was suddenly unbearably glad to see Gansey and Blue joining him. For some reason, although he had arrived with them, he felt as if he had been alone for a very long time, and now no longer was.

"That thing. Is it one of Dad's secrets?" Matthew whispered.

"You'll see," Ronan replied. "Because I'm going to tell you all of them."

63

The Gray Man couldn't think of a way to get rid of the other treasure hunters without having to confront his brother.

But that was unthinkable.

The Gray Man thought about the card Maura had drawn for him. The ten of swords. The absolute worst it could get. He had thought that it meant leaving behind Henrietta, but now he knew that although that was terrible, it wasn't really the worst thing that could happen to him.

The worst thing had always been his brother.

You're going to have to be brave, Maura had said.

I'm always brave.

Braver than that.

For so long his brother had haunted him. Taunted and teased him from hundreds of miles away, even as the Gray Man studied and trained and became ever more dangerous in his own right. He'd let him take everything from him.

And what, really, was keeping him from facing his brother now? Fear? Could he be any more deadly than the Gray Man? Could he really take anything more from him?

The Gray Man thought of Maura's smile again. And he thought of the fuss and noise of 300 Fox Way, of Blue's bright banter, of the tuna fish sandwich at the deli counter, the haunted blue mountains calling him home.

He wanted to stay.

Persephone had patted his knee. *I know you'll do the right thing, Mr. Gray.*

As he drove, the Gray Man stretched one hand into the backseat and dragged his gray suitcase onto Greenmantle's meters. Driving one-handed, glancing from the rain-slicked road to the case every so often, he first found his favorite Kinks album.

He put the disc in the CD player.

Then he fetched out the gun he had hidden in the kitchen cabinets at Pleasant Valley Bed and Breakfast. He checked to make certain that Calla had not cleverly removed all the bullets. She had not.

He got off the interstate.

He was going to stay. Or he was going to die trying.

In the rearview mirror, he saw two cars get off the interstate behind him. Up ahead were two bleary-eyed truck stops — nothing said exhaustion like the wide-awake lights of a truck stop. He chose the larger one.

Already he could recognize his brother's silhouette behind the wheel of the farther car. Age had not changed the set of his chin nor the shape of his ears. Age, the Gray Man guessed, had not changed much about his brother. Fear tickled in his gut.

Through the speakers, the Kinks confessed that they no longer wanted to wander.

The Gray Man pulled up to a pump.

Here is the thing the Gray Man knew about gas stations after dark: They were the best and worst place in the world to kill someone. Because here, between the pumps, in this insomnia light show, the Gray Man was well-nigh invincible. Even if there were no other cars getting gas, he had two different cameras pointed at him. And the cashier monitoring those cameras was only a panic away from an emergency button. Only the most casual of killers would strike between these gas pumps. Too kill someone here was to be caught.

The Gray Man's brother would not get caught. He was dangerous not because he was reckless, but because of the opposite.

And the treasure hunters — they probably were not killers at all. Just specialized thugs with a skill for breaking and entering and enough tact to not break something valuable once they had it.

Sure enough, the Gray Man's brother didn't even pull close to the pumps but instead pulled into the darkness beside a trash bin to wait.

The other car hesitated as well, but the Gray Man rolled down his window and waved them over. After a pause, they pulled up the other direction, driver's window to driver's window.

They were just a pair of young roughs, both looking tired and frustrated. The one in the passenger seat held a bank of devices on his lap. The Gray Man glimpsed a sea of candy wrappers and soda bottles, a blanket balled in the backseat. So they'd been living out of this car for at least a few days. The Gray Man didn't really begrudge them trashing his rooms back at the bed and breakfast. Probably how he would've done it, before he knew any better. Well, probably not. But still, they weren't as bad as the two he'd left in the woods.

This is why you're the best, Greenmantle had said.

It was true. The Gray Man really was the best.

It was quite clear they hadn't expected the Gray Man to stop, and if they had, they hadn't expected him to be leaning easily on the window with the Kinks shouting, *Silly boy, you self-destroyer!*

"Good evening," the Gray Man said pleasantly. The station smelled like very old fried food.

"Hey, man," said the driver, an uneasy cast to his voice.

"I see you're following me," the Gray Man said.

"Hey, man —" protested the driver.

The Gray Man gently held up a hand. "Let's not waste time. I don't have what you're looking for. I lied to my employer. I pretended the unusual readings were because of the object so he'd keep paying for my room and board while I looked for it. And then I told him I took it to try and get more cash out of him. Which didn't work, as you can tell."

They stared at him, too bewildered at first to immediately reply.

"Hey, man," said the driver, a third time. The passenger scrubbed a hand over his face and then pensively thumbed the still-glowing meters in his lap. "How do we know you aren't lying to *us*?"

"For what purpose?" the Gray Man asked. He gestured toward the Mitsubishi. "Let's be honest. I could easily lose you guys in this."

He thought, anyway. Probably. It looked fast.

The two of them seemed to think so, though, because they both frowned.

"Look, I'm only stopping out of professional courtesy," the Gray Man added. "I can see you guys haven't been in this business as long as I have, but I'd hope you'd do the same for someone else in my position." He wanted to tell them they could search his car, but that would sound too eager. Too guilty. They'd think he'd dumped it.

More frowning. The guy in the passenger seat said, "What about the readings?"

"I told you. I lied about the readings because I knew I could get away with it for a while. They're only from the fault line. You can drive up and down the mountains if you want to see for yourself. Follows them pretty perfectly."

They wanted so badly to believe him. He could see it in their bloodshot eyes, their flattened lips. They'd been sent in pursuit of a ghost, and not many besides the Gray Man had the patience for that. They wanted to be done, to go after more concrete spoils.

"But what do we tell our man?"

"Hey, what do I know?" the Gray Man asked. "I'm the one who's on the run 'cause mine didn't believe me."

"True point," commented the guy from the passenger seat. There was a pause, and then he added, "I've got to piss."

The Gray Man had won.

"Here. Put my number in your phone," the Gray Man said. "We can keep in touch."

They exchanged numbers. Passenger Seat went into the station to pee. Driver said, "Well, *hell*. Do you have a cigarette?"

The Gray Man somberly shook his head. "Gave them up a year ago." He had never smoked.

Driver jerked his chin back toward where the Gray Man's brother waited in the shadows. Rain streaked through the pale beam of his headlights. "What about him?"

"Cagey Guy, you mean? I don't know. I guess I'll have to talk to him out of the cameras."

The driver looked up sharply to where the Gray Man pointed. "Oh, man. I never even thought of them."

The Gray Man tapped the end of his nose. He said, "That's a tip. Okay, let's stay in touch."

"Yeah," the driver said. "Oh, hey —"

The Gray Man stopped rolling up the window. He tried not to hold his breath. "Yeah?"

The driver cracked a grin. "I like the license plate."

It took the Gray Man a moment to remember what it was.

"Thanks," he said. "I like to tell the truth when I can."

He rolled up the window and pulled forward. As he did, his brother eased forward in his car, too. It was a slithering little coupe, something that probably looked elegant back in Boston. The lights striped over the top of it as it pulled forward to follow the Gray Man.

A truck stop was the best and the worst place to kill someone. Because outside of the camera-laden gas pumps there was often a parking lot for weary truck drivers to snatch some sleep. Sometimes it was only room for ten or fifteen semitrucks. Sometimes it was twenty or forty. They were rarely lit, never filmed. It was only trailers and fatigue-drugged drivers.

This truck stop had a massive parking area, and the Gray Man led his brother's car to the very farthest edge of it. He stopped behind the grubbiest of the semitrucks.

This was it.

This was really it.

The Gray Man felt every point of those ten swords piercing him.

Every gray day wanted him. It would be easiest to just give in.

The Kinks sang, *Night is as dark as you feel it ought to be.*

The coupe pulled alongside the white Mitsubishi, driver's side to driver's side. And there he was, unassuming and soft looking. He'd grown a tidy beard that somehow emphasized the sympathetic curve of his thick eyebrows. People always thought he had a friendly face. There was a lot of talk about sociopaths having frightening eyes, but not the Gray Man's brother. When he needed to blend in, he was as warm and as intimate as you could hope for. Even now, sitting there in the coupe with that curled smile, he looked like a hero.

Dean, we're just going to try this one thing.

"Well, little brother," said the Gray Man's brother. He knew from long experience that his voice alone would paralyze the Gray Man. Like a snake, it gave him plenty of time to digest his victim. "Looks like it's you and me again."

And the voice had the effect it always did: a poisonous venom of memories. A decade flashed in the Gray Man's head.

blade

cut

slice

burn

pick

smear

scream

The Gray Man took the gun from the passenger seat and shot his brother. Twice.

"Really," he said, "it's just me."

He put on a glove from his suitcase and transferred the Post-it note from his steering wheel to the inside of his brother's car.

Then he turned up the music, rolled up the window, and got back on the interstate.

He was going home.

EPILOGUE

A secret is a strange thing.

There are three kinds of secrets. One is the sort everyone knows about, the sort you need at least two people for. One to keep it. One to never know. The second is a harder kind of secret: one you keep from yourself. Every day, thousands of confessions are kept from their would-be confessors, none of these people knowing that their never-admitted secrets all boil down to the same three words: *I am afraid.*

And then there is the third kind of secret, the most hidden kind. A secret no one knows about. Perhaps it was known once, but was taken to the grave. Or maybe it is a useless mystery, arcane and lonely, unfound because no one ever looked for it.

Sometimes, some rare times, a secret stays undiscovered because it is something too big for the mind to hold. It is too strange, too vast, too terrifying to contemplate.

All of us have secrets in our lives. We're keepers or kept-from, players or played. Secrets and cockroaches — that's what will be left at the end of it all.

Ronan Lynch lived with every sort of secret.

His first secret was himself. He was brother to a liar and brother to an angel, son of a dream and son of a dreamer. He was a warring star full of endless possibilities, but in the end, as he dreamt in the backseat on the way to the Barns that night, he created only this:

Article 7
Further Condition

UPON MY DEATH, MY CHILDREN SHALL BE ALLOWED FREE
ACCESS TO "THE BARNS," ALTHOUGH THEY MAY NOT ONCE AGAIN
TAKE RESIDENCE THERE UNTIL ALL HAVE REACHED THE AGE OF
EIGHTEEN.

Then, when he woke, they all helped to put Aurora Lynch in
the car. And in silence, they drove her to the GPS coordinates
marked in Gansey's journal.

There was Cabeswater fully restored. It was spreading and
mysterious, familiar and eerie, dreamer and dreamt. Every tree,
Ronan thought, was a voice he might have heard before. And
there was Noah, shoulders slumped, hand lifted in an apologetic
wave. On one side of him, Adam stood, hands in pockets, and on
the other side was Persephone, her fingers twisted together.

When they carried Aurora over the border, she woke like a
rose blooms. And when she smiled at Ronan, he thought, *Matthew
does look a little like her.*

She hugged him and said, "Flowers and ravens," because she
wanted him to know she remembered.

Then she hugged Matthew and said, "My love," because he
was her favorite.

She said nothing at all to Declan, because he wasn't there.

Ronan's second secret was Adam Parrish. Adam was different since making the bargain with Cabeswater. Stronger, stranger,
farther away. It was hard not to stare at the odd and elegant lines
of his face. He stood to one side while the Lynch brothers revived
their mother, and then he told them all, "I have something to
show you."

As dawn began to pink the bark of the trees, they followed him deeper into Cabeswater.

"The pool is gone," he said. "Where the fish changed color for Gansey. But now —"

Next to the dreaming tree, the pool had been replaced by a slanted and sheered rock surface. It was striated and cleaved with deep scratches, and the deepest of them cut all the way through the rock and into the ground. Cool blackness beckoned.

"A cave?" asked Gansey. "How deep does it go?"

Adam said, "I haven't gone in. I don't think it's safe."

"What's the next step, then?" Gansey asked warily. It was hard to tell if he was wary of Adam or wary of the cavern.

Adam said, "Make it safer."

He glanced at Ronan, eyebrows furrowed, as if sensing Ronan's eyes on him.

Ronan looked away.

The third secret was the cavern itself. When they finally returned to 300 Fox Way, the sun was well up. To Ronan's shock, a white Mitsubishi sat on the curb. For a moment, he thought — but then he saw the Gray Man waiting on the front step with Calla. His presence here instead of hundreds of miles away was not probable, but it was not impossible.

As Persephone climbed the stairs, Calla said accusingly, "This is your fault. Did you know this was going to happen?"

Persephone blinked her black eyes.

"Mr. Gray?" Blue asked. "How —"

"No," Calla interrupted. "Later. Come with me."

She led them upstairs to Maura's bedroom. Pushing open the door, she let them take in the sight.

A candle was melted on the carpet. Beside it, in a square of strong daylight, a scrying bowl was knocked askew.

"Who did this? Where is Mom?" Blue demanded.

Calla wordlessly handed her a note. They all read it over Blue's shoulder.

In a hasty, water-stained scrawl, it said, *Glendower is underground. So am I.*

ACKNOWLEDGMENTS

I'd like to thank the usual suspects, but particularly Jackson Pearce, without whom this book quite literally wouldn't exist. I'd like to thank Brenna Yovanoff for the beginning and Tessa Gratton for the end.

The team at Scholastic continues to be amazing, particularly David Levithan, ever tolerant of my foibles, and Becky Amsel, ever enabling my foibles. Special thanks as always to Rachel Horowitz and Janelle DeLuise for getting me read all over the world.

Blue Ridge Mac: You saved my life, on deadline, not once, but twice. I won't forget that. Ponies for all of you.

Agent Laura Rennert: You also saved my life, on deadline, not once, not twice, but repeatedly. I won't forget that, either. Ponies for eternity.

As always, I'm useless without my family. Dad, thanks for dragons. Mom, thanks for hours and hours and hours. Ed, you had to live with Kavinsky for fourteen months. There aren't enough ponies for that.